Praise for Paula Fox and her novels:

"Paula Fox is so good a novelist that one wants to go out in the street to hustle up a big audience for her. . . . Fox's brilliance has a masochistic aspect: I will do this so well, she seems to say, that you will hardly be able to read it. And so she does, and so do I."

—Peter S. Prescott, *Newsweek*

"Brilliant. . . . Fox is one of the most attractive writers to come our way in a long, long time." —*The New Yorker*

"As a writer, Fox is all sensitive, staring eyeball. Her images break the flesh. They scratch the retina. . . . Fox's prose hurts."

—Walter Kirn, *New York*

Desperate Characters:

"A towering landmark of postwar realism . . . a sustained work of prose so lucid and fine that it seems less written than carved."

—David Foster Wallace

"Absorbing, elegant. . . . What gives this slice of life its timeless urgency is Fox's spare yet penetrating prose, shifting imperceptibly from present to past, external to internal, revealing the hushed despair, absurdity, and latent violence that lie beneath the most humdrum words and routines." —*Entertainment Weekly*

"Among the best things we have in contemporary literature—original, enduring, charged with intelligent, articulate life and with the tension of modern survival: brave, witty, alarming, and quite wonderful."

—Shirley Hazzard

"A piercing portrait of a modern couple at bay. . . . Relentlessly honest, brilliantly crafted, passionate." —John Gabree, *New York Newsday*

"A reserved and beautifully realized novel." —Lionel Trilling

"*Desperate Characters* takes its place in a major American tradition, the line of the short novel exemplified by *Billy Budd*, *The Great Gatsby*, *Miss Lonelyhearts*, and *Seize the Day*. . . . Grueling and brilliant."
—Irving Howe, *The New Republic*

"A brilliant performance, quite devastating in its mastery of the brutish New York scene."　　　　　—Alfred Kazin

Poor George:

"The best first novel I've read in quite a long time. . . . A merciless uncovering of the exurban wastelands of the spirit."
—*New York Review of Books*

"Compared by critics then and now to Chekhov and Melville and Muriel Spark and Nathanael West and Batman and Robin, really, and rightly. She's good, she's good, she's more than good."　　　—Jonathan Lethem

"Like a sealed bottle of pure mid Sixties. . . . *Poor George* feels fresher after a third of a century than do most novels written yesterday."
—Jonathan Franzen

The Widow's Children:

"Chekhovian. . . . Every line of Fox's story, every gesture of her characters, is alive and surprising."
—Christopher Lehmann-Haupt, *New York Times*

"Demonstrates once again Fox's original unsettling talent. . . . Astounding in its portrayal of the textures of emotional life, moment by agonizing moment. . . . Fox releases conflicts and passions of great intensity, and sets them simmering, combining, and exploding like volatile liquid elements."　　　　　—*Saturday Review*

"Compelling. . . . It has in it, especially apparent in the wit, a worldliness which it could not do without, and which is that of someone who has lived long enough to have learned a great deal. . . . Remarkable."
—*New York Review of Book*

A
Servant's
Tale

PAULA FOX

INTRODUCTION BY MELANIE REHAK

W. W. NORTON & COMPANY

NEW YORK LONDON

For information about permission to reproduce selections from this book,
write to Permissions, W. W. Norton & Company, Inc.,
500 Fifth Avenue, New York, NY 10110

ISBN 0-393-32285-8 pbk.

W. W. Norton & Company, Inc.
500 Fifth Avenue, New York, N.Y. 10110
www.wwnorton.com

W. W. Norton & Company Ltd.
Castle House, 75/76 Wells Street, London W1T 3QT

1 2 3 4 5 6 7 8 9 0

To James Harvey, Sheila Gordon,
and Robert Lescher

It is true that children pick
up coarse expressions and bad
manners in the company of servants; but in the drawing room,
they learn coarse ideas and bad
feelings.   *Aleksandr I. Herzen*

One foot in Eden still, I stand
And look across the other land.
                    Edwin Muir

Truth and Consequences

Introduction by Melanie Rehak

Truth is messy. If you have read any of Paula Fox's deeply affecting and humane novels—and most probably even if you haven't—you know this. You also know that it is necessary. Truth can be beauty, certainly, but more often than not it tends to consist of pain and disappointment; that naked moment when the scales fall from your eyes for good and there's nothing left to hide behind. If you can deal with that and still find a way to live, then the beauty part, the part when you're strong enough to go forward with your eyes open, kicks in. This is the reality that all of Fox's characters come across sooner or later, and seeing how each of them chooses to meet it has much to do with why her books are so compelling.

It's not, however, a hugely popular reality. It's too harsh for that. Most of what we're taught about how to navigate the world involves compromising the truth or even avoiding it entirely in order to preserve comfort—both our own and other people's. For this reason, it seems almost inconceivably brave of Fox to have opened *A Servant's Tale* with the anguished cry of a man who has lost everything, including his pride, and knows it. "*Ruina! Ruina!*" he writes in a note to his wife as he prepares to go off and die alone in a swamp, the victim of circumstance, ignorance, and a greedy sugar cane plantation owner. He is the grandfather of Luisa, the novel's narrator, and all of this has taken place long before the real action of the story begins on the Spanish-speaking Caribbean island of San Pedro in the 1930s. Time and constant retelling have served to burnish the tale of his downfall to such a high sheen that the idea of defeat has become a regretfully large portion of Luisa's heritage.

But who wants to read a book that announces its grim stance so unabashedly, in the very first words of the text? Why let yourself in for 300-odd pages of something that has all the hallmarks of misery?

The simple answer is because it's written by Paula Fox. *A Servant's Tale*, like all of her novels, is built on an astonishing sensitivity to the inner lives of its characters, expressed in prose that conveys that sensitivity so clearly, so honestly, that it's hard to understand how she does it in the same words I'm using to write this introduction. Instead of being weighted down by its portrayal of the often desperate struggle to forge an existence in the face of all kinds of adversity—emotional, financial, racial—*A Servant's Tale* holds the composite parts of this effort up for observation and forces us to think about them not, ultimately, in a hopeless or judgmental way, but in a way that provokes the beginnings of real understanding.

It is Fox's particular gift to make us feel glad, as opposed to burdened, that we take on this challenge when we read her books. There are enough pressure points in *A Servant's Tale* to ensure that almost no one will escape a cringing moment or two of self-recognition in its pages (and, by association, a moment or two of self-knowledge), and this comes as an oddly exhilarating relief. The story, divided into four sections, revolves superficially around the decisions and losses of one person, but its concerns are far greater than that. It is a book about the trials of immigrant life, about paralysis brought on by fear of change, and about the tensions inherent in every family that cause us to make decisions we only fully understand later. Because Fox is a writer who never shies away from the enormous paradoxes that complicate each of us, *A Servant's Tale* is also a forceful exploration of what Luisa comes to understand as "the pity in love." In other words, it's a book about what it means to be a thinking, occasionally frightened person on the way to discovering that life is not a matter of either/or.

When the novel opens, Luisa is a little girl on San Pedro, in the village of Malagita. Her father is the son of the sugar cane plantation owner (the same family that destroyed her mother's father), her mother a maid in that owner's kitchen. Luisa tears through her days with a ruthless curiosity, intense in her desire for knowledge as only a child can be. (It's not hard to understand why Fox has had such success as a children's book author once you see how brilliantly, how easily she observes the world from a child's point of view.) In a passage characteristic of Fox's writing for both its plainspoken language and the searing afterimage it leaves, Luisa insists on finding an explanation for something that's bothering her, a doll that has been emitting a rancid smell: "I took a knife and cut the doll open. Out fell fruit pits wrapped in bits of rag. But the pulp still clung to a few pits, and on one wriggled a small worm the color of the flesh of a mango." It's a shocking moment—rotting innards revealed in a way that simply can't be denied—and it becomes all the more awful once you've read further into the novel and watched Luisa grow from this ferociously inquisitive little girl into a woman whose only desire is to know as little as possible.

Fox effects this quietly tragic, troublingly familiar transformation before our eyes as she moves Luisa and her parents from Malagita through a series of dreadful New York barrio apartments, the dead-end grunginess of which is palpable on every page. Luisa's father is solely responsible for the decision to leave Malagita—he's desperate to escape his tyrannical mother, who gives him the money to do it, plus there are rumors of revolution—and he's the only one who wants to be in New York. Her mother refuses to learn English and succumbs to cancer early, slipping silently away from the class conflict of her marriage. Luisa herself chooses to escape the fate her father has handed her by defying his wishes that she become educated and aligning herself with her mother. She becomes a maid.

It's the only conscious decision she makes for almost the entire book, and though it seems uninformed in some ways (another character tells her accusingly that it's "not a choice. You're just going along") Fox makes it clear that it's actually a perfectly reasonable path for her to settle on. Diminished by all that's been taken away from her, Luisa orchestrates her survival by focusing on one dream: getting back to her beloved island. Cleaning houses is a way to earn the money to get there, and it also provides her with the means for a different kind of travel:

My work, done and every day undone—was the dull, mechanical movement of a treadle. I dreamed of another life. I wondered if I had become the ghost of the plantation, if the people of the village, walking along the dirt roads at twilight, staring up at the slowly darkening sky, would, sensing my presence, shiver and retreat indoors. Yet it was the very monotony of my servant's life that freed me to return in my thoughts to Malagita.

So Luisa makes a life for herself, blocking out everything in the external world from the burgeoning civil rights movement to her father's very existence, to the lives of the wealthy New Yorkers in whose apartments she spends her days (this latter group an eccentric, often hilarious bunch worthy of a book of their own). Like so many unwilling exiles, she's there but not there. Even a brief marriage that produces a son doesn't do much to pique her long-lost curiosity. At one point, she refers to her closest childhood friend, Ellen, now an ambitious African American lawyer whose head is understandably full of ideas about Luisa's education and political awareness, as "poisoned with information."

A rapid succession of events—a death, the disclosing of an affair between her son and one of her employers, that much-longed-for trip back to Malagita—eventually forces Luisa to understand that some facts are unavoidable, a hard truth if ever there was one, and a realization that comes awfully late for her. Nonetheless, it's impossible to see her as pathetic, and this is a grand achievement on Fox's part. Luisa is childish, but she's hardly the simpleminded servant, the faceless, silent presence she imagines herself to be. She has too much dignity for that.

She also has too much wisdom, albeit wisdom she doesn't always comprehend. Think of her comment about being poisoned by information, and now think about your own life. Can you claim that you've never been overwhelmed by trying to keep up with the constant influx of news and gossip and cultural noise? That you haven't felt lost in the din on occasion?

Reading Paula Fox is the best antidote I can think of to being lost in this way. No, she won't give you any answers. She won't tell you that everything works out in the end. But you've heard that before anyway, haven't you? And you know it's not true.

—May 2001

Part One

"*Ruina*! *Ruina*!" my grandfather, Isidro Sanchez, had scrawled at the end of his farewell note to my grandmother, which, she recounted, in a voice still astonished after all the passing years, he had written only an arm's length from where she sat mending a tear in the shirt he was to wear the next morning when he had been summoned to see Antonio de la Cueva, the proprietor of the sugar plantation of Malagita, to answer, among other serious questions, why he had not fulfilled his cane quota and therefore could not guarantee his rent for the coming year.

"He looked up from time to time," Nana told me. "He stared at my hands in a way he had when he was thinking. I finished my sewing. He began to fold the note. He did so precisely as he made paper boats for our children, and he wrote a word on it. By then, the point of the quill pen must have been almost dry, it scratched loudly. He placed the note at the center of the table. He stood up and took his hat from the peg on the wall; he didn't tell me where he was going. When he walked out of our house, I didn't know that I would never see him again in this life. In the morning, I woke up alone in our bed. I rose and ran to the table and picked up the scrap of paper, pretending to myself it would be figurings and sums. The children were shouting for their breakfast, especially your mother, who always made more noise than the others."

When my grandmother recited the last sentences of the note, I recited them with her. I knew them by heart.

"I am going to land that not even the de la Cuevas would want," my grandfather had written. "I am abandoning you and my children."

"Do you think he was a bad man?" my grandmother asked me.

"No, Nana."

"He was a saint—as you must have guessed by now. He went to the Estremadura swamp. He died there of starvation."

My grandmother had kept little else that had belonged to Isidro Sanchez except his note. Before I could read, Nana let me look at the yellowing piece of paper but not touch it. When I followed with my eyes the twice-written *ruina*, I imagined I could hear a hoarse cry, Isidro's anger. It was like a curse with which a person suddenly renounces reason.

I didn't think of him as a saint but as a man who had run away in the dark, leaving behind him only a twice-written word like two thorns.

"Then I was alone with my babies," Nana recollected, her voice low yet charged with the dismay she must have felt that morning long ago. "We owned nothing by then. Not the cane shoots, the farm, the implements, the pasture, the wagon road, not the oxen or the cart, not my little vegetable garden, not my own bed. The proprietor of the plantation owned it all, possibly even my underpants." She paused and placed her warm hand on my head. "But in those days everything was serious. Each thing had its importance and was not as it is now where one thing is the same as another, and there are no more stories. So Antonio de la Cueva felt some shame, some small responsibility, and I was given work to do for the de la Cueva family, mending their linen. After all, I was not the widow of some *colono*."

That was true. Isidro Sanchez had not always been a farmer without land. He had had his own on which he grew his own cane, and he had taken it to the de la Cueva mill to have it ground and to sell it. But as the de la Cuevas bought up more and more land, they paid him less and less for the sugar from his cane. At last his farm was surrounded by their land and it was swallowed up. That happened many years before I was born, when there was still yellow fever, and the great sugar latifundio ruled our island country, and the plantation owners could put a private railroad line through a farmer's land and were not obliged to pay him for wood or water, sand or stone, or anything else they made use of.

Without land, my grandfather had nothing to leave to his two sons, and like the other workers, he had to wander about the countryside looking for work during the dead time when the de la Cueva mill was idle. One morning, an official of the plantation told him that he was neglecting the cane field that was his responsibility, that it was full of Don Carlos weed. The de la Cueva company would destroy the weed, but Isidro Sanchez would have to pay all the expenses arising from their effort. Also, there was crucial repair needed on certain fences which Señor Antonio de la Cueva had been hoping Señor Sanchez would have taken care of, for the sake of his own dignity, at least. Those fences would be a further expense to Señor Sanchez. And, finally, there was the matter of his cane quota.

It was that evening that my grandfather wrote the note to my grandmother, printing her name, Rafaela, carefully on a fold, and left his home, Malagita, and then walked several days and nights until he reached the Estremadura swamp on the northeastern coast of our island of San Pedro.

.   .   .

In my infancy, neighbors or their children must have taken care of me during the hours my mother worked in the great house. My mother didn't tell me so but after I was a grown woman, I once saw on a street somewhere, a child of nine perhaps, her back bent with strain, hoisting up a fat baby with her thin arms, and I knew exactly how it felt to cleave to such bony, narrow shoulders.

Mamá did tell me that soon after I had learned to walk, I set off on long journeys by myself, and she would grow frantic searching for me in bamboo clumps or in the cane or on the slope of a hill where a few *guayaba* trees grew wild. "A mad traveler," she called me, shaking her head. She would smile reluctantly at her joke. "*Luisa, la viajera loca.*" But at once she would cross herself, pressing the narrow oval of her thumb nail against her lower lip. Only the mother of Jesus could protect her against the destructive power that might be unleashed by words; she knew that if she spoke of my journeys too often, I would one day fall into the canal that ran through Malagita and drown.

My memory begins with the slow passage of a solitary rider on a short-legged island horse as it struggled along the dirt road spring rains had made impassable for ox carts. The rider's face is hidden by his collar, the horse snorts and pants as it lifts its hooves from the mud like a fly caught in molasses. I am sitting in the doorway of our *bohío*, my knees and bare feet wet with rain, watching the rider and his horse toil through the watery half-light.

That would have been during the dead time when the sky was dark with rain and rain clouds, and the chimneys of the silent mill loomed through the wet air like the trunks of immense trees. In that season, Malagita lost its human look little by little and sank into the mud and waterstreaming underbrush and night and day seemed the same.

In December, in the dry weather, the harvesting of the cane and the grinding of it began. The mill ran day and night and the black smoke poured from its chimneys. The roads dried and hardened and Malagita and its dwellings seemed to rise up as though pulled by ropes. All around it the fields glittered where the sun's rays struck the machetes of the cane cutters with needles of white light.

The plantation was like a wheel and the great house of the proprietor was its center. Antonio de la Cueva had been dead for many years. Only six months after what remained of my grandfather's body had been discovered in the swamp, de la Cueva had gone to look over his *cafetal* up on the mountain slope where the coffee plants grew in the shade of banana trees, and on his way down had been thrown by his horse. "Broken like a dry stick," said Nana. "He had been too pleased at the good harvest he saw coming. God punishes for certain pleasures."

Antonio's widow, Beatriz, lived on and operated Malagita with the help of her oldest son, Leopoldo. But he died a week before his fortieth birthday when the small airplane he was flying fell to earth, crashing against the mountain. It was said in the village that the crash had been no accident, that Señor Leopoldo had chosen to die because of his mother's heartless demands upon him, demands that could have been made properly on a steward but not a son. When I was born, the daughter of her younger son, she was already old and had begun to suffer from periods of craziness. Although she was my father's mother, she did not acknowledge my birth, or my existence, any more than she took notice of my mother's presence in her kitchen as a maid of all work. "But don't imagine that if your Papá, Orlando, had married your mother before you were born, it would have made a difference to a woman of the type of Beatriz de la Cueva," my grandmother told me sternly.

When I had just passed my sixth birthday, Nana took me to the cane field. She held my hand tightly in hers as I gazed at a man whose face I could not see because of the shadow cast by his broad-brimmed straw hat.

"That is Ortiz," she said. "He is the best cutter in Malagita when he's sober."

Ortiz grasped a stalk of cane in his left hand, slashed away the leaves, then with a long swing of his machete which made me shudder, he cut the cane just above the ground. He glanced up at us briefly, his jaw working as he chewed on a twig which poked out from a corner of his mouth. He bent again, swung the stalk to the left and brought it back sharply against the machete blade, cutting it into two sections. From one, he lopped off the green top.

"For horses and for the cattle," Nana explained, and shook my arm when I began to turn away. I sighed with uneasiness as Ortiz cut the sections into even pieces. He spat out the twig. For an instant it gleamed with his spittle in the sunlight. He moved on to the next stalk.

All around us in a clearing that grew larger as Ortiz and the other cutters swung their blades, women and children bent to pick up the fallen cane, doubling over themselves like loops of thread, then bearing what they had gathered to wagons across whose boards lay thick chains. One wagon was already filled, and a man was yoking up to it a pair of oxen while another man guided them with a goad. The oxen would haul the wagon to the weighing station Nana and I had passed on our way to the field just as the sun had risen. A mule, its head drooping, had been standing there next to an enormous hoist. On narrow railroad tracks, a long line of cars had stood empty, their thin slatted sides casting shadows across the dusty floors, and leaning against them had been several silent men, the bottoms of their trousers wet from the damp high grass they had walked through.

The oxen swung their great heads from side to side through haloes of circling flies. The heat of the sun bore down like a weight. The massive animals strained to haul the wagon; its great rough wheels creaked and slowly turned. The tall figure of Nana in her black dress bent and straightened up over the ground as she worked. Now far away, the cutters advanced down the rows of cane. They never looked back; sometimes they shouted, raising their heads briefly, or burst into yelps of laughter. They were tearing the field of cane apart like a flock of angry birds. We crept behind them on the earth gathering up what they had left for us.

I grew dizzy and afraid. It was the first morning of my life I had not been free to run about, to stop doing one thing and to start another at will. I flung myself at Nana's skirt. "I can't! I can't!" I cried.

She gripped my arm. I snatched up a piece of cane and began to chew it, the familiar thick sweetness of its juices giving me an unformed hope.

"In a few days you grow used to it. Then you won't think of it," Nana said. She placed her hands on my face. "The heat . . ." she muttered. She went to where a water jar leaned against a stone and brought it back and held it while I drank. Over its spout, I glimpsed a man on a horse riding toward us. He held the reins loosely in one hand, a cigarillo in the other. Nana took away the jar as the man dismounted. He stared at us while he patted his clean white jacket. Smoke rose from his cigarillo straight up in the still air. The horse suddenly lifted its tail and farted tremendously.

I hid against Nana, crushing the cloth of her skirt against my mouth to stifle my laughter. She shook me, saying under her breath, "The over-seer . . ."

When I looked at him again, he was so close he appeared to be about to topple over on me. I could see a thin line of black dirt beneath each of his fingernails as he thrust his hand toward me.

"What is that?" he demanded disgustedly. His face was cold and stern but there was some weakness around his eyes which opened and closed rapidly as though still affected by the blast from his horse. I knew that he felt he had lost his importance.

"Luisa Sanchez, my granddaughter," said Nana as though she were speaking to a toad.

"Take her away from here," he said.

"Don't talk to me as if I hadn't been present when your mother gave birth to you!" Nana cried. Some women nearby straightened up from their work and watched us intently.

"My birth has nothing to do with this," the overseer shouted. "It has to do with her birth. You shouldn't have brought her here."

"Who told you that!"

"I don't have to be told. You know the reason yourself!" He flung his cigarillo on the ground and stamped on it violently as though it had been a scorpion.

"Nothing is her fault," Nana said. "She is a child."

"You aren't her only grandmother," he replied, stretching out his thin corded neck.

"There is nothing baser than a man who follows imagined orders," said Nana.

The overseer suddenly bent over and gripped my waist and lifted me up high above him. I tried to squirm out of his hands. I felt their moist clutch through my dress. He laughed aloud and tightened his grip.

"Put her down," Nana said. "We'll go away."

At that, he lowered me to the ground. I smiled at him because now I knew what the hope had been that I had sucked into my mouth with the sweetness of the cane; it had been to escape from this field with its mute women and children.

Nana was silent as we began to walk back to the village. She waited patiently when we reached the weighing station and I paused to watch the men hook up the locomotive to the line of cars that would, later, be filled with cane.

When she spoke at last, it was only to say, "I wanted you to be like the rest of us, to save you from a harder life."

Nana and I often walked together on the plantation roads in the late afternoons when a damp, cooling breeze sprang up and pressed against our skin like cloths dipped in a stream. Often, she spoke not one word. When I stopped to touch a lizard as green as the slime that collected along the sides of the canal, or tried to steady with my glance the quick movements of a parrot in a bamboo thicket, she waited, motionless, and if I looked up at her to see if she was about to urge me on, her face appeared so tranquil she might have been praying.

We had come to the Malagita surgery and Nana stopped, as she nearly always did, to peer through the bars of the window. Standing on tiptoe, I, too, was able to see into the room where sick people were, nearly everyone said, made sicker by the village doctor. Three of the narrow beds within the bare room were empty. On the fourth, Dr. Baca lay asleep in his black suit, one of his hands holding an unlit cigar resting on the floor. "Working for the poor," Nana remarked. "Look! He hasn't taken off his boots." Dr. Baca snorted loudly as though in response. I darted away from the window. "He heard you," I said.

"He never hears anything," declared Nana.

We passed an open place where no grass grew, where the ground was as smooth as a floor. On holidays, the men of the village played pelota there so fiercely, with such wild cries, that once when I had been watching them from across the road, hidden behind a clump of bamboo, and

had seen a man fall to the ground, I thought he had died and was astonished when he rose a few minutes later like Jesus resurrected. At the
furthest edge of that bare, trampled space stood a large thatched hut.
When I had gone in there one morning early, after I had passed through
the village and seen not a living thing except a dark cloud of gnats hover-
ing over a dead tortoise, I found a deep pit in the earth and reaching into
it, had drawn up handfuls of dusty feathers. Nana told me about cock-
fights when I showed her what I'd found; she scattered the feathers in the
yard behind her cabin, saying there were men like stones, roused from
their stoniness only when they could torment creatures far less brutish
than themselves. I didn't go again to that place where men played their
games. Sometimes I thought a dream was taking me there against my
will.

Off by itself near a grove of mango trees stood the village jail. The
shutters were closed over its two windows so we were not able to see if
someone was inside the cells. The jailer slumped on a bench against the
wall near the door, staring sleepily down at his tracking dog which lay
on its back at his feet, its muzzle open, its purple tongue lolling, its terrible
teeth glistening with saliva, and its balls hanging down sideways across
its belly like overripe figs. The jailer gave us a sun-dazed glance, then
lowered his head.

"What an ugly sight," Nana said as we walked on. "How dusty they
both were! They must roll in ditches together. You'd think merely looking at them would stop men from drinking and fighting. Señora Galdos'
nephew, who was in jail last month for two nights, says the jailer and the
dog eat together like man and wife."

Right after the jail, the village began to crowd up against the road.
Some houses were on stilts and below them hens scratched in the dirt or
ran with violent haste from one spot to another. Other houses squatted
on the ground, *bohíos*, such as the one I lived in, built of heavy cane stalks
plastered with mud. But our cabin was the color of the red earth of Malagita, while these cabins had been painted yellow or blue or white so
that even during the rainy season, they appeared to be less sunk into the
earth, more a part of the air. A few had floors made from the trunks of
the royal palm. From windows and doorways women spoke to Nana,
greeting her, asking after her health, as though they'd not seen her for

weeks—they sought her out if she did not make at least one daily appearance on the road—and smiling when they looked down at me in a way that had troubled and puzzled me from the first time I took notice of it.

I took deep breaths of air, sweet and throat-tickling with the dark smell of cane juice which boiled in the huge cauldrons in the mill and reached everywhere in Malagita. The mill ran night and day now; that powerful smell blotted out the stench of animals and the scent of flowers alike. I felt strengthened by it as though it fed me. I ran away from the old women squatting in their doorways smoking their corncob pipes, and from the women who held babies which Nana touched as she talked as though they were objects of devotion. I ran toward the *plazuela* where royal palms, their trunks the color of ashes, rose high in the air, circling a small park. From beneath a palmetto a small dog as yellow as soap fled at my approach and crept into some thick underbrush where I had once seen a bright little snake crawling out of its old skin, a sight I longed to see again.

Just as the dog's tail disappeared, the noon whistle blew in the brick clock tower. I clapped my hands to my ears. The whistle's sustained shriek was like a knife that pierced my hands and entered my skull. Nana, who had caught up to me by then, pulled my hands away from my ears. "It's stopped," she said, but the shriek had turned into a silver snake I saw fleeing along the edge of the sky.

The tower stood at the entrance to the park. A black iron grating surrounded it like the one which enclosed the grave of Antonio de la Cueva in the graveyard near the chapel. The tower contained not only the terrible device which made the whistle but also loud, toneless bells that rang for fires, for hailstorms and, at times, for special Masses when everyone not at work in the mill was obliged to go and kneel on the cement floor of the chapel while Father Céspedes demanded of God that He restore Señora Beatriz de la Cueva to her senses.

On each of the tower's four sides was a clock face as large as a wagon wheel. I had never seen the hands move, although I knew they did just as I knew the sun rose and set although I hadn't caught the sun in motion either. Nana shook me gently. "What are you staring at?" she asked me. "The sun," I said. "Leave the sun alone," she said.

In the distance, I heard the sound of horse's hooves. I thought of the overseer and his strong hands. Birds sang in the park which was nearly always empty of people except in the early evenings when mothers strolled among the trees with their children, or on Sundays when those people who had dressed for Mass wished to prolong the pleasure of wearing their best clothes, and so spent all the time they could spare from their tasks sitting on the stone benches where I watched them with amazement as they smiled and spoke in low voices, and I stole secret glances at their shoes, at the cloth that covered their knees and arms. They held their heads erect, their hands were quiet on their laps—people whom I could barely recognize as the same ones I saw on other days, the women, barefoot most of them, laboring at their washtubs, the men, their feet in canvas slippers, wearing shapeless trousers, on their way to the mill.

A girl was singing louder than the birds, monotonously, insistently, a popular song my mother sang. I could see the girl down the road hanging up laundry in her yard. Nana bent to embrace me, her cheek resting briefly on my head. "I don't know what will become of you," she said as she often did, and sighed deeply. "Go on home now . . ."

I waited. She had said nothing to me about what had taken place in the cane field. I looked at her mouth where the explanation was hidden; the flesh of her tightly closed lips was as ridged as a nut's shell. I began to swing my foot back and forth so the reddish dust was lifted and scattered by my toes. I knew it would annoy her as all idle movements did. I wanted her to speak—to tell me about the invisible event which had taken us from the cane, back to the road to the village, and which I had not understood just as I could not understand, or see, the motions of the hands of the clock or of the sun, spaces where hidden forces changed everything.

She spoke at last, her voice severe. "It was bad of you to laugh at the overseer. A serious matter."

I bowed my head, remembering the soft, sickening stirring of the little snake as it abandoned its old skin. Out of the corner of one eye, I glimpsed Nana's legs, her black stockings with the tiny even stitches of her mending like the feet of millipedes. Suddenly she began to laugh. I looked up and saw her lips grow smooth as they stretched with laughter. I threw my arms around her waist.

"Yes, yes, it was comical," she admitted. "That horse . . ."

"Why did he make you take me away?"

"So you wanted to stay!"

"No!"

"He pretended he was protecting you because you are Orlando de la Cueva's child. He only wanted to feel important. In fact, he was punishing you, pushing you away from the only life that's possible for you."

I looked at her dumbly.

She took hold of my shoulders and gave me a little push. "Go . . . go," she called as though I was already far away from her but with the sudden tenderness that so often flooded her voice no matter what she was talking to me about, and seemed, like the smell of the cane, to be part of the air I breathed.

I ran off, knowing she would remain where she was, watching me until the moment I turned at the curve of the park. Only then, when I knew she could no longer see me, would I feel the pinch of anxiousness that had come to me at my first sight of her, a worry which I had never felt until that moment because, until the morning I had discovered her in Malagita, I had wandered everywhere as though there was nothing that could hold and keep me, nothing that I would wish to hold and keep.

Our *bohío* was on the outskirts of the village and it had a name: the house of the Chinese. Years before, a Chinese man had lived in it and had kept a garden where he grew vegetables the people of the village had never seen before and would not buy from him or even accept when he tried to make a gift of them. He had had an important job at the mill, work not entrusted to an ordinary plantation worker. His importance had been in his eyes, the way they could see and measure in an instant if the machines which spun the cane juice were throwing off too much molasses. When I asked Mamá what had happened to him, she told me he had moved long ago to the capital, Tres Hermanos, and by now was probably dead.

"Then he can't come back and take our house away?" I asked.

"Don't be stupid," she said. She crossed herself. She was afraid of the dead.

I imagined him creeping toward the doorway in the moonlight, looking in at us while we slept, watching us as he had watched the machine in the mill with those clever eyes glowing like the light from our lamp when Mamá turned it up.

I dug in Mamá's vegetable garden for his bones until she discovered the holes I made. I dug near the outhouse and found the skull of a small animal. From the ceiba tree, I took a seed pod and broke it open and pulled out the white silk inside. I covered the skull with the silk and set it at the base of the tree. The next day there was no trace of it. After that, for a while, I was haunted.

I asked Nana if the Chinese man had died in Malagita. Nana said he had simply disappeared. The Chinese, she told me, were not like any other people. Her own grandmother had lived during the time when there were still black slaves in San Pedro. A few Chinese had been brought into the country to work. When the owners of the cattle ranches and the coffee plantations tried to treat them as they treated the blacks, flogging them, or beating them with rough sticks, they would kill themselves from the shame of it.

"My own grandmother told me of these things—and when they didn't kill themselves, they'd slice up someone else with their long knives."

Even if the Chinese had died in the capital, he might return to his house. I was afraid of his ghost. How he must have hated the villagers who had refused his vegetables! How lonely he must have been, going to his machine in the mill, coming home to this cabin off by itself! Yet my fear of him was half sham—I entertained myself with it—although there were times when the dread of him appearing to me in some unimaginable form drove me wild, especially on those nights when Mamá worked late at the great house and I was alone, stifling beneath a ragged old blanket we used only in the months when the nights were cold, but with which I entirely covered myself so that no matter which way I moved I wouldn't be able to see anything preparing to spring at me from a corner of the cabin.

Still, my fear of the ghost of the Chinese was as nothing compared to my fear of the pigs which wandered freely on the open land between our cabin and the village. In all my travels, I had never gone near them, but to reach Nana's house without circling the entire village, I had to pass through the herd.

My mother and my grandmother did not speak to each other. If they passed in the village, they averted their faces. Until I was four years old, I hadn't known I had grandmothers. Someone must have spoken of Nana within my hearing, and once I'd heard of her, I wanted nothing in the world but to see her.

"Me? You ask me!" Mamá had cried. "I won't take you to see that woman who deserted me! Who told you about her? I suppose it was Isabel Galdos. My God! Go on! Go to see her. Let Isabel Galdos take you! As for me, I expected this from the beginning. One betrayal leads to another. Ay!"

She would say no more to me about what Nana had done to her. And although she protested loudly, I didn't believe she really wanted to stop me from finding Nana. In any case, Mamá's prohibitions never had much force. She could startle me with her loud cries, her storms of weeping, the way she would strike her own body with her fists, but I knew that in the end she would yield to me with a sigh, forgetfulness already on her face—what *had* all the trouble been about—her expression one of gratified sadness.

But although it hadn't been Señora Galdos who told me about my grandmother—who it was I don't remember—she did give me directions to find her in a long whisper close to my ear when she had come by one day and found me alone in the cabin. When I said, dismayed, that I'd have to walk among the pigs to reach Nana, Señora Galdos looked at me with surprise. I thought I saw a touch of malice glinting in her eyes. It would not have been the first time I had seen adults take pleasure in the discomfort of children.

There was no other way unless I spent most of the morning walking around the village. There were the pigs, rooting in the earth beneath a scattering of trees, their gray backs dappled with the shadows of leaves. Each morning as I approached within a few yards of the herd, a sudden movement of one of them would send me running, gasping for breath, back to my door. I threw stones at them. I wept, alone in the hot stillness, and through the water of my tears, they seemed to flood the ground like a gray, filthy stream. One day, I picked up a stick and, holding it above my head, went sobbing among them. They gave way, running stiffly on their stick legs as their quick-moving yellow eyes passed over me; it was like being observed by creatures who had no light inside them.

I found my grandmother sitting on the ground in front of her cabin smoking a little pipe. She put it down and held out her arms. "My beauty!" she exclaimed. "My darling!" She touched the tears on my face which had not yet dried. I told her at once about the pigs.

She held me close to her. In her dark, low, firm voice, she related a story about pigs inhabited by devils and how Jesus had made them rush into the sea and drown themselves and the devils inside them.

"When you pass among them," she said, "whisper His name. They won't harm you."

She hugged me for a long time, singing little songs to me. She examined my toes and fed me pieces of something wonderfully sweet that she had made from coconut. It was on that first day she told me I had another grandmother, Beatriz de la Cueva.

From then on, I went to visit her almost every day. But it was many weeks before I lost some of my fear of the pigs, even though I called out, *Jesus! Jesus!* so loudly I set the village dogs to barking. I hated the pigs' smell of damp clay, the senseless twitching of their curled tails.

Mamá was in the cooking shed.

"A man called Ortiz made Nana take me away from the cane," I told her. Her hand gripped the handle of a knife. It rose and fell as she sliced a banana for frying. She cast a distracted look at me when I squatted on the ground.

"Stand up!" she cried. "You look like a little old woman!"

I stood, very slowly, to irritate her. Her short, round arm was squeezed by the sleeve of her black uniform which she had pushed up to keep it from soiling. She lifted out lard from a can with a wooden spoon she'd exchanged for the knife, and dropped it into a pan. When the lard had melted and grown hot, she dropped in the banana slices and as they crackled she turned them from side to side.

"Ortiz lifted me into the air. Then he threw me down on the ground," I said loudly.

She dropped the slices on brown paper and salted them. The heat from the shed and the warmth from the sun, now directly overhead, made me feel thick and sleepy.

"Be careful!" she warned me. "You'll become a storyteller like my Mamá. Stories and lies—they're all the same." She handed me a banana slice so hot I had to toss it from one hand to the other. I hopped away to the road that went past our cabin and sat in a rut made by the wheel of an ox cart. Quite suddenly the day darkened and almost at once rain fell heavily, emptied out of the sky as though from barrels. Just as suddenly, it stopped. The sun shone as brightly as before. Nearby, I saw a frog no bigger than the nail of my smallest finger. A thin, yellow line ran down its green back; it jumped into my open hand as I spread my fingers on the ground, and I held it loosely, feeling its tiny, wet flutter of movement.

I had lied about Ortiz throwing me to the ground because I had wanted Mamá to question me the way Nana did in a serious, interested voice. I tightened my fingers. I could have crushed the frog the way the village boys crushed lizards but I let it go.

The plantation steamed. Beyond the chimneys of the mill, I could see all the way to the red tiles of the great house. When sunlight struck the thatched roofs of the *bohíos*, they looked on fire, but the tiles of Señora de la Cueva's *vivienda* drank up the burning rays and kept their look of coolness. Beyond the roof, far, far away, was the slope of the mountain where Antonio de la Cueva had been broken like a stick, and where the small coffee plantation still flourished. Near the summit of the mountain, the dark stone tower of an old fortress rose above the trees.

Nana had told me that on the side of the tower hidden from view there was a great cliff from which the Spaniards, who had once owned our country, had hurled prisoners into the sea. Thousands, she had said. The few who had escaped had dug tunnels with their bare hands out into a forest whose trees had long since been cut down to make ties for the railroad. The old fortress was deserted now except perhaps for spirits, dangerous spirits, Nana had said, because their lives had been filled with so much suffering and terror. But even before the Spaniards came, there had been suffering on the mountain. Nana had told me of Indians who fought among themselves, who ate their prisoners, and who flayed the skins of their enemies and wore them like capes.

The palm fronds, the blossoms of climbing vines and tangled creepers, twined around the branches of the mango trees, a grove of which stood on the other side of the road—all gleamed with raindrops. Beneath the mangoes, a flock of silver-feathered guinea hens sheltered.

My mother passed from the cooking shed to the cabin, carrying dinner on a plate, black beans and rice—Moors and Christians, Papá called them. I followed her, water dripping from my hair onto the dirt floor.

"For God's sake, dry yourself," she said. She set three places at the table as she always did. But Papá did not come today.

I ate with a spoon. Mamá used one of the two heavy, silver forks Papá had brought us from the great house. After we had eaten, she would wash the fork, wrap it in a piece of cloth and place it next to the other one in a basket beneath her bed where she also kept a pair of shoes Papá had bought for her in San Isidro.

We ate, the silence stirred softly from time to time by Mamá's sighs. A distant cry came from somewhere. Was it a man? A woman? I was suddenly alarmed. Was the voice summoning me? "Mamá?" I looked up at her. Her face was blank. She frowned slightly. She was still in her working time. A faint breeze sprang up; I saw through the doorway the moving leaves of a palmetto.

After dinner, Mamá would go back to the kitchen of the *vivienda* from which she would not return until dark. I could not imagine her moving quickly at her work. On Sundays, after she had returned from early Mass, she would lie on the bed, one wrist resting on her forehead, her fingers curling loosely, her eyes half-closed so that she looked as though she was dying. But on those rare Sundays when Papá was with us, she cooked all day and swept out corners of the cabin she never glanced into unless Papá was there. Even then, she moved so slowly, it made me want to shout with impatience and run away from her.

Once in a while, she brought home food from the *vivienda*, dishes that had been sent back to the kitchen from the Señora's table and which the servants, already stuffed with eating all day long, permitted Mamá to take away. For this purpose she always carried a tin bowl to work with her. When she came home with it empty, we had fried eggs and beans and rice for supper.

One evening as I stood in the doorway where I usually waited for her, I saw her running down the path that led to our cabin from the canal which flowed between it and the de la Cueva gardens. Even from where I stood, I could hear her praying and calling on God to help her. The guinea hens woke and filled the night with their agitated cries which bubbled like water rushing over stone.

"Don't touch me!" she called out. She leaped into the cabin and with a sob of relief, placed a large platter on the table, at the same time letting fall the tin bowl from beneath her arm. In the candle light, I saw a golden pudding quiver. Around it, on the rim of the platter, were birds in flight and between each one, a spray of smoky blossom.

My mother breathed heavily as though she was still running. I had never tasted *flan* before although Nana had described it when she spoke of all the things she had cooked during the years my grandfather had owned his own farm.

"La Señora sent it back to the kitchen," Mamá whispered.

"Why are you whispering?"

"Hush!"

She passed her hand over the pudding in a way that made me think of the little chapel, of Father Céspedes' hands fluttering over the altar.

"It's not only a piece of something," she said reverently. "It's the whole of itself. I couldn't bear to empty it into the bowl. No one saw me take the platter—how could I have done that? If it breaks . . . Oh! If it breaks!"

We ate it all. It was wonderfully smooth. I felt sick, the thick taste of eggs in my throat. Mamá washed the platter with our drinking water. While she dried it, she sat on the bed, holding it over the mattress as she turned it slowly around. I leaned against her and reached out to touch one of the birds whose shape rose against my finger.

"No!" she uttered, pushing me away. With both hands, she carried the platter to the table where she lowered it gently. I woke once during the night. Mamá was bending over it, motionless and hunched as I had seen her stand before the votive candles in the chapel. I felt lonely to see my mother standing there as though worshipping, her shoulder and one arm touched by the moonlight which came through the window and which, even as I was staring at her, was suddenly shut off by clouds so that Mamá simply disappeared. I was afraid to call out, to startle her. I felt swollen as though my inside was larger than my outside.

She left earlier than usual in the morning carrying the platter in the cloth with which she'd dried it.

"Pray for me, Luisa," she said. "Pray that I don't stumble. Pray to the Mother of God I keep this safe, that Ursula Vargas doesn't see me with it in my hands . . ."

I had never been to the kitchen of the *vivienda*, but I knew from Mamá all the names of the other servants. Ursula Vargas was the housekeeper, "a snake," Mamá said, crossing herself to ward off snakebite. Mamá was so afraid of her that I had become afraid, too, and sometimes I would say her name out loud when I kicked open a nest of biting ants, or when a wasp flew circles around me.

Mamá was the only woman from the village who worked in the kitchen. Except for Brake, her English valet, Beatriz de la Cueva's servants came from Spain. A maid of all work had fallen ill during her first week in Malagita. She was sent back to Spain, and it was her place which Mamá took.

She had been fourteen years old when Ursula Vargas had walked through the village looking for a girl to work in the kitchen. When Señorita Vargas saw Mamá, she was bent over a tub in Nana's yard washing clothes. She looked strong. Much later, Vargas learned that she could read and write, accomplishments which might have counted against her if Vargas had suspected them.

Nana said, "Such women never imagine there is a single thing they don't know. If Vargas had asked your simpleminded Mamá if she'd had any schooling, Fefita would have told her. But the schooling made no difference although it might have if Vargas hadn't seen her that day. Only a minute and your entire life changes. We weigh no more than feathers. But there's no use in thinking about that—life is the way it is, cry as you may. I had a sense—a warning—that something was going to happen when I looked to see that Fefita was doing what she should. She fell into such dreams, she had to be reminded some days to put one foot down before the other in order to walk. And I saw someone observing her from the road, a woman in a black dress, the material of special quality, not widow's cloth. Well, then, we needed money. What was I to do? The sum was so small, it's hardly worth mentioning. But we had no choice. I let my daughter go. I knew there would be a calamity."

"Was that me?" I asked, happy to be sitting in her lap, my legs dangling above the smooth dirt floor.

"Don't be so pleased with yourself," she said. "It wasn't your doing."

When Nana said *calamity* in the strong, stirring way she pronounced certain words, I couldn't connect it with anything concerning Mamá.

Mamá, unharnessed from the yoke of her work, slumped as though dazed by a blow. Only her hand, when it held her palmetto fan, moved with purpose. Above its movement, I often saw her eyes slide from me to the doorway, to the few objects in our house, the table, her bed, my straw mattress in the corner, the basket that held the forks, as though she could not understand what she was doing among these things in this place.

When Nana rested and smoked her pipe, leaning in her doorway, gazing out wordlessly, her wash done, her house swept, her mending put aside, she looked ready to spring in an instant to a horse's back.

My mother's voice wandered, trailed off, misted with sighs. Did she know what she thought? Was she thinking? Her own tears so often took her by surprise.

I didn't see the money that Mamá was paid, but Nana showed me a few coins once, putting them in my hands so, she said, I could feel their weight. Nana did a little of this and that—fancy sewing for a confirmation dress, making sweets from coconut, or another kind of sweet made by boiling milk for hours. When she gave predictions to women about their futures, she didn't take money. Some people in Malagita called Nana *Rafaela de la mala fortuna* because all her predictions were of calamities.

"It's a calamity to be born," she said often, "and a worse one to die."

There was a witch on the outskirts of the village who never predicted anything but who was said to have caused harm to those she'd taken a dislike to. Women left food in front of her hut. Sometimes she stole a goat and killed it. Señora Galdos swore she had seen her rolling in blood. No one dared accuse her of stealing because of what she might do in revenge. But Nana, when we spoke of these matters, told me that only God could work magic. The old witch had fooled people, not a difficult thing to do if you had the skill. It was probably the only way she knew how to take care of herself. The world was full of people, Nana said, for whom life was utterly impossible, made so, often as not, by other people. "Still, don't stare at the old woman or speak to her," she warned me. "Malice is enough of a calamity."

I had seen the witch once, her face splotched with raw, pink patches as though parts of it had been peeled like fruit. She had been carrying a long stick. When she saw me staring at her, she beat the air with the stick and howled like a dog.

"Is it all right to touch Enano's hunchback?" I asked Nana. Enano was an old dwarf who lived in a partly collapsed shed with his ancient mother. All the children of the village touched his hump for good luck.

"What do you want luck for? It's nearly always bad." She looked at me with a sad expression. "Don't forget, Enano is somebody's child."

In the tin tub in which Nana bathed me twice every week, I watched her brown hands break the surface of the water as they searched for the rag, a bit of soap. I widened my index finger and thumb and a bubble grew between them. I blew it free. As Nana spoke, her breath cooled my skin. Her head, covered with rippling black hair, was close to mine.

"Your fourth toe is exactly like my fourth toe," she said. "When you are seven, you must bathe yourself."

I stood up, she dried me and dressed me. She took strips of rough brown paper and rolled up the strands of my brown hair and tied the strips in knots. Then we sat and ate hard crackers and fruit. She said that Dr. Baca, whom I knew she detested, was a glutton and would eat himself to death. She had had a dream about Father Céspedes in which she had seen him in the moonlight stepping across a large puddle. When he lifted up his black skirt, she saw that one of his feet was cloven like a goat's hoof. She said the de la Cuevas had eaten up the country like termites eat wood, and that the souls of the farmers whose land they had gobbled would weigh like stones upon their heads and keep them earthbound forever.

I stared at Nana's hair where it began on her forehead growing back in waves, delicate hairs like plumage. She made a prediction about me. "No one will take care of you when I'm dead. You must learn to take care of yourself." I saw Nana dead, lying on the dirt floor. I sobbed, and she embraced me. "Hush," she said. "Now, I'll tell you a story." She handed me a cloth to dry my tears.

"At the foot of the mountains in the north of our country," she began, "there were once many caves. In time, they collapsed, and their substance changed the soil and made it good for growing tobacco. The land is not open there as it is here but closed in by mountains so steep you must descend by ladders. I heard of one place where eighty ladders were let down so men could get to the bottom to plant the tobacco. They need oxen to plow so the strongest men carry down the calves. But once they're there, they can never be brought up again. Do you know why?"

She wiped crumbs from my lips with her fingers. "Think!" she said severely.

"The ladders fall?"

"Ah, Luisa! You're not thinking!"

"What's the difference between a story and a lie?" I asked.

"A lie hides the truth, a story tries to find it," she said impatiently. "All right, then, listen. The oxen don't remain calves any more than you'll remain a child. They grow too big, and the men can't carry them back up the ladders. They live and die on those small plots of land at the foot of the mountains."

I strained to grasp her meaning. She watched me closely, then took my hands in hers. "Don't worry," she said soothingly. "You'll see it all someday."

I understood enough to know that Nana saw what others couldn't see, that for her the meaning of one thing could also be the meaning of a greater thing.

For my mother, a thing was only itself. She could see what was in front of her, the wash piled in the basket, the tiny stones she snatched triumphantly from a handful of dried beans, the shreds of sugar cane that clung to my clothes after I had sucked out the sweetness from a stalk, the endless lines of ants which in certain months moved in wavering lines across the floor of our cabin, the heel of a shoe, one of the pair Papá had bought her, that had broken off the only time she had worn them, and which she would hold close to her face, staring at it. She always brought things close to her eyes as though they did not enable her to see but were dark windows behind which something struggled to look and understand.

I didn't behave toward my mother as the other children of Malagita did to theirs. It was Nana whose hugs and kisses I sought. It was she whose words I remembered and thought about, like thrilling stories one could hear over and over again.

When, at Mass, I noticed Mamá staring raptly at the image of St. Joseph which stood in a niche near the altar, I didn't believe she knew what she was praying to him for. With strange satisfaction, I saw the little pimples of wax on the bare feet of the image, and places where the blue of his robe had run into the pink wax of his skin.

I described the *flan* to Nana.

"Leavings," she said scornfully. "Droppings from the old woman's table."

I looked sorrowfully at an ugly little doll made of rags which Señora Galdos had given me.

"What's mine?" I asked.

"Nothing!" cried Nana fiercely. "None of us owns anything. Those bits of soap I wash you with? Theirs. Do you hear that hen clucking? She is not mine. Not this house, not the pins in my hair. All I had was my daughter and Orlando de la Cueva took her."

She made a sudden gesture with her hand; curving her fingers, she seemed to try and seize the air.

The paper twists pinched the skin of my head. I sighed, wishing it was time to undo them. I'd have curls then that looked like the shells of land snails and they'd last just long enough to reveal to Mamá that I had been at Nana's.

"You've been to see her! That woman who abandoned me when I needed her most—at your birth when I was in agony for thirty-six hours!" She would cry a little and bang a pot with a wooden spoon and sniffle. She'd be thinking about something else soon enough.

I stared at the peak of hair on Mamá's forehead. It was like Nana's, so smooth and silken in its ripples. Her eyes, too, were like Nana's, deep-set, dark, heavy-lidded. Was it what she saw that made her look so different from her mother?

"Does Papá look like his mother?" I asked her.

Mamá moved uneasily in her chair; the tiny silver crochet needle with which she had been making a narrow line of lace slipped out of her hand. She felt for it in her lap, her head bowed.

I asked again. She made an odd protesting sound as though something unpleasant had touched her skin.

"She doesn't come to the kitchen," she said at last, pushing the crochet needle against her finger. "And I never leave it except when there are guests from the capital and I must take them their breakfasts."

I imagined suddenly that between the kitchen and the rest of the rooms in the *vivienda*, there lived a herd of pigs, packed between walls, astride tables and chairs.

"Papá visits her," I said.

"At least *she* has a heart," Mamá said broodingly.

A breeze brought the smell of jasmine into the cabin. We both looked up and sniffed. Mamá's face grew dreamy. Her long lids slowly shut. "This life . . ." she murmured.

"Does my other grandmother, Señora de la Cueva, know about me?" I shouted. Startled, she opened her eyes and began to crochet rapidly.

"She knows everything," she replied.

When I asked Nana the same question, she said, "For Beatriz de la Cueva, you are a bedbug."

Holding a huge wooden spoon in both her hands, she stirred the liquid in a black kettle over an open fire. She was making *dulce de leche*.

"My stupid Fefita," she said. "She gave them the only thing she had a right to withhold. About what else could she say yes or no? And as if it was nothing—when it was all that belonged to her!"

"What was nothing?"

"Nothing."

"Oh!"

"Don't kick up the dirt. You'll put out the fire!"

"But what are you talking about?" I wailed.

"Luisita, even if I say it, you wouldn't know what I was saying. It is a thing between men and women."

I stood still, the fire's heat against my legs no less intense than that which rose to my face. I was ashamed to keep anything from Nana, but I was about to. I didn't know why I wanted to conceal from her that I already knew about the thing between men and women, although it was only as she had spoken those words that I realized I knew. "The thing between" was what had awakened me on nights when moonlight, or the paler light of stars, illuminated the cabin, and revealed on Mamá's bed the shape of something like a horse and its rider, galloping in place as though mired in deep mud, until, at last, the rider fell from his horse, and I saw it was Papá, his leg sliding slowly over the edge of the mattress until, with a start, he drew it back, slipping it beneath the cover so I no longer had to see his flesh, so white in the unearthly light.

"Hush! We'll wake her!" Mamá had whispered on one such night, and I had held my breath in horror lest she should see that I was awake. It was how I felt now, why I would not look at Nana lest she see in my face the reflection of the picture in my head. Was it because of that that Nana couldn't speak to Mamá? Why—because of that?

"Don't you want to see her sometimes?" I asked.

"Yes," she answered at once. "I want to."

"Papá's mother is not angry the way you are. She sees him all the time."

"Nothing matters to that woman except what she desires."

She stirred the bubbling milk steadily. It was thick, and as brown as sugar. She had a grave, listening look on her face. I suspected she was missing Mamá, and I felt desolate as I often felt at night, alone in the cabin, waiting in the doorway for the sight of Mamá's figure hurrying from the canal footbridge.

I told Nana news that was already several weeks old but which I'd forgotten, although it had troubled me at the time. It was that Papá had told Mamá he would not allow me to be confirmed. Nana did not seem surprised. "There'll always be trouble between them," she said. "It began in sin after all."

"Mamá screamed when he told her. For a year, she's been thinking about my confirmation dress." I had been thinking about it, too, and I had been angry and bewildered at Papá's words. "Whatever she becomes, I won't have her crossing herself like a primitive every moment of the day," he had said. "You can take her with you to your Masses. But that's all."

"Your Mamá screams as other people yawn," Nana said.

"I would have had a white veil for my face. And white shoes," I said resentfully.

Nana stopped stirring and looked at me.

She went to Mass during the week in the village, but on Sundays, she walked three miles to a neighboring village to attend the Mass in the church there so she would be in no danger of meeting Mamá. Nana prayed often—whenever she felt like it, she said—but she made fun of Father Céspedes, of all priests, calling them black beetles.

"You know nothing," she said to me. "You've had no catechism. Say a Hail Mary for me."

"Ave Maria," I said.

She laughed. "What's to become of you?" she asked the sky. She began to stir again. "You can't work in the cane. You can't pray."

"When will the *dulce* be ready to eat?"

"It's not for you," she answered. "I'll sell it for a few pennies. After all, I don't have a rich father to help me through life!" And she laughed again.

The church bells rang for six o'clock Mass. It was time for me to go home, although Mamá might still be at work. I kissed Nana, who held me close for a long moment, then I ran through the village, swept home by the pealing of the bells, the air drenched in scents of jasmine and cooking cane, past the *plazuela*, through the herd of pigs which seemed, magically, to make way for me, all the way to my door from where I saw, standing motionless in the shadowed room, my father, his flat hat on the back of his head like a black halo.

.   .   .

"Who should I love better? God or you?" I once asked Papá.

"I am the one who feeds you," he had answered. "I am the one who is here."

It was a lie. My mother fed me. I knew that from the beginning. But his lie pleased me, and I often repeated it to myself as though it had been a kindness, a kind touch on my hair.

It was the beginning of my life that my mother spoke of on each anniversary of my birth. Oh—the strain of trying to show her sympathy as she described her labor! I dreaded that day!

Mamá would awake with a cry, "Ay Dios! It is today!" And even before she rose to wash herself and to dress, she would begin the story.

"Seven years ago, on the thirty-first of December, at this very moment, I was six hours away from the end of my suffering. My labor began little by little—I thought it would be easy, such small pains, they almost made me laugh—but then, as night came, the pain turned into

knives, here, down here—" and to show me where, she would throw
back the cover and stand and press her hands against her lower belly—
"cutting, cutting, all through the night until noon the next day, the very
last day of the year, 1926, when you finally released me."

She would look at me intently to make sure she had my attention.

"The pig," I prompted her.

"Ah, the pig! They were killing the pig at the great house for the New
Year's celebration. They were cutting its throat, and I thought its screams
were my own."

I told her I had to go to the outhouse. Reluctantly, she let me go. When I
returned, she began the next part of her story, how Dr. Baca had been in
Tres Hermanos to collect money from a winning lottery ticket, how the
old midwife had died the first week of December, and how her daughter
was so frightened of birth labor, she had hidden in the cane where no
one could find her. One of the women of the village had done what had
to be done, but so brutally, said Mamá, that she would never be the same,
down there, and again she pressed her hands against her lower body as
though she had to urinate.

By then, I was frantic at her sobs, the way she swayed as though about
to fall, and I was crying along with her. At last, she finished. She dried
her tears on her nightgown and mine by pressing her moist palms against
my cheeks. Then she knelt down and told me how I had been wrapped in
a clean shirt of Papá's and placed against her breasts. A smile, as foolish
as the one I had seen on the face of Enano, the hunchback, when I touched
him for luck, stretched out her small, puffy mouth so I could see a tooth
gleaming. She cradled herself with her arms, then playfully reached out
a finger and touched my nose.

After she had washed herself, after she had boiled milk and strained it
for morning coffee, she brought me a small linen towel on which she had
embroidered my initials in orange thread: L. S. Around its borders ran a
narrow line of crochet. What was I to use it for, I asked her sullenly, seeing how gay she was now that she had made me so miserable.

"Keep it in memory of me," she said. Her words reminded me vaguely
of something I had heard Father Céspedes say in the chapel.

After she had returned home from the kitchen that evening of my sev-

enth birthday, she began to take on against Nana, thoughts of whom, I
supposed, had rankled in her throughout the day.

"Anyone would think, with two of her children dead, and one son in
North America as good as dead, and only me left, she would have—if
she weren't such an unnatural woman—come to help me in my need.
Imagine! She sat there on the floor of her cabin like a stone. Señora Galdos
went to her to beg her to come. All she did was to blow smoke at her
from her pipe!"

"Nana told me a great fire will lick up our whole country soon like a
communion wafer."

"When will she set the fire?" she cried and let out a shriek of laughter.
It was false laughter; I could hear the effort of her breathing as she tried
to keep it going like someone blowing on a flame.

"She was right about the hailstorm," I said.

"It's not important to be right about such things," Mamá said. "It's
important only to know when your children need you."

Nana's house was one of the few in the village which had a tin roof.
The small hard pellets of hail had struck it with such force it had sounded
as if a carpenter was driving nails into it. Nana and I had watched from
the doorway as the hailstones rolled across the ground. A watery coldness rose from them such as I had never felt before. Malagita, the cane
fields stretching far and wide around it, seemed suddenly pitiful. I imagined the land as Nana had told me it had once been, empty, no cities, no
villages, a wilderness, just the way the Spaniards had found it when,
weak and exhausted, they had landed on the shore of the island. But they
had been strong enough for murdering.

"Three brothers, Pedro, Vicente, Tomás, anchored their ship in Bajía
Vieja four hundred years ago and claimed the island for Spain," related
Nana. "A week later, Pedro, the oldest, killed Vicente the youngest. Vicente had praised Pedro for his piety in deciding to name the island, San
Pedro, after the saint. But Pedro replied he was giving his own name to
the island, Isla de Pedro, not the saint's. When Vicente observed that
Pedro himself was named after the saint, Pedro kicked him to the ground
and stabbed him with his dagger. He was buried in the forest that grew
there in those days, just above the beach, but his bones were never found."

"How do you know Pedro kicked Vicente?" I asked.

"Tomás kept a diary. It's in the National Museum in Tres Hermanos, and your sweet grandfather saw it with his own eyes. Even so, if it had not been written down, one knows how Spaniards are."

"And then what happened?"

"As is their custom, they murdered all the natives they could find. They fought among themselves for the land and, naturally, the ones with the biggest holdings were the biggest brutes. Black people from Africa did the hard labor. After a time, the cattle ranchers found there was more profit in sugar. From then on, cane decided everything—it ate up the land, and because there are only four or five months of hard work to make it into sugar, it left people idle for the rest of the time and there was hardly any work for them to do so they could earn their living. But in the end, Spain lost the island to the United States, and that country gave San Pedro its freedom."

As she pronounced the last word, she pulled down the lower lid of her right eye with one finger, a sign in Malagita that what you have heard or what you have said is not to be taken seriously.

She looked amused with herself. I was suddenly angry and stamped my foot.

"Then whose country is it?" I demanded.

"Beatriz de la Cueva and others like her own this country," she said, and this time she made no sign but looked at me gravely, the little smile gone from her lips.

"She came with the three brothers?"

"Ay! Luisa! That was four hundred years ago!" She began to smile again. "Well—perhaps she did. Perhaps through an oversight, she didn't die. Now—pay attention. First came the criminals and soldiers and the priests. Then the ancestors of the de la Cuevas."

"Are we Spaniards?"

"We are everything except, thank God, English. It was the English who brought the black slaves." She took hold of my chin and cupped it with her hard, narrow hand. "I see a touch of the Chinese there—in the corner of your eyes."

I didn't care about being this or that. I was thinking about Brake, the

English servant in the *vivienda*. How I would like to see him, to see what it meant to be English!

"You had an uncle, Aldo," she said, sighing. "He had blue eyes and his hair was red. He died when he was four. Blue eyes, enormous, like the sky."

I began to look around the room for the doll Señora Galdos had given me. I had lost it somewhere. I wanted to find it so I could take it apart and see what she had stuffed it with. There were lumps like little stones under the bright red cloth of its body, and in the last few days the doll had begun to stink like rotten fruit. Last week, Señora Galdos had called to me from her window as I walked on my way to Nana's, and asked in her silly voice, "Where is your precious little baby?" and when I held out the ugly thing, which I'd just been smacking against the trunks of the royal palms in the *plazuela*, she uttered cooing cries of the sort I had heard women make when a new baby was thrust into their arms for them to admire. If, after I had ripped open the doll, Señora Galdos asked to see it, I would say it had died of *viruelas*. Since she had pretended it was alive, I could pretend it had died. There was something about Señora Galdos that made me behave in a sullen, bad-tempered way even though it was she who had told me where Nana lived, and afterward, the one who took me to Nana's when I was ill and needed the nursing that Mamá had no time to give me.

The graveyard was full of babies who had died in the first few weeks of their lives, and of older children like my Uncle Aldo, sickened by a disease frequently called the will of God when neither the village doctor nor any of the two or three *curanderas* in the vicinity, thought by the women to be far more gifted than the doctor, and certainly kinder and less coarse in their ministrations, could find a cure for them.

I wondered if Nana had forgotten how often she had told me about Aldo of the blue eyes, and of the death of another son, Felipe. Or was it that thoughts of her dead children were always in her mind and she had to let them out so she would have room for other thoughts?

Felipe had been two years younger than Aldo when he'd fallen beneath the hooves of a horse ridden by an old man carrying his ancient father across the saddle—"so old, his bones showed through his skin . . . it was as though death carried death,"—Nana had said—fleeing to the mountain along with the rest of the people of Malagita who had learned that an army of Negroes, rebelling against the hideous conditions under which they labored in the nickel mines to the north, was marching across the country, burning plantations and murdering everyone in them, and that it was only a few hours from the village.

As it turned out, the Negroes had not been within sixty miles of Malagita. They had killed several officials of the company who owned the nickel mines, and they had burned down their own wretched shacks. Many of them were shot, and the rest imprisoned when they were caught by soldiers from the United States who had been sent to our island to help put down the rebellion.

If they had reached Malagita, they would have found only Nana in her cabin, holding her broken, dead child across her lap. She had sent Federico, the oldest, to the mountain with a neighbor's family. My grandfather was away looking for work in the capital. My mother was not born until a year later. "All for a lie, my poor little son was trampled to death," Nana said.

The bitter suffering of adults was everywhere, in the voices of the women who came to visit my mother on those Sundays my father was away, in the faces of the men without work who hung around the jail or the little store, and, toward the last weeks of the dead time—before the mill started up—and when food was scarce and the monotony of the long days had worn the men down until they crackled with worry and rage, in the very air of the village so that you seemed to breathe it in and taste it, like you tasted the black acrid smoke that poured from the burning heaps of rubbish on the outskirts.

Only Enano, the hunchbacked dwarf, showed no anger, no sorrow. And Mamá, although she groaned as much as any other woman in Malagita, perhaps more, was so changeable in her moods that it didn't seem possible any deep bitterness had taken root in her nature. She didn't appear to grow older but to remain always the same, a small, plump woman, rushing fearfully from the cabin to the *vivienda*, returning to collapse on her bed and whisper to God who floated somewhere above in the great blank sky.

No one asked to be born, Nana said, but when babies were born in our village, people collected around the house of the mother like bees around blossoms. If it was an especially difficult labor, Dr. Baca took the mother to the surgery and women gathered at the barred windows, calling out words of comfort, groaning with her as her suffering grew more intense. Later, when the infant had been born, the men lost their look of mysterious preoccupation, their intense impatience in the company of their wives, and smiling, gathered around with the women to observe and admire the new baby.

If it was a girl, her ears were pierced eight days after her birth. Once, I pushed my way into a crowded cabin where I watched a woman set fire to liquid in a spoon, dip a needle into it, then plunge the needle into each ear lobe of the tiny infant whose cries brought a gratified smile to her father's face. The bloodied little white threads which were pulled through the holes made wet, pink circles on the baby's cheeks. "*Pobrecita . . .*" everyone murmured. Poor little thing.

"Look!" called Nana. "Here's this miserable piece of a thing Isabel Galdos made for you!" She held up the doll I had dropped on a heap of corn husks near the doorway and forgotten. "Piece of a thing." That amused me all the way home.

I took a knife and cut the doll open. Out fell fruit pits wrapped in bits of rag. But pulp still clung to a few pits, and on one wriggled a small worm the color of the flesh of a mango.

.   .   .

My own father did not see me until April, at the end of the *zafra*, the harvest, when I was four months old. Mamá had gone back to work in the de la Cueva kitchen a week after my birth, leaving me in the care of one or another of the village children, those who were too young, or too weak, to labor in the cane. Mamá would come home to feed me, running so as not to waste a minute of the time Ursula Vargas had grudgingly given her, and—she told me—holding her breasts so they would not hurt her as she ran.

As I slept and woke in the basket that was my first bed, my father was occupied with the duties which arose from his engagement to Ofelia Mondragon, the daughter of the owner of a plantation to the east of Malagita. It is only her name that I recollect. What his duties were, as her future husband, I never learned. But I imagined the principal one was to murmur her name over and over again, as I did, upon hearing from Mamá how Ofelia was jilted on her wedding day.

On that morning, Papá arrived at my mother's cabin in his wedding clothes and sent home whatever child was guarding me in my basket. Mamá found him sprawled on the bed ignoring my cries. She was frantic, as usual, with all the work she had left undone at the *vivienda*. When she saw him, she let out a shriek, she told me later, that she knew could be heard all the way to Nana's cabin.

"Now!" she had shouted at him. "And on this day! Finally! Finally you've torn yourself from the side of Señorita Mondragon to come and see your own child!"

She had snatched me up from the basket and thrust me at him.

"Put her away at once where I can't see her," he had said.

She had nursed me, keeping her back to him. He had undressed and left his bridal clothes in a heap on the floor, and when she lay down beside him on the mattress he had brought her a year before from the *vivienda*, he had told her he had refused to marry Ofelia, that when he'd risen that morning and thought of his bride who was about to become his wife, how proper and dull she was, how she babbled from fright and emptiness, a black hole seemed to open up at the edge of his bed, and all the while he had dressed, the black hole remained there, waiting for him, and he had known he could not go through with the wedding. Beatriz de la Cueva, he had told Mamá, declared that by jilting Ofelia, he had finished off his proper life, and that whatever he did after this day was of no consequence at all. It was, my mother told me years later, the only time Papá had reported to her anything La Señora said. From now on, he had told her, he would live with her.

It was a scandal in Malagita for nearly a month, talk about it lasting at least a week longer than an earlier scandal I had heard Mamá and Señora Galdos discussing when they didn't know I was just outside the door, trying to make a *casilla*, a little cage built of twigs in which I planned to trap a pigeon. This other scandal concerned one of Papá's uncles who had come from Cadiz to visit his sister. A week after he had arrived, two cutters had discovered him on the ground between two rows of cane, his hand gripping the penis of the fourteen-year-old son of a mill supervisor. Señora Galdos had remarked that, clearly, Señor de la Cueva had known nothing of the rapidity with which good cutters can move down a row, for surely he must have heard them slashing away. The uncle returned at once to Cadiz, the boy had been thrashed by his father, and thereafter was called Gomez, *la mariposa*, until the day he was sent away to a Jesuit seminary in the capital.

I had never heard Mamá laugh with so much freedom. I began to laugh with her, giving away my presence.

There was silence from the cabin. I heard a cracked giggle from Señora Galdos. Mamá appeared in the doorway. She looked frightened.

"Don't repeat what you heard to anyone," she said to me anxiously.

I didn't know what I'd heard. It had been the surprise of her laughter that had aroused my own.

My father's offense in jilting Señorita Mondragon and coming to live in our cabin had no clear result for Mamá. She continued to work in the kitchen. Brake, the Englishman, and Ursula, the housekeeper, treated her exactly as they always had, a local girl who had to be watched closely in case she forgot what she'd been taught yesterday. And Señora de la Cueva, on a rare visit to the servant's wing, passed by my mother without a word or a glance.

Although La Señora had told my father his life was finished, he continued to visit her when he wished to. When Mamá once asked him timidly, "And La Señora? Is she well?" he replied coldly, "Keep still."

My father did not speak Spanish as we did. It seemed a different language from ours, as unfamiliar as the English and French he could speak. I might not have noticed his singular accent with such interest if it had not been on the question of language that Mamá actually defied him. Even I had recognized that her weeping, her protests against one thing or another, were only forms of surrender to him. But she would not change the way she spoke, not one word, and when, once, in a fury, he leaped from his chair, picked it up and threatened to hurl it through the doorway, exclaiming that she was a stupid peasant who had turned one of the world's great languages into jungle mutterings, she glared at him with eyes grown enormous, glistening like candle flames, and through her fleshy little mouth with its color of red buds, came one, harsh, contemptuous word, "Idler!"

My father slowly set the chair down. Without looking at her, he went away into the darkness outside. I followed her worriedly as she moved with agitated steps about the cabin until she told me to go to bed and leave her be, for God's sake.

It was true that my father did no work, or none that I knew about. I knew that like Dr. Baca and a lot of others, he played the national lottery. The *lotería* preoccupied the men of Malagita. I had not heard of anyone winning it except for Dr. Baca. Whenever Mamá found one of Papá's discarded lottery tickets with its long printed list of numbers, she would tear it into tiny pieces and burn it.

Dr. Baca rode a gaunt horse when he traveled to an outlying district where a man might have nearly severed his arm with an ill-aimed swipe of his machete and was too weakened to come to the surgery. I had heard his horse panting as though about to expire one morning when the doctor rode by our cabin. He was a huge man. A quantity of black hair grew out of his ears and nostrils. When he visited Papá, I went to my bed at once. Mamá sat on a stool close to the door. The men drank rum until they were nearly insensible. After Dr. Baca had staggered out into the dark, Mamá dragged my father to bed, removed his clothing and rolled him over the mattress like a sack until he was pressed against the wall. Those nights he kept us awake with his loud snores and mutterings— some other language we could not speak properly.

She never told me so but I guessed why she sat on a stool near the door. It was so she could get out of our cabin quickly. There was violence in my father that threatened to erupt in ways that it was, I felt, dangerous even to imagine. He cursed, he raised his hands, doubled them into fists, then left the cabin as swiftly as a knife hurled through the doorway.

Nearly as frightful as the way his skin would turn so white was a look I had caught on his face one night when Mamá and I were clearing away our supper dishes. He was standing still, his arms limp at his sides. On his face was an expression like that of a man I'd glimpsed through the window of Dr. Baca's surgery who had been hurt by some machinery in the mill and was looking down at the blood as it poured from the wound on his wrist.

Papá didn't touch me. He ordered me to call him Papá, not *Papi*, as the other children in the village called their fathers. He would not answer me if I asked him a question in a voice he judged to be too loud. When he was home, he made me wear the shoes he had bought for me although they were so big they constantly slipped off my feet. He taught me to use a fork. He made Mamá comb my hair even if I was just about to be sent to bed.

I was unable to explain Papá to myself. His moods, his words and actions were so often unexpected, the reasons for them hidden.

But because of the mysteries of Papá's ways, more than because my ears were not pierced and I was not taught catechism or because I was the illegitimate grandchild of the proprietor of Malagita, I felt a strangeness about myself, a certainty that made me miserable yet beguiled me, that I was not part of the common life of the village, and I began—when I don't know, since, as I learned in later life, one passes almost insensibly from thoughtless certainties to the knowledge that little if anything is certain—to see and hear with the eyes and ears of an outsider.

.   .   .

In Malagita, only the doors of the jail and the store were locked, and, naturally, the entrances to the *vivienda*. I could go to Nana's cabin if I wanted, whether she was in it or not. But such a painful desolation took hold of me one early morning as I sat alone in her chair by the door that from then on, as soon as I came within sight of the cabin, I halted, waiting until I caught sight of movement inside or heard her singing some wordless song at the back.

Often she was out in the fields searching for special grasses with which she could make concoctions. These she gave to the women who were more apt to consult her than Dr. Baca, especially when their sicknesses came not from a visible wound but were deep inside them, sending out slow, frightening waves of pain from unknown organs whose shapes they could vaguely distinguish when they pressed their palms against their bodies to show Nana where they thought the trouble might be. It took me a while to comprehend that Nana was one of the village *curanderas*, perhaps as long as it took me to realize she existed even when I wasn't with her.

She was paid for her services in goods and food. But for the sweets she made, and for which she was known all over the countryside, she demanded money as she also did for mending linen from the *vivienda*

when it was handed out to her because there was too much work for
Beatriz de la Cueva's own seamstress.

There were whole days when I could not see her, and when I complained of it, she asked if I would like her to starve to death? "The first
thing is to feed oneself," she said. "After that, there may be time for talking."

Left to myself, I often followed one or another of the roads that led
out of Malagita. Some workers lived outside the village, and during the
working time when women were alone—those who were in the last days
of their pregnancy, or in poor health—they invited me in to visit them
when they saw me poking along the dusty road. They questioned me
about the great house and its affairs, and I repeated to them Mamá's frag-
mentary utterances from which, I suppose, they pieced together a sense
of the life of the *vivienda*; they caressed me and gave me food. What I said
appeared to fill them with pleasure.

Ursula Vargas, I told them, never sweated. La Señora's personal doctor, Dr. Aguirre, ate not only the food on his own plate but everything
La Señora left on hers, and his hair was jet black and so thin, Mamá told
me, that one of the serving maids had counted exactly four strands of
it combed straight across his narrow skull. Emilio, the chief cook, had
temper fits that were so terrible the other servants locked themselves in
their rooms until he had recovered himself. I told them how glad Mamá
was that she could come home every night, unlike the other servants, so
she could sleep and not be waked up by La Señora for whom day and
night were exactly the same, and who would demand a bowl of soup at
three o'clock in the morning, or, discovering a small tear in her pillow
slip, would order the seamstress to mend it, no matter what the hour.

They asked me about Calderío, the estate manager, who had taken
the place left vacant by Leopoldo de la Cueva and my father, and whom
they called *maricon*, a word that meant nothing to me but made laughter
slide across their lips. I had seen him only once and then at a great distance as I peered through the huge front gates of the *vivienda*. He was
sitting in a high-backed cane chair, his long, thin, insectlike legs crossed
at his ankles, his feet resting on the patterned marble of the veranda floor,
a broad hat tipped over his face. "Dreaming of fat boys," said old Señora
Nuñez.

On other days, I went to a swamp where, among willows and reeds, edged with floating purple flowers, a small pond lay as unmoving as water in a bowl but croaking like a giant frog with the voices of the hundreds of frogs that lived in it. For hours, I watched birds, the *tacos*, whose brilliant yellow wings flashed like sunlight among the clumps of palm, and parrots, the mossy green of their feathers like the endless band of green light which sometimes lingered on the horizon after the sun had set. In the reeds, I found a nest of brown eggs. I broke one open. A bloody clump fell liquidly to the ground. In the mass of it, a tiny beak stuck out, the color of a fingernail.

I passed near the railroad track on the way home, and if the cars were loaded with cut cane, I pulled a stalk from the open sides. Was it stealing? It was my grandmother's cane, I told myself. The brilliant lizards winked around my feet as I chewed the stalk but slipped away like water when I reached out a hand to touch them.

Wherever I went, I could always see the mountain, the long slopes, the gray tower of the old fortress.

"Is there really nothing inside the tower?" I asked Nana.

"Spirits. I told you."

"Indian spirits?"

"Spirits have no race."

"They go in and out through the tunnels," I said.

"What tunnels? You're being a little pest today!"

"The tunnels you told me about, the ones prisoners dug so they could escape."

"Spirits have no need of tunnels."

I began to dig tunnels everywhere, with sticks, with sharp stones, with a big spoon I had taken from our cooking shed. I broke the handle of the spoon and buried it beneath a tree. Mamá held her head and cried, "My God! My spoon is gone. Someone has stolen my spoon!"

"A spirit," I muttered.

"Did you take it?" she demanded, shaking me.

I said I had never seen the spoon. She had to leave for work. I sat in the doorway, feeling a lassitude, a weakness so profound that when Señora Galdos walked by, a basket on her head, I did not even raise my head to look at her.

"*Negrita!*" she called. "Come with me, help me pick guava."

I shook my head. I would never go anywhere with her though she often asked me, and I wouldn't set foot in her cabin.

She put down her basket and came to sit beside me. She took my hands and kissed them, smoothed my hair and cooed like a dove. I leaned against her shoulder that smelled of sweat and something sweet, almost like jasmine.

"Poor thing," she murmured. "What a life for you. With that *Papi* of yours."

I admitted nothing.

"You might as well be an orphan."

I realized how pitiful I was. I felt stronger. At the base of the tree where I'd buried the spoon, the earth showed no sign of having been disturbed. Perhaps I'd only imagined breaking the spoon. But when Señora Galdos had gone her way, guilt returned to take her place beside me.

That night Papá began to teach me to use a fork but he grew impatient at my clumsiness, and he gripped my fingers and pressed them around the handle and jabbed the tines against my mouth. They pierced my skin and blood dripped into the bowl of yellow rice. My mother dipped a rag in water and held it against my lip. "Brute!" she whispered.

Papá drew back from the table, his eyes nearly shut, his mouth tightly closed as though he were shutting himself away inside his own flesh where he could not be reached or touched.

How I hated him for that! I wanted to shout out to him that I had broken the spoon, and that I would break the great ugly silver forks whenever I got the chance. But I was afraid as I stared at him in the dim light, burning with hatred for him yet afraid of the shadowed hollows of his face. The spoon no longer mattered. When I looked at my mother as she wrung out the bloody rag into a basin, I felt a mute and sickening contempt for her. That night, I lay awake and listened to my parents breathing; rays of moonlight briefly touched his nose and chin, her neck and plump shoulder. Then the moon set and the room was black. The world seemed an arid, blackened place like the cane fields after the stubble was burned to the ground. I felt utterly alone. Morning came. It was Sunday. Mamá looked down at me, surprised. "You're awake," she noted sleepily.

I watched her dress for Mass. From their bed, Papá spoke.

"I don't want Luisa to go with you anymore," he said.

"You can't know what you're saying," she said. I got up and began to dress myself. Papá was suddenly by my side. He gripped my arm. Mamá cried out and grabbed my other arm. I heard the insects humming outside. Although it was early, I could see how hot the dirt of the road looked, like small puffs of brown fire. I shrieked as they both pulled at me.

"You'll twist off her arm!" Papá shouted.

"Without God, she has no use for arms," my mother cried.

My father let go of me. He took a thin cigar from his shirt pocket and lit it and went to the doorway, standing there with his back turned to us.

"Orlando," my mother implored. "Please!"

I sat on my bed on the floor and tried to rub away the red marks of their fingerprints on my arms.

"It's nothing to you. And it's too late for me—because of what I did with you. But she—" She drew a deep breath. Fervently, she called out his name, "Orlando! Orlando!"

He continued to stand where he was. She spoke to his back, but quietly now as though she was already in church, praying.

"She is your bastard. Even if you won't allow her to be confirmed, at least . . . let her go with me to Mass. For God's sake!"

My father stepped outside. Mamá fell against the wall, weeping into her hands. I went to the doorway. Papá was walking quickly down the road. He didn't look back.

Several weeks later, Mamá dressed herself in her best clothes. From the basket beneath the bed, she took a round paper box of rouge and rubbed the pink powder into her cheeks. With a stone she drove a nail through the heel of her broken shoe and blunted the point of it inside the shoe. Soon my father appeared riding Dr. Baca's horse. Mamá told me to go to Señora Galdos; she would not be home until dark. Papá lifted her on to the horse, she clasped his waist, and they rode away. I ran to Nana's where Mamá knew I would go.

I told her Mamá had put rouge on her cheeks and gone off with Papá on the horse.

Nana stared at a picture of the Virgin Mary which was tacked to a wall. "For God's sake," she said softly. "I can't believe what I'm thinking." She would not say what that was. At dusk she sent me home.

The tower on the mountain was as red as fire, but it had turned black by the time I came within sight of our cabin and darkness was pouring into the sky as though it came from the chimneys of the mill. They were home. I could smell food. I went first to the cooking shed. In a pot, a huge fish lay coiled like a snake on a nest of onions and tomatoes.

In the cabin, I found Mamá sitting on Papá's lap, the heel of her shoe once again hanging loose. Papá raised a glass to his mouth. Mamá's arm was around his neck. As I walked in, she drank from his glass and laughed softly. Papá's black hat was on the table near a bottle.

"*Hijita!*" Mamá cried. "My love!" She rose unsteadily from Papá's lap. Her whole body was convulsed with giggles. She half fell upon me.

"Daughter," she said again as though identifying me. "Your Papá and I were married in San Isidro this day." Suddenly she began to cry.

"I'm hungry," Papá said.

"You are no longer Luisa Sanchez," my mother told me between sobs. "You are Luisa de la Cueva."

She staggered out toward the cooking shed and I reached beneath the bed, into the basket, and took out the towel she had embroidered for me. I traced the initials L. S. with my finger. I didn't care what they had done that day. My name was Luisa Sanchez.

After their marriage, Papá did not oppose my going to Mass with Mamá, but she no longer insisted upon it. The little girls of Malagita showed me photographs of themselves wearing their white dresses and veils of white lace. They watched my face to see if I envied them. But by then, I bore my differences with some fortitude, partly because a certain distinction came with them, partly because I knew there was no escape from them. I rarely went to the little chapel and after a certain event occurred, I never went again.

Beatriz de la Cueva was ill, and Father Céspedes came to the village to hold a special Mass. Mamá was given time off from work to attend it, and she took me with her. Father Céspedes' knees creaked loudly; his voice droned on forever. It was noon on a day of intense heat. We knelt, sat, stood, knelt. Suddenly, I fainted. I regained consciousness and found myself lying in the aisle. Mamá's face was hidden in her hands from which dripped the black beads of her rosary. I crawled up the aisle and tumbled out the chapel doors onto the road. A man passing by at that moment, pushing a wheelbarrow loaded with sacks of lime, picked me up and wheeled me to the surgery.

Dr. Baca held my wrist in his fat, dirty fingers. Then he blew cigar smoke in my face.

"Go home," he said. "Follow your father's example. Stay out of churches."

Hidden in the folds of the black lace scarf Mamá wore to Mass was a little card on which was a picture of Jesus. His heart was pinned to the outside of his white robe. Three drops of bright red blood fell from it. Each thorn of His crown was like the transparent beak of a nestling. His eyes were the color of cocoa. He looked as if He was melting in pain and goodness.

It was to Jesus Father Céspedes directed his pleas for Señora de la Cueva's health. It was to this bleeding heart he prayed. I touched it, a puff of silken paper that bulged out like a frog's throat. I would have liked to cut it open as I had cut open the doll, to find out what was inside it, but the very thought of doing such a thing frightened me so much that it made me shout and run around in circles to force it from my mind.

Mamá said that most of La Señora's sickness was craziness. She herself had once seen her leaning from one of the great windows of the *vivienda*, calling out, "*Mi Coronel! Mi Coronel!*" until she was seized by Dr. Aguirre and her nurse and taken back to bed.

"What *coronel*?"

"There is no *coronel*," Mamá replied. Sometimes I hung around the gates of the *vivienda*, hoping I would see La Señora leaning from her window and crying out passionately for her colonel. How could there be anything she wanted that she couldn't have?

Whenever I heard someone speak of her, that day I would watch my father with burning interest. But it was not possible to ask him anything about her.

I told Nana that La Señora de la Cueva was really my grandmother now that Papá and Mamá were married. Nana snorted. "You are Luisa Sanchez in the eyes of God," she said.

I was not fooled by the eyes of God; it was in Nana's eyes that I remained Luisa Sanchez; she had claimed me for her own. But I was not sure to whom I belonged.

Papá was at home more often. I did not like to be alone with him even though he rarely spoke to me; he didn't ask me where I was going or when I was returning, and hardly seemed to notice me when I stayed around the cabin. In his presence, I felt dangers, unnamed, unknown. One morning when I guessed he would be staying home, I walked with Mamá to the canal, waiting until she had crossed the footbridge before I scrambled down the bank to the water.

Often, there was an old man fishing there. He called me *hija* and as soon as he saw me, he would begin to chatter with great liveliness. He had no teeth, and I had difficulty in understanding him. But I liked him to call me daughter, and I liked to see the strong tug on his line that pulled it deep into the green water. He pointed to the teeth of a barracuda he had caught.

"If we had been bathing in the canal, he would have eaten us. Look how he is staring at us from the corner of his eye!" He shrieked with laughter, his pale gums gleamed in the sunlight, and his spittle sprayed the side of my face. Suddenly, he snatched up my hand and placed it between his gums and pressed them together. I shuddered from head to toe and pulled my hand out of his mouth. "I am an old barracuda with no teeth," he shouted after me as I clambered up the bank.

There were many old men in our village who had little to do except to find people who would listen to them. But the women, even the oldest ones, tended the chickens and pigs and goats and their gardens. They took care of each other when they were sick. Dr. Baca was sent for only when every other possibility had been tried. If he found a pot of magic herbs in a woman's cooking shed, he would hurl it to the ground. When she knew he was coming to examine her, a woman would hide her herbs, or her doll made of wax and straw, or a small cross she could carry hidden in her hand, made from the wood of a tree that grew with its roots in the air. If she was too sick to conceal these treasures, her neighbors would do it for her. Everyone knew Dr. Baca was indifferent to any woman's belief in witches and magic; he simply didn't want to see evidence of it.

I wondered what he thought about little card pictures of Jesus. There was no one in Malagita whom I dared ask such a question, not even Nana.

.   .   .

When I first begged Mamá to take me with her to the *vivienda*, she crossed herself and cast a glance at heaven.

"Where do such ideas come from?" she asked wonderingly. "How could you imagine such a thing?"

I looked at her mutely. The next day I asked her again. And the day after that.

When she returned from Mass on Sunday, she said I could go with her the next morning. I would have to stay out of the way, keep silent, touch nothing.

For the first time, I walked across the footbridge over the canal with her. Down on the bank, the old man was fishing. My skin prickled as I remembered the feel of his wet gums. I stared down at the water, straining to see in its slow moving green depths the knife-toothed fish. Mamá yanked my arm. Her face was tight with urgency. The cries of the guinea hens dwindled as we advanced toward a high wall of green, a living fence that spread so far in either direction, I could not see where it ended.

"There," Mamá said as she pushed me in front of her through a small opening. I stepped into an enormous garden where paths of white pebbles wound around great mounds of flowers like platters heaped with food. She held my wrist and pulled me on toward a long flight of steps which led up the side of a building whose whiteness dazzled like sunlight. At the foot of the steps, a man crouched grinding coffee beans. Grapefruit trees grew nearby and among them another man tended a small fire.

"Will *she* be there?" I whispered to Mamá as we walked up the stairs. She slapped my arm. "This is only the kitchen and the servants' quarters," she said irritably. We stepped into a corridor. A bell rang shrilly as we passed along it. On each side were small rooms with stone floors furnished with a bed, a chest of wood and a chair. In one room sat an elderly, thin woman sewing on something. She looked up as I peeked in, nodded to Mamá and ignored me. "The seamstress," Mamá said. "A *gallega* like the others."

"A *gallega?*"

"From Galicia where her servants come from—except for Señor Brake and me."

By then we had reached the kitchen. In silence, two men and a woman worked intently at long tables. Knives rose and fell, things were stirred in huge bowls, pans were pushed into a stove as black, and, it seemed to me, nearly as large as the engine which pulled the cars full of cane to the weighing station.

Several bells rang at the same time. I looked up at a black box attached to the wall in which small numbered white squares, fluttering like hummingbirds' wings, made the servants jump about like fleas and speak excitedly among themselves. Three big trays appeared on a table. Mamá snatched a white apron from a hook and wrapped herself up in it. I was pushed here and there as the servants rushed to fetch various objects and place them on the trays. Mamá seized my shoulder. "I must take Dr. Aguirre his breakfast today," she said. Later, she explained to me that the bells which summoned the servants were connected by electric wires to the rooms of La Señora, Dr. Aguirre, and to the guest wing where visiting businessmen who were involved with the commerce of the plantation always stayed.

She took a stool from beneath a table and put it in a corner. "Sit there," she ordered me. She lifted up a tray and left the kitchen. My heart pounded. One of the men came over to me. He was plump, and his head was covered with tight little curls that looked dusty like a parrot's tongue. He lifted my chin in his hands and gazed into my eyes.

"So this is the grandchild," he said, and laughed like a friendly boy. "Would the grandchild like something good to eat?" When I nodded, he patted me on the head as though I were a dog. Soon, he brought me a piece of white bread and a large white cup filled with coffee and milk. "My name is Panchito," he said, winking at me, "and you can always count on me."

When Mamá returned, she showed me the servants' bathroom which was on the other side of the kitchen near the storerooms where food was kept. Our own toilet was a lime pit, a few boards straddling it, one with a hole in it, a thatch to keep off the rain. Here were a tub as long as a bed, a marble basin, and the toilet. I gazed down into it. Mamá reached over my shoulder and pulled a chain and a great gush of water pounded toward me. I fled into the hall. Mamá, following me, smiled triumphantly.

Throughout the morning, I never saw the servants slacken in their work although Panchito found time to hurry over to me now and then and sing a snatch of melody or hand me a slice of fruit and wink and smile. When it was noon, and time for the servants to have their dinner—La Señora dined in the evening—Mamá took me back to the bathroom, lifted me up and placed me on the seat where she held me in a determined grip. I clenched my bottom and cried out to her to let me go. She shook her head. I struggled to climb up upon the seat but she held me fast. It was true I had to urinate. At last I did, crying a few tears, wondering how it was that Mamá could make me do anything at all, especially such a dangerous thing. She was not the same in the *vivienda* as she was in our cabin. I was a little afraid of her. She let me pull the chain myself. I watched the swirl of water rise and subside; I would like to have pulled the chain many times, but she pulled me away, muttering, "Enough joy . . ."

As we walked back to the opening in the green wall, Mamá moved more slowly than she had in the early morning. I was able to see that at one end of the garden there were large cages in one of which I could glimpse the flicker of birds' wings, in the other, the quick movement of small animals. "Monkeys," she said with disgust. At the other end, beyond the flower beds and flowering trees, stood a small, pink house surrounded by a low stone wall, its tile roof supported by six slender white columns. I had never seen anything which struck me as so entirely beautiful except, perhaps, the wings of Nana's hair, or the color inside the petals of certain flowers, and like these latter, the house touched me with a vague sense of loss, of sadness, which ugly, broken things never did.

I heard a low murmur of voices. From around the corner of the pink house two yellow-haired children walked sedately, their hands clasped. An old woman in a white dress, its cloth so stiff it stood out from her body like the shell of a tortoise, followed them carrying a basket which she set down on the ground. Each child took a fully clothed doll from the basket, the old woman opened a book, and all three fell silent. It was like a dream, or like one of those images conjured up by the heat on days when the air shimmered like water.

"Who are they?" I whispered.

"The grandchildren of La Señora," Mamá replied.

"Papá is *their* Papá?" I asked, astonished.

"No, no," she replied hastily as she began to shove me impatiently toward the opening. "La Señora had another son, Leopoldo," she explained. "He died when his airplane fell on the mountain—"

"Our mountain?" I interrupted.

"Yes. Those are his children. His widow is French." We went out of the garden and onto the neglected land where only bamboo thickets grew. I noticed how Mamá had worn a little path in the ground that led to the footbridge. As we walked along it, she remarked with a certain satisfaction, "I've heard the widow wants to go back to France, but La Señora won't permit her to take the children. So she stays. Poor thing."

"I'm her grandchild, too," I said. Mamá hurried on.

A long time later, the woman from France spoke to me on a late afternoon in the garden. I had been piling up the little white pebbles from the paths into mountains when a long shadow fell across them.

I heard an exclamation. I looked up, expecting it was one of the servants to tell me to leave the garden before Brake brought out La Señora in her wheelchair for an afternoon airing. But it was a person I hadn't seen before, a tall woman, stooped, narrow-shouldered, thin, her blonde hair in an untidy knob at her neck, staring down at me with a troubled expression as though my presence at her feet on the path had alarmed her. I stood up awkwardly, prepared to be ordered away. She advanced one narrow foot toward my piles of pebbles as though she intended to scatter them, then withdrew it.

"Who are you?" she asked.

"Luisa," I answered, unsure which other name the situation required.

"Everyone in this place is called Luisa," she remarked in a voice that was hopeless and harsh. She shrugged and went on past me, along the path to the pink house.

"Those children are your cousins by blood," Mamá told me as we came within sight of our cabin. "It means nothing. It isn't worth anything."

I never met my cousins. I glimpsed them and their mother only once again, and then at a distance. But I didn't forget her. She had spoken to me as one adult speaks to another; a powerful accumulation of unexpressed feelings, of unstated thoughts, had pressed up against the few words she had spoken to me. The strangeness of it stayed with me a long time.

How miserable our cabin looked to me that day! Even when I thought of Nana's cabin which held everything of importance to me, it now seemed fit only for creatures that crawled on all fours. I caught sight of our outhouse. Its close, hot stench reached to where I stood. Mamá had gone directly to the cooking shed. Soon, the smell of codfish frying in oil triumphed over every other smell, even that which emanated from the tangle of jasmine blooming on a bit of trellis the Chinese man had erected for some climbing plant so long ago. The house of the Chinese was not a house at all, just the barest shelter. I knew what a house was now.

I returned often to the kitchen of the *vivienda*. The servants paid scant attention to me, except Panchito, the cook's assistant, and Brake, the Englishman. I knew Brake found me amusing, the way a child senses such a thing. He was entirely bald. His eyes were pale blue, and I could see his eyebrows only when he stood out of the sunlight. He spoke our language very slowly, one word following another after a long interval during which his bloodless-looking, thin lips worked patiently, as though silently practicing. When he noticed me, he would bend slightly and bow. "How are you today, little girl? What are you planning to do? Nothing wicked, I hope."

Someone would pull back a chair from the large marble table in the middle of the kitchen on which I had seen Panchito roll pastry until it was so flat and thin you could see the marble through it. Brake would sit down. Mamá would set a cup of coffee before him. He drank it with little quick sips like a bird. Like Ursula Vargas, he was treated by the other servants with diffidence. I knew he was "higher."

Once a week the silver was polished, and the vile smell of the paste used to clean it drove me out of the kitchen. When I came back, the branched candlesticks, teapots and coffee urns, the heavy knives with their curved handles, the platters I could have sat upon with room to spare, were spread out upon the tables glowing as though struck by moonlight.

Panchito's knife, when he chopped vegetables or meat, moved so rapidly I could not follow its motion. I watched him take out the guts from a great red fish which lay upon a wooden board.

"If you watch closely," he told me, "you'll see his eye close when he has given up hope that he can return to the sea." He cut off the head and threw it into a pot of boiling water, then lifted me up high to see. The eye had turned white like phlegm.

"He knows now," I said.

Panchito laughed and hugged me and called me his little doll. Ursula Vargas was observing us from the door. The next day she complained to Mamá that I was getting in the way. I was sent out to the garden.

I went to watch the caged birds and the monkeys. A large gray monkey gripped the cage wires in his black twig fingers and observed me fixedly. His speckled yellow eyes flickered like tiny flames. Around him, the long-tailed spider monkeys flung themselves about like ropes of fur. I felt the old monkey's ill will. Panchito gave me a handful of rags soaked in alcohol and said it would make them drunk like men. I pressed the rags through the cage. The monkeys snatched them and held them to their faces, closing their eyes. They seemed to go mad a minute later, and the cage rang faintly like coins falling as they hurled themselves against it. But the gray monkey pulled the rag apart with his small, hard hands and bared his teeth at me.

Panchito purchased pink sheets on which were printed songs that were being played and sung in the capital, brought to our village by an old man who carried them tied in bundles on his back. Mamá begged to borrow them. "Only for one night," she said, looking at Panchito with timid yearning. He rolled up the sheets and handed them to her. She thanked him many times. I was ashamed that she was so unaware of the way the other servants were watching her, the disdain I thought I perceived on their faces. When we walked home, she clutched the songs in one hand, trying to make out the words in the deepening dusk, and held my shoulder with her other hand so she wouldn't stumble. I didn't understand the desperation with which she read and then tried to sing those songs; she seemed drunk and foolish like the monkeys who had buried their faces in the alcohol-soaked rags.

She sang while she prepared our supper and while she set three places on our table. Papá, who was at home that evening, asked her to stop her wailing. She sat down and sang on.

"Trash!" he shouted.

She pushed herself back violently from the table and stamped her feet on the floor.

"Is your head empty of everything that matters?" Papá snarled.

I put down my spoon very carefully so it would make no noise.

Mamá was on the edge of her chair; she clasped her hands and sang of a girl named Lupe, deserted by her love and longing for him. Papá stood up and went outside, turning in the direction of the cooking shed. A minute later, I heard the crash of pots falling. Mamá looked at me and stopped singing.

"Go and see what he's doing," she whispered.

I went out into the dark, into the moist night air. The path to the shed was worn as smooth as our floor. Around me, I felt gathering everything I feared, the spirit of the Chinese man, the herd of rooting pigs, the gray monkey which had glared at me as one beast glares at another. I was so frightened, I began to pant like Dr. Baca's horse.

I never once thought of Nana—fear and desolation had severed me from the consciousness of her presence across the village. Somewhere, Papá was hidden in the dark. Inside the cabin, Mamá sat motionless, her gold tooth gleaming in the light, her hands smudged black from the ink which had run off the coarse pink paper of the song sheets. There was no comfort anywhere.

I heard a movement, the soft thud of footsteps. Papá stepped toward me from behind the shed.

"I've decided that you are going to school," he said flatly. "Even your Mamá can read—as you have heard tonight."

He walked on quickly. In the light from the cabin doorway, I saw he was going toward the village, to get drunk with Dr. Baca, I imagined.

"What did he say?" Mamá asked me eagerly. A few grains of rice clung to her upper lip. She had been eating all the while I had been outside.

"He said you are as stupid and bad as the monkeys in the garden," I said. She gasped. I turned my back on her so she wouldn't see that I was smiling. I heard her stand up. Then suddenly she was on me, her hands slapping wherever they fell, upon my back, my face, my arms. I crawled away from her at last and hid myself beneath the cover on my mattress.

"*Hija, hija,*" she groaned. Gradually her breathing slowed. The tips of her black working shoes pressed against me. I moved close to the wall.

"Go to sleep," she said softly. "Yes! Go to sleep right now! When you wake, you may already be as old as I am and know what I know."

Papá didn't come home that night. I didn't sleep until the sky began to lighten with dawn.

.   .   .

One morning, a week later, Papá did not leave the cabin after he took his coffee, and when Mamá told me to hurry and get ready to go with her to the *vivienda*, Papá said, no, he was taking me to school. He ordered me to wash myself and to put on the shoes he had bought for me in San Isidro. They fitted me now.

I had heard about the school from Nana but I was not interested in it—I didn't think it had anything to do with me. The teacher, Señora Garcia, Nana had said, was another of those people in Malagita who served Beatriz de la Cueva too well, although she should have known better, being an educated woman.

For the first time, I walked to the village with my father. As we passed among the morning shift of workers on their way to the mill, I was aware we aroused an odd and furtive attention in them, that their faces were tight with a meaning I could not pluck out. When Papá yanked me into the chapel, I was relieved we were out of sight.

He walked straight to the altar, neither kneeling nor crossing himself, then veered and went behind it to a door I had not noticed before. He looked back and motioned me on impatiently as he opened it. I heard a woman's voice say, "Good morning, Señor de la Cueva."

When I looked through the door, I saw a room larger than our cabin. A woman I had glimpsed about Malagita stood in front of a blackboard. She was large and clean-looking and her skin was very pale.

"Señora Garcia," Papá greeted her in a courteous voice. He inclined his head slightly as he spoke as though with respect. "This is my daughter, Luisa, who knows nothing."

She smiled at me and said, "Good morning, Luisa." I ducked my head, unable to speak, burdened with my ignorance.

"Come home directly after school," Papá said. "No more of this vagabond life for you."

He bowed to the teacher and left. I passed my fingers over the scarred surfaces of a little desk. "You can help me," Señora Garcia said. She showed me how to erase the blackboard. I thought of Brake as I breathed in the dust of chalk. It was alien, dry and white, utterly different from the melting, fragrant, half-rotten taste and smell of Malagita. Señora Garcia wrote on the board.

"Your name," she said. "Luisa de la Cueva." She pronounced it with faintly mysterious emphasis. I squeezed my toes inside the hard leather shoes and thought of how cool the earth would still be in the *plazuela* at this time of the morning. It seemed good to be stupid. I wagged my head as I had seen Enano do and tried for his foolish smile.

Señora Garcia touched my hair lightly. "You'll see," she promised. "It will be all right when you learn to read."

I gazed at the warped planks of the floor, a dented kerosene can in a corner, at the cracked wood of the desks, at the armful of soiled books she had gathered up from her table and was now clasping to her chest.

Only in the kitchen, the servants' quarters, the garden of the *vivienda* were things whole and perfect. As she asked me to do, I placed a reading book on each of seven desks.

During the two years I attended Señora Garcia's classes, there were never more than seven students. A few minutes later, they arrived. The oldest was a boy of twelve, and I, at eight, was the youngest. They were the children of technicians who worked in the offices of the plantation and whom I had not seen about the village. The children I had occasionally played with, the sons and daughters of ordinary laborers, wore clothes which were either too large for them or too small, and went barefoot except when they attended Mass. Their laughter, like their anger, burst forth from them unexpectedly and was loud and harsh. But my classmates spoke softly. The three girls laughed with their hands covering their mouths. The boys' hands were clean. In time they all grew friendly enough, but they rarely waited for me when the whistle blew at noon and we were sent home for our dinners, and they didn't tease me as they did each other. Sometimes, when it was my turn to read aloud, or to work out a problem on the blackboard, I felt they were waiting for me to do something unexpected and shocking, and that it was such a possibility which kept them guarded and distant.

After I began to recognize letters, I drew them with a pointed stick in the dirt, filled in the lines with stones, then kicked them all apart.

In the reading book, there was a picture of a house. I showed it to Mamá, watching her face as I pointed to its shuttered windows, the curved, smooth roof, the flowers planted all around the veranda, the heavy carved door.

"Our house is nothing but a hole," I told her. "The windows are just holes like our toilet."

"God made the world," Mamá said stolidly.

I observed to Nana that neither she nor Mamá lived in real houses.

"Is that what you've learned?" she asked sarcastically.

"Only my other grandmother, La Señora, lives in a house," I said.

Nana lit her pipe and went to sit in her doorway. I heard her speak to a neighbor woman. Once she stepped outside and scattered the chickens scratching in the dirt in front of the cabin. When their squawks had subsided, she remained in the door. The afternoon was hot and silent. In the close little room where I had been cherished, I was now abandoned. I couldn't escape—she filled the doorway with her long back. When she turned to me, I couldn't see her features, only a dark, menacing shape, the sun behind it.

"Señora de la Cueva is not your grandmother except in the sense that a hen is connected with the egg it drops into the straw. She is hardly more than that to your father since nothing he does signifies anything to her. All you have is me and your mother. Don't trouble your brain about houses, what they are and what they aren't. It's a pity you're the only one, a pity you don't have a little brother or sister to take care of. It would give you something to think about beside yourself."

She had never spoken to me so coldly. I was afraid to look at her. I bowed my head. Suddenly, she knelt beside me. She put her arms around me and I burst into tears. She said, "I know how hard it is for you."

Seven months later, my brother, Sebastiano, was born. He did not live long enough for me to take care of him, or to distract me from the puzzle of myself and Beatriz de la Cueva.

.   .   .

A week before Sebastiano was born, La Señora left for one of her twice-yearly visits to Tres Hermanos, where she was to spend a month in the suite of rooms always kept ready for her in the best hotel in the capital. And on the day of Sebastiano's birth, and his death, Papá himself went to Tres Hermanos, for *negocios*, he told my mother.

"Business," she said scornfully, shortly after he had left for the weighing station where he would board one of the small Malagita trains which would take him to the main, and only, public railroad line. "He has no business—he's going to see the old woman in her hotel and pretend he isn't a husband and a father."

I was getting dressed for school. She stroked my hair. "Papá won't know if you don't go to school," she said coaxingly. "Come with me to the *vivienda*. Panchito has been missing you. *Hijita*! Really—I can hardly move about. Señora Garcia won't mind if you're not in school. Ay! I'll teach you a song."

She looked at me out of wide, frightened eyes. "Yes?" she questioned, then picked up Papá's cup and drank the few drops of coffee he had left. There was a loud, sudden spattering of water between her legs. She looked down.

"My God!" she whispered.

"I'll stay with you, Mamá," I cried, and ran to my mattress where I sat down, hiding my face with the cover.

"It's the water," she moaned. "Go find Dr. Baca!"

Through my fingers, I saw her stretch her arms toward the ceiling with such strain it seemed she was trying to lift herself up to it. The seams of her dress ripped from beneath her arms down to her swollen waist. She flew at me suddenly and seized a handful of my hair and twisted it.

"Do you hear!"

I tore myself loose from her and ran from the cabin. I ran through the herd of pigs, cursing them, and past the calm, empty *plazuela*. Dr. Baca was in his surgery, gripping with both of his hands the bony jaw of an old woman, trying to force open her clenched mouth. The smoke from his cigar, burning on a plate near a case of instruments, filled the air with sour pungency. He saw me in the doorway and released the old woman's jaw, and she whimpered and tapped one yellow tooth with a long, yellowed fingernail.

"My Mamá—" I began.

"Never mind. I'll come," he said. "You take yourself off. I knew it would be soon. Go to your Nana's for the day." He looked down at the old woman. "*Tía*, if you don't let me look down your throat, I can't find out what's making you choke in your sleep," he said in a gloomy, bored voice. She opened her mouth slowly, but the doctor had already turned away and was dropping instruments into a case. I left, taking the road from the village that led toward pastures where goats grazed and fed. I wasn't going to school where, what with the speed news traveled in Malagita, the children would soon know that my mother was giving birth. I would not be stared at this day. For once, I didn't want to see Nana. I wanted to be lost—to be not known by anyone.

It was early June, the time when the heaviest thunderstorms came to San Pedro. As I walked through a grove of almond trees, there was a great rumbling in the sky. The first loud drops of rain spattered on the leaves, then a torrent fell. I ran across a field to an abandoned shed which had fallen in on itself, and I crawled into the brown moldiness while the sky thundered and insects ticked in musty clumps of wet straw beneath my arms and legs. I fell asleep out of utter loneliness.

When I awoke, a wet breeze was blowing. It was sweet to taste and I gulped it down like fruit. Now the sky was pale like Mamá's face after she had stopped weeping. I walked back through streaming underbrush onto the muddy road. Birds called among the vines and flowering trees. I was wild with hunger, and I began to run toward home.

Even before I reached the doorway, I could hear the turbulent sound of distressed women. Father Céspedes was there, standing just in front of the cabin, wearing his broad-brimmed priest's hat. When he saw me, he turned to the room and called out something I couldn't hear, then stretched his hand toward me. I looked quickly at his small feet in their neat black boots buttoned at the side. Which one was cloven? Señora Galdos appeared behind him, her face awash with tears.

"God has taken your sweet little brother to heaven," Father Céspedes said, trying to place his hand on my head, but I kept out of his reach, too occupied with eluding his touch to take in what he had said. I considered going back to the shed, but there was nothing to eat there in that miserable place where I had taken shelter. And night was coming, a vast, slow spreading of darkness across the wan sky. The world looked dead.

Suddenly, I understood what the priest had said. At that moment, Señora Galdos reached around him, took hold of my arm and yanked me into the cabin. A faint shriek, *Ay*, sounded from near my mother's bed. She lay upon it, her belly shrunken. Her eyes were closed, below each one a violet shadow. The women sitting near her looked at me sternly, silently. Mamá opened her eyes and saw me.

At her cry, "Luisita,"—as though at a signal—the women began to wail. Señora Galdos pushed me to the bed. Mamá reached out and embraced me so violently, I fell across her. I heard Father Céspedes praying loudly and irritably as though he was trying to drown out the women.

"You must see your brother," cried Señora Galdos. I crawled out from under Mamá's arms which lay upon me like earth. She sobbed as two women led me to our table where, between two lit candles a mound of cloth lay. Someone's hand lifted up a corner of it. I saw a human face not much larger than my palm. The skin of it was blue. A little wrinkled mouth was open as though it had begun to form a word.

"The will of God . . ." droned the priest tiredly as I ran out of the cabin and down the path to the canal. The heavy rain had stirred it out of its usual sluggishness, and small waves slapped the banks and the water was darker than the sky.

For a while, I stood there on the bank, half dreaming, imagining myself hiding beneath La Señora's bed in the great house. Then I glimpsed at a great distance a horseman riding; he seemed to draw behind him a black line which split the earth and the sky and was as straight as those that Señora Garcia drew on pieces of paper on which I wrote the words I learned to spell. I turned toward home. I saw Father Céspedes leaving, and just after him, several women. When I looked inside the cabin, only Señora Galdos was still there. I was dazed with hunger, and I took the bread she gave me and began to eat it so quickly I choked. Mamá was quiet; she seemed asleep. A slight wind sprang up when the last ashy light had gone from the sky, and the flames of the candles swayed above the dead baby on the table.

I fell asleep but awoke often. In those brief moments of consciousness, I saw Señora Galdos dozing in a chair or speaking softly to Mamá. Once I heard a curious exchange between them. "Imagine!" Señora Galdos exclaimed. "Think what he gave up for you! Never a day without enough to eat. Such furniture! The life of a king! You have a great responsibility."

"What is that?" Mamá asked in a weak voice.

"To discover what is in his mind," replied Señora Galdos.

"Why isn't he here?" my mother whimpered.

"I heard Dr. Baca had gotten a message to him through Calderío."

"Sebastiano," Mamá pronounced faintly. "At least, he was baptised. At least, Luisa was baptised. Orlando might have prevented that."

"You'll have another."

"God spare me," said my mother.

My brother was buried the next day. The sky was burning blue although rainclouds were already gathering in the east. The box was very small in which Sebastiano lay, and the hole in the ground was shallow. At the other end of the cemetery was the curving iron of the grilled fence which surrounded the grave of Antonio de la Cueva upon whose tombstone a long-winged marble figure stood, seeming about to leap to the ground.

Many of the people of Malagita had come to the cemetery. I heard a man say that the priest had demanded a huge fee for the burial service because it was a de la Cueva infant, although not a bastard like the other one. Señora Garcia bent to kiss me at that moment so I did not see who had spoken. When the long ceremony was drawing to its close, I saw Papá and Dr. Baca at the edge of the group around the little grave. I saw how people looked at my father, how curiosity made their faces so naked. When he stared back at them, they quickly turned away.

The grave was covered with earth. The sky was clouding over, the air already steamy with the morning's heat and the coming rain. When people embraced me, they lifted me up, holding me close to them, and I felt suffocated and embarrassed. Mamá swayed toward me, then fell against Señora Galdos and buried her face in her hands. A young woman carrying a sleeping baby said, "That Rafaela is heartless."

I went to Nana's that afternoon—no one asked me where I was going. I was forgotten.

"Won't you ever speak to Mamá again?" I asked her.

"Never," she replied, but with an uncertain note in her voice I had not heard before. She stared at me for a moment. "You're filthy. Why didn't she bathe you?"

"She was too—"

"Don't talk to me of sorrow," Nana said.

She heated the water to give me a bath. "Take off those dirty clothes," she said. She seemed brusque and cold as she dragged out the old tin tub and filled it. I no longer fitted into it and had to sit on my heels. The day was dark. I could see through the doorway how lifeless the light was. Soon the rain would turn the earth around my brother's grave to mud. I thought of the closed, wooden box, creatures burrowing around it. I thought of the dead, thick, gray sky. What did it matter that I had learned to read? It was absurd to be bathed, to have my hair rolled up in pieces of brown paper, to stroll with Nana, after the end of the storm that was coming, in the rain-soaked *plazuela*.

Drops of water spattered my face, Nana's tears.

"Poor infant," she whispered. She leaned toward me, her arms came through the water and gripped me, and we huddled there like that until the water grew chilled. Then she sat back on the dirt floor and looked at me deeply. Slowly, a smile touched her lips.

"Are you heartless?" I asked her.

She thought for a while. "Yes. I think so. A little," she said.

She sent me home earlier than she usually did. As I passed through the *plazuela*, I recognized some men I had seen that morning in the cemetery, and I wondered if the sombre intensity with which they were speaking had some connection with the death of Sebastiano.

Mamá was sitting on her stool by the door, holding in one hand her card of Jesus, his silken heart dripping its three drops of blood. She smiled at me gently, absently. A few feet from her, my father leaned against the wall, his feet crossed at his ankles, his head bent to one side as though he was listening to her breathe.

We ate a soup Señora Nuñez had made for us of potatoes and beans and pork. My parents' silence at the table seemed empty of troubling emotions; the only sounds were the humble noises of eating.

Just before I went to sleep, Mamá came and knelt for a moment beside my mattress. She held her chest as she leaned over me and said she would have to go to a *curandera* to get a potion to dry up her milk. She spoke peacefully, confidingly, and took my hands, pressing them against the swollen skin of her breasts. I drifted off and knew no more until Papá's voice awakened me in the black, moonless night.

I heard him say the president of San Pedro had run off to France, taking with him the treasure of the country, money he had collected from his criminal acts over the years. Armed men were roaming the streets of Tres Hermanos. During a motor ride on the Cristobal road which led from the capital to the sea, men had hurled stones at Papá's mother in her limousine car, and she was returning to Malagita as soon as arrangements could be made for a guard of soldiers to accompany her in her private train.

I saw a movement in the dark, a thickening of it, and I imagined Papá was sitting up. His voice grew loud and agitated.

"They'll call it a revolution," he said. "It will end in yet another death of the country—we won't stay for that."

"Where will we go?" Mamá's voice asked in alarm.

"The United States," he said. My mother gasped. I heard a soft thud as Papá fell back on the bed. Their voices dropped into murmurs. I felt a great shaft of fear as though someone holding me over the canal with two hands had taken one hand away.

In a few days, Mamá went back to work in the kitchen of the *vivienda*. I watched her the first morning as she walked toward the footbridge, her head bowed. There was a sorrowing, heavy look to her body. I wondered if she was thinking of Sebastiano, a presence, a name, which had fluttered so briefly between two darknesses. She had been quiet, almost calm, since the funeral; she had hardly spoken. I would have liked to cause her such an important sadness. I felt alone, friendless, I didn't want to go back to school.

It was not that the children were unfriendly. They called me Luisita, and I knew Marina Lopez, the daughter of a clerk in the plantation who was also the official village photographer, well enough to spend an afternoon with her now and then. But there was a space between me and the others; it was filled with my special, and irregular, history that could not sink into the past because its story was not only mine but also Beatriz de la Cueva's. Of late, I had begun to suspect that the solemn way grownups treated me was false, that, really, I only served to remind them of their own seemliness.

On Sundays, if I met children on their way to the chapel, they would gaze at me gravely, self-importantly, and, I sensed, with a touch of pity. At such moments, I realized I was no more acceptable to them than the chief gardener's son whom no one permitted in their cabins because he would urinate when he felt like it, indoors or out. I had heard Panchito discussing this boy with the cook. The cook said that it was only because the gardener was so skilled at his work that La Señora continued to employ him. Panchito remarked that the cock of the gardener's son was more familiar to the people of Malagita than the true cross. They had laughed with the hard laughter evoked in men, I had begun to learn, by their bodily differences from women.

The three soldiers who had ridden back to Malagita from the capital on La Señora's train to protect her, hung around the *plazuela*, smoking cigarettes and shouting at each other as though they were miles apart instead of sprawled out on the same bench. The people of Malagita never went near them. One day they disappeared and were not seen again.

In the afternoons after school when I had nothing else to do, I stayed in the garden of the *vivienda*. Brake would warn me to stay out of sight if La Señora was to be taken for an outing in her wheelchair. I had found hidden places from which I could spy on the children of the French woman, whom Mamá had called my cousins. I watched them from a distance and hated them distantly. They were like pictures of children in a school book. Gradually my interest in them withered and blew away, although my belief that they knew nothing of my existence continued to give me an odd feeling of triumph.

My mother had nothing more to show me in the kitchen. I had begun to feel contempt for the servants, even for Panchito, and their enslavement to the ringing of the bells, the quivering of the small numbered squares in the black box on the wall that caused them all to leap about and run into each other and cry out in alarm.

Beyond the *vivienda* and its gardens and the nervous life of the servants, the village waited for the mills to come to life. One night I went out to catch the large night beetles that carried lights in their tails. I knocked them from the branches of trees and put them into a jar Mamá had given me. When I had collected five of them, I held up the bottle and the yellow glow showed me the night earth, the patch where yams grew, and the path around it to the outhouse. All at once shrieks and shouts burst from the village. I ran into the cabin. Mamá looked up from her lap where tiny circles of crocheted ivory-colored thread lay like a handful of flower petals. "They're fighting," she said resignedly. "The men have nothing else to do."

The next night I was awakened by the distant beating of a drum. It was a stupid sound, but the intervals between the dull thuds were ominous. I knew that some of the women in the village went to a small forest a mile or so away from Malagita where moss hung thickly from the tree branches, and where they took part in ceremonies of witchcraft.

The village grew sick as a person becomes sick, fevered, sometimes delirious, sometimes sunk in lassitude. Dogs were beaten, and children kept their distance from the men. One day, a boy came down the road as I left school with Marina, shouting that a flock of white owls was roosting in a tree near the pond. Nana had told me these owls drank the holy oil from the sanctuary lamps in churches. We all ran to the pond, joined along the way by other children.

The owls filled the branches of the tree which shadowed the pond. A boy flung a stone at them. Soon, other boys were flinging stones. An owl was hit and fell straight into the pond where, as the boys continued to stone it, it turned around in the still water. The other owls appeared dazed; they didn't fly away but stayed motionless in the tree.

Two outlying cabins were set on fire, and an old woman died in the flames. For a few days, a special policeman from San Isidro questioned various families in the village to try and find the culprit, and the lethargic jailer and his dog followed the policeman at a respectful distance. The guilty person was not discovered.

"The country people keep themselves down," my father remarked.

Mamá said nothing.

"Of course—it's easier to be ignorant, not to think. To be like you . . ."

"Ave Maria . . ." groaned Mamá.

"For me, this world is a hell of thought. For you, only the present moment exists. Why don't you sing one of your beautiful songs about broken hearts?"

"Orlando! Leave me be!"

The whiteness of my father's face at that moment was like the whiteness of the sun's rays glancing off the canal.

I wished I were Marina Lopez or the daughter of Señora Garcia who had been sent away to a convent school in the capital. I had eaten food in the *vivienda* undreamed of by the other children of Malagita, and our cabin was filled with many more objects than I had seen in any other cabin—it seemed to amuse Papá to take things from his mother's house and bring them to us—yet I longed to be anyone other than myself.

Glancing out of the door one evening, I saw a monstrous figure, winged and deformed, making its way toward the cabin. It was Papá, carrying on his back one of the great, cane rocking chairs from the marble-floored veranda of the *vivienda*. As he set it down on our dirt floor, a heap of soft, silken children's dresses fell from its seat.

"Let her wear them to school," he said. "She looks like a gypsy child."

Mamá was sighing and gasping with admiration over the smocking, the lace collars, the material of the clothes.

"They were about to be thrown out," he said, then added in an ironic tone, "by my generous sister-in-law."

The girls gathered around me in school the next day and touched the cloth of my dress and murmured like doves—how pretty!—but they didn't ask me where it had come from, and I didn't tell them. The boys looked at me from the corners of their eyes. I felt as though I were made of honey.

I stopped by Nana's. She drew me to the door, to the light. "Another joke of Orlando de la Cueva's," she said. Her hand reached toward the embroidery on the bodice of the dress and twitched over it like a small bird. I drew back, thinking she meant to rip it apart. But her hand suddenly dropped. She shook her head, then softly said, "Well—why not?"

"Papá brought three dresses for me," I said. "And before that he brought me two books, written in English."

"Don't forget the English brought the slaves."

"From my cousins," I said. "They sent them to me."

"No," she said firmly.

"All right," I agreed. "But the dresses and the books once belonged to them. Now they're mine."

"Your grandfather could read. But he gave all that up when the de la Cuevas descended on him like buzzards."

"Where did my grandfather come from?"

"Where we all come from," she replied. "Seville and Africa."

I didn't go directly home that afternoon but wandered around the village, the folds of my dress soft against my knees. I passed by Señora

Garcia's house. Señor Garcia, who was said to have studied the law, and worked in Señor Calderío's office, was standing beneath a tall tree whose leaves were red as flames. Next to him was a stool and upon it rested a square black box which he gazed at so intently—his hands pressed together as if he was praying, his chin resting on his fingertips—that he didn't notice me as I stood on the road watching him. A black tube rose from the box, widening outward like an enormous ear that was listening to his prayer. Gripping the stool and box in his arms, he shifted them about on the ground until he found a spot that seemed to satisfy him. He rocked back on his heels, smiling, then caught sight of me and waved a long arm in my direction. "Come over and see our new victrola, Luisa," he called.

I jumped out of the watery sunlight, across a narrow ditch still running with smoky water from the afternoon rain, and into the long shadow cast by the Garcia house which was as substantial as the surgery, a real *casa*, not a cabin, with both grilles and shutters at the windows. The front door opened, and Señora Garcia came out and walked to us on a neat path, her hands drifting across the flowering bushes which grew along it. The Garcias kept no chickens to scratch in the dirt or pigs to stir up the earth.

Señor Garcia was explaining how the victrola worked. I barely listened. I was looking down, covertly, at my yellow dress, thinking that because of it I was standing here with my teacher and her husband, all of us smiling, while above us the narrow red leaves of the tree rustled with the specially sweet air which always followed rain. Señor Garcia carefully lowered a thick rod, attached at one end to a corner of the box, until its tiny point touched the edge of a ridged black platter. At once, I heard the drowsy whisper and rattle of gourds, the beat of a drum, and a high, thin voice, penetrating as the whine of a mosquito, singing words I had heard before when Panchito had sung them to me one afternoon in the *vivienda* garden a few weeks earlier. The Garcias laughed, carelessly, happily. We might all have been children together. I, too, began to laugh, and to sway to the music, moving my feet back and forth as Panchito had taught me.

Señora Garcia's laughter ceased abruptly. She grabbed my shoulders and held me motionless, pressed so closely against her I could feel her hipbones. She bent over me.

"You mustn't do that! Don't shake your bottom that way!" she said in my ear. She put her finger to her lips as though to warn me not to question her. Señor Garcia was clapping his hands in time to the music. I backed away from them. Her mouth opened but closed at once as though she'd changed her mind about whatever she was going to say. Instead, she nodded as if in agreement with herself and turned, smiling, to her husband who had cupped a hand behind one of his large, pale ears and was stooping over the victrola.

I went back to the road. The long, slanting light of late day lay across the village. Among the trees, birds rose and dipped, busy and noisy at this hour. After a while, I began to walk slowly home. When Enano shuffled past me, groaning a word of greeting and offering his hunchback to be touched, I shouted at him to get away from me, then fled when I saw the look of bafflement on his huge, sad face. The obscure shame I had felt as I had waited on the road, hoping the Garcias would summon me back, grew more intense with each step I took.

In the cabin, I sat huddled on my mattress against the wall. One strong ray of yellow light from the setting sun struck through the doorway at the floor. I wished it were night, and I asleep.

What had I done? I didn't believe that Mamá could explain anything to me, but when she came home, I described to her what had transpired at the Garcias'. While I spoke, she set the table for our dinner. She peered into the bowl she had brought from the *vivienda*, grumbling over its contents. She sat suddenly down on the floor and took off her shoes, stretching out her short, plump legs. "My knees are a hundred years older than I am," she said.

"Mamá!" I cried.

She looked up at me, her gaze focused at last.

"You must be careful now," she said, getting to her feet and beginning to undress so that she could put on the ragged old dress she wore at home.

"You're going to be nine years old soon."

I ran outside and flinging up my arms frightened the guinea hens until they flew apart scattering jasmine petals as they tried to get away from me. Mamá called from the cabin.

"You mustn't let Panchito touch you anymore. Do you understand?"

I recalled at once the afternoon Panchito had taught me a few steps of a dance. We had been standing near a great bed of purple flowers from whose centers dripped sticky yellow tongues. He had taken my hands in his and sung me the song Señor Garcia had played on his victrola. His soft, round body had seemed close to dissolving as he jiggled and bounced, urging me to imitate him. Ursula Vargas had stepped out of the kitchen onto the platform at the top of the stairs. She had called out his name in a sharp voice and he had gone to her without a backward look at me.

Suddenly, like grasping the sense of a word which, until that moment of illumination has been only a mysterious association of letters, I knew what I was to be careful about, and I knew why Señora Garcia had so coldly interrupted my dance.

"Eat!" Mamá said. I shook my head. She looked at me curiously. She rose and came to me and smoothed my hair. "Between men and women —" she began. I pushed away her hand. She looked vaguely uneasy then shrugged and left me alone.

As soon as I lay down on my mattress, I fell asleep. But this day was not over. Hours later, Papá woke me. The sawing and whirring of insects outside in the dark sounded like tiny imitations of the machinery of the mill played by a victrola.

On the table lay a black and white board upon which stood carved black and white figures.

"I'm going to teach you chess," he said.

"Let her sleep," my mother protested from the bed.

"Pay attention," my father commanded me, ignoring her. "These figures are called men. Moors and Christians, like the beans and rice."

A long time later, my arm reddened by the slaps Papá had given me each time I forgot the knight's move, and clutching a Christian bishop in my hand, I lay my head down on the board and he allowed me to go to bed.

For days we played chess as soon as Mamá had cleared away the supper dishes. One night, I ran away to Nana's cabin, slipping past Papá as he was setting out the men on their squares. The village streets were dark save for a flickering light here and there which cast a yellow glow on the red earth like the light of the night beetles.

I woke Nana.

"I'm afraid," I said and began to cry.

I slept in her bed and each time I woke, I felt her arms around me. I could smell her hair and skin. My finger made the knight's move on her shoulder.

Just as the sun was rising, Nana peeled an orange for me. She gave me coffee and milk in a bowl and watched me drink it with a concentration that comforted me.

When I returned home, Mamá had already gone off to the *vivienda*. Papá was asleep, the sunlight falling on his face. For a while I observed the delicate tremors of his eyelids. Then I dressed for school without waking him and went back to the village.

Papá did not come home that night or for the next three weeks. The chess board disappeared like the three soldiers who had guarded La Señora. But the shape and feel of the black and white men stayed with me for years, and they seemed to move of their own accord like an army advancing through my thoughts.

.   .   .

When Papá finally returned, he brought news from the capital. There had been riots, he told Mamá. And there was a new president, so ancient he would likely have to be carried into the palace like a tray of bones. He wouldn't last long, Papá said. Then the Negro sergeant, Galda, would cut off a few heads and plant his great bottom in the palace.

"It will go on like this forever," Papá said. "Monkey thoughts and monkey uniforms."

"What difference does it make to us?" Mamá asked, and shrugged her shoulders as though answering her own question. She went to the cooking shed and I followed her. She stirred a pot of cornmeal mush. The old fisherman had given her a fish and she began to tell me how she was going to cook it, how good it would be with the cornmeal. My father appeared outside the shed.

"You deserve Galda!" he shouted. "All of you!"

"All of us!" exclaimed Mamá. "A fine thing to say! What can I do?"

"You could learn something."

Mamá picked up a morsel of fish and dropped it into hot lard.

"I have learned how to support three people," she said loudly and turned the fish over, jiggling the pan.

Papá's harsh laughter drowned the noise of the small explosions of fat.

"And what do you imagine one needs to live in this garden of paradise?" he mocked. "There's fruit on every tree, palm thatch for shelter, pigs for New Year, and the climate is so mild one could go naked if it weren't for Catholic lewdness."

Mamá placed the fried fish on the cornmeal. With a rag she picked up the pot and turned away from the stove, her face moist with steam. She walked rapidly to the cabin. I ran after her, hoping Papá would go off to see Dr. Baca.

After a few minutes, he came inside.

"Your daughter's feet are nearly ruined by her shoes which she long ago outgrew," Mamá said, filling my plate with food. "The dress I wear to Mass is nothing but mending."

As though he hadn't heard her, Papá began to speak again about matters of the country, politics, a subject that held no interest for me— who would rule San Pedro now, what the plantation owners wanted and would get, what the tenant farmers might do, and how the country people, *guajiros*, who had come to the city calling themselves revolutionaries, were looting—robbing people poorer than themselves. He put down his silver fork.

"You're not listening," he said.

"You're only speaking this way to make me feel ignorant. It's what men do. You're like other men, after all."

He looked at her keenly for a moment. "You didn't think I was?" he asked mildly.

Her face flushed and she began to eat quickly as though intent only on filling herself.

"I've made inquiries about traveling to the United States," he said. Now Mamá put down her fork.

She raised a stricken face to him, at the same time grabbing my hand. I tried to pull away. Her grip was so strong, I thought she might pull me onto the table.

"Fefita," my father said warningly. "No tears. Did you think I was playing some game when I spoke of it before? Do you think I can live the rest of my life here? My only company that coarse idiot, Dr. Baca? Or drinking English tea with my mother who has invented her own insanity to protect herself from giving a thought to anything but Malagita, her domain, who continues to pretend I've come from the capital to visit her, that I don't live a few hundred yards from her in this *casucha* . . ." He stared fixedly at each wall as though silently saying a version of the stations of the cross. Mamá burst into a great sob, and Papá got up and flung himself through the doorway.

She held her face in her hands, tears leaking through her fingers.

"How will we get there?" I asked her. She only sobbed louder. I repeated my question. She lifted her wet face from her hands. "Where?"

"The United States."

"*Hija*—we will fly like witches for all I know." She looked at the plate of food my father had hardly touched. "You can take care of yourself, can't you?" she asked me with a wet, forlorn smile.

"Where is it? That place."

"Everyone knows where it is," she muttered. She stood and went to the door. "Out there," she said. "Everywhere."

I felt a sudden sad affection for her. I went and stood beside her. She rested her warm arm on my shoulders and we both stared out at the night.

Moonlight shone on a broken cart someone had abandoned across the road. Each rough board was lined in silver, and the long pointing shaft shimmered like moving water. My hands would be warmed if I touched the swelling trunks of the trees. Bamboo clumps and flowers were the color of ashes, indistinguishable except for their shapes. A rooster crowed and from far off, another rooster answered faintly. The silence deepened, then was broken by the rapid, choking bray of a donkey.

Nana had told me a story: The devil announced he was bored with four-footed creatures and was going to kill them all. When he got to the donkey, it gasped in terror, "Not me! Not me! Not me!" And was still crying out in terror although the devil had so enjoyed the donkey's voice he had promised to always spare him.

"What will happen to us?" my mother asked softly. I knew it was not a question she expected to be answered.

My father returned the following evening but he said nothing about the United States. I believed now that we were going away. What this belief meant, I didn't know, only that in the ordinary movements and habitual gestures of each day a vast uncertainty lay. Although it was we who would be leaving, it was the village that seemed to recede until it was like a place I saw from a great distance, far less substantial than the tower rising from the old fortress on the mountain. I felt I could see right through the cabins, the classroom, the cross-encrusted walls of the chapel, as though everything was made of transparent, flimsy stuff. In silence, in my heart, I said good-bye each day.

It was the end of November, the last of the rainy season. Soon there would be no morning dampness smelling of wet leaves and frogs. The harvest would begin; the idle men would return to the mill to tend the crushing machines and the boilers—great open cauldrons which turned the cane into raw sugar—once more the black smoke would pour from the chimneys of the mill and tar the skies above Malagita.

Just before the yearly resurrection began, San Pedro was granted a miracle. A hurricane veered away just before its full force would have struck the island. Great waves beat upon the island's shores. The water in the canal rose to within a few feet of the footbridge. The winds scattered animals all over the village. Goats grazed in the cemetery after the wind had died down, and pigs rooted in the park. A few chickens, blown into thickets of palmetto, were impaled on the sharp points of the leaves. But there was no tidal wave such as had drowned hundreds of people on other islands in the Caribbean. No one was hurt in Malagita, although some buildings were damaged.

Beatriz de la Cueva ordered a line of poles sunk into the earth around the *plazuela* and the clock tower and electric lights were attached to them. Mamá said it was because she was grateful to God for sparing San Pedro from the horror of the hurricane. But Nana said it was not gratitude at all—La Señora was incapable of such a feeling—but an attempt to prevent the workers from realizing what was happening in the capital by offering them a diversion, a useless thing. For once it seemed to me that Nana spoke foolishly.

Mamá and I went one evening to look at the lights. Among a group of people who were strolling about and speaking excitedly, I noticed Señor Garcia staring up at the electric lamps which hung from the poles like giant egg sacs such as I had seen attached to the tails of the cockroaches Mamá could not rid our cooking shed of during the rainy season. The undersides of the great fronds of the royal palms were the color of pineapple flesh. The light touched the railing that girdled the park and fell upon my bare feet and Mamá's black working shoes.

"Science . . . science . . ." murmured Señor Garcia reverently as he walked past us.

Beatriz de la Cueva, I thought.

"What a blessing!" exclaimed Señora Galdos, clasping me to her with too much passion as usual. She was pregnant, and her immense belly appeared to lead her about like an animal she was chained to. I thought I could hear the baby muttering inside of her, telling her that she was much too old for bearing children as some of the village women had said, laughing at her behind her belly.

A greater wonder than the electric lamps was soon to follow. A moving picture had been ordered from the capital by La Señora, and was to be shown in the village. Mamá, who had been charmed by the electric lamps though she had long been accustomed to electricity in the *vivienda*, showed no interest in going to see the picture. Papá remarked contemptuously, "You don't even know what a movie is!" and she replied that that was reason enough not to bother with it. In that case, he said, he would take me.

"You've just revealed everything," he said to her. "What a perfect expression of your peasant incuriosity."

"Take her!" cried Mamá. "May she have joy of it! I'm too tired, you brute! Your mother destroys us all with her caprices! I want to sleep, to rest . . ." She fell heavily on the bed and turned her back to us.

Not far from the clock tower was a wooden structure where the moving picture was to be shown. I had peered through the windows at the long bare room, wondering what its purpose was. Chickens sometimes wandered into it and the floor was green with their droppings.

By the night of the showing, the floor had been washed clean. Upon it stood rows of small wooden chairs which opened out like scissor blades. That I should be sitting next to my father on such a public occasion kept me in a state of painful excitement. The air was thick with tobacco smoke and noisy with the voices of the village people; they were stirred as though a great joy possessed them.

A small balcony jutted out from the back wall only a few feet above our heads. It remained empty until just before the picture began. Then my two cousins and their mother entered it and sat down, their blond heads dusted with yellow light which poured through a large circular hole above their heads. Papá glanced up at them, a faint smile on his thin lips, knowing and derisive.

The room was plunged into darkness and seconds later, upon the bare wall we faced, words appeared and disappeared. A great sigh passed through the audience as five smiling people appeared on the wall, their mouths moving silently but animatedly. They sat down to a table laden with food. Three were children who bowed their heads over their plates as a round-faced young man spoke and a young woman clasped her hands in prayer.

The story was nearly incomprehensible. Scenes were abruptly separated from each other by lines of words which Papá whispered to me, without troubling to translate them from the English in which they were written. The young man had to leave his family and travel to a crowded city where he fell among evil people who forced him to drink rum. He fell asleep from drunkenness and woke to find himself lying beside a railroad track next to a corpse. He fled from there, his eyes huge with terror, and he wandered about cities and grew old, his beard as white as the snow which fell almost throughout the entire movie, and which never melted away from his shoulders and his rag-bound feet. He returned home at last and saw through a window his children, now grown, and the woman, her braid as white as his beard. Once more there was a laden table. The woman carved the flesh of a huge, roasted bird. It seemed to me that her eyes glinted with madness. The old man, clutching the long stick with which he helped himself hobble, drew away from the radiantly bright little house and vanished into a thick haze of snow.

Soon, the wall went black. A light came on. The moving picture was over. Only the shuffling of people's feet broke the silence as we filed out into the night.

Papá walked on the other side of the road away from me. I imagined Nana alone in her cabin. I thought of her black hair turning white. A great hush hung over the village, broken once by a thin startled cry of a night bird. An awful grief took hold of me. I began to cry out loud, helplessly. I couldn't stop, though I was appalled by the noise I was making.

I had not told Nana that Papá had said we were going away. I had been afraid to tell her. I gulped and sobbed and pressed my knuckles against my mouth. Papá kept his distance and his silence. When we got home, Mamá took one look at me and cried out that I had been harmed—what had he done to me! Papá said it was the moving picture. I was too impressionable, he said, as a consequence of Mamá's own lack of restraint.

She shook me as though to shake out an explanation. The bearded old man, his rags, his aloneness, these were things for which I had no words. I couldn't have explained why I thought Nana was staring at me through a window, unable to get to me, her hair as white as snow. At last Mamá pulled me onto her lap and for a while, I bore the convulsive squeezing of her arms, the muttered accusations against Papá who, in any case, didn't hear them since he'd fallen asleep.

.   .   .

The harvest began; the chimneys smoked. I forgot the moving picture and thought less about leaving Malagita. When I walked to school, I kept to the middle of the road; it was the time of year when great spiders came out of holes in the ground and walked about on jointed, furry legs and when the wasps Nana called the devil's little horses began to build their nests.

Señora Garcia had loaned me a book about a man who sets out to discover a lost continent in the sea, and I was thinking about him one morning, saying his name over to myself, as I came within sight of the chapel.

A group of men were standing in front of the doors. Father Céspedes was among them gesticulating violently, shaking his head from side to side. Suddenly he darted forward and grabbed Lazaro Quintana, who was a head taller than he was, about the waist and tried to force him to the ground. Another man broke into laughter. Lazaro bent over and lifted up the priest until his little buttoned black shoes showed, helplessly hanging, toes pointed downwards. The laughing man struck Lazaro across the back. He dropped Father Céspedes as though he'd been a sack. I felt a hand on my arm and looked up to find Nana standing beside me.

"Come with me," she demanded.

"I have to go to school."

"There'll be no school."

When we reached her cabin, she said, "You'll stay here today."

Silently, she made herself coffee but forgot to drink it and went to stand in her doorway, looking out intently. "Come here and tell me what you see," she ordered me.

I looked out. "Nothing."

"Look at the mill."

"There's no smoke."

"Yes. That's it," she said.

Men were walking along the road in groups of four or five, speaking excitedly among themselves. I saw Señora Galdos in the distance talking to several women.

"What is it?" I asked. A man I remembered, Ortiz the cutter, passed by. Nana called out, "How is it, Ortiz?" "We'll see," Ortiz replied grimly.

"Aren't they cutting cane today?" I asked her.

"Let the wind cut the cane," she said. She seemed suddenly elated. She turned back into the cabin and spread her arms wide and looked straight up at the ceiling. Her mood alarmed me. I began to tell her hurriedly about how Lazaro Quintana had lifted up the priest.

"I saw it all," she cried. "So it begins!"

"What begins?" I shouted in exasperation.

"The revolution," she declared. She took a metal box from beneath her bed and opened it and took out a sheet of paper which she handed to me. "You can read now," she said. "Read this." I held it as she explained to me that it was a legal paper called a contract, and that my grandfather had been forced to sign it, and that when I finished reading it, I would see his signature, firm and clear as it always was, even under such conditions.

Not all the words were known to me but I read enough to understand that my grandfather had had to pay a rental on everything he used, that he had to repay all loans by March thirty-first of each year, and that he could only grow crops permitted by the Company. The Company was not required to pay my grandfather for cane ruined by delay—if the mill was not operative for any reason—and he was never to demand a reduction of his rent even if the Company took land from him for which he paid rent and used it for various purposes such as extending the railroad line or experimenting with new types of cane.

It was hard to read the paper. I skipped much of it. My grandfather's signature was just as Nana had described it. It seemed to have been written by a different man than the one whose last desperate word had been *ruina*.

I could hear her breathing as though each breath pained her. I looked up into her gaze, so grave, so heavy with a meaning I couldn't make out. I pressed the paper into her hand and turned away, not knowing what she wanted from me.

"You'll understand one day," she said in the fateful voice with which she made her predictions.

I would have told her then that Papá was going to take me away if I had not felt so uneasy at the strangeness of the morning. Outside, it had grown still and no one passed the cabin for a long time.

Nana's mood changed. A look of hopelessness came over her face.

"What can we do?" she asked sadly. "You'll see. They'll call out the soldiers . . . they always do. Malagita will be full of them, misguided brutes, peasants wearing their first pairs of shoes, hardly better off than we are. We're too weak . . . too weak."

But the soldiers didn't come. The revolution appeared to have passed through Malagita that day, pausing only briefly, then going on somewhere else. The mill started up, school resumed. Señora Garcia did not mention the missing day. When I reported to Mamá how Lazaro Quintana had picked up Father Céspedes as though he'd been a doll, and described how the priest's little feet dangled in the air, she threw up her hands and thanked God the men were back in the fields and the mill where they belonged.

A revolution was a pitiful thing. It made people think something different was going to happen. Afterwards, there was a kind of mortified silence. Even Nana told me to be quiet, to not speak of it, to stop asking questions.

A week after Nana had called upon the wind to cut the cane, a woman came screaming down the central road to Malagita, past the cabins, the *plazuela*, the surgery, all the way to the chapel where she stood trembling violently as people gathered around her, as we, having run out of the schoolroom, past the altar, up the aisle, despite Señora Garcia's demand that we stay at our desks, stared at her in excitement and fear.

In the bright sunlight, she turned in circles, moaning. Women clutched at her. The men implored her to calm herself.

"A hanged man!" she gasped out. "The birds have taken his eyes—"

The crowd gathered her up like a fish in a net and carried her away back down the road. Señora Garcia pushed us into the chapel where she made us kneel, ordering us to pray to God to save us from any more horrors.

The story of the hanged man was all anyone spoke about that day. A suicide was unheard of in our village. He had been old, in his fifties, his wife dead, his children scattered. It was true, Señora Galdos informed everyone, that birds were vicious creatures and had pecked out his eyes. Someone recalled that he had not attended Mass since the death of his wife. The old fisherman opened his toothless mouth and proclaimed that he didn't wish to speak ill of the dead, but he knew that the man had been a drunkard. But Nana said the man had hanged himself because the revolution had failed.

As I walked home late that day, I saw Mamá hurrying from the *vivienda*. "Don't speak of it!" she called out. "I've heard everything."

She reached the cabin a minute before I did and went in. Just as I reached the threshhold, I heard her gasp. I looked in. "My God! He's brought the suitcases," she said.

They stood side by side on the floor near the table. I went to them and felt the smooth leather, the metal locks. Mamá grabbed my hand. "Don't abandon me," she muttered. "Leave them be. Don't touch them."

It was after dark when Papá appeared at the door.

"What is that you're eating?" he asked with unusual mildness.

"You can see, can't you?" my mother replied sullenly. "You know what an egg is, don't you?"

He walked over to the suitcases, picked them up and carried them to another part of the cabin and set them down. With his back to us, he said, "In ten days, we're going to Tres Hermanos. There is a ship leaving for the United States—"

"—I can't!" Mamá interrupted. "Orlando, I can't."

"I've had some luck," Papá went on quietly. "I've bought our passages. There's something left to take care of us, for a while, at least."

"Nothing I wish matters," Mamá said. "Will you turn around and look at us? Can't you reflect about this awful thing you're doing?"

Papá walked rapidly to the table. He snatched up her spoon.

"Do you want to remain a child forever? Why aren't you using the fork? Why isn't she using the fork?"

"Luck!" exclaimed Mamá. She laughed. "So you've won the lottery at last! Is that it?"

I thought Papá would leave then as he often did in the middle of a quarrel with her. But he remained in the door, staring out, his body motionless, a kind of intent look about him as though he was braced against something he'd glimpsed moving in the dark.

"Are we going to come back?" I whispered to Mamá. She was staring down at her rice and egg, her hair tumbling across one cheek.

"I don't know," she said. "I don't know anything."

No one spoke. A faint smell of lard lingered in the air. The fried egg on my plate was cold. I broke it with my spoon, and when the yolk spilled over the rice, I turned away in disgust. "Eat your supper," Mamá begged me softly. It was too late; I had no appetite left.

Before school the next morning, I went to Nana's. At last, shuddering as though I stood in a cold rain, I told her. She held me in her arms so long, I felt suffocated. I pinched her ears until she let me go.

"You'll be lost, lost—and I—now he is taking you away from me altogether, first Fefita, now you . . ."

"I won't go."

"If only your Mamá could refuse—if she could refuse anything."

"I'll refuse."

She seized me again. "You can't," she whispered. She let me go and went to the door and cursed the chickens.

"I could hide," I said.

She laughed bitterly.

"I can run away."

"Where can you run?"

"I could stay with you. They wouldn't miss me."

She turned back into the cabin. "Perhaps," she said, staring down at me.

That evening, Señora Galdos gave birth to a son. Her labor had been long and difficult. At the end of it, she ran out onto the road, knelt and, at the same moment, the baby tumbled out onto the earth. She named him Pedro.

.   .   .

My mother tried to pack her cooking pots in a box. Papá caught her at it and grabbed up the pots and flung them to the back of the cabin.

"You don't understand . . . you can't understand . . ." he repeated over and over again.

When he had gone, she slipped her little card of Jesus and His bleeding heart into a cloth pocket in the side of one of the suitcases. "Don't tell him," she said to me.

.   .   .

One day after school, I found Papá waiting for me outside the chapel. The children paused to stare at him. I felt the blood rise to my face. I felt on fire. He stared back at them steadily until, whispering among themselves, they set off toward their homes.

"Tie your shoelaces," he said to me impatiently. I squatted down on the road to do as he had ordered. On his boots, I noticed a pattern I hadn't seen before circling over the leather like the path of a worm.

From stubbornness and anger, I didn't ask him where we were going, not even after we had passed through the gates of the *vivienda* and crossed the veranda to the broad, carved, wooden doors, not even after he opened one of them and motioned me to walk through.

But in the immense room where I found myself, I was overcome with the desire to hear a human voice. "Are we going to see Mamá?" I asked. Alma, a young maid from Galícia, entered through one of the many doors which opened into this room, carrying an armful of flowers. She began to arrange them in a vase which stood on a table before a mirror. As her hands worked, she watched us. I smiled at her reflection but there was no sign of recognition on her face.

"I'm taking you to my mother," Papá said. I followed him down a wide corridor until he paused and rapped softly at a closed door. A woman in a white dress opened it. Behind her, I glimpsed a bed piled high with pillows; above it a roof of cloth hung in pleats like a half-opened fan.

"Señor Orlando," the woman said, "I'm afraid she has forgotten you were coming today. She has had a bad week."

"It doesn't matter," Papá said. I hung back. He took hold of me and pushed me forward toward the bed.

An old woman reclined against the pillows. Her hair was piled up on her small, narrow skull like the beaten white of an egg. Below thick, black eyebrows, her narrow eyes were closed, each lid tinged with red as though the creased, ashen skin had been stirred with a drop of blood.

"Mamá?" Papá asked in a hushed voice. "I've brought the little girl."

She opened her eyes slowly, scowled as though puzzled, then looked at me for a long moment.

"Do you speak French?" she asked in a queer, dead little voice.

I shook my head, unable to answer, my voice trapped in my throat like a thick bubble.

She moved restlessly against the pillows. "I want a cup of coffee," she said to the woman in white.

"Not today," the woman said soothingly. "The doctor said tomorrow, perhaps."

"Perhaps," the old woman echoed grimly. "Perhaps I will die tomorrow."

She turned her gaze on me once more. I was terrified. It was such a chill gaze, blank as the white moon on cold nights.

"You will never be truly cultivated until you learn to speak French," she said. Her eyes closed, her thin hands fluttered once then slipped beneath the coverlet.

"Mamá?" Papá whispered.

She didn't open her eyes again, staying behind them like someone who has locked a door on the world.

"We will leave Malagita on Sunday," Papá said as we passed once more through the immense room. Alma had gone. The tall yellow flowers filled the air with their sweet, spicy fragrance. I wondered which door led to the kitchen, to Mamá and Panchito and all the others. The significance of Papá's words weighed little at that moment. I could only ponder the mystery of my presence here and my mother's in the servants' quarters.

"Go home now," Papá told me as he closed the gates. For once, a command of his suited me. I watched for Mamá long before she was due to come up the path, and when at last the shadow of our cabin lay across the road and I saw her, I ran to meet her, more astonished now at the event I was about to recount than when it had happened.

"Papá took me to see La Señora."

She stood still. "My God . . ."

"She asked me if I could speak French."

Mamá took my arm and hurried me into the cabin where she sat down at once, drawing me close to her and staring at me.

"Did she give you anything?"

"No."

"How much time were you with her?"

"A few minutes."

She nodded. "I felt something. I was folding linen. I remember now. I stopped suddenly—I shivered. I must have known you were there."

"Alma told you."

"No, no. I felt it, I tell you."

Mamá was only interested in her clairvoyance. In any case I didn't want to talk about La Señora anymore. The wonder of the visit was fading. Nothing had happened after all. Had she even known that I was her granddaughter? "The little girl," Papá had said to her. I took off my tight shoes.

"And she gave you nothing at all?"

"Nothing."

"That was all she asked—if you could speak French?"

I looked at her coldly and said, "She didn't even know who I was."

"God will punish them both. Unnatural mothers, the two of them . . ."

"We're going away Sunday," I said. She crossed herself.

"I know," she groaned. "When I think of it, my heart beats so fast it takes my breath away."

We stared at each other for a moment. She began to undress wearily.

"In three days," I said deliberately.

"In three days," she echoed.

.   .   .

The servants had given her gifts. She cried over them—a tablecloth embroidered by the seamstress with clumped designs of fruit and birds in rather harsh colors, a book of prayers printed on paper as coarse as that of the song sheets. "Pearls," she exclaimed, holding her hand out to show me a tiny pair of earrings. "Real pearls." She wiped her eyes with a little soiled cloth she had taken from the pocket of her black uniform. "I would never have thought it of Ursula Vargas," she said tearfully.

"Will you keep still?" snarled Papá.

They quarreled all evening. Even during the night I awoke to hear a kind of low mumbling of mutual exasperation and complaint.

Tomorrow I would say good-bye to Nana. Tomorrow I would sleep for the last time on this mattress, in this corner from which I had so often seen the moon traveling across the sky. And the night after that, I would be—where? In what place could I possibly be the night after that? On a train? On a ship from which I couldn't see the land? Could there be a sea without end? I felt as if the three of us had already set out into a darkness that would take us further and further from Malagita—until we were so far away we could never return.

.   .   .

"I know," Nana said. "I've heard." She set down before me a cup of thick chocolate. "This is the way the Spaniards make it," she said.

I had no appetite for anything.

"Drink it for strength," she said, touching my hair with the whole of her hand as though she was gathering me up, her voice tranquil, as if this was any other morning.

A horse appeared in the doorway, stretching its neck around so its head hung inside the cabin, a bridle trailing on the floor. A man's hand grabbed the bridle and pulled the horse away. The man himself peered in at us. "Here is the animal, Señora Sanchez," he said. "I'll need her back by Monday."

"You'll have her," Nana promised. "Tie her up to that tree over there by the tub."

He led the horse away. I saw clumps of dried earth on its rump.

"We're going to hide," Nana said. "We're going to run away." She handed me a sack stained with circles of grease. "Food for later," she said as she folded a blanket over her arm.

Clutching the sack, I stayed where I was. It is Nana, I told myself, but fear dazed me.

"Don't be afraid," she said softly. "What I'm doing is correct. God doesn't mean to have you taken from me." She took hold of my arm and pulled me to my feet and led me out of the cabin to the horse.

Nana sat sideways on the padded cloth that covered the horse's back. She reached down her hand. I gripped it, swayed against the sun-warmed pelt and felt myself lifted against it until I was sitting in front of her. She picked up the reins. "*Anda! Anda!*" she called. The horse turned out to the road and, slowly switching its great tail, took us out of Malagita.

"Where are we going?" I asked her.

"To the old fortress."

"But the spirits—"

"No," she interrupted quickly. "That's a thing one believes in now and then."

I could smell the fried bananas in the sack. The heat of midday filled me up like a thick, hot soup; we rocked gently on the mare's back. My eyes had already closed as I felt Nana pull on the reins to turn off to some other road.

I woke to feel her arm holding me against her. Far ahead of us, I saw the mountain, the gray tower. We stopped at a small pond where the horse lowered its head and drank. The land around us was deserted. There were no cane fields here. I no longer cared where we were going. We went on. Sometimes the horse's hoof struck a stone. The shadows of the trees lengthened. I could feel Nana's heart beating strongly.

"The mountain is too far," I said. "It's moving away from us."

I heard a church bell, as muffled as though it rang under water. The horse halted. Nana kicked its sides but it would not budge. She slid down to the ground and held out her arms for me. The horse turned its head to watch Nana as she lifted each hoof. "Nothing," she muttered. For a moment she seemed bewildered. She took the sack from my hand. "Never mind. We'll eat now, you and I and the horse, too. After that, perhaps, she'll be willing to take us a little further."

She spread the blanket by the side of the road. "Here," she said. "This will be our little house for a while."

We ate rice and bananas with our fingers. Afterward, she took two scarves from her pocket and tied one around my head and one around her own. The bats would begin to fly soon, vague, smoky shapes in the fading light. "I'll have a little tobacco," she said. She puffed for a few minutes on her pipe. Her shoulders drooped, and I saw a deep line on each side of her mouth I had not noticed until that moment.

"They won't know I've gone yet," I said.

She sighed. "We can't be sure of that."

She got up and walked to where the horse cropped and took its bridle to lead it back to the road. "We'll go on," she said.

Far to the west a single line of smoke rose straight into the air. Light slid slowly from the trees like honey, and lay in long, narrow, golden pools upon the ground. The dark flowing over us from the east streaked each blade of tall, wild grass, the trunks of trees, the undersides of leaves, and brought with it a strong smell of earth. The horse's head drooped sleepily. Only the small regular thuds of its hooves broke the silence. The moon rose; it seemed to flutter like a white moth behind two thin clouds. At some point, Nana gathered up the reins and we halted. She slipped the padded cloth from the horse's back and spread it on the ground beside the road. She tied the bridle to a nearby sapling.

I sat on the cloth and looked at her. The moonlight showed her face, still with patience and hopelessness. The United States was a great hole to the north which would swallow me. I knew Nana could not save me from it. She sank to her knees, looked up once at the sky, then lay down beside me. When I awoke, my body was chilled in the places where it had not been warmed by hers. She was asleep, her head resting on her clasped hands.

The early light unfolded like the petals of a rose. Across the road flowed a stream, and I knelt and splashed my face and cupped my hands to drink. When I turned back, Nana was sitting up watching me.

"Maybe they won't mind leaving me," I said.

Nana shook her head slowly. "I've done a stupid thing," she said. She got up and led the horse to the stream where it dipped its head and drank. When she came back, she took an orange from a small string bag.

"The tower isn't any closer," I said.

"It is closer. But it makes no difference."

She climbed onto the horse and held out her hand. "We'll go on. I can't bear to turn back yet," she said. I understood that she had given up.

Not much later, I heard distinct hoof-beats.

We plodded on. In a few moments, Papá, riding Dr. Baca's horse, drew abreast of us. He seized the reins of our mare. Nana turned her face away as he led the horse in a wide circle until we were facing in the direction of Malagita. For a little while, he kept hold of the reins, riding next to us so that my leg was between the great, rough, horse bodies, then he let go. We followed him to the village. The journey which had taken us half a day and the night ended as the shriek of the noon whistle blew.

Papá, to my amazement, rode straight to Nana's cabin. All these years I had thought—but what *had* I thought? How could I have imagined that we were all invisible to each other? In my unknowingness, I had been like the ants I sometimes followed, watching their struggle to carry a hibiscus leaf to their nest, unaware of me, my foot raised to crush them and their leaf into the dirt.

Nana slid off the horse and held out her arms for me. Once I was in them, she held me out, away from her, her face expressionless. "Go home," Papá ordered me. "I must return the horse."

I struggled in Nana's arms and tried to get close to her. In that instant, as I clutched at her skirt, Mamá stepped out from Nana's cabin.

The two women stared at each other without speaking. Papá wheeled the horse around and rode off in the direction of the surgery, turning once with stiff reluctance as though against his own intention, to glance at Mamá and Nana who had still not spoken or moved.

Suddenly, my grandmother flung out her arms. "I can't! I can't bear it!" she cried.

The two women ran toward each other. They stood for a while in a silent, fierce embrace. It was Nana who released Mamá first. Then she picked me up, swaying with my weight, and held me against her. She kissed my forehead with dry lips and put me down.

"No more . . ." she whispered. She entered her cabin, making a violent gesture with the hand she held behind her back as though to push Mamá and me away from her.

We walked past the now silent clock tower and rounded the *plazuela* toward home. I looked up at Mamá. There were no tears on her face. I did not know what I wanted to ask her, how to speak of the great puzzlement I felt. For the first time, we walked together through the herd of pigs. I saw our *bohío* ahead. It already looked empty, more than empty, as though it had been abandoned years ago.

.   .   .

Mamá, Papá and I set out from Malagita before dawn. We stood beside the suitcases, waiting for the train that would take us to Tres Hermanos. When it came, Papá pushed us both up three high steps to the platform.

We slept that night in a little hotel, in three cots lined up against the wall like those in the surgery. In the morning, we boarded a ship. Mamá went to our cabin from which she didn't emerge until the end of the journey. I stayed on deck to watch the sharks Papá had told me I would see once the ship was beyond the harbor, and they were there, just as he had said, turning up their white bellies in swift passage through the water. As I leaned on the railing, I wasn't thinking about sharks. I was dreaming of the day when I would return to San Pedro, now a bluish haze receding on the horizon. All at once, even as I stared at it, it vanished. There was only a waste of sea and sky.

That night, I lay beside my mother in our lower bunk. I whispered to her, "I'm going back. You'll see."

She clutched me to her. "We'll never go back," she said.

"I will!" I cried.

"Hush! Stop! Go to sleep!"

"Nana will take care of me."

She pinched my shoulder. "Fool! She can barely take care of herself. She has nothing."

"Then—La Señora will take care of me."

"My poor crazy child . . ."

"Yes!" I shouted. "She will! She must!"

Papá opened the cabin door. I heard my mother's heart beat loudly. He climbed the little ladder to his bunk above us. For a moment his legs dangled down, his feet like two pale fish swimming near my head, then he drew himself up into his bed.

The ship rocked gently as a cradle absently touched, the engines rumbled ceaselessly. My parents slept. But I lay awake, my eyes open and straining in the dark as though in that way I could catch time out, arrest it, even as it bore us implacably northward.

Part Two

Once out of the narrow hallway of the tenement we were living in at the time, my mother depended upon me to speak for her, to stand between her and the cold, racial glare of Broadway shopkeepers whose sluggish ill will never lost its power to quell me even as it aroused a desperate desire to hear, directed toward Mamá and me, the plain justice which their voices expressed when they served other customers, Irish or German, I guessed, or similar, proper folk, who so complacently placed their canned fruit and vegetables, their white bread and dusty potatoes, on the wooden counter while the grocer, with a pencil stub, rapidly added up the prices with a self-important flourish, then rang up the total on a huge cash register whose drawer shooting out with a loud bang to receive bills and coins always made Mamá start as if at that same instant she had discovered there was no money in her pocketbook to pay for our few purchases, canned milk or vinegar, or three brown eggs.

It was only in Mr. Salazar's *bodega*, after a hasty, frightened run from our flat, that Mamá moved with a touch of ease as she estimated the ripeness of plantains, or slipped her hand into a sack of black beans, or touched with one finger the fleshy white roots of sweet cassava in its open wooden crate.

Here in the dim, tiny Spanish grocery store on Broadway and 158th Street, which always smelled of cat urine and cockroach poison, of spiced sausage and coconut candy, Henry Salazar, a tall, elderly, unsmiling Cuban from whose steel-framed spectacles the left lens was missing, weighed lard and onions, and, when asked for it, went to a cubicle at the back of the store and returned with what always looked to be the same gray slab of pork banded with lines of dried dark blood. From this he carved rough chunks, throwing them on his scale until a customer cried, "*bastante!*"

Below the counter, he kept a stack of lottery tickets for sale, and near a shelf of boxes of Dutch Cleanser and cakes of yellow kitchen soap, a telephone. It was this last which drew customers to the *bodega* as much, if not more, than Salazar's meager stores of what the neighborhood Irish children called "spic grub."

Salazar charged two cents for each use of the telephone; he kept the pennies in large glass jars on a shelf off by themselves. Some storekeepers displayed jellybeans in jars, offering a prize to whoever could guess the correct number of candies in them. I tried to guess at the calls for help the pennies in Salazar's jars represented, how many inquiries made to remote authorities for news of lost relatives.

Once when I'd been sent for a bottle of milk, a woman was behind the counter weeping into the phone. "Send a police—send, please—" she gasped out. Salazar was wrapping a loaf of lard for another customer who stared aghast at the weeping woman. "Send doctor . . ."

When she had replaced the receiver, Salazar put down the lard and held out his long hand. Dazed, she stared down into it. "*Dos centavos*," he said gravely. She stroked her cheeks, shook her head. "He swallowed rat poison," she said. "He's dancing—on his back—on the floor." The other customer put the two pennies in Salazar's hand. As I left, I heard the clink of them dropping into a jar.

After Mamá had carried her groceries in a cloth bag back to the kitchen of our tenement flat, she would sit on the edge of a stool near the sink and stare at what she had bought. She kept one foot on the floor; the other dangled like a child's. Her body was heavy and shapeless in a dress of dark material, and she slumped, exhausted after her perilous journey. Slowly, she would begin to put things away.

Nearly every day when I got home from school, I found Mamá sitting on that stool, one elbow on the counter, staring into the sink, waiting for me to lead her out into the New York streets as if she was blind and deaf.

We had been in New York City for five years. She had not learned English despite the months she had worked in a perfume factory across the Hudson River in New Jersey.

But she managed to keep the job for a year, traveling by subway, then by bus, to the bench where she sat all day long in front of a machine that stoppered bottles of scent, surrounded by women from whose mouths issued a blizzard of language, white and cold, she said to me, like the snow, hard, she said, like the patches of ice on the sidewalk in winter before which she would shudder with dread as I yanked at her arm or grabbed folds of her worn black coat to drag her on and into one of the flats where Papá had moved us because of a rent concession. Several times we moved because he needed more space for boarders who would rent from us one of the linoleum-floored cubicles along the hallway, each furnished with a bureau, a chair and a spindly bed.

It was one of those boarders, Maura Cruz, who found Mamá the job in the perfume factory, and who, with frantic insistence, tried to compel Mamá into becoming an American. And when she was fired from the perfume factory—as a consequence of her inattention, many unstoppered bottles had drenched the skirts and legs of the talkative women further on down the assembly line with the powerful if synthetic aroma of spring flowers—it was Maura who found her work she could do at home. This job, making beaded bags, required only that she deliver her completed work once a month. But the wholesale office to which she had to take the bags was so far downtown that she complained the subway ride was nearly as long as our journey from San Pedro. I had to go with her, she said, because she would not be able to argue with the man who was to pay her for her labor, and whom Maura referred to as a thieving Jew.

The thieving Jew had a dingy little office at the front end of a dark loft near Delancey Street. He was middle-aged, a tired-looking man who barely spoke to us, taking the beaded bags, one at a time, from the sack in which Mamá had carried them, and looking at them so closely he seemed about to press them like handkerchiefs to his eyes. We made thirteen trips to him. Each time, he paid Mamá exactly the sum Maura had told her to insist upon. One late afternoon, he told us he was bankrupt.

"No more business. No more money," he said when he had counted out eighteen dollars, placing the crumpled bills in Mamá's hand. "Is he lying?" she asked me in Spanish. I glanced at him. Before I could answer her, he said, "No, I'm not lying," so diffidently, so mildly, that I felt a rush of sympathy toward him, and surprise that he understood our language. He smiled at me abstractedly, then turned away, placing his hands on the rough table he used for a desk and leaning on them, a grimace of pain on his nearly hidden face.

After these trips, we returned home to find the early winter dusk waiting for us at the top of the subway stairs, or else the long, hazy evenings of summer when men and children gathered beneath the street lights on our corner, shouting at each other in a language that was not Spanish or English but an agitated, harsh mingling of both. A year after Mamá lost her job in the perfume factory, she explained to me, "I couldn't pay attention to those bottles that flew past me. How could I—with those women always talking?"

"You didn't have to listen to them."

"Ah, but I did! They *wanted* me to know how ignorant I was. They watched me when they talked. I was drowning, I tell you."

I knew she understood more than she let on, but Mamá's inability, or refusal, to learn to speak English was like an ailment which ate away at her nature. Even the country folk who rented rooms from us for a few months, and who often came from remote rural districts in Cuba or Puerto Rico, even those *guajiros*, so ignorant that our chain-pull toilet alarmed them as Beatriz de la Cueva's servants' toilet had once alarmed me, would press me—whom they treated in this regard as an authority because I went to school—to help them speak as Americans spoke, to teach them to unlock their tongues so they could pronounce, without that Antilles accent to which they attributed so much of their social and economic misery, those particular words which began with the treacherous *th*, or those that ended with the perverse, unspellable *ough*, or the homely *ing* which was, said a young woman from San Juan, exactly like the sound made by a *saltón*. "In English, a *saltón* is a grasshopper," I said. "*Que barbaridad!*" she commented.

The Great Depression was not unique to these immigrants who had experienced so much want. When Papá told one of our boarders, Enrique Machado, that there had been sixteen million unemployed people in 1933, the Cuban shrugged. "Hombre! You get a long ride on the subway for a nickel," he said, as though offering proof of a prosperity kept out of his reach only by his inability to sound like everyone else.

Mamá clung to the old language like a shipwrecked person might cling to a plank, caught in currents which were carrying her ever further from the shore.

.   .   .

During our first summer in New York, in 1936, Papá had told us that the gift of money made to him by his mother, and which we had not known about until that moment, was half spent. I think Mamá had known Papá had not won the lottery. She had guessed that he had borrowed money for our passage and settling in the United States from Dr. Baca, or some other crony he had had in Tres Hermanos.

When she learned where it had come from, Mamá was so outraged that Papá had made a secret of its source, she went to her bed and lay down upon it and vowed she would not rise again to cook meals and wash and iron for a man who had insulted her so deeply by not confiding in her.

"I am a fool!" she cried bitterly as Papá stood in the doorway of the kitchen, and I lurked in the dark hall near their bedroom.

"I, who each day take pennies and nickels to that *bellaco*, Salazar, to buy that *porquería* he sells that I make into meals to keep you alive—I, whose every day is full of misery—how can I clothe the girl? How can I keep her so she doesn't go among the American children like a beggar? Where am I? What is this terrible place you've brought us to?"

"She has no sense," Papá muttered while Mamá sobbed convulsively. "She's forgotten she is in her own country."

This earlier news, that we were not immigrants but American citizens, and which Mamá had learned in San Pedro before we had even embarked on our ship and which, I suppose, had made no difference in her life that she could grasp, was given to me when I was first enrolled in the public school on Amsterdam Avenue. With his customary, disdainful curtness, Papá had told me that his father, Antonio, had been an American citizen, relinquishing his Spanish citizenship long before he went to San Pedro to claim his own father's legacy to him of the plantation of Malagita. I had been astonished to think, those first days among the school children whose language I could not yet speak, that I was an American like them, even though I had been born a bastard.

Papá went to the bedroom door. "We have rent from the boarders," he said defensively. "Don't forget that."

"The boarders!" exclaimed Mamá. "The boarders steal into my kitchen in the night and eat what little food is left. They don't pay the rent except when it suits them. My daughter teaches them for nothing. The boarders! Don't speak of them!"

Papá went down the hall and out the door, slamming it behind him. I peeked into the room. Mamá was sitting on the edge of the bed. She looked more frightened than angry.

"Should I make supper?" I asked her.

She moaned faintly. "No, no. I'll get up. I'll get up in a moment." She held out her hand, and I went and held it. It was moist and lay slackly in mine.

"Look, you see. Now I know there was a certain sum—well—I can see the very last cent of it. What can he do? He's not fit for finding work. What will happen to us, Nena? Do you remember the Estradas?"

An old woman, Mrs. Estrada, and her granddaughter, Alicia, had lived down the hall from us when we'd first moved in. I hadn't seen them for months.

"I didn't tell you. You know, she was very clean, that old woman. She made a pot of soup for her little Alicia every night. She, herself, was not eating the soup. One morning when you were at school, the police came. She had starved herself to death, you see. They had nothing. In this country, you can die of hunger, never mind what that fool Enrique Machado says. In San Pedro, there was always something to eat. But here? Who would know about it if you died in your bed like Mrs. Estrada? Only when the police come."

I imagined I could hear two pennies dropping into one of Mr. Salazar's jars.

A week later Maura Cruz came to us to rent a room and, eventually, to find Mamá her jobs in the perfume factory and for the thieving Jew. But Papá did not work for some years.

.   .   .

When I watched Mamá ironing a shirt of Papá's as she bent over the sheet-covered plank balanced on two straight-backed chairs that she used for an ironing board, her own dress unpressed, her lips moving as she talked to herself, I wanted to kick away the plank, its clumsiness and inadequacy proof that I would never be able to enter that world which I had begun to suspect lay beyond our barrio.

Papá's shirts always were ironed. Each morning he polished his black shoes with a frayed rag. Each morning he shaved with his straight razor so closely he seemed, daily, to have scraped away more of the thin flesh that veiled his prominent cheekbones and sharp chin. Directly after I left for school, clattering down the narrow stairs that led from our flat to the entrance hall, I could hear his footsteps behind me. I had even less idea of where he went than I had had in Malagita.

Our first flat had been two tiny rooms in a damp basement next to a coal chute, its door lit faintly by a dusty bulb that hung from a low ceiling from among a thicket of narrow pipes which gurgled and shuddered along their length day and night. From our one window, we saw above us the feet and ankles of passersby. I thought we had come there to die— or that the place was the hell Father Céspedes had described with such satisfaction. After we left there, Papá always managed to get the top floor flat in most of the dirty brick tenements in which we lived. Once we were given a six-month rent concession. On the first day of the seventh month, Papá moved us out to a new and identical railroad flat. Indeed, they were like rusty, railroad cars—narrow high-ceilinged halls, three or four bedrooms off them, a kitchen with a deep sink, next to it a grooved metal counter, a parlor at the end of the hall with two windows opening to a fire escape. In one flat where we lived almost a year, a young rent collector, whose father owned the building, came on the first day of the month and stood nervously in the doorway, his nostrils pinched, his lips tightly closed to shut out the smell of our life.

The first time I ventured out into the street by myself, feeling all around me the vast, people-choked city, it seemed to me that Malagita could not exist. As I stood there, not daring to leave the entrance of the building, I felt such a shocking loss, I begun to cry aloud. Mamá heard me from our basement rooms and came to get me and lead me, sobbing, into their dark depths.

We began to accumulate things; a collection of iron bedsteads which, when I touched them, gave me the taste of vinegar on my tongue, thin mattresses covered with coarse-stained ticking, a metal table in one of whose snapping joints I broke my finger, my father's armchair, a present Mamá had bought him when she was working at the perfume factory and which she had paid for over eight months on an installment plan, and about whose worm-pink cover Papá never ceased to make sarcastic comments, wondering aloud if my mother's brain contained any other idea of color than pink. Long after the color faded, he would point a derisive finger at it and shake his head.

When we moved from the basement home, we had Papá's suitcases and two boxes of bedding, a few pots, a small, black iron Mamá had to heat on a stove, and a plunger with a broken handle which Papa had found in a garbage can, and which we had to use often for the toilet in that most wretched of all our homes. On our last move, which we made the year I was seventeen, in 1943, during the war, we had fourteen boxes. On the top of one I carried, I saw Mamá's Sacred Heart, the same one I had watched her slip into a suitcase in Malagita so long ago. The stuffing had leaked out of the heart which was now collapsed, and Mamá had handled the card so much there were dark splotches on the face of Jesus so that He looked as though He'd been in a street brawl.

We rarely heard from our boarders once they shut our front door behind them and went down the stairs to the street and to different lives. But as we moved from flat to flat, each within a radius of a dozen blocks or so from each other on the east side of Broadway, two of them, Maura Cruz, and the short, explosive Enrique Machado, remained with us for years, moving with us and helping transport our household goods. My father lent his strength only to carry the detested armchair. Once we passed another family on the move. The man and his two sons averted their faces as though to show they were not like us, but the woman, gripping several stuffed pillow cases, gave us a look of wry commiseration.

.   .   .

At waking one's body is without age. It is like the body of someone newly born. That moment in which one is most insensible begins to fill up with the sorrowful presentiment of an absence. I recall how the morning light first touches the top of the tallest royal palm and the face of the clock tower, then a narrow dirt road still cool from the night's moisture and a ditch beside it in which deep shadows run like water. It gilds a palmetto, the fronds of a thatch above the dried red mud walls of a *bohío* and sends a radiant shaft across the earthen floor to a low bed where it reveals who it is I grieve for, Nana. She is covered by a sheet around which she has crocheted a border of *margaritas*, her braid of black hair touches the floor, her long lids are shut but will soon open; as mine have; when she wakes to another day and slowly remembers, as I have remembered, what she has lost.

.   .   .

My mother and I had a violent fight. One morning she felt ill. I made up her bed for her. Beneath the thin mattress, I found six letters I had written to Nana.

"You didn't mail them!" I screamed with rage and panic.

She put down her cup of coffee and clutched her breast. Her hair was frazzled, the sleeve of her pink robe torn. "*Hija* . . ." she muttered.

"My God! How could you! How I hate you!"

She flung cup and contents at me. It struck my chin; the coffee splattered on my blouse.

"*Atrevida!*" she cried. "First, Orlando, now you!"

All these months I had imagined Nana reading my letters, touching them. I was beside myself. Sobbing, I yelled, "Yes, I dare! I'll call the police!"

Papá and Maura Cruz ran into the kitchen.

"Stop this noise at once!" he ordered.

Mamá had risen from her stool and was advancing toward me, her hands above her head balled into fists.

"You sack of rot!" I shouted.

"Oh! I'll kill her!" swore Mamá.

Maura Cruz threw herself bodily against Mamá. Papá picked me up, his arm hard around my waist, and took me down the hall and flung me on my bed. He slammed the door shut with such force that flakes of blue paint rained from the ceiling to the floor.

I cried tears of pure rage for a long time. I fell asleep. I woke to shame. There was silence in the flat. I had missed school. What excuse could I write out for myself which Mamá would sign in handwriting more like a child's than mine? I had to use the toilet. There was no one in the hall. When I returned to my room, Mamá, fully dressed, her hair tidy, was sitting on my bed.

"I mailed the letters while you slept," she said softly.

I lay with my head in her lap.

"She can read, you know, but she can't write—well, perhaps, a word,

two words. It was my father who was really educated. So I thought—
I see how wrong it was now—that there was no value in sending the
letters you wrote. But—perhaps it's because I'm so sad that I don't do
much . . . well, Nena, I wrote a note myself, though she can't answer it.
But I thought, someone might answer it for her. So I asked her for the
address of my brother, your Uncle Federico."

"You went to the post office by yourself?"

"By myself," she said humbly.

She stroked my hair. "Such a pretty color," she said. "What would be
the American word for this color?"

"They have no word for it," I assured her, wanting to shield her from
any uncertainty.

"Brown," she pronounced rather grandly after a moment of thought,
rolling the *r* as though it were a small wheel inside the word. Her hand
rested on my head. "That was a horrible thing you called me."

"Oh, Mamá . . . I didn't mean it."

"Tell me," she said, "what were you going to call the police for? And
where were you going to get the two pennies for Señor Salazar's big
jars?" She suddenly began to laugh. It was a sound of deep hilarity such
as I had seldom heard from her.

I couldn't think what I'd had in mind for the police to do. Her laughter
trailed off. She touched my ear. "There's no use in calling them," she
said pensively. "They don't like us here."

.   .   .

After mailing my letters and her note, Mamá developed a craving to hear
from her mother. For several weeks, she crept off every afternoon to a
Catholic church, ten blocks south of where we lived, to pray for word
from Nana. I had passed her once on Broadway but she didn't see me.
She was keeping close to the store fronts, her face frightened but resolute.

She didn't like the church. "God is someone else in this country," she
said. At first she had gone to confession but she couldn't understand the
words the Irish priest rattled off behind his wooden grill in the confessional box, and she was ashamed of how few English words she had
with which to disclose her sins.

"*Orgullo*," she said to me one afternoon as she slipped her rosary into her old black pocketbook and tied a scarf around her head. "What is that in English?"

"Pride," I answered in surprise. When she returned that day, she told me the priest had asked her if there were missionaries in San Pedro. That was, at least, what she thought he had asked her. "As though we were Africans . . ." she exclaimed indignantly. Years later, she asked me how to say *desesperacíon*, and when I said, despair, she bowed her head as though she had heard a fatal judgment. By then, she had given up confession and rarely went to the church, such a huge place, the air cold even in summer.

But her prayers for word from Nana were answered. A month or so after my letters had gone out, a reply arrived from San Pedro written in a careful, rounded hand by my old teacher, Señora Garcia:

Your mother received with great happiness her granddaughter's letters. Everything Luisa wrote is beautiful to her. She hopes there will be more letters so that she can hear Luisa's voice over the thousands of miles that separate her from Luisa herself. Señora Sanchez has good health. But La Señora de la Cueva is more crazy than ever. (I write this because Señora Sanchez commanded me to. I don't agree.) The last address she has of Federico in New York City is a restaurant called Salamanca. She sends embraces and kisses to her children so far away.

My father, with unusual alacrity, agreed at once to try to find the Salamanca restaurant and inquire after Federico's whereabouts. But when Mamá took two pennies from a milk bottle in which she kept change and held them out to him, he pushed her hand away impatiently, saying he wouldn't set foot in that Cuban's store but would find a public telephone somewhere.

Mamá and I sat together silently, staring at Señora Garcia's letter. "Your Papá's lonely," she said suddenly.

I was preoccupied by the answer to Nana I was fervently composing in my mind, describing to her how Mamá and I had squeezed next to each other in the pink armchair to read Señora Garcia's words over and over again. "Lonely?" I repeated disbelievingly.

I saw a slow blush spread over Mamá's face as if, unintentionally, she had revealed something intimate, and perhaps shameful, about my father.

Papá had found a telephone number for the restaurant and had actually spoken to Federico himself. He refused to answer Mamá's questions—how did her brother sound? Was he happy? Had he asked after her?—except to say that Federico had promised to visit us very soon.

The following Sunday at noon, there was a loud, impatient banging at our door. Maura, whose bedroom was nearest the door, got to it first and opened it. My uncle Federico, his wife, Aurelia, and their son, my cousin, Atilio, brushed past her and in single file marched down the hall to the parlor where Mamá, moved to tears by the occasion—she hadn't seen her brother for nineteen years—had risen to her feet and was holding out her arms.

Uncle Federico embraced Mamá with an odd, finicking haste, cast a glance at me, then, with a measuring stare, looked around at the room. He sat down on a straight-backed chair, opened his mouth and in a rapid, heavily accented but utterly confident English, related to us his first struggles in the United States, how he had overcome every handicap, how he had risen to the position he now held as maître d'hôtel at the Salamanca restaurant which was, naturally, downtown, and was famous for Spanish cooking, the world's greatest cuisine, mistakenly credited to France by ignorant people who imagined that in Spain everyone did nothing but eat rice and beans all day long to the accompaniment of castanets.

At first, Mamá had cried out to him to speak in Spanish, or, for God's sake, to go more slowly in English. But she soon fell silent, the strain on her face as she had tried to follow what Federico was saying replaced by a look of dejection of which, perhaps, she was conscious, because she gave him an occasional, hesitant smile as though to gainsay it. Federico did not notice her smiles; all along his eyes had been fixed upon Papá who, to my surprise, seemed to relish my uncle's every word.

Nana's son! It was hard to believe, although he resembled her more than my mother did. It was a clownish resemblance like that left of the original faces of the subjects of portrait photographs after Maura had tinted them with special paints, work she did in the evening for extra money.

Atilio, several years older than I, kept on his little hat which sat ridiculously in the middle of his fiercely curling black hair. His plump, sullen face was as smooth as an almond. He made a dumb show of his reluctance to place his bottom on anything in our parlor. He was wearing a vest as well as a jacket, and the heat—it was August—made him sweat, drops of it running down his forehead. I saw his Mamá take a large, violet handkerchief from her pocketbook, and looking to see that Uncle Federico was not watching, wipe her son's face and the sides of his short, thick nose, exactly like her own, while he stood scowling at her.

Federico, like many people who never need pause to think, didn't run out of subjects. He spoke of gala dinners at the Salamanca, of his professional acquaintance with the important people who frequented the restaurant, of the Ford automobile he was considering purchasing from a certain priest—he couldn't reveal the priest's name at the moment, but he was a man of some political power in the Latin community—who was offering it for sale, and of the mountains northwest of the city where he had taken Aurelia and Atilio for a week's holiday last summer.

"What!" he exclaimed, although no one had said anything. "You haven't been out of the city yet? Incredible! Ah, Orlando, you must see this wonderful American countryside."

My father held a cigarette to his mouth. So quickly, it seemed one bland motion, Uncle Federico whipped out a box of matches from his pocket, fired one, lit the cigarette and made a slight bow. Aurelia, whose corset stays I could see poking against the fabric of her dress, had gone to stare out the window while Mamá went to the kitchen to make coffee. Federico spoke of the excellent condition of the upholstery in the priest's Ford, the number of patrons who could be seated in the Salamanca, the cost of his holiday, and the spaciousness of the Sanchez apartment on the upper east side of the city.

"You have a refrigerator?" he asked Papá who shook his head, an amiable smile on his lips. "Ah, yes. Then you have an icebox. So did we, at first, didn't we, Aurelia? But now of course, we own one," and he smiled grandly. Papá nodded again as though he shared Federico's consciousness of his own consequence.

He asked Mamá, just before he left, "And how is our Mamacita?" He looked over her head at once as though silence would be preferable to an answer.

"I had not spoken to her for years until just before we left Malagita, then we—"

Federico interrupted her with a noisy sigh. "Yes, she's difficult, our mother. She has a difficult temperament. Old-fashioned ideas, you know."

Mamá looked hopefully into Aurelia's sudden stare of interest. "It was because of Orlando and me that she wouldn't speak," she said gravely.

"Don't you have a radio?" Atilio whispered to me. I shook my head. Maura Cruz leaned out into the hall where we were all standing.

"Who's that little monkey?" she asked in a loud whisper, pointing a finger at Atilio. There was a movement to the door, and the Sanchez family, accompanied by Papá, stepped out of the flat into the hall.

"Good-bye, my little niece," Uncle Federico called back. Papá closed the door and Mamá went to the kitchen. I followed. She was sitting on the stool, holding a cup beneath a trickle of water from the tap. Her dress was the same color as the cheesecloth through which she poured boiled milk for our coffee. A hairpin was about to fall from the knob of hair at her neck. Maura ran into the kitchen and stood there with her hands on her hips, her face intent as she looked at Mamá.

"Let Orlando go with them!" Mamá suddenly shouted. "Those Americans!"

"That boy looked exactly like a monkey," said Maura.

Mamá wiped her face with a dishrag then looked at it with disgust. "My family," she muttered. "That was my nephew and my brother." She caught sight of me. "Take down the clothes in the bathroom," she said harshly.

Had she guessed I was counting up the ways in which Aurelia was superior to her? Aurelia's hair was short. I had smelled the thrilling, scorched odor of her permanent wave. The seams of her stockings ran precisely down the middle of her thick calves. Her dress was pressed, her corset, immense, a coat of armor, powerfully holding her together.

I went to the bathroom where our clothes were hung to dry on three cords stretched above the bathtub. Except for a pair of Mamá's mended stockings, everything was damp.

The wooden handle of the toilet chain was loose. Above the toilet, a narrow window let in a few inches of light that had a gray bloom to it like a rain cloud's. The sash was askew; it could neither be raised nor lowered. Kneeling on the toilet seat, I saw an identical window set into a dark wall a few feet away. As I peered through the uneven opening, I became convinced all the air was leaking away, down to the invisible place below from which I'd sometimes heard the barbed yowling of cats. I ran out into the silent hall. If only I could find my way to the Sanchez apartment glowing with light on the upper east side! What did it matter how awful the three of them were if they had escaped from the barrio!

.   .   .

The Sanchez family did not visit us on many occasions, but Papá often went to the Salamanca late at night at closing time to pick up Federico and go with him to some club on the east side. I visited the Sanchez home some years later. I was not as surprised as I might have been the first day I met them to discover that their apartment was not so different from the railroad flats we had lived in. Only its furnishings—monstrous, overstuffed chairs squatting side by side in the living room on a carpet the color of Mercurochrome, glass tables cluttered with china statues of shepherdesses, squirrels and birds, and a radio in a large cabinet on top of which stood a vaguely sacramental plaster figure of a man clutching a staff around which someone had tied a purple satin ribbon, and the in-termittent, clanking shimmy of the refrigerator—were to substantiate Uncle Federico's claims to material success.

There were a few "clubs" on the west side, too, small abandoned stores furnished with a few folding chairs, a few card tables, where Latin men gathered in the evenings. When Mamá sent me on a late errand, I could hear the cadenced clack-clack of dominoes as they racked them up, the released excitement in their voices as they shouted and quarrelled and laughed over their games. They were, in their club, triumphant exiles. They kept their hats on. For adornment? Protection? I hated those hats. I hated the way the men strutted around each other, crowing *Oye! Oye!* —listen! listen!—and when, one such summer evening, I saw Papá through a dusty window moving among other men with a bodily ease, an expression of leniency on his face I had not seen at home, I hated him. But he never wore a hat, not even in the iron cold winters.

More and more frequently, he was away from our flat. But, as in Mala-gita, Mamá would set three places at the kitchen table, and when he did not come, would cover his food with a plate and put it aside for him.

If she begged him for money, holding up a patched coat which I had long outgrown, and pointing at me—"the girl grows so fast . . . she must have a new coat," he would push her aside. "Don't pester me," he would say.

Somehow Mamá kept me clothed. After she stopped working, she would filch change from Papá's pockets, and borrow from Maura or Enrique Machado, and gradually amass enough to buy me a sweater or material to make me a dress which she sewed by hand, dragging her stool to the window to get as much light as possible.

I cannot remember my father saying good morning to me; I recall only an atmosphere he brought about by his intent watchfulness to which I awoke each weekday. He didn't make my lunch or pass a comb through my hair—Mamá did that—but it was the force of his silent insistence that pushed me down the hall and out the door to school.

Yet he was indifferent to what I was taught as long as I could speak and write English. Often, he made me read to him from a newspaper, correcting my accent or demanding I explain the meaning of a word. If my explanation was wrong, he closed his eyes for a long time. I stared at his shirt to see if he was still breathing, imagining that, finally, he'd died of disgust at me.

One morning I found a dollar beneath the jar of change. I took it.

I didn't go to school but to the Red Robin movie house on Broadway and waited beneath the marquee until it opened at ten A.M. I sat through three entire programs, a serial, a cartoon, a travelogue on Naples, Italy, and two movies. I'd left my lunch at home. As my hunger increased, I grew aware of how weak a form my defiance of Papá had taken, knowing that despite the intimation of eternity aroused by a whole day at the movies, I would have to go home eventually. I was thirteen—there was no other place to go.

When Mamá saw me, she covered her mouth with her hand as she did when she was frightened or scandalized. I shrugged with the last of my courage. "Ay! Did you take it? He knows you took it," she whispered. I could have denied the theft. Not only boarders wandered through the flat but their friends and cousins.

Papá stood in the doorway of the kitchen. "Did you go to school? What did you do with the dollar?" he asked wearily. I wished only there had been more money for me to steal, an amount substantial enough to have shaken him.

"I went to the movies," I said insolently, looking over his shoulder at the window as though I found the fire escape more interesting than he, as though he was nothing to me. "I bought a candy bar," I added. "And this magazine." I held it up, rolled in my hand. He reached out to take it. He stared briefly at the photograph of a movie star couple on its cover, then began to rip its pages into pieces, letting them fall to the floor.

"Orlando! What are you doing?" my mother cried.

He beckoned me to follow him, and I did, sweat breaking out on my palms. In the bathroom, he took his leather strop from the nail where it hung. "Hold the rim of the tub," he said neutrally. When I did, he hit me, quickly, four times, with the strop. At each stroke, I felt a wave of faintness; the knocking of my heart was random and violent, as though it had broken loose from whatever contained it. My father was beating me. I felt a depth of helplessness I had experienced only on the ship that had carried us away from San Pedro.

I remained where I was, leaning over the tub, while he returned the strop to its place and left the bathroom. A few seconds later, I heard the clatter of the front door as it opened and closed. The rim of the tub was wet where I had gripped it. I went out into the hall. Maura was peeking through her door which she'd opened a crack. Mamá stood in the kitchen doorway. I didn't know I was crying until I felt my cheek to brush away what I had thought was a flake of paint. The two women suddenly moved toward me. They stopped a few feet away and clutched each other as if I was a disaster they dared not approach. Then Mamá reached out and touched my blouse that had come loose. Maura went to her room and returned with a small jar of vaseline. Slowly, Mamá lifted the blouse and stepped behind me. She moaned. I heard Maura draw in her breath. Barely touching my skin, Mamá began to spread the vaseline on my back.

"You didn't stop him," I accused her.

"Oh, my God! When have I been able to stop him!" Mamá cried.

She handed the jar to Maura. "Come, we'll eat supper now—now, before he comes back. I've made chick-pea soup. Hush! Hush!" She took my hand and led me to the kitchen. Maura ate with us as though it was a celebration. I was too tired to listen to their agitated voices. I wrapped myself in invisibility like the hero of the serial I had watched that day at the movie.

Papá returned just as we finished eating. Maura slunk out of the kitchen, rolling her eyes heavenward.

I will do as I want, I thought. Later.

At that moment, I heard the sound of claws on the hall linoleum, and into the kitchen walked a short-legged dog. Its filthy mustard-colored fur grew in spikes, its eyes gleamed red in the dim light from the bulb which hung from the kitchen ceiling.

"My dog," Papá said in a somewhat subdued voice. He clicked his fingers and called softly, "Jamon!" The animal sidled toward him. It seemed very old. It moved like a mechanical toy—I expected to hear the whirring of machinery.

Mamá raised her fist and took a step toward Papá. The dog growled. My father broke into hectic laughter. Abruptly, the dog sat down and gazed up at him. "A man has his friend!" Papá declared.

Mamá wept. She pressed her palms together and lifted her face to the ceiling.

"God send me home," she sobbed. "Give me back my life . . . let me work like a slave in the cane—take me away from this place, this man. I am abandoned!"

She choked and coughed, then she picked up the skirt of her dress and wiped her face. Papá made a sound of revulsion. Mamá came to me and pressed my face against her chest; her arm around my back pained me, but I didn't move.

"Take me to the store," she murmured tremulously. "I have to buy bread for tomorrow."

She released me and took her cloth bag from a nail. Papá and the dog were gone.

She made herself ready for the street. She smoothed her dress. Her fingers caught up and twisted loose hairs into the coil of hair at her neck. She took coins from the jar, holding them up close to her eyes to make sure what they were, nickels or dimes—she never carried more money than she thought she might spend—and then, as always, she went to the kitchen window and looked out briefly. Each time I saw her do that, I had the fancy that, for an instant, she gave herself an indulgence, a dream that it was a small village which lay about us.

"Oh—come on!" I exclaimed. When she turned from the window and looked at me, she seemed afraid. Was it because I had spoken so harshly to her? The welts across my back were as much her doing as Papá's. She had known what he was going to do when he led me from the room. How could I have thought she was imagining anything at all when she stared out at the roofs and chimneys that stretched to the horizon? Her nature, her self, had leaked out of her like the stuffing from the heart of Jesus.

She took a hesitant step toward me. "I won't let him do it again!" she burst out. "I didn't even know what he was going to do. Next time—" She gave a hasty look around the kitchen, then grabbed up the blackened iron from the stove and brandished it, her eyes not leaving my face. She paused as though she waited upon a judgment from me on her intention. I tried but I could not visualize Mamá hurling the iron at my father; I could only see her pressing his shirts.

.   .   .

On our night errands, as we went down the stairs to the street, we descended into a more concentrated broth of the smells of our own life, the earth odor of beans, thick and placid, the piercing, lurid stink of bugkiller, the smell of ironed cloth to which the raw odor of the yellow soap in which it had been washed still clung, and, as though the building had been steeped in it for a hundred years, the stench of drains.

But—"*Que sabroso!*" Mamá would say if we passed the door of the fortunate people who were going to eat pork that night. As it fried, it vanquished all other smells; celebratory and consoling, it was a bit of prosperity crackling away in a dark little kitchen like our own.

There were scents of perfume, too, of pomade, lotions and powders from the five-and-ten on Broadway, and their lingering, thin sweetness emanated from flats where women like Maura Cruz lived, women who hoped to bleach and dye and perfume themselves into Americans, who wore heels that made them totter forward as though the wind pressed at their backs, who wore rattling beads and clanking bracelets upon which they spent whatever they could salvage from rent and food.

Maura counseled Mamá to make herself pretty for Papá. Lowering her voice, an insinuating smile on her lips that was not enough to mask her jittery uncertainty, she exclaimed, "Negra! That's how it's done with men, like this. Here." She rubbed two spots of orange rouge on Mamá's slack cheeks, standing back and narrowing her eyes. Mamá gazed back at her timidly. "Wait!" cried Maura. "Take these!" She handed Mamá a pair of earrings. "Wear them!"

But Mamá, glancing at herself in Maura's powder-clouded hand mirror, shook her head. "Orlando doesn't care for clowns," she said gravely, and handed the earrings back to Maura, and went to wash the rouge from her cheeks, refusing the jar of cold cream Maura held out to her.

Mamá had given up Maura's dream of pretty women a long time ago. With the fitful energy of prolonged grievance, she contended with each day's petty irritations, the way Jamon would drop his haunches suddenly and deposit a small hard turd beneath a table, the personal debris Enrique Machado left in the bathtub, the insolence of cockroaches, my own body which grew and lengthened in ways that made us both desperate as I took up more space and required more cloth and leather to cover myself.

My father, periodically wearied by his acquaintances in the "club," would sit all day in his chair in the parlor, brooding and silent except for an infrequent word to Jamon who never left his side when he was home. Mamá would flutter around Papá, reciting our needs like an enraged prayer.

"Go to your mother!" she shouted at him one evening. "Write to her! My God! The impossible life here—this is no country for people who have nothing."

"My mother died last month," Papá said laconically.

I was leaning out of the window, my hands pressing down on the rusted bars of the fire escape. I leaned further out. "*Hijita!*" screamed Mamá. "You'll fall!"

I drew back into the room. They were staring at me, Mamá with her hands pressed against her throat, Papá, expressionless, half-risen from his chair. My hands were gritty with dirt. I looked down at them fixedly. La Señora was dead. It was not possible. In that moment the death of a hope I'd not known I'd had, so nebulous, I couldn't put a word to it, but knew it had been hope by the desolation which followed its loss, made me feel faint and ill. My legs trembled. I imagined all of Malagita following its mistress into a hole in the ground. I had not written to Nana in months, my early resolve to write her once a week weakened, then defeated by the unanswering silence. What would happen now?

"Wash your hands," Papá ordered me.

I didn't obey him but stood stubbornly where I was, desperate to hear more. He muttered something. I wondered if he'd called me a donkey as he sometimes did. He turned abruptly and started to leave the room. Mamá caught hold of his sleeve.

"You must talk," she implored. "What kind of a man says nothing when his mother dies?" He pushed away her hand. "I went downtown to see the Malagita representative—" he began.

"—What?" Mamá interrupted. "What are you saying?"

"Calderío was made executor. The French cow and her children inherited it all." He shrugged. Mamá looked dazed.

"Then ask *her* . . ." she said dully. "Ask the Frenchwoman for something. You are the son."

"I'll ask her why she's a cow," Papá said. Jamon rose up, tried to scratch his ear and fell down. "Did you imagine that we were going to be rich someday?" Papá asked, his voice swelling into a shout of accusation.

Mamá put her arm around me and led me from the room, down the hall. "It was because he set himself against her . . . from the beginning," she said.

She halted in front of the bathroom. "Wash your hands, my love," she said so gently I thought my heart would break. "Try not to soil your school clothes so much . . . I'm very tired."

.   .   .

Maura was fired. The factory where she had worked was going out of business. The photographer who occasionally gave her portraits to tint told her not to bother coming around so often—customers couldn't afford the extra money for color. She wept as she brought us news. "What will I do? Oh, what will I do . . ." she moaned. Her terror filled the kitchen. She'd seen a man dressed in a woman's coat lying dead in a gutter

on Broadway. She'd seen thousands of people lining up for one dishwasher's job at a Child's restaurant. The country was going down. A
woman she knew had stood on line for three hours to get free soup.
And when there was only one old man standing in front of her, she had
fainted from hunger and exhaustion. The rich had hidden themselves
away, guarded by savage dogs and armed servants. Would Orlando put
her out on the street now that she couldn't pay her rent?

Mamá reached across the table and clasped one of Maura's thin hands
in her own. She said nothing. There was an eerie quiet. Against the
kitchen window, the darkness pressed. Surely it was a thicker, blacker
dark than that of mere night! The hands of the two women lay on Papá's
overturned plate—he had not come home yet—and on the stove sat a
pot that held the last of the soup we had been eating for several days.
That night, it had tasted mostly of stale lard; I knew it was because Mamá
had taken a wing and the neck of a chicken she had used for flavoring out
of it and put them in a saucer on the kitchen windowsill to give to Papá
when he came home.

Except for what the pot held, I noticed suddenly, there was no food in
the kitchen—not even the can of drippings Mamá kept near the stove.
Had we come to the end of everything? Mamá murmured something and
released Maura's hand. I looked down at my school book, at the poem I
had been trying to learn by heart and that I would be required to recite
aloud in school the next morning. I didn't know what some of the words
meant; I didn't know if I'd ever seen a daffodil.

Sometimes, Maura would test me when I had to memorize a poem or
learn some dates in history. I looked at her. I could see the patches of
damp from her tears on her bony cheeks. The ends of her hair were still
reddish but the dye had faded and gone rusty. Only the black roots she
hated, and which sprang like wire from her narrow skull, looked living.
Timidly, I pushed the open book toward her, feeling a pinch of con-
science that I should be looking at her so critically yet wanting something from her. She stared down at the page a second, then slammed the
cover down.

"Daffodils!" she groaned, her eyes filling with fresh tears. "*Que
mierda!*"

A cracked bark of greeting from Jamon announced that Papá had come home. I heard the door slam, his slow footsteps down the hall. He came to stand silently in the kitchen doorway, Jamon crouching at his feet. Mamá rose from the table and started toward the stove. She halted suddenly and stared at Papá. He was wearing a long, white jacket buttoned up to his neck, and a square white cap. Across the front of the cap and the pocket of the jacket were stamped initials: N.Y.C.

She started toward him. He held up one hand as though to prevent her coming closer.

"What? Are you a garbage man?" burst out Maura.

"Garbage?" echoed Mamá. "Orlando? You have work?"

He came to the table. Maura got up and left the room. I thought I glimpsed a fleeting smile on her lips. Papá turned over his plate and stared down into it.

"Orlando?" Mamá questioned.

"I'm going to sweep the gutters," he said to the plate. "I have work as a street-sweeper."

Mamá opened the window and brought in the saucer of chicken.

"I'm so happy," she said. "So happy."

"Don't speak anymore," he said quietly. "I ask you not to say any more."

.   .   .

Papá kept his first job almost a year. Jamon mourned his absence by the front door, growling at us when we came near him. One afternoon when I came home from school, I met Mamá on the stairs dragging Jamon by a piece of rope tied around his neck. "He's making a sty out of the house," she said breathlessly. She pulled on the rope and the dog bumped down a step. I took him from her and yanked him down the stairs and out into the street where he did everything in a minute in front of our building, standing stiffly on his legs, trembling slightly. He dragged me back into the hall as though in horror of the outdoors. With Papá, he would go anywhere, but when I tried to lead him up the street, he would snap at me with his yellow blunted teeth.

When Papá stroked him, Jamon's head hung down. His eyes shut until only a moist gleam showed where they were; strings of saliva caught among the whiskers of his muzzle. Papá's hand moved back and forth across his frizzled fur. Papá's lips were slightly parted so that I could see the chalky white of his teeth. When the stern and orderly motions of his hand ceased, Jamon would lower himself slowly to the floor where he appeared asleep. Papá would observe him briefly, then, his own eyes closed, would lean back in the pink armchair. Nothing was permitted to interrupt this occurrence that took place every evening just after Papá came home from sweeping the streets of New York City. Even if supper was ready, Mamá would go to stand silently at the parlor entrance and wait until dog and man were motionless before she asked Papá to come to the table.

All day long the dog yearned for him. When Papá opened the door, his head was already bending toward the animal. The dog groaned, Papá murmured his name, and they went down the hall to the parlor. I was drawn again and again to this scene though it filled me with distress, and a painful restlessness I could not put a name to.

We began to eat meat again. I was aware, as I bit into a piece of beef, how long we had been living on thin soup and rice and scraps of salt pork. Mamá bought a little blue rug to lie beside the bathtub on the cold white tiles of the floor. "The pink one was nicer," she told me, "but you know how your Papá hates that color." She bought me a blue sweater nearly the color of the rug, and I wore it until my wristbones poked out of the sleeves and I could hardly pull it over my head.

Papá, too, made purchases, mysterious objects which he kept in their boxes in a corner of the front room, and about which Mamá soon stopped asking questions since they provoked in him that scornful dismissal of any concern of hers that wounded her so.

One Saturday morning he awoke Enrique Machado, who always slept late into the day because he worked half the night in a bowling alley, and took him off for several hours. They returned carrying long wooden planks which they took to the parlor. Machado went out again and came back shortly, clutching a dirty canvas sack full of tools which I recognized as belonging to the super who lived in the basement. When Mamá and I heard the sound of cardboard ripping, we went to look. The boxes were open. Papá and Machado gazed down into them. "Leave everything," Papá said. "First the mounting for the parts." He didn't look in our direction.

Not until Mamá and I had finished supper, and Mamá had put Papá's dish into the oven, did the noise of sawing and hammering cease. Except for Machado's frequent trips to the toilet—we all knew he had a weak bladder; frequently, during the night, I would hear the weak, hesitant trickling of his urine, then the brief convulsion of the toilet and its long aftermath of gurgle and drip—they hadn't left the parlor.

Maura had gone out somewhere. The silence after the din of the afternoon was profound. Suddenly there was a roar, a voice singing, an immense earsplitting hammer of a voice that struck the pot on the stove, the dishes in the sink, the thin glass of the kitchen window, and made them clink and rattle.

We ran to the front room. The boxes lay overturned and empty. On a wall of planks which extended halfway across each of the parlor's two windows, were affixed wires, switches, and metal objects like huge mouths, and it was from these last that the terrible noises were issuing. Machado stood transfixed, but my father was laughing and hugging himself in a frenzy of joy. Mamá clapped her hands to her ears. He looked at her as though he had forgotten who she was. He stepped to the wall and with a strange, exaggerated delicacy, touched a knob. The roaring ceased at once.

"'*I Pagliacci*,'" he said with a mercilessness that seemed to condemn us all. He began to right the empty boxes and to carry them away down the hall. "*Un gran talento*," Machado said admiringly.

When I arrived home from school later than Papá did from his job, I could hear the enormous radio a block away, bands, orchestras, talk, singing, and sometimes a mad twittering of canaries. It was like the shapeless uproar I sometimes heard from the Broadway "clubs" but pitched up so high that people passing by stopped to stare up at the top windows of our tenement, their expressions bewildered and outraged. The police came twice, called by indignant tenants. The second time, they warned Papá that if they were called again, they would take away his contraption and arrest him for disturbing the peace.

A few days after that, he lost his job. He could no longer support his radio, which constantly required new parts and new refinements. He returned to his armchair where he sat, day after day, staring at the now silenced speakers upon which dust had begun to collect. Mamá would not touch them.

Maura, who had fled the apartment to escape the radio, even after long days of searching for work, came back early to her room and unmade bed. Machado was the only member of the household who still went out to work. Mamá eked out meals. There was a brooding quiet throughout the flat. What were we drifting towards? Each night, I wondered if we were eating our last meal. Sometimes Mamá and Papá fought about Maura's not paying her rent, but their anger was lifeless, their voices plaintive, and Papá's threat to evict Maura, without conviction.

The flat was a place I never wanted to be. Walking home from school, always hungry, always angry because I was hungry, I imagined the dark hallway, the blue painted walls, the swollen lumps of plaster, the narrow, stale, silent rooms.

I pretended that the sidewalk would emerge at the cooking shed in Malagita, that I would see Mamá as she had been, her hair pinned neatly to her head, her plump, smooth arm and hand holding a wooden spoon to turn slices of frying bananas, the sweet, warm darkness all around, the lamp flickering in the house of the Chinese a few yards away.

Then I would start at finding myself in front of the entrance to our tenement next to the step, a garbage can half-emptied by a stray animal, a few pieces of coal on the sidewalk that had fallen from the coal chute that led to the basement. When I thought of Papá at such a moment, I knew he was crazy, not like an actor imitating insanity such as I had seen in the movies, but crazy in life.

.   .   .

I asked Maura to test me on the lines of a poem I had to memorize, but she told me not to ask her anymore—she had too much to think about these days. "Find somebody with a job to help you," she said. By thinking, she meant lying down on her bed and staring up at the ceiling, her door open a crack so, she explained to me, she would not feel she had been thrown into her grave.

When I passed by her room and glimpsed her prone body, her still face, she seemed to be floating, and later, when I peeked through the door and saw her eyes shut, I imagined she had been carried far into her misery until she had fallen asleep within it, as though it had nursed her into forgetfulness.

Over the years, children came and went in my school. Families moved out of the neighborhood or came apart when one of the parents, usually the father, ran away and disappeared. The children were sent to relatives in the south or back to the Caribbean islands from which they had come. When I was in the eighth grade, Ellen Dove transferred into my school from a Catholic school a few blocks away where my father had, in the past, often threatened to send me when he judged I wasn't learning enough, or that my American accent was becoming "vulgar." I knew he wouldn't have been able to. The Catholic school cost money.

Ellen's braid of thick black hair was tied at its end with a narrow blue ribbon. Her clothes were always freshly ironed, the white cuffs of her cotton blouse starched and gleaming against her brown, narrow wrists. She was lighter-skinned than some of the other Negro children in my class, and she kept herself apart from them as well as from the rest of us. I watched her all the time. I waited, in the mornings, for her to appear at the classroom door, tall, slender, and, to me, uncommon.

She grew aware of my attention. She would turn to me and smile, her eyes shining through black, thick lashes. She would lift one hand and crumple her fingers just slightly. I woke in the mornings, thinking about her. We became friends. She came to my school in March. When the days grew warmer, we walked down to the Hudson River. Just north, the George Washington Bridge gripped the two shores. We found a countryside of small woods and bare slopes. We watched the river flowing past, the boats, the huge ships which came upstream to anchor. Ellen tested me on lines of poetry: *I have a Rendezvous with Death*, I quoted. "The *z* is silent," she said. She told me about the future. I had not thought about it before. This future flourished on the banks of the Hudson, far from the tyranny of the present. It had a smell, the buoyant, clear, watermelon smell of the river, and the chaste, plain, green fragrance of the new grass.

Ellen stayed after school doing her homework, or else she went to the public library. Her mother didn't want her to go home to empty rooms. Her neighborhood was only a few minutes walk from mine, but it was darker, menacing. In her building, there were vacant rooms. The hall fixtures lacked bulbs; animals sheltered in corners and men slept in bundles of rags in the abandoned flats whose shattered doors hung open.

Mrs. Dove washed the walls and floors of her three rooms every weekend, standing on a milk crate to reach into the corners beneath the tin ceilings. One Saturday when I was visiting Ellen, Mrs. Dove, finished with her cleaning, filled a glass with chips she struck from the cake of ice in her icebox, then she poured grape juice over them. Only when Maura opened a new bottle of nail polish—she hadn't had the money to buy any for months—and spread out the thin fingers of her hand, the yellowed nails curved like the beaks of birds—had I seen such anticipation of pleasure as I saw in Mrs. Dove's face, exactly like that on Maura's when with a tiny brush, she made the first, steady stroke of red lacquer. I shivered. Mrs. Dove, glancing at me over the rim of her glass, put it down. "Want some?" she asked. Perversely, I shook my head.

She kept framed photographs on a small table covered with a woven cloth. The largest picture, a family occasion, stood in the middle. In it, a dozen or more people sat around a large table spread with a white tablecloth. Wineglasses, crumpled white napkins and cutlery lay about. Everyone was smiling at the camera except for one elderly white woman whose hair was screwed into a bun on top of her head. Her chin thrust out and up as though she was trying to escape the constriction of a heavy necklace coiled around her throat.

"My grandmother," Ellen said, her finger touching the old woman's face. "The table we once had. The tablecloth . . ."

Behind the brightly lit table and the dark faces, among which the one white face glowed like a bulb, stretched a large room bulky and shadowed with blurred furniture. "Her mother?" I whispered, looking toward Mrs. Dove who was standing in front of a window. "Daddy's," replied Ellen.

"One of my grandmothers was crazy," I said. "But she had everything."

"The other had nothing?" Ellen asked pensively.

"She had me."

"So did the crazy one."

"She didn't want to know that."

"There's a man on the roof," Mrs. Dove announced. Her throat was very long, her skin darker than Ellen's. She was staring at something across the street. Ellen and I went to look. "He's in trouble," she said.

The man was leaning over the roof edge of the tenement facing the Dove's flat. It was drizzling and twilight had come, a deepening of the gray light. Through the holes in his shirt, the blackness of his skin was startling. He gestured at the sky. His mouth was open as though he was shouting.

"Maybe he's fixing the roof," Ellen said.

"Nobody fixes roofs around here," Mrs. Dove stated. "He's lost his mind is what it is."

"Oh, look! He's going to fall!" cried Ellen.

Mrs. Dove thrust up the window and leaned out so far it seemed she might fall herself.

"Get down off there," she called.

The man twisted his head violently about as if something had stung him. He caught sight of us crowded at the window.

"Moses grew tired," he shouted. He began to sob noisily. A tiny old woman rose up behind him, gripped his arms and walked him backwards to the shed that housed the stairwell.

Mrs. Dove shut the window and went to turn on a standing lamp. "Moses grew so tired," she said, passing her hand across the black fringe of the lampshade, "that Aaron and Hur had to hold up his hands because only when he was holding them up could Israel prevail." She stood stiffly in remote holiness.

When Mrs. Dove said a religious thing—I could usually tell it was by the pressing gravity of her voice—I had a tormenting desire to laugh. At the same time, I felt rebuked just as when a teacher spoke in a distant sombre tone of voice about Helen Keller's struggle—or someone else's who had been born blind, crippled or in terrible poverty—to overcome misfortune, and whose noble character was a reproof to us, in whom, the teacher implied, lack of character was already so apparent.

Mrs. Dove sighed and turned away from us standing mutely before her. I glanced sideways at Ellen. She shut her eyes and felt the air pathetically with her hands, pretending she was blind. How I loved her!

She walked with me downstairs to the street where we paused and looked across at the building into which the man on the roof had been led by the old woman.

The street had its own darkness. I couldn't remember it in sunlight. A man leaned against a stoop looking blank, poking with a toothpick among his teeth. A dog cut back and forth across the pavement as it ran past us. There were blackened patches of fur and skin along its bony back and sides as though it had been singed. From somewhere nearby, we heard a wordless human howl.

"Maybe that's him," Ellen said. "Maybe he wants to go back up to the roof and talk Bible with Momma."

Would he have fallen over the edge if Mrs. Dove had not called out to him? Perhaps he didn't want his life. The one person I knew who always wanted his life was Uncle Federico. I imagined that he ate it up, day by day, like a meal. Mamá and Maura often called on God to let them leave this world.

"Thad's coming tonight," Ellen told me. I had met her brother once. He was twenty, the only person I had known who went to college, although I had heard of others. The same teacher who read us inspirational stories about Helen Keller, had told us of certain students from our own school who had gone on to what she called "the higher education." They had seemed like people in history books. I thought of them in their wheelchairs, crippled, deaf, mute, ascending a steep hill to that higher place which, the teacher made clear, the rest of us would never reach. But Thad was a tall, thin, quick-moving man, his head a cap of reddish curls, his skin pale. There was nothing wrong with him. He had stared at me after Ellen had said, "This is my best friend."

"You and me could be spies," he had said. "You're Spanish, aren't you? You don't look the way you're supposed to, either."

"You, a spy!" Ellen had exclaimed to him. "Not you! Not the way you go round saying Negro Negro Negro."

"You'd be surprised—how much harder having a choice makes things," Thad had told her.

"You'd better go," she said now. "We're both shivering."

I hesitated. "I didn't tell you about Papá's boarder," I said. "This morning, when I went to the bathroom, he was pressed up against the wall and when I started past him, he grabbed me here." I showed her, putting my hands over my chest. "And he pushed me back against the wall and lay against me."

"Jesus!" breathed Ellen.

"Mamá opened her door, and he turned so fast, like a cockroach, and ran into his room."

"Did you tell?"

"Just you."

"What if he does it again?"

I took out the pair of scissors from my pocket that I'd stolen from school and showed them to her. "No. He won't. Now I keep these under my pillow, and take them with me whenever I hear Machado in his room."

"The teachers count everything."

"I don't care."

"Would you kill him?"

The one unshattered streetlight went on just then at the end of the block. I felt heroic. "Yes," I said loudly. She put her arm around my shoulders and leaned her head against mine so that I felt the thickness of her braid. "That man's watching us," she whispered. "I'll walk you to the corner."

I saw the man on the stoop flick his toothpick into the street and walk down the stoop. We started toward Amsterdam Avenue. Ellen glanced back. "It's all right," she said. "He's gone the other way." She pressed my arm. "What did it feel like?"

I wished suddenly I hadn't told her about Machado. An old shame kept me silent. As though she were standing there beside me, I felt the grip of Señora Garcia's hands on my shoulders when she had stopped me from dancing that long-ago time in her garden in Malagita.

I worked the blades of the scissors in my pocket. I had an impulse to swear I'd not known Machado had been in the hall waiting for me. It was senseless. It was Ellen's hand, not Señora Garcia's, that now grasped my shoulder. "Tell me," she insisted.

We had walked several blocks and were nearly at my door when I said, "I don't know how it felt. I hate him."

"Look!" Ellen said. She was staring into an unshaded window on the first floor of my building. A man, his shirt half covering his buttocks, squatted on the body of a woman whose arms were raised high above her head, gripping the iron bars of a bed. Her face was rigid. With a violent lift, the man swung up his rear end, then, as if exhausted, let it drop back. The woman's mouth turned downward slowly as though she tasted something of inexpressible bitterness. I heard laughter. Two men were standing behind us a few feet away, watching as we were. I grabbed Ellen and we fled into the hallways and squeezed ourselves behind the stairs. I don't know how long we crouched there silently. When, at last, I looked out the men were gone, and no light fell on the sidewalk from the unshaded room. We gave each other a haunted look. Ellen ran down the street to the avenue. She turned once but she didn't wave.

I went to Maura's room where I found her sitting on the edge of her bed staring at the wall. I knew she had been waiting for weeks to hear from Uncle Federico whether he could get her work in the kitchen of the Salamanca. I had heard her weeping in the night. Papá wouldn't allow her to eat with us, but Mamá always left her a plate of something on the stove. After Papá had gone to bed, she would tiptoe down the hall to get it.

She looked at me irritably; whatever she had been thinking about, she wanted to keep on with it.

"Times are getting better they say," she said angrily. "But not for me."

"Maybe you'll hear from Uncle Federico tomorrow."

"That bastard, excuse me for saying so about your relative, but I've been down there three times." She snorted. "He says he wants to know me better, he wants to be sure I can do the work. 'Do you know how to wash lettuce, querida?' he asks me. Very serious, you understand. He's an important man, after all. Excuse me, but he washes his balls in olive oil, the pig!"

I was struck. Was such an extravagance possible? Did he really?

Maura spread out her fingers. "I should have stayed in Havana," she said. "At least, the climate is good." She looked at me inquiringly. "What is it, Negrita?" she asked with a certain kindliness.

"On the first floor, through the window—" I hesitated.

"What, what? Tell Maura . . ."

I stared at an opened tube of lipstick on her bureau; a hairpin was sticking out of it.

"A man was on top of a woman. He had on a shirt, but she was naked. Her face—she looked like she was dying, like she was poisoned . . ."

Maura began to giggle. She covered her mouth with her hand, then took it away. "Dios! I wish I had a cigarette," she said. She reached over to the bureau and snatched up the lipstick tube and scraped at it with the hairpin. "All gone," she said, showing me the pin. She folded her hands. "Don't you know about that whore?" she asked, a faint smile on her lips. "That's how she advertises, so everyone walking by can see what they'd get. She has her *ataques* in public."

"What is that? *Ataque?*" I asked.

"A woman can't talk about that," she said broodingly. "It's something that can't be explained." She looked miserable suddenly. I backed out of the room.

.   .   .

A few weeks later, Enrique Machado grabbed me again. I bit his cheek. He raised his hand to strike me but at that instant Papá's voice, raised in complaint, came from behind the door a few feet away. Machado's hand dropped to his side, his thick pale tongue sought for and found blood from the wound I had given him. He stared at me with frightened, startled eyes. I ran, trembling, into the bathroom.

"I'm as cruel as Papá," I told Ellen. "When I saw the blood on his cheek, I wanted to shout—good!"

"God!" Ellen cried. "That's right. You did right!"

"If I hadn't lost those scissors, I might have killed him."

She gasped; her eyes shone. I grabbed the books she was carrying home from school. "I'll carry them," I said loftily.

She was always loaded down with books. At night, when I thought of her a few blocks east of me, I imagined her, her head bent toward the light from the fringed lamp, reading, learning—getting ready, she'd say wryly—while I dreamed of Malagita. For Ellen, freedom lay ahead.

She and Thad and their mother were close. A steady warmth of concern glowed in Mrs. Dove's rooms, defended by order, religiosity, an intention to make the most of fleeting chance. Wordless love bound them together. It warmed me when I was there, and it forced me into a more bitter awareness of the irritable pity I felt for Mamá, and my intensifying suspicion that feebleness lay behind my father's unpredictability and white-faced rages.

He had never had any nerve, I told myself. He was unable to relieve the meagreness of our lives, finding a job only when there wasn't a spoon of rice left in the kitchen. Sometimes I recalled what Mamá had described to me years before, how Papá had stripped himself of his bridal clothes and left them on the dirt floor of our cabin the day he had jilted Ofelia Mondragon. Perhaps some other man had been left there on the floor along with the clothes. Whoever he had been, he was dead now.

.   .   .

Ellen's father had been a construction engineer in Dayton, Ohio. In those days, a Negro in such a profession was singular. "He had very good manners," Ellen had said. "If you'd just heard his voice, you would have thought he was a regular Ohio fellow, better educated than most."

In Mrs. Dove's scrapbook, I saw newspaper photographs in which his brown face appeared among those of the white dignitaries who attended ceremonies for the opening of a new school or office or apartment building. "My white Gran, his mother, told him to watch out, not forget this had been a slave country." The city administration changed. Mr. Dove lost his contacts and found himself without work. He sold the furniture in those rooms whose grandeur I had surmised from the dining table in the picture Mrs. Dove displayed among pictures of dead relatives. They had lived well; they hadn't saved money. Mr. Dove finally got a job as a janitor in an apartment house he had helped build.

"Down the coal chute," Ellen had said. Mrs. Dove had once given dinner parties and held musical evenings for Negro musicians who couldn't get work. She had had table linen and a china service for twelve.

"What happened to your father?"

"He began to drink," Ellen said. "Momma had to leave him. She brought us here with her and after a long terrible time, she got a job as a cook-housekeeper for a rich widow. He moved in with Gran. He died a year later, drink, I guess, and Gran only lasted another few months."

Ellen was interested in my history. Yet even as she questioned me, her alert gaze on my face, I felt, as I answered, a restlessness in her that made me conclude she couldn't quite take seriously any trouble that didn't have to do with color. "Was your Nana telling you you had ancestors that came from Africa?" she demanded. "I don't know," I replied truthfully. "You'd know if you'd been born here," she said.

"Look at me," she said. "I haven't got rhythm. I'm not going to be Fredi Washington and sing with the band. But I'm not going to be some woman's *girl* like Momma."

"You get the best grades."

"What will I do with them?"

The teachers all liked Ellen. She had an eager, appreciative way of listening and, like her father, very good manners. "I'm an example," she said once, "and I can't seem to help it."

When a teacher heard my accent, she would frown.

"Luisa, say this: He has filled the hungry with good things."

I repeated it. The teacher heard the throaty *g* I couldn't get rid of.

"Gree! Gree! Gree!" she would cry. It was as though one of the caged birds in Señora de la Cueva's garden had flown from Malagita to the classroom to shriek at me with its inhuman craziness.

On a spring morning when the classroom windows were open for the first time that year, a wild fragrance drifting in like a spirit would make me feel anything was possible, but only for a moment. Hope would drown in the smell of dust and chalk and stale paste.

Ellen and I no longer went to the banks of the Hudson to dream of our future. We clung to each other, but we were peevish, arguing sluggishly about which street to walk home on, which teacher was the worst, movie stars.

"John Boles, Leslie Howard," she said disgustedly. "Those old white things—curdled milk."

"I hate Leslie Howard."

"No, you don't. I saw how you jumped when he got shot in that picture."

We were weighted with gloom. We intoxicated ourselves with scorn for the movies in which people our age grinned and clapped their hands and danced in their fine clothes to unseen orchestras like happy monkeys, for our schoolmates, for the whores on Broadway we had come to recognize and whose days began as we came home from school, for the lewd janitors who emerged from dark basements at twilight to pick their teeth and ogle us.

Only the mention of Thad brought light into Ellen's eyes.

.　　　　　　　　　.　　　　　　　　　.

Maura got the job in Uncle Federico's restaurant. She soon reappeared as her old self, dingier, but redheaded as fire, jingling her bracelets, wearing skirts that seemed, as she walked, to wrap each buttock separately, her voice as shrill as ever when Papá was away, insisting to Mamá that she leave him or else dress herself up and win his love back. Enrique Machado went to prison for five years. He was caught by the police in a pawn shop at two in the morning, a trumpet gripped in one hand, a diamond ring in the other. My gladness shamed me. I would try to pity him, but then I would recall the horrid knobbiness of his body as he pressed me up against the wall.

Papá, who played the *lotería*, won two hundred dollars. We moved in a week into an identical flat. We got a three-month rent concession and a new boarder, a thin, short man whose hair pomade had a nose-prickling sweetness. Mamá thrust my old winter coat at Papá; she pressed it against his shoulders, his face, until he pushed her away. But he gave her some of the money from his winnings. I had a new coat, the first new garment I had had in several years except for the shoes Mamá had bought with money borrowed from Uncle Federico.

"One day I will repay you," she would say bravely. "You'll see."

"Perhaps," Uncle Federico would reply.

I touched the navy blue cloth of my coat and each of its five large white buttons. Most of my dresses were cut down from Aunt Aurelia's discarded clothes. She was fond of prints that depicted large flowers in tropical colors. When Mamá had finished remaking a dress for me and I had put it on and gone to stand on her bed to look at myself in the mirror on her bureau, my light brown hair and pale face seemed to float, disconnected, above the brilliant material.

We didn't see the Sanchez family often. We never had a meal with them. They usually came on a Sunday morning—if the weather was warm and clear—never in winter or in rain. Aunt Aurelia in a flaming dress, her plump fingers curled tightly around the clasp of her pocketbook, would exclaim at the earliness of the hour she had risen to go to Mass, or to make her confession. All the while she was speaking, she would watch Mamá with a sly look as if she knew Mamá hardly ever went to church. I imagined Aurelia behind a black, dusty curtain of a confessional, striving to discover in herself some tiny failing.

One Sunday, Uncle Federico brought us, in a finger-smudged cardboard box, the remains of a cake from a birthday party given the night before in the Salamanca. Setting the box in front of Mamá, plucking off the top, he thundered, "There! A souvenir for you alone!"

Three cracked red sugar roses sat on the white icing, and curving letters in green icing spelled out: *Happy Birt*. My mother gazed down at the cake. I had not noticed until that moment the dark circles beneath her eyes. The flesh of her face drooped like a cloth held loosely by two hands. Her fingers, resting on the rim of the box, looked waxen. I felt as if it had been my own, the effort she was making to thank her brother.

"Thank you," I said abruptly. Papá suddenly left the kitchen where we were all standing around the table.

"It was specially ordered," Uncle Federico said tentatively. Could he have been struck, as I was, by the strange, confused expression on Mamá's face, her silence? I willed her to speak, hoping the sound of her voice, stuck now behind her twitching mouth, would assure me she was not sick, not crazy, but the same woman who, when I had had the illnesses of childhood, fevered, crying out with the agony of earaches, had brought teas of herbs, wool cloths thickened and yellowed with Vicks, cold rags for my burning skin, who had made meals out of nearly nothing, the lamenting spirit of all our narrow crowded flats who had managed to keep our days in some kind of order.

"Looks like somebody stuck their fingers in it," Atilio remarked. Aunt Aurelia smiled smugly as though he'd said something intelligent.

How long had it been since I'd last heard Mamá sigh and speak aloud of her troubles to the ceiling, above which God looked down, watching her suffering?

"Thank you Federico," she said at last, her voice barely audible. I went to my room and lay down on my bed. Only a minute later, Atilio appeared in the door. He grinned, leaped to the bed, grabbed the blanket, held it tight across my shoulders, and pressed his wet lips against mine.

With my fists, I pounded his oiled little head and heaved up with my hips and legs, thrusting him off me. He fell with a thud to the floor. He crouched there for a second, looking up at me balefully, then stood and said, "You bitch! What do you think girls are for?"

I aimed a kick at his groin. He laughed and covered that part of himself with his hands and swaying his hips like a woman, minced out of the room.

I heard my uncle's voice as he proclaimed the new prosperity that was coming to the United States, the greatest country in the world. Uneasily alone in my room, perplexed by the lingering sensation of my cousin's plump lips, I got up and went down the hall to the parlor. Atilio was staring dully at the speakers on the wooden boards Papá had yet to dismantle. Aunt Aurelia was gingerly touching some mending of Mamá's. For the last few months, she had been doing a little sewing for neighbors who, almost as poor as we were, paid her for her work with eggs or rice or a bit of pork. The Jews, Uncle Federico pronounced, were responsible for the war in Europe. Of course, there would be profit in it for our country. He touched his sleeve and smiled. He often smiled when he touched himself or his clothes. "Adolf Hitler is a person of consequence," he said, nodding at Papá. "We may have to deal with him ourselves."

"There's not the least chance of that," Papá said.

"Oh, yes. The Jews will drag us in. Roosevelt adores them," declared Uncle Federico. I stopped listening.

Later, after they had gone, I found Mamá in the kitchen in front of the stove, her hands clasped. I felt a painful urgency, I must embrace her! But I couldn't. Only a few hours earlier, I had pitied her so, recalled her goodness.

"I'm going to look for work," I told her.

"Not yet," she said quickly. "Next year, when you're fifteen."

"I can get a job at the five-and-ten for the Christmas weeks."

"Once it starts, it will be for the rest of your life," she said as she turned to me. With a certain shyness, she touched my face. "You must keep going to school."

"I can do both."

"Not yet," she repeated.

Jamon, who had become increasingly unsteady on his legs, staggered into the kitchen and stared at us, panting.

"Give it a little milk," said Mamá.

I placed a saucer in front of him. He stared at it for a long moment then with a scrabble of claws, his head bowed, went out of the kitchen.

"Atilio held me down on my bed and kissed me," I said.

"That too," she said softly. "Once it starts . . . wait . . ."

Disheartened, yet not knowing what I wanted from her, I started to leave.

"The kissing ends very soon," she said. She was staring down at the saucer of untouched milk. She pushed it with her toe until the milk splashed on the floor. "He shouldn't have done that," she said without conviction.

"Mamá?"

"Oh—don't ask me anything," she said. I went out the door. "Forgive me," her voice trailed sadly after me.

.   .   .

Uncle Federico was boastful, sure that what he called his thoughts were the last word on everything. Only rarely had I seen uncertainty in his expression. That had been when he noticed his son and wife whispering together intently, standing apart from him.

He admired the customers of the Salamanca who tipped him well because it was in their power to do so. They were winners, they had influence, which was what counted. He had some himself. With it, he helped Papá get his second job in the United States, and one he kept. Among the regular patrons of the restaurant was the owner of a fashionable food store on the east side. Uncle Federico was not mean but neither, I believed, was he generous. I guessed that he had boasted to this customer that his brother-in-law was the son of a wealthy plantation owner in the Caribbean—he would not name the island of San Pedro; he would be afraid no one would have heard of it—at that moment without employment. I could almost hear him uttering my father's name, the length of it giving it a significance that would be to Uncle Federico's credit.

I saw Papá once at his place of work two years later when I went to tell him that Mamá had been taken to the hospital. He was standing behind a counter piled with jars of jam, cellophane-wrapped baskets swollen with fruit and boxes of candy and figs and cakes. An elderly woman, the only customer, walked slowly from basket to basket, poking at the cellophane with a gloved finger. Around her neck were draped two long pieces of dark fur, their tips, two snarling little animal faces whose glass eyes glowed at her waist. Papá was not looking at her; he didn't see me. He looked haughty, indifferent, another customer, perhaps, who had mistakenly wandered behind the counter.

The doctors sent Mamá home from the hospital the next day. Her violent stomach pains, they said, were the result of nervous agitation. She would have to go on a diet of bland foods. She looked somewhat rested and consumed, with satisfaction, the last of a dish of highly spiced sausages and beans Maura had cooked for me the night before.

All the time Papá had been without work, my uncle had treated him with deference, glancing, as he spoke, at Papá's face, as though to read there that he had not given offense. But once Papá had been hired— through his introduction—Federico changed. He interrupted Papá continually. He frequently grabbed his shoulders, held him tightly, and even rocked him back and forth like a large doll. I could not tear my glance from the sight of my father's rigid body locked in Federico's fleshy arms. I waited for an explosion, for Papá to free himself and hurl my uncle to the floor. It never came. Did my mother embrace him? If she did, did he look the same as when Federico held him? So blank-faced?

My cousin, Atilio, left his apprentice's job in a machine-tooling shop to go to Canada. From a port there, he would take a ship to England where he would become a soldier. My uncle brought him to us to say good-bye. He was beside himself with pride and agitation. He clutched Papá's face between his hands. "My little son," he cried. "Under the *bombas.*" Mamá began to cry, and Aunt Aurelia sobbed, hiding her face behind her new pocketbook which bore two enormous gold letters, *A. S.* (Maura, who had glimpsed the Sanchez family trailing down the hall, remarked later, "One more *S* on that *mierda* pocketbook would have made it perfect!")

Atilio was taciturn as usual. When no one was looking, he stared at my breasts and bared his teeth at me.

When the room grew quiet, the women ceremoniously drying their faces, my father looked penetratingly at Atilio. "Why are you volunteering?" he asked.

"*Porque este muchacho es un hombre valiente!*" cried Uncle Federico driven by emotion into speaking Spanish.

Atilio shrugged. "Well—you know—I like to see places, get around . . ."

I was sent to make coffee. When I returned, our farewell to Atilio was interrupted by Jamon. He raced madly into the parlor and halted in the middle of the room as if he'd run into a wall. He swayed—something seemed to be stretching his neck, pulling it from his shoulders—then sank to the floor, turning slowly until he lay on his back. His legs gave a violent quiver, were almost instantly still, and stuck straight up toward the ceiling. He was dead.

Aunt Aurelia burst into offended howls. Atilio emitted a bubbling screech like laughter squeezing through a hole but Uncle Federico, faced with the ultimate loser, tiptoed out of the room and into the kitchen where he remained until Papá, his jaw clenched, picked up the corpse and took it away. He didn't return home until very late.

He must have gone to bury the dog near the river. It was the only living thing he ever showed affection toward, and I didn't believe he would leave Jamon for the garbage men. He told us nothing—not that we asked him anything. Mamá had given up questioning him. In any case, he was rarely home.

He had bought a small radio which he kept on a box near his armchair in the parlor. Some Sundays he turned it on and leaned forward to hear a concert. Once he had played a radio too loud. Now it was tuned so low, only he could hear it.

　　　　　·　　　　　　　　·　　　　　　　　·

I found a job, two hours every afternoon, all day Saturday, in a variety store on Broadway. It was narrow and long like a tenement flat. The dusty air was steeped in the odor of camphor. In the display window rose a pyramid of pink or blue felt slippers, around its base, school copybooks and small white saucepans. I was to be paid fourteen dollars a week. On the first day Mr. Dardarian, the owner, handed me an envelope with my pay in it, the world was a different place.

I walked the streets until the cold drove me inside, my finger tips inside the envelope in my pocket, touching the bills. A tide was carrying me away from the life my parents had made, or so it seemed to me that day. I felt a joy that was nearly vengeful.

At home, I handed the envelope to Mamá. She took out the bills, hesitated, then counted out five of them and handed the rest back to me. Her small roughened hand rested briefly on my arm; she gazed at me silently. I went to my room where I spread the nine dollars on my bed. I gathered them up and put them in an old shoebox that also held the letter Señora Garcia had written for Nana. When the box was filled with dollar bills, I would buy my passage for San Pedro. With equal conviction, I believed that I could, and couldn't, do such a thing.

A few weeks before my fifteenth birthday, on December eighth, the United States declared war on Japan. I began to read the newspaper Papá brought home each evening.

In the variety store, a metal globe of the world stood on its base among boxes of crayons and sets of jacks, checkers, and china-faced baby dolls the length and width of my thumb. On the globe's surface, in pastel seas, lay the red and green and yellow continents. I touched the eastern edge of America. That I should be standing in the passage between the counters of the store, snow beginning to fall on the street outside, Mr. Dardarian running his hands up and down behind his suspenders as he leaned over the cash register, and yet be there, where my finger touched upon the metal replica of the round earth, was like an invention, a story, as impossible to grasp as the daily news of bombings and battles, of ships exploding and sinking, of men drowning in those painted seas.

We lived in a village of sorts, our barrio. Even when soldiers began to appear along its streets, young men a few of whom I vaguely recognized, transformed by the thick, coarse fabric of their uniforms which gave them a look of competence, I couldn't imagine where they were going, what might happen to them. Neat, superior in their purposefulness, they came home from training camps to flats like ours to say goodbye. When I saw them and imagined them dead in another country, it was as though I'd learned that the small boys in the street who shouted, bang! bang! could, with their cocked index fingers, really kill.

I read the society columns of the newspaper, followed the beautiful child contests, the comic strips and Hollywood gossip. I stopped reading the war news except for those stories that reported the landing of spies from German submarines along the coast. Mr. Dardarian nailed up a poster on the store wall that read: *A slip of the lip can sink a ship*.

Maura began to roll her own cigarettes because of tobacco rationing, but Mamá hid the rationing booklets Papá brought home. I found them beneath a bunch of dirty rags in a kitchen drawer. One afternoon, Mamá sat on her stool in front of the sink, clutching the handle of the broom and as it gave way under her weight, began to fall from the stool. I took the broom from her and helped her upright. "*No puedo*," she said breathlessly, her face averted as though ashamed to tell me she couldn't— couldn't anything, I knew she meant.

Papá bought a record player and records and had a telephone installed in the parlor. I don't recall it ever ringing. Mamá refused to iron his shirts on the old plank. For a while, he took them to a laundry. Then he brought home a real ironing board. She broke its wooden legs in front of him. "*No puedo*," she cried. "*No puedo más!*"

At night, Papá polished his shoes and listened to his records. He seldom spoke. As he moved fastidiously through the shabby rooms, he grew to seem a prosperous stranger. Yet he gave Mamá money. One evening, I heard him order her to buy a dress, shoes, a coat for herself. "I command you . . ." he said. I knew she wouldn't, couldn't.

My throat was parched. I spent a good deal of my pay on bottled sodas. I had the curious thought that I was slowly drying up and would eventually crumble like a leaf in late autumn. I dreamed of being discovered by someone and carried bodily away from the flat, the barrio. In the dull labor of school, I saw no promise of rescue. When I glanced at Ellen, three desks away, her head bent over book or paper, it seemed to me I could almost hear the sound of her intention; it was like a distant, ringing bell that would not be silenced.

I went with her to the library. "Get a card. Look for something," she told me. I didn't understand my bleak stubbornness. I couldn't rid myself of it. I didn't get a card. Instead, I watched the librarian and the readers as I waited for Ellen. She came to me carrying a thick history of Mexico. "Did you know that you are a colonial?" she asked. She had begun to be disappointed in me. "I can't get out," I said to her. "You don't want to enough," she said.

She took me to a museum downtown. In enormous halls, huge stuffed animals stood in file. There were masks and fish, great round stones carved by men who had lived in Mexico before the Spaniards came.

Afterwards, we walked along the edge of Central Park. Ellen was whistling tunelessly to herself. She was whistling, I thought, because I wouldn't talk with her about what we had seen in the museum. How could I speak? I felt crushed by its immensity, the carvings of vanished people, the dead animals, the hundreds of glass-eyed brilliant birds in their cases. And I was uneasy on the broad avenue where there were no small stores and tenements, only huge buildings across from the park at whose windows I looked in vain for a figure or a face. An ancient man was walking slowly toward us. His white hair grew thickly like a wool cap, he carried an umbrella frame upon whose bent ribs a few fragments of black cloth still clung.

"Little nigger girls . . ." he remarked as we circled around him.

Ellen walked swiftly on. I touched her arm as we started down the subway stairs. "We shouldn't have come down here," I said.

"Don't say that!" she exclaimed angrily. "I'll go where I want to go. Anyhow he didn't mean you." Not looking at me, she added, "Color runs."

A train came along. My relief at the knowledge that in a few minutes I would be on the familiar streets and then, at once, my bewilderment that I should be relieved at returning to the place from which I wanted so desperately to escape, made me forget Ellen's anger, even her presence.

.   .   .

Thaddeus was coming for supper, Ellen told me one afternoon. Mrs. Dove had said I could come, too. When Ellen opened the door to me that evening, I saw Mrs. Dove cutting her son's hair. She had brought the fringed lamp close to the chair. Her glasses glittered with reflected light as she bent, snipping at the tight reddish curls which clustered at his neck. They both looked up at me at the same time. Mrs. Dove greeted me with her usual gravity but I noticed that her lips trembled as she spoke. She had buttoned her blouse unevenly. Thad smiled. "My fellow spy," he said.

Four places were set at the table. A small vase held daisies. They looked fresh. I guessed Thad had brought them; they were not wilted and faded like the flowers Mrs. Dove brought home from the apartment of the woman she referred to as "Madam."

As Ellen leaned toward me, I glanced at the room. It was not just that it was clean, I realized, but that something had been grappled with to make it look the way it did, an insistence that it yield up whatever comfort was to be gotten from it.

"Thad's been drafted," Ellen whispered. "She's terribly upset." Mrs. Dove put her hand on Thad's head and pressed it gently forward. The scissors snipped. Thad grinned up at us as we watched silently.

I knew that Mr. Dove's insurance had helped pay Thad's college costs and Ellen's tuition at the Catholic school. It hadn't been enough. That was why she had come to the public school and why Thad had a night job at Grand Central Station where he wore a red cap and carried travellers' suitcases. He could have gotten a job anywhere, Ellen told me, but where it asked *race* on the employment forms, he always wrote *Negro*. It was harder for him than if his skin had been dark, she said. White people hated him because he was wearing their skin.

"Luisa!" he exclaimed once during supper. "That's the prettiest name!"

He spoke of his classes, about the two men he shared a small apartment with, one a sleeping-car porter, the other a short-order cook. He said nothing about being drafted. Mrs. Dove remained silent except to offer us food. As she carried the coffee pot to the table, she began to falter; she swayed suddenly and the pot fell from her hands, the coffee splashing on the table cloth and on my arm.

"God!" she burst out, with such a depth of feeling that I imagined she would push the table to the floor and leap from a window. Instead, she took my arm in her hands and began to wipe off the hot coffee with the hem of her skirt as though I'd been a chair.

"Momma, Momma," Ellen called to her pleadingly.

She dropped my arm. "It's wrong. It's wicked!" she cried. "No Negro man in this country ought to be taken into that white man's army. Not one!"

Thad had fetched a rag and was mopping up the coffee from the table. Mrs. Dove went to the chair where Thad had been sitting when she cut his hair; she sat down and stared straight ahead, smoothing her skirt over and over again.

"You're wrong, Momma," Thad said. He took a flattened cigarette from his pocket, lit it and drew deeply.

"Since when have you taken up tobacco, Thaddeus?" his mother asked.

Thad said, "You think when we come back, things are going to be the same? They won't be. They're not going to put the brooms back in our hands."

"They will be the same," Mrs. Dove said flatly. "It was after your father started smoking that he began to drink, Thaddeus."

"Momma? You've got to understand my being in the army is a bigger chance for me than a college degree."

Mrs. Dove laughed bitterly. One side of her blouse collar pushed up against her chin, a few strands of hair had worked themselves free of the black pins that had bound them. She had clenched her hands so tightly, I could see her prominent knuckles.

Hatted and gloved for church on Sunday mornings, she had looked calm and unshakeable like one of the great ships Ellen and I had seen riding at anchor on the Hudson.

I got up to help Ellen with the dishes. She looked at me briefly. "Your arm okay?"

"It was just a few drops," I said. She was silent. I felt she wanted me to go home. Nobody was talking. I was there. They were holding back, waiting until I'd gone.

"I'd better go," I said.

"I'll take you," Thaddeus said.

"I'll be all right."

Mrs. Dove looked at me with surprise as if she'd forgotten I was there.

"No. Thaddeus will take you home," she said with her customary tone of certainty about what was fitting. That night I had seen her shaken. Like her gloves and her hat, the certainty was, perhaps, something she put on like a garment. As I looked around the room I admired so much, I visualized it empty, as desolate as those other rooms I passed in the halls where homeless men took shelter.

Thad and I were the only people on his street.

"Do you feel bad?" Thad asked. I nodded, wondering how he had guessed. He took hold of my arm firmly.

"Sometimes I miss my grandmother," I said. He held my arm tighter. He probably didn't know much about me.

"She's back there—where I came from."

"You can go there someday," he said.

Maura had been saving for a trip to Havana all the time she had been our boarder. During the time she was out of work, she had used up the money. Now she had begun to save again. I didn't believe she would ever return to Cuba. Once in the United States, I wondered, could anyone ever leave? "I'll never have enough money for that," I said. I knew it was too late. It wasn't only distance that had sealed Malagita away from me; it was the years.

"That's the wrong way to think," Thad said earnestly. "If you want to visit your Gran, you've got to start the work of it now. You have to make deep choices. When my mother knows Ellen has to have a new coat, she arranges her whole life for that. She'll start thinking about the winter in April. In the summer, she'll let the apartment get dark before she turns on a light. She's thinking about the pennies she's saving for the coat. I've seen her slice a tomato so thin, you'd be fooled by what you see, how she can make one tomato go such a long way. If she finds out that woman she works for is going away for the summer—she doesn't get paid then —she listens around to see who's getting married so she can get the sewing work for the wedding. She's always thinking about that coat."

He didn't understand. It wasn't a visit I wanted but the way it had been. He kept at me about choices. He was beginning to sound like Mrs. Dove when she talked religion.

We had come to the corner of Amsterdam where there were people. Thad was talking so loud, I was afraid they'd think we were fighting. But nobody paid us any attention.

"It's a hard way to live," Thad said. "You miss a lot." He rummaged in his pocket. "Wish I had another cigarette," he said. "I only buy loosies. You know about them? Three for a nickel."

I hesitated, then I said what was in my mind. "I'm going to be a servant. I'm not good in school the way Ellen is. I'm going to have to get real work soon, not just an afternoon job. And—oh, I have to get away!"

He let go of my arm. We had reached my corner. I felt cold and miserable. I was sure I had lost his good opinion, if he'd had one of me. What I'd said so loudly, so boldly, had taken me by surprise. He'd forced it from me, talking about things I couldn't do. But something had come together in my mind the minute I'd spoken, fragments of a picture of myself in a black uniform with a white apron. I felt a sour triumph. I was going against him—he was dreaming. I wasn't.

"That's not a choice. You're just going along."

In front of my building, I looked up at the whore's former window. I felt my face turn red. Thad was smiling.

"You've forgotten," he said. "We're spies, Luisa. We can go anywhere. We know how to disguise ourselves."

But he didn't disguise himself. I realized all at once that he wasn't *safe*, that he might not even get back to his mother and sister tonight without mishap. He suddenly hugged me. "Don't be so scared," he whispered, drawing me up the steps to the door.

"You know I live with two other fellows?" I nodded. "One of them can't sleep," he went on. "I mean, never. Except for a few minutes then he wakes himself up with terrible dreams. They make him cry out. Well —it's more like roaring, you know? He's a few years older than I am. He didn't finish the sixth grade. He went to work when he was twelve, he started drinking, too, got into fights all the time. He's stitched up all over his face and neck. He wanted to be a cook on a ship. He wanted to travel. When he gets really drunk, he says to me the next day, 'I shipped out last night . . .' He's a short-order cook. When he comes home from the restaurant, he falls into bed . . . so tired . . . but the second the light's out, he's wide awake. That's the insomnia.

"He smiles about me going to school. He says, 'Go to it, Thaddy! Do it!' but he doesn't believe anything. He gets up at noon, his feet find his shoes. He drinks a soda, has a cigarette, drinks from the pint he keeps on the floor next to the bed. Then he goes off to his job, jokes with the customers, plants his feet in front of his stove. I've seen him there, shaking the french fries, cigarette hanging from his mouth, his bottle handy. When he comes home and lies down, someone else wakes up—the life in him that can't get out—and it walks around the room all night."

I saw the new Cuban boarder coming down the block. He nodded to me briefly but stared at Thad for a long moment before he went past us into the building.

Thad was looking at me with a serious, intent expression. I felt a stirring of happiness. It made my breath come fast. He was thinking about me; he might, at any second, say words that would make my life clear. He didn't speak. The agitation I felt was suddenly too much to bear. "There have to be servants," I burst out.

"You've made up your mind," he said, "without thinking. You don't know enough yet."

"I know I have to get away."

"But—to what?"

"And I'm really a foreigner."

He laughed. "Who isn't?" he asked.

"I'd better go up."

"You can't be a servant as long as people think servants are slaves," he said.

"Your mother—" I hesitated. "She's a maid."

"She takes what they give her," he said, "and she judges them."

He pressed my hands with his then walked away toward Amsterdam. I watched him until he had disappeared.

I saw him once again a few months later when he came home to say good-bye to his mother and Ellen before he was sent overseas. He smiled at me and pointed to his chest, his soldier's jacket.

"My new disguise," he said. "Would you have known me?"

He had no idea how much I had thought about him since we had stood on the street and talked.

"I wouldn't have known you," I said. "It's such a good disguise."

.   .   .

When I was unable to sleep, I dressed and stole down the stairs to the doorway of our tenement and looked out at the street, at the cats which came out at night to search for food, at a man or a woman hurrying some place, their faces glimpsed briefly in the light of the street lamp, mysteriously shadowed. Sometimes, a man, once a small boy, sat on the steps of another tenement down the block, or across the street, and I would wonder about them, wonder what had driven them from their rooms, if, like me, they had started up from their beds the moment the light was turned off, or if they had fled from a family battle, the loud cries of which frequently shattered the nighttime quietness of our street like glass smashing on the pavement.

As I leaned in the doorway, it would seem to me that I could simply leave the barrio, simply walk away.

Thad's letters from England often contained messages for me. When Ellen repeated them with a touch of sternness, they sounded no different from those of my teachers who tried to goad me into greater effort. Thad had taken me on like a missionary takes on a heathen, intent on saving a soul. It both touched and irritated me. The line was drawn. Ellen and Thad—and even my father in his disaffected and belittling fashion—on one side, I, on the other. They wanted to drag me across the line into a life that required an effort I was unable, or unwilling, to make. To me, being a servant promised a kind of freedom. I was wild with impatience to leave home; I was convinced of a secret power to make things go my own way. Yet I was troubled by thoughts of how Ellen and Thad would judge me, just as I had moments when I longed to astonish my teachers. I made one attempt to alter what I felt was inevitable. One night, I heard the Cuban boarder, Carreno, telling my father that the men in the machine shop where he worked as a turret-lathe operator, were being drafted at such a rate they had begun to hire women. "Women," he repeated mournfully. "They will disrupt everything," Papá declared with bitter conviction.

The next morning, I stopped Carreno as he hurried down the hall, and asked him the name of the shop. I didn't go to school. As I rode downtown to Fourteenth Street where the Moskowitz Diamond Die Company was located, the thought of Thad's approval of what I was about to do, that thought which had so lifted my spirit that not a second seemed to have passed between the moment Carreno had given me the address and the moment I had dropped my nickel into the subway turnstile, utterly vanished. I felt a cold alarm that made me start forward at each stop, half rise to my feet to get off and run to the uptown platform.

In the small front office of the company on the twelfth floor, a middle-aged woman who smelled rather sickeningly of violet perfume, daintily touched one dry curl on her forehead. "We don't need nobody now," she said. Behind the closed door next to her desk, I heard the dull pounding of machinery.

"I heard they were hiring women," I said.

"We're going on a war footing pretty soon," she said. "You'd have to get clearance because of the stuff we'll make then."

I stood in front of her desk, mute, longing for her to take my arm and lead me beyond the door. I imagined myself at an unimaginable machine, working levers. "You know what clearance is?" she asked, narrowing her eyes shrewdly. I shook my head.

"F.B.I.," she said, "and that's no fooling."

"Mr. Carreno told—" I began.

"Him!" she snorted. "That fruit!"

I turned toward the door to leave.

"You in school?"

"Yes."

"Stay there," she said. She was smiling; it was a dry little smile that barely changed her face. "There'll be plenty of jobs for a long time," she said. "Long as the war goes on."

When I got home around noon, a stream of light lay along the hall, flowing like water in a gutter. Mamá was sitting in the kitchen on her stool in her nightgown looking down at a newspaper. She was so absorbed, she didn't hear me. She bent over the paper and drew a line with a stubby pencil. As I moved closer, I heard the faint whisper of her breathing. Her fingers were as thin as twigs.

"Mamá?"

"Ssh . . . I'm nearly finished."

The children's page of the newspaper lay open on the sink counter. She had been connecting dots with her pencil and now they formed a cartoon dragon with a forked tongue.

I left her and went into the parlor. A book was lodged in Papá's chair. I didn't bother to read the title; I didn't care what he read. Presently, I heard the slow, reluctant sound of her footsteps. She stood for a moment in the parlor doorway, blinking in the light, then went to the armchair where she groaned faintly as she sat down. She glanced at the book with an odd, startled expression and drew her body away from it.

She had been shrinking for months, dwindling like a piece of ice under the flow of water from a tap. I had noticed, but it had been only noticing—I hadn't thought about it. She had been a girl, only a few years older than I was now, walking swiftly down the path from the *vivienda*, dressed in a black uniform, looking anxiously and eagerly for me. As I struggled to recall the face of that girl as it emerged from the dark, it seemed to me I could smell the odor of flowers and pigs, that I sat waiting in the cabin for her to pause at the door, to say, "Ay Dios! I'll make our supper now."

"Why aren't you in school?" she asked timidly.

"I'm not going to school anymore," I said. She looked bewildered and plucked at the book. When she had it in her hands, she turned it from side to side and dropped it on the floor. Perhaps she was beyond caring whether I went to school or not.

"I'm going to look for work as a maid."

Her hands flew to her breasts, then, with a terrible cry, she covered her face.

"No," she whispered. "Ave Maria! Don't do that."

I walked to her and touched her shoulder. She flinched. I felt a kind of horror. There she crouched, she, whom I'd imagined long subdued by suffering, even become insensible to new blows, was sobbing, shaken, as though it was the first time she had surmised the black heart of life. I began to rub her back. Gradually, her breathing grew less labored. She murmured something and moved away from my hand, turning up her wet face to me.

"It won't be the same for me as it was for you," I said.

She shook her head. "You don't know anything," she said.

"I know I have to work," I said coldly.

She stared at me a moment, then lifted her arms. I saw how thin they were as her sleeves fell back. I bent to embrace her. I barely felt her hands against my back, they lay there so lightly. I smelled her, the soiled gown, the neglected flesh, the musty odors of a body which had lost a guiding discipline. There was another smell, sharp, rancid, fleeting, I couldn't put a name to.

She was thirty-three. She died eight months later of cancer, a few days after her thirty-fourth birthday. By then, I had started my life as a servant.

.   .   .

Papá was holding a rolled newspaper in one hand that drooped toward the floor. Until I walked in front of him and could see his face, I thought he was asleep, but his eyes were open, his gaze on the window. I looked and saw a building like ours. On its roof, the ropes women hung laundry on in warm weather stirred and tugged at the leaning poles to which they were attached. Daylight dwindled in patches on the dark brick of the wall. The darkening sky pressed thickly down, pulpy and plum-colored. One star gleamed.

My father took no notice of my presence. After a minute or so, I heard the rustle of the newspaper edges as he struck it on the floor.

"I've quit school," I said. Almost at once, like three hard exclamations, the doors along the hall closed, shutting Mamá and Maura and Carreno into their rooms.

The newspaper dropped at my feet and unrolled. I saw the word, *Stalingrad*, and I bent to read the headline that told of the surrender of the German Sixth Army. Papá stood and kicked the newspaper away and walked to the window.

When he turned back to the room, his face was calm. He looked at me steadily. I was frightened. Yet I felt distant too, my life a small point of light far away from him, in a place he couldn't reach.

"I had no reason to hope for more," he said quietly. "But I did hope."

"For what?" I couldn't help asking.

"For—something. You're not stupid."

"I have a job," I said quickly. "On Long Island. I'm going to be—" I forgot for a moment what the ad in the newspaper had said. He waited by the window. "I'm going to be a live-in maid."

He nodded once. "Well—you've taken after her," he said. He laughed briefly. "After us," he added.

He returned to his chair, picking up the paper on the way. He shook it open.

I walked down the hall toward my room. Mamá's door opened. She peered out at me, her eyes wide with alarm. I shook my head. "It's all right," I said. "What can he do?"

When I passed Maura's room, she reached out and grabbed my arm. I shook her off. "*Hijita*! Don't be so tough!" she protested. Carreno's door remained shut.

.   .   .

Ellen, as my father had, gave way before the force of my intention. I had said nothing to her about the job until I had gotten it. As I described its particulars—twenty-five dollars every two weeks, every other Sunday and one day a week off, my own room and bathroom—she looked at me with dislike. It wounded me bitterly even as I suspected it rose from her own uncertainty about her life. Well, then. Let them both see me as a hopeless case! She was still a schoolgirl, and Papá had to come home every night to the barrio. I was getting out.

On the banks of the Hudson, she and I had played at magic lives. But I had already had a magic life in the garden of Malagita, in the great kitchen where I had been shown the reflection of my face in a silver tray.

Neither Atilio nor Thaddeus had been heard from for some months. "My little son is under the *bombas* and has no time for writing letters," Uncle Federico said. I had seen newsreels of the bombing of foreign cities, fires cleaving the darkness, people running, shadows of confusion and alarm, the bomb craters in the gray light of day piled with the debris of buildings which only hours earlier had been filled with the living.

During the last week I lived at home, I wished the *bombas* would fall on the city, imagining that in the terror they would bring, in the destruction of all that proclaimed itself permanent, I would be released from doubt, set only on survival.

The morning before I was to take the train from Pennsylvania Station to my job in Forest Hills, I shopped for my mother. Later, I took the broom and swept all the rooms, gathering up the dust on a piece of cardboard I found in Carreno's room. I paused there. One of the drawers in his dresser was half pulled out. I looked in and saw a few pairs of rolled black socks, a yellow embroidered shirt made of thin, transparent stuff, and a magazine. I picked it up and it fell open in my hands. I dropped it back at once into the drawer, but not before I had seen a clumsy drawing of two naked men, one standing with his head thrown back, the other, kneeling before him, his mouth clamped on to the extended cock of the one who stood, hanging from it like a garment of flesh. For a moment, I couldn't catch my breath, and I stood motionless, burning as though sheathed in heat.

I looked at the objects on the dresser, a photograph of a caged parrot, a saucer holding a piece of pink soap, a spidery object which I gradually recognized, as I began to breathe normally again, as a hairnet. There was a dark smudge on Carreno's pillow. Shuddering faintly, I bent forward and sniffed the perfumed residue of his hair pomade. On the wall was tacked a card of a painting of Saint Sebastian. I had begun to count the arrows which pierced his body when Mamá came into the room.

"One would have been sufficient," she remarked dryly. I laughed too loudly, too long. She grew alarmed. I reached out to touch her, but my hand fell away. I felt too great a revulsion for flesh at that moment.

"Watch out for the sons," she said.

"He's eight years old," I said. "And the other child's a girl."

"Watch out for the father, then."

"Oh, Mamá!"

She took a step toward me. Her eyes filled with tears. "You've grown so tall," she murmured.

I took a very small step away from her. She was staring at the card of Saint Sebastian.

"Sebastiano," she said softly. "He would have been ten now."

For a moment, I couldn't think what she meant. Then I recalled all at once: the swaddled body of the dead baby on the table, the little mouth open. He would be bones by now, no more than a handful.

"I'll be back twice a month," I said.

"Perhaps you'll miss me sometimes," she said seriously, thoughtfully.

"I will," I said. I didn't believe I would.

.   .   .

On my free Sunday mornings, I took the train to New York City, away from Forest Hills where the Miller house sat in a row of similar houses on a curving street—each with a glassed-in sun porch and a narrow cement path leading to a white painted door, each, I supposed, with a refrigerator that was never empty, and rooms which at night were flooded with light that had a penetrating, meddling force the daylight seemed to lack and in which the dozens of things I dusted and polished and wiped, furniture, vases, China boxes, clocks, lamps, books, looked ownerless like objects in a store, an accumulation the purpose for which had never been clear.

I returned to the barrio, to our flat, where I opened the door into a dark hall and found myself in a passageway to a different country, and I walked quickly past the rooms, catching sight on my way to the kitchen of our belongings, each a relic of struggle, fought for, gained, abandoned, the flaws that had first placed them within our grasp defeating

any effort to make them whole: cracked iron posts of bed frames, drawers that couldn't be closed sticking out of bureaus, shaky chairs.

But on Wednesdays, my weekly day off, I stayed downtown in the
city. I learned the streets and avenues like lessons. When I got hungry I
ate in cafeterias where it was not necessary to speak to anyone, only
push a dollar through a grill and gather up nickels from a smooth metal
tray and deposit them in slots next to glass boxes which held sandwiches
and cakes. In the ceaseless noise, among throngs of people, I made my
choices of what to eat in private, silent pleasure. In the vast movie theaters
where I often spent the afternoons, the speech of actors filled the dark
with inhuman emphasis. Sometimes the film broke, then their voices,
accompanied by the slap of torn film, changed into a kind of slow, bestial
roaring.

It was not in the Miller house where I felt out of the barrio so much as
it was on the city streets where I took any direction I wished, where any
choice I made, a candy bar, a walk through the aisles of a department
store, a movie, seemed a deliverance from all the constraints of my life,
and was quickened by an anticipation I had not felt since I had last run
down the dirt roads of Malagita to visit Nana.

Only now and then, when I lifted a sandwich or a cup of coffee to my
lips, and caught a smell of cleaning fluids and powders which had clung
to my fingertips, was I reminded of my labor which maintained the order upon which the Miller's domesticity rested.

                    .   .   .

"Your goal is fifteen minutes a shirt," Mrs. Miller had said with a bark of
laughter. After I had learned to iron, she brought me handfuls of frayed
lingerie and I began to learn to mend, but I could never make the stitches
as small and fine as the ones on Nana's black stockings. After I washed
up the dinner dishes, I could go to my room. The garden view that had
been promised in the ad was of a scraggly, overgrown hedge. But, at
night, the sky was enormous, and when I opened the window, I could
smell trees and earth.

"Anybody ever call you Lou?" Mr. Miller asked. "Like a nickname, I
mean?"

"Not yet," I answered.

He had come into the kitchen to make himself a cup of tea. I wrung out a dishcloth and spread it on the sink rim to dry.

"I'm going to call you Lou. Okay, Lou? My wife tells me you made it through two years of high school."

"Almost three," I said.

"You can't get any place without an education," he said, a tremor in his voice. "You're always at a disadvantage. You could go to night school, you know. Don't forget. You've got two languages already. You speak Spanish, don't you?"

"Some," I acknowledged.

"Well, then. You're ahead of the game."

He looked at me expectantly.

"I don't think Spanish counts, Mr. Miller," I said, hanging up my apron on a hook behind the basement door. Mrs. Miller had found the apron on a chair one day. Although she was usually good-tempered, she had told me with scarcely restrained irritation that unless I was wearing the apron, it must always be out of sight. I had begun to learn that being a maid was more than cleaning.

"Lou, you've got a right, in our country—"

"I'm glad to be working for you," I interrupted. He stared at me a second, nodded, then took his tea and went to the door. "Okay, Lou. It's your life," he said with a touch of disappointment.

It *was* my life, hidden from the Millers in my room, in the streets I wandered, in my thoughts.

I didn't care what they called me. I knew more about them than they could guess about me. June and Alfred, I called them in my thoughts after I'd seen their first names on the mail which I spread out on a table in the hall each morning. Yet I liked them. It was not their friendliness so much as their curiosity about me which partly dispelled the coolness I had felt toward them once they had hired me, once I had put on one of the two aprons Mrs. Miller handed me the first day I went to work for them. For all their efforts to make themselves comfortable with my presence, I knew I held mystery for them.

I surmised, had I been a Negro servant, they would have seen me as a flat surface. Not in their most private thoughts would they have considered me more than a dark-skinned vacancy. As it was, there was an odd, shifting equality between us; we were all working people together, except, of course, I didn't set them tasks. I sensed I must relinquish nothing of my secret life.

I suddenly perceived that for Ellen to distinguish herself by acquiring a profession was a matter of the life or death of her spirit—that to be unknown was ordinary, but to be cancelled out as a creature undeserving of interest, was an unnatural death in life.

In the Miller household, it was the children, Lisa who was seven, and Benjamin, nine, who made me feel a vague, continuing apprehension. They did as they liked. "We love our children," Mrs. Miller said to me with an emphasis that suggested she thought hers an unusual sentiment. The children never closed a door or picked up anything they had dropped or put anything back from where they had taken it. It was as if their hands were unable to grip things.

At the table, they pouted and pushed away their suppers. Mrs. Miller pleaded with them to eat. She told them about poor people who didn't have such good food.

"Isn't that so, Luisa? Aren't there little children in the world who don't have enough to eat, who'd be glad to have what's on these plates?" she asked, rolling her eyes at me to urge me to confirm what she had said. I could only nod as I looked at the plump little girl, sprawled in her chair, her mouth turned down in complaint, the boy idly stirring his milk with his finger. Grimly, I scraped their untouched suppers into the garbage can while Mrs. Miller spoke worriedly about bacteria and disease. But she kept leftovers from the meals she ate with her husband and made use of them.

Sometimes I played cards with the children or read to them when the Millers went out of an evening. But I felt wary of them, aware of the unchildish appraisal in the faces they turned up to adults, and of the deliberateness with which, I judged, they misbehaved. One morning, I woke to find them standing by my bed. I supposed they had been watching me while I slept.

"Please don't come into my room," I said.

"It's my house," said Lisa.

"We can go where we want to," Benjamin added.

"Not in this part of it," I said, trembling with anger. "Not this room. Only if and when I ask you."

Lisa looked frightened. "Will you ask us?" she said and began to cry.

I was ashamed, and I pitied them. I sat up and embraced them both, drawing them onto my bed. "I'll ask you," I promised. "Don't cry. It's all right."

After that, I began to like them better, and I gradually learned that they, too, had their secret lives, refuges from the weight of that love that seemed to measure and record every breath they drew.

.   .   .

On a Sunday in October, just as I had put out my hand to brush back a strand of Mamá's hair so I could see her face and try to gauge if my effort to persuade her to go to the clinic was having any effect, there was a pounding at the front door. I heard Papá walking down the hall to open it.

"You haven't taken off your coat," Mamá murmured reproachfully.

"Are you going to live out your life on this damned stool? My God! Do you sleep on it?" I cried in exasperation.

"Oh—leave me be!" she exclaimed.

"You're sick," I protested. I turned and seized the tap to try to stop its eternal leaking.

"It can't be fixed," Mamá said.

"Will you go if I take you? I'll take you next Wednesday on my day off."

"My coat is torn. I can't find the right color thread to mend it."

"I'll find the thread. I'll mend it," I promised.

Uncle Federico appeared at the kitchen entrance, his shoulders hunched over, his face stricken, naked without its customary bullying smile.

"Horrible news," he announced. He walked in, Papá a few steps behind him. As Mamá slid from her stool, Maura, looking half-asleep, staggered into the kitchen wearing her green winter coat over her nightgown.

"Coffee," she croaked. "Por Dios!"

"You wait for your coffee!" Papá said with ferocity.

"Atilio, my little son . . ." muttered Federico. Panic gripped me. Would we now have to mourn Atilio's passing? "He's in a hospital somewhere in England, his little body burned," Federico said, tears coming to his eyes.

"Ay, Dios mío!" cried Mamá.

"Only just after he had been made an officer. But he wrote the letter himself—just a few lines, but, poor boy, he always thinks of his *papi* and his mama and their worry."

"Will he be crippled?" asked my father.

"Of course not," Federico answered with sudden irritation. "It is only his left leg and arm, and the new American techniques are the best in the world."

"I'm so sorry, so sorry," Mamá said. "Aurelia must be suffering."

"Of course. The mama always suffers," Federico said quickly. "The woman stays and suffers," he added, giving me a dark look. "But I have other news, also very bad," he said. "It's about our Mamá, Fefita. And you must remember the good part—she is now released from suffering—unlike my poor Atilio. I received information this morning that a hurricane struck San Pedro. No ordinary thing. They've said the winds are 167 miles an hour. And there has been a tidal wave."

I saw Papá cast a fleeting, resentful look at Mamá. I knew then that he had already heard of the hurricane. While I had been making my bed in Forest Hills, Papá had been listening close to his radio, secretly listening, while Mamá sat on the edge of their bed waiting for the strength to come with which to begin another day. As though I could feel that first slight menacing stirring of wind in the palms, that special faint stirring that comes after a long stillness, after the sky has turned the color of saffron, I cried out, "Nana!"

From Mamá came a faint echo of my cry, a hopeless protest that died away at once.

Federico gazed up at the ceiling. "We won't know for days—if ever. The devastation is terrible, the cane crop ruined, infants carried out to sea, people have no houses—"

"—Shut up, idiot!" shouted my father. "Shut up!"

Federico was stunned. Maura ducked out of the kitchen. Then Federico raised his hand as though to strike Papá. Mamá caught hold of it and he grappled silently with her. As they struggled, Papá, pushing me aside, strode out and down the hall.

I went after him, catching him just as he reached the door. I yanked at his jacket so hard I had it off his shoulders. He turned to face me, his thin mouth opening like the mouth of a fish gulping at air.

"Mamá is dying," I gasped out. "You bastard! You terrible bastard!"

He tore himself from my grip and, to my amazement, dropped to his knees. He covered his face with his hands and swayed there on the floor before me. I thought he'd gone mad.

"Forgive me!" he groaned. "Forgive me . . ."

I backed away from him, vaguely aware of Maura breathing noisily nearby. I turned to her, intending to tell her to go away. But as I glared at her excited face, I heard the door bang shut. He had gone. Federico was coming rapidly up the hall. "Stay with your Mamá," he ordered me. There was no heat of feeling in his voice, only the usual note of self-satisfaction.

In the kitchen, Mamá was crying. Maura shuffled in. Almost admiringly, she remarked, "Fefita, you will cry away all the water in yourself."

"Papá did something crazy," I told them. "He kneeled and asked me to forgive him."

"If that one kneeled, it was because God broke his legs," Maura sniffed.

How deeply entrenched she was in our lives! My sudden dislike of that fact made me walk quickly to my mother and take her arm to lead her to the bedroom, sheltering her with my body from Maura who followed us to the door. "Excuse me," I said coldly, and shut her out.

Mamá collapsed on the bed. I sat near her on its edge. "She may not be dead," I said.

"I would never have seen her again, Luisa," Mamá said. "What I feel—" she broke off and looked distractedly about the room. "What I feel is that everything is running away from me so fast!"

"Please. Please let me take you to a doctor. I know you're really sick."

"Not yet," she said. "I'll go. One of these days. You, poor thing. You loved your Nana. Remember? I remember. You watched me in the mornings, wanting me gone. Yes, yes . . . you wanted me gone so that you could run off to her. I always knew when you'd been there. You came home with those little curls all over your head."

I cried. She put her arms around me and rocked me back and forth in the old way that had once seemed to drag me into her own mourning but for which I was now grateful. She wiped away my tears with her cold hands. She smiled faintly. "As you said, she may not be dead," she said. "You know what they say about people as clever as my Mamá—they can swim without getting their clothes wet."

She shivered, and I looked around for something to cover her with but she put her hand on mine and said, "No. I'm all right. But I'm tired. I'll sleep now."

I went to my own bed where I lay motionless, feeling light and without substance. Carreno snored in the next room.

Only a few of the houses of Malagita could have withstood such winds. The *vivienda* would be untouched, its prodigious doors and great shutters closed against the storm, its servant houses blown away. Somewhere among the vast rooms, the Frenchwoman and her children would have listened to the violence outside, knowing themselves to be safe. The clock tower would stand. And perhaps the marble angel that had stood on the tomb of Antonio de la Cueva.

From the door of Nana's cabin, she could survey the whole territory of her life. When she saw me running down the dirt road toward her, she had smiled, and when I'd flung myself against her, she had laughed out loud.

I heard Papá returning home later. I got out of bed and looked down the hall to the parlor. I could see his arm on the arm of the chair. I saw him lean forward to turn on his radio and bend his head close to it.

"Forgive me," he had said. My mother had shown no interest in that extraordinary request of his. Had she known what he had meant, I brooded. From his crimes, I chose only one, the loss of Malagita.

　　　　　·　　　　　　　　　·　　　　　　　　　·

My mother died in the second week of December.

I was playing Parcheesi with the children at the kitchen table one evening when Mrs. Miller came to say there was someone on the telephone asking for me.

I had hardly picked it up when Maura's voice shouted in my ear, "Luisa! Luisa!"

A gust of fear blew through me. "Don't yell," I told her. "I can hear you."

At once, she began to wail.

"Maura, for God's sake . . ."

"Your Mamá . . ." she cried.

I knew then what news was coming to me from this first telephone call of my life.

"Your Papá and I are at the hospital on 168th Street." She said with a sudden, crazy brightness. Almost at once, her voice sank until I could hardly hear it. "I found poor Fefita in her bed tonight, unconscious. Your Papá and I rode in the ambulance with her."

"Is she dead, Maura?" When there was no answer, I said, "She's dead."

"Yes. Only fifteen minutes ago. She never said a word. Nena? Are you there? She had made her bed, she had packed most of her clothes in a box."

I could not seem to release the deep breath I had drawn. Maura was calling my name again. I heard myself saying as though from a distance, yes, yes. She was asking me to come as soon as I could, to bring cigarettes—she was going mad with my father so silent.

In the living room, Mr. Miller shook the pages of a newspaper.

"I'll be there," I said and hung up.

I went and told the Millers. She stood up, a magazine sliding from her lap to the floor. She held out her hand. I looked at it as it curved to rest upon my arm; it looked so strange to me at that moment. More brusquely than I intended, I shook it off. Mr. Miller had gone out of the room and was now back wearing his coat. "I'll drive you there," he said.

"No!" I protested, alarmed by a kind of helplessness induced in me by their concern.

"Get your coat," he said as though I hadn't spoken.

"This is your Christmas present from the children," Mrs. Miller said, tearing red tissue paper from a package. She pressed a pair of white wool gloves into my hands. "You can make use of them tonight. It's very cold."

In the car, Mr. Miller told me that his mother had died when he was five. He had some idea of how I felt, and being a foreigner too, because Jews were always, in some sense, foreigners, no matter what they were, and was my father there at the hospital? Is that who had called? And take all the days I needed, they'd manage. And money. Did I need money? He could advance me my pay, or even—

His voice began to falter. I had said nothing. The unanswering silence of one person makes language futile. After a while, when I was able to speak, I thanked him. He stretched out his right hand and rested his small, pale fingers on my wrist.

Maura and Papá were in the visitors' room, sitting across from each other like strangers. When they saw me, they stood up. Maura came to me, tears beginning to form on the already swollen rims of her eyes.

How old was my father? No birthdays had been marked except mine. Mamá would take from a drawer a little package wrapped in colored paper, and Maura would pick out a bangle of hers and give it to me. Two years ago, on my sixteenth birthday, I had thought—this is how old Mamá was when I was born. Now she was dead.

Over Maura's shoulder, I stared at my father, at a place on his upper lip where he had missed a patch of dark beard. His eyes were shadowed, half-closed; he had slipped one hand beneath his jacket so that it sheltered against his body.

To whom could I speak of my mother's life? A nurse came into the room and lit a cigarette. An old man in a brown bathrobe peered in, then slipped around the door and sat down on a bench where he stared fixedly at the floor. Maura was talking of the funeral to Papá.

It was not that I hadn't loved her. It was not that.

"Where is Mamá?"

"They've taken her away," Maura said.

"Where?" I cried out. The old man stood up and left abruptly. "Where?"

Maura put her arm around me and led me to the window. Below, I saw the Hudson between its luminous banks, blacker than the sky. Softly, steadily, Maura told me that there was a special place in the hospital where bodies were prepared for burial. I heard the tone of invention in her voice. "They dump them in the river," I said. Her grip on my shoulders tightened. The strength of her stringy arm surprised me and tempered the desperate and confused anger I felt as I stood there, my forehead pressed against the icy windowpane.

At the end of the Mass which Maura had arranged, and which was held in a small chapel of the church Mamá had once gone to, I wept from exasperation when the Irish priest extolled Mamá's virtues as a wife, a mother, and a pious Catholic. She was to be buried twice; once in the ground, once by the uncomprehending, indifferent priest. Aurelia sobbed loudly into one of her chiffon handkerchiefs but Uncle Federico was silent until the service was over and we were outside on the sidewalk. There should be a meal after the funeral, he muttered, didn't Fefita deserve a funeral meal? No one answered him. He sighed and looked up at the church doors then quickly away to the more comforting sight of the automobiles passing by on the broad street.

The snow held off until Mamá was put into the ground in a crowded cemetery just outside the city limits. Uncle Federico drove us home in his rackety Ford after dropping Aurelia off at their apartment house. She had bent over the seat toward Papá as though to kiss him, and he had pulled away from her so quickly he had pushed me forward so that I fell on my knees against the car door. I saw a look of dread on his face; his lips trembled, his eyes seemed to start out of his head. It passed in a second.

By evening, the bars of the fire escape at the parlor windows each held their narrow weight of snow. The wind blew great clouds of it across the roofs; where it caught the light, it shimmered like silken cloth.

Papá sat in his armchair, his hand covered his mouth and nose. He raised his eyes briefly to look at me. Was he going to say nothing to me? I started to leave.

"Wait," he said.

I paused at the door.

"You don't know how I feel."

"No. I don't. How could I?"

"Some people—like your mother—are broken early."

"By others . . ."

"Your Spanish has become so coarse," he said. It was strange but I hadn't realized we were both speaking Spanish.

"I wonder if you remember what *alegría* means?" he asked me. "It was the great thing she had when I first knew her. Gaiety, they say here. It's not the same. Do you know she made me laugh? How she could make me laugh! Away from those dead rooms, how I laughed. Do you know she prayed to *me* as well as to her Jesus and Mary?"

I found I could not look at him. "There was no place for me in Malagita," he said. "Not a corner, not a crack."

"I know what I know," I muttered.

"You don't guess at all that you don't know."

"Aren't you sorry?" I burst out.

"Sorry," he repeated grimly. "My God! Sorry!"

We had no more conversations. Two days later, I went back to Forest Hills where Mrs. Miller assured me that I need do nothing until I felt better. It was work I wanted.

In my room at night, when I knew the children were asleep, and there was no danger of their wandering into my room, I took out of my drawer the two massive silver forks I had found among Mamá's ragged underwear. They had become tarnished, nearly black. I had taken polish and cloth from the kitchen, and I worked on them until they glittered.

Everything else which had belonged to her had been thrown out by Maura, who, during the time I spent at home, had cleaned and cooked our meals and silenced Carreno when he started to speak of Mamá, as though to show him—and us—that it was only she who had the right to grieve for her.

I had written a note to Ellen, telling her of Mamá's death, and saying I would stop by on my next Sunday off on the chance I might find her in.

On Sunday, I found Mrs. Dove just home from church, I guessed. She was wearing her hat and gloves. She studied me for a moment. She was most sorry to hear of my mother's passing on, she said. I observed how carefully she removed her hatpins, smoothed her hair, stretched and pressed the fingers of her gloves.

"She was very sick," I said.

"It takes a long time getting used to. The sorrow never goes away."

She placed her hat on a table. "Won't you have supper with us?" she asked.

"Thank you, but I'd better go home."

"Well, yes. I suppose your Daddy must be expecting you."

I looked at her grimly. The sympathy on her face was plain to see. Of course, Ellen wouldn't have talked to her about my father. She called him "the knife" and it was a kind of understanding, enough for me. We had not often spoken of him. I hadn't known how to.

When Ellen came, I was sitting by the window, staring across at the roof where long ago she and I had seen a madman. She put her hand on my head. "I'm so sorry," she said.

"I asked her for supper but she has to go home," Mrs. Dove said.

"Let's go out and get some coffee," Ellen said to me.

"Ellen, I'm making your supper. You can have coffee here."

"I'll be back soon, Momma," she promised.

We walked up Amsterdam to a dark little bar where she turned in. "I want a drink," she said. "Maybe two." She lit a cigarette then put it out absentmindedly. The bartender said, "You need a few more years to get my drinks. I'm not serving you, baby."

"Yes, you are," she said. She smiled so splendidly, so knowingly, I didn't see how anyone could refuse her anything. He didn't.

"How is your father?" she asked.

I shook my head. "I've never been able to tell. I can't now. I hate to go back there. Mamá's gone, my grandmother lost in the hurricane . . ."

"People disappear," Ellen said sadly. "So quick—and they're gone."

I spoke of the Millers, how kind they'd been. I could hear the insistence in my voice. "It's not hard work," I said.

"It's demeaning."

"What is, Ellen? What is!"

"Just the doing of it. Being a maid like my mother. Because you don't have any choice."

"She sees to you," I said sharply.

"I know, I know . . . Momma didn't know what else to do. She was a lady." Ellen laughed. "A colored lady. You know what? We used to have a maid. Thad teased her about that."

"Thad," I said, suddenly gladdened.

"He's in Paris. Imagine that! It's the good thing about the war. Thad got to Europe."

She tossed down her drink. She's so skillful, I thought, meant for the world.

"I'm going to City College," she said. And added fiercely, "That's where I'm going."

I told her more about the Miller household. I said too much. I knew my words would return to me in the rooms I dusted and swept, and when I looked at the discontented, nervous children, and when I shut the door to my room without believing anymore that the door would ensure my privacy. "I guess," I said, "there is kindness that doesn't mean much."

As though my concession required her to make one, Ellen said, "Maybe you had good luck. Momma worked for some beasts before she got to old Madam. Her graciousness was severely tried when we first came to New York. Christian suffering, she called it."

"I've got to go," I said. "Maura Cruz has been doing so much. I'm only going there for her sake. He's never even thanked her."

"Luisa? Won't you try something else? Make your father pay for it. There are so many things you could do! You could learn anything."

I was thinking about something else. I wanted to ask her if she was in love. I glanced at her stern face and felt silly.

"I'll walk you," she said, in the old, sweet words. She held my arm close to hers all the way to my block. "Don't worry," she said. "You're the one that's earning your own living."

It was an indulgence, but I was grateful for it.

"Are you in love with anyone?" I asked.

She laughed. "Oh, Luisa! That's movie stuff!"

We were standing in front of the window where we had seen the whore at her work. She had moved out so long ago. Now, two children peered at us through the folds of a limp sheet that served as a curtain.

"You can sleep in Thad's old cot—if you don't stay at home on your days off," she offered.

We embraced. The enlivening warmth of my feeling for her carried me all the way to the door of the flat. I heard the sound of men's voices from behind the door, a shout, laughter.

There were people in the parlor. I went to Maura's room. She was sitting on the edge of her bed, made up heavily, dressed, her thin legs crossed at the ankles, around one, a thin gold chain. When she saw me, she cried, "Ay, Chica!" and put her finger to her lips. She stood up and came to the door and peered down the hall.

"He has them here all the time now, those good-for-nothing drunks," she whispered.

I noticed her suitcase on the floor. She followed my glance. "It's not possible for me to stay," she said. "It's a madhouse of men."

"I won't see him," I said.

"He'll know you're here. He always knows who comes in and goes out."

"I'm going right now. I only came to see if you were all right."

"Thank you, Nena. I'm glad someone in the world cares about poor Maura. You have some things in your room."

"Nothing I want."

"Carreno's gone, too. Your Papá sleeps in his room."

"How will I find you?"

"I know of a room nearby I think I can rent. I'll leave the address with Señora Alegre downstairs."

"*Alegre!*" I repeated. "Is she happy?"

Maura gave me a bewildered look. I put my arm around her. I could smell her hair dye. She sobbed briefly. I left right away and went quickly down the hall and the stairs to the street. I glanced up at the tenement and suddenly realized that what I hadn't wanted to see was Mamá's stool by the kitchen sink.

.   .   .

In March, another death occurred. Thaddeus Dove was killed while on a weekend pass when he tripped on a mine in a farmer's field a few miles north of Paris. A few months later, the war would end, the defeat, Mr. Miller would say, of the old terrible world of the past.

Thad had written home that he loved the French countryside, the stone villages, a café he had found in one of them where he could warm his feet on a brazier of hot coals and drink a glass of red wine. It would have been spring there, too, the earth spongy and damp as it was down near the Hudson. I knew how he had looked, a tall, thin, young man, walking across the thawing ground, thinking hard about his life to come.

Part Three

When the weather was bad and the children were kept indoors, I sat with them on the floor of Benjamin's room, turning the glossy pages of a volume from his set of the *Book of Knowledge*. On drowsy afternoons as rain pattered against the windows or snow fell thickly, we mused over what we found explained and illustrated in these books. Commandingly, they scorned or accepted facts as they did food. When I thought of the numbed way in which I had swallowed the information fed me in school, it seemed comical to me that I bothered to argue with these children for whom dislike of something meant that it wasn't so. She didn't want the sky to be black forever and ever, Lisa exclaimed tearfully after I had read a long paragraph about the darkness of space. Benjamin pressed a page of the book between his fingers. A tree couldn't be sliced thin enough to make paper, he asserted, crankily insisting I turn the page at once.

One evening, Mrs. Miller placed before me on the kitchen table a loosely-bound book. In its coarse paper, I could see actual slivers of wood. I started to call Benjamin, childishly gratified at the thought of confounding his stubbornness with proof of what we had read about the manufacture of paper. I suddenly perceived what I was looking at; it was not a photograph of random sticks of wood but of people peering between slats of a shed blotched with tar as black as the sockets of their eyes.

Mrs. Miller was staring at me fixedly. "Turn," she said.

The next picture was of a pyramid of children's bodies in front of which stood an American soldier, his hand on his forehead as though to shield his eyes.

"Belsen," said Mrs. Miller, her voice barely audible.

Soon the newspapers were filled with photographs of death camps. At breakfast, the Millers read a newspaper thrown against the door each morning by a boy on a bicycle. In the evening, Mr. Miller brought home a late edition. It was a gray spring. The humid air carried a smell of earth into the house as the Millers sat silently, Mrs. Miller reading passages in the paper Mr. Miller passed across the table to her after he had marked them with his pen. Each evening, after I had gathered up the papers to put out with the garbage, I read what Mr. Miller had checked. A one-paragraph story caught my eye. It concerned a retired clockmaker who had undertaken to repair the bomb-damaged clock on a town hall in Germany. He had been drawn into the works and killed. There was no more than that.

The clock works must have been huge, must have started so violently, so suddenly into motion that they had begun to consume the old man before he realized what was happening to him. Perhaps the people of the town had gathered on the street below, looking up at the clock, waiting for a sign that it was working again. All the while the old man, caught in the wheels, was dying.

.   .   .

I felt obliged to return to the flat in the barrio. Papá was standing in the kitchen drinking coffee. He was moving, he said. He had found a room further uptown. "It's only one room," he noted as he wrote out the address. I would stay at the Millers' on my night off, I said. He looked momentarily uneasy. "I didn't intend to suggest you couldn't visit," he said.

I wanted to tell him that I didn't care what he was suggesting but I only muttered that I had some clothes to pack.

"By the way," he began softly. "Did you happen to see among Fefita's things those two silver forks? You remember? I was fond of them. They seem to have disappeared. Carreno was a low type . . . I thought he might have—"

"—No," I interrupted firmly. "I've not seen them."

"Well, good luck then."

"Can you tell me where Maura went?"

"I know nothing of that old bitch," he replied.

I snatched up the scrap of paper with his address and started to leave the kitchen.

"Yes! That old bitch!" he repeated with ferocity.

"She was a comfort to Mamá."

"She weakened her."

I glanced at his polished shoes, his starched shirt. I thought of him alone, paying attention to himself, nursing his rage.

"These women who slink about the place," he muttered.

We parted without saying good-bye.

I stopped at Mrs. Alegre's flat on the second floor. She leaned against her door, an elderly woman with bald patches on her skull. She was drunk, and she smiled at me loosely and intimately. Maura hadn't been able to find a room, she told me. Maybe she had gone to New Jersey. She'd turn up one of these days.

I walked quickly to the subway, oppressed by the barrio as though it still had some claim upon me. Maura had dropped into darkness. There was nothing left that mattered to me uptown except Ellen Dove, and she would soon be gone.

My father had brought us here, leaving behind him all that he'd disdained, Ofelia Mondragon, Malagita, his mother, so rich she could settle the question of who belonged in this world and who didn't.

Let him have this waste of streets! One room would suit him. Without the grieving presence of my mother, he would have nothing to recall to him that he hadn't made a choice, only evaded one.

.   .   .

In the heart of the winter, I abandoned my trips to New York. On my days off, I listened to the radio the Millers had given me for my birthday or, when the family was out, took a book from Mr. Miller's shelves. Most of his books were about plant management—he was vice-president of a small company that made radio components—but there were a few novels, among them one about a poor Mexican community in California. I didn't like it, but it aroused a new appetite in me. I went on to a long novel which I kept under my bed, the awareness of its presence drawing me through the day to the moment when I could close my door and read.

"How do you like *Gone With the Wind*?" Mr. Miller asked me one evening.

They had searched my room. I turned my back on his encouraging smile. Why did it matter to them what I read? My heart fluttered with apprehension. The book was all right, I said coldly. The next morning I replaced it on the shelf. It wasn't until years later, after I had seen the movie which had been made from it, that I learned how the story ended.

I had liked finding my place in the evenings, reading until my eyes grew heavy. Like the heroine, I, too, fell in love with a man made unobtainable by his uprightness and perfection.

I wore Mrs. Miller's discarded clothes. "Here's a blouse that would look good on you," she had said to me one morning. "It doesn't suit me." I wanted the blouse but I didn't want to take it. She sensed that. "Don't be silly," she murmured. "Take what you can get."

Occasionally, she gave me something new she had changed her mind about after wearing it a few times. "Too late to return it," she would say lightly. I marvelled at such extravagance, and in time, I got over my reluctance to benefit from it.

She watched sharply over my work, holding up the shirts I ironed, looking through each window to make sure I'd not left cloudy patches, running her hands over the surfaces of tables. More and more she came to sit with me while I ate my meals in the kitchen, speaking to me of her worries about Lisa and Benjamin, about the people who were moving into a new apartment house a few blocks away, people, she said, who were "not like us."

"Like me?" I asked.

She looked shocked. At my question? Had it balked some ritual unthinking movement of her mind?

"Oh, Luisa—you *are* like us!" She'd flushed at her lie.

Near the end of the time I worked for them, Mrs. Miller began to confide in me more intimately, but in such a roundabout way she might have been giving me instructions on the universal nature of man. "Their heads fill up with business," she said. "They don't grow up—they become competent."

As though ashamed of these clues she gave me of regret and dissatisfaction, she was always more rigorous the next day in her attention to what I was doing; she would recite the day's tasks to me as I stood in the kitchen, a recitation that had in it a touch of the dry, rebuking tone of a classroom.

I knew they were fond of me. I saw it in their faces—relief, too—when they returned from an evening out to find me drowsing in their living room, waiting up to tell them the children had eaten well—I always told them that—and had gone to sleep when they should have. It could only have been fondness of the narrowest sort. My life did not intrude upon them. I was a pair of hands, the household's nurse.

I wasn't ungrateful. I guessed that in the scale of things they treated me well. I was no harried girl hurrying through the night carrying leftovers to a mud hut. At some point, I told them my mother had been a servant, and yes, Malagita had been exotic—leaving them to put what meaning they would to that word. I kept to myself memories of an earthenfloored room flooded with moonlight and the scent of jasmine, a room utterly unlike any room of theirs, undefended against the outdoors by locks and jammed-down windows, where I had risen from my bed and taken only a few steps to find myself on an endless road, the mountain rising in the distance toward a vast sky. I whispered the Spanish words— *jazmín, luz de la luna, campo,* as fervently as Mamá had once said her rosary.

Mr. Miller's company was diversifying, he said, and had bought a plant in Delaware where he would have to move himself and his family. Alarm at the coming change transformed the placid, uneventful days. The children shammed illness. They fought with each other until they fell exhausted into their beds. The Millers bowed to their tyranny, giving in to every whim as though to forbid them anything at all would bring down their house. It was not their children's hatred they were so afraid of, I thought, but of their own of their children.

I saw my own fate fly ahead to Delaware joined forever with theirs. I couldn't go with them. When I told them so, Mrs. Miller looked at me as though I'd broken her heart.

"The children," she breathed, "they'll suffer. They're more attached to you than they are to my mother, their own grandma."

"Mr. Miller said the house he found is very nice," I told her. "The school is only a block away."

"What does all that matter!" she cried with a passion that seemed to throw away her whole life.

"It matters," I replied with sudden impatience. I retreated to my room.

When we said good-bye, when I stood by the front door with my suitcase among their packing cases, and I saw the distress and uncertainty on Mr. Miller's face, my spirit quailed at all our unknown destinies.

"Luisa, what will you do now?" Mr. Miller asked sombrely.

"I'll stay with a friend's mother for a time," I replied, "until I find a new job."

"I've written a letter for you," Mrs. Miller said. "You'll need a reference." I took the white envelope from her. Lisa wrapped her arms around me. She had grown so much, her head now rested on my chest. I bent down to kiss the snarled, curly hair that she had not allowed us to brush for days. I heard a wordless exclamation from Mrs. Miller. She looked at me a long time, then bent her head forward until her cheek rested against mine. "We'll miss you," she said.

She told me she'd written down their new address and put it in with the reference. "You'll write to us?" I nodded. I walked down the cement path, turning once to look back. The children were watching me, each standing in front of the narrow window on either side of the door. I knew I would not see them again.

On the train to the city, I read the letter. It said I was dependable, responsible, honest, and competent. It said I had worked as a maid for two years and never given cause for complaint, and that I was very understanding with children. It recommended me highly. It was the first good report card I'd gotten.

.   .   .

"Where are you staying?" Papá asked me.

"With Ellen Dove's mother. I can stay there until I get a job."

The room he had found for himself faced the west as had the hospital waiting room. He was a changed man from the one I had seen the night Mamá had died; he had put on weight, there was faint color on his cheeks although that may have been only the reflected glow from the setting sun. The window glass looked liquid, a down-running watery trembling. The giant letters on the Jersey shore, *Jack Frost Sugar*, suddenly lit up.

In a corner stood a carefully made-up cot, a light blanket wrapped around its thin mattress like a bandage. On one of two pegs near the door there was a hanger with a dark blue jacket, the one he wore to work. A cup drained on a small counter. The old armchair was pulled close to the window. Within reach of it stood a large record-playing machine, its doors open, revealing the spines of albums of music.

Papá had left everything of our barrio life behind him. This is what he had always wanted, this bare, clean room. I felt a grudging sympathy.

"Do you need money?" he asked, lifting the top of the record-player and peering into it.

"I've saved . . . I don't need any."

"I'm sorry you have no formal training." He glanced at me, then quickly away.

"But I have."

"Maid's training," he said.

"I prefer it."

"Do you?" He lifted the arm of the player and lowered it carefully. When he looked back at me, I thought I saw a glimmer of interest in his face.

"It's my fault," he said. "If I had taken care of my life, if I'd been firm and seen to things . . ."

"I've been to see Uncle Federico," I said. "I thought he might know of work."

Papá gestured toward the window. "I've grown fond of that sign," he said, then added ironically, "After all, is it any less grand than the pyramids of Egypt?"

"He says he'll ask for work for me among the restaurant clients," I spoke deliberately as if to a child.

"He's too dim-witted to be able to help you," Papá stated.

"He helped you, and Maura."

"He opened the kitchen door and Maura ran in like a rat, and like a rat, ran out again."

Sweat suddenly broke out on my forehead. "You're so cruel," I said in such a low voice I wasn't sure he heard me.

"You don't understand," he said quietly. "I can see that. You don't realize that I'm sorry. I've learned you can't do much about anyone's life. Not your own either. One is carried along, stranded here or there. One day, you find yourself stranded in a place you want to be. That's all. Accident, chance, luck. I have a little money now. Like you, I've saved. You can have some of it. It might help you to become stranded in a place you'd be happier in."

The room had grown dark. It looked smudged, less clean, too empty. I tried to form words, to say—thank you. My lips were frozen. His offer tasted bitter to me, not water but some medicine for thirst.

In the voice of his new, strange serenity, he said again, "I'm sorry," and he leaned toward the record player and took an album from the shelf.

As I closed his door and went down the hall, I heard music, a woman's voice singing, heavy, languorous, in a language I didn't recognize.

.　　　　　　　　　.　　　　　　　　　.

"That isn't what I'd wear for an interview, Luisa," Mrs. Dove said tentatively. "It's not the right thing."

I glanced down at the rough tweed skirt of a suit Mrs. Miller had given me. The shoulders were too tight but it fitted me well enough, I had thought.

"You look very nice," she said, "but the woman you're going to see might get the wrong idea."

She wanted to let it rest at that with no further explanation. I started to take our breakfast dishes from the table. She took them from my hands, saying, "I'll do that. Save your strength."

During the week I had spent with her, she had treated me with a distant religious benevolence, a formality, that had enlarged the small rooms. Even about the tweed suit, I thought I had heard a devout note. Once I had seen her disheveled by anguish. She had recovered herself, yet as though the convulsion of her sorrow at Thad's death was still rocking below the surface, there was a kind of disarrangement about her. There was a look of absence on her face, her gloves were soiled, strands of hair escaped the pins she pushed so sternly into the knot of hair at her neck. She ate her meals as though it was a hard and hopeless duty.

I glanced at the scrap of paper on which Mrs. Dove's Madam had written the name of the woman I was to be interviewed by, an actress and grandniece of hers. I would have to leave or I would be late. As I started toward the door, Mrs. Dove called out, "Wait!"

I paused. She was uncapping a tube of cream and rubbing it into her hands. I could smell almonds. When she looked at me, her face was transformed by a knowing, derisive smile. She held up her glistening hands and waved them. "You're a young white girl. They'll see you different from how they see me—but not so different as you might think. You're looking for servant's work. Don't push clothes like that in front of their eyes."

"The woman I worked for gave me this suit," I protested.

"To wear out of her sight," declared Mrs. Dove.

I changed my clothes and put on an old wool skirt Mamá had made for me, and a brown cotton shirt. As I walked past her to the door, Mrs. Dove reached out and caught my hand, holding it a minute.

"Disguises," she said. "You recall my boy's joke about disguises? Although you can't live if you're not seen plain by someone. I believe God sees me plain. I don't care about anything else. I hope I didn't hurt your feelings." She released my hand. "You'll be all right," she said. She was the only person who had not questioned my decision about becoming a servant. I wondered about that.

.   .   .

Eloise Grant from Hollywood, in New York to act in a play, asked me if I had seen her in the movies. I looked covertly around the living room of the apartment she had explained she had sublet, a room in which the entire Miller house could have fitted. I saw huge locked cabinets black with layers of wax, scuffed leather couches and armchairs resting on an enormous stained rug. On the wall hung a gilt-framed mirror in whose murky, dusty depths, I thought I saw storm clouds forming. In what way could such a place be made what Mrs. Miller had liked to call "shipshape"?

Miss Grant, smiling, awaited my answer.

"No," I blurted out.

She laughed. "One in a million," she said. "That's cute."

"I don't go to movies often," I explained, somewhat abashed.

"Don't worry about it. I'm not vain. I don't know what my great-aunt told you. But I'm strictly temporary. Plays die suddenly like people. The second it closes, that's it, and I'm off to the coast." She paused and scowled at a dark oil painting of a man on his knees praying to a skull. "Just the place to have a crack-up," she said. Had I been hired?

"Please call me Eloise," she said.

I called her Miss Grant. At her frequent parties, I wore the short black uniform with a white starched apron she had bought for me. In the top button of the uniform, just below my chin, she would place a red rosebud. The bartenders were out-of-work actors, slender, radiant young men who closely observed the male guests and who often complimented me on my hair, my figure, even my legs; their impish smiles meant to tell me not to take what they said to heart.

In the mornings, Miss Grant made up her face while her first cigarette of the day burned down in an ashtray on the dressing table, her own, she explained to me, which she'd had shipped to New York from Hollywood. "When I look into that particular mirror," she avowed, "I know exactly where I am."

She would throw down her mascara brush and walk naked around the huge apartment, make phone calls, drink coffee, suddenly fling herself onto the sofa and grab up one of the dozens of magazines she sent me out to buy. I lined up her beautiful shoes in rows in her closet. They had been made by hand in colors she taught me to name, fawn, apple green, oxblood, cerise, French blue. "They have destroyed my poor tootsies," she said complacently.

She was usually asleep when I arrived. The silent apartment was brooding, smelling of the brandy-soaked fruit Miss Grant loved to eat and had delivered to her from some fancy food store, perhaps the very one where my father worked. Several times, I found evidence that a man had spent the night, the butt of a cigar, or on a table, extra glasses and plates on which the rich decay lingered of a meal sent up from a nearby delicatessen, and once a raincoat dropped over the back of a chair, its sleeves touching the floor. I left it there. It was gone by the time I started vacuuming.

Maura had made up her face as though it was a photograph she was tinting. Miss Grant studied herself a long time. With a slow, steady hand, she would transform her rather plain features into those of a woman who looked like a model in a magazine advertisement. Her distinction was her forehead, exceptionally high, white and unlined, a dome, below which her face went about its work of expressing the impulses that struck her continually. Her face throbbed like a heart. Above it rose the cool-looking lifeless forehead like the shell of an egg.

Her play ran for nine months. A few weeks after it closed, she packed her crocodile suitcases, her steamer trunk that opened like a great book, and returned to Hollywood, leaving me with two nearly empty bottles of French perfume, a cream-colored, watered-silk affair she had called a cocktail dress with an enormous artificial flower at its neckline, and a different view of the uses of money than I had learned from the Millers.

In the furnished room on 125th Street, a block or so from Riverside Drive where I had moved a few days after I began to work for Miss Grant, I tried on the dress. Its sleeves reached just below my elbows; its hem stopped several inches above my knees. I bundled it up, intending to throw it away. Instead, I kept it for months until its useless beauty oppressed me so much, I put it in the garbage one morning on my way out to work. Its intimation of glamour had faded away like the magic of a charm invoked too often, too frivolously, and not meant for me in any case.

Miss Grant had given me an introduction to a business woman, an old friend of hers, whose small apartment on the east side I cleaned once a week, ironing her blouses and handkerchiefs in the morning, sweeping and dusting in the afternoon. From Miss Doris Mathes, whom I saw twice, once to be interviewed, once when a severe cold kept her at home, I had gotten another job, two days cleaning and occasional help with dinner parties, with the Geldens, a middle-aged couple who were acquaintances of hers.

I shopped for my employers, occasionally served meals, changed their linen, got to know dry cleaners and Chinese laundrymen, took telephone messages, played their radios, poured Lysol into their toilet bowls, and from their soiled sheets and plates, their wastebaskets and garbage cans, found traces of their human passage through the nights and days from which I was able to deduce their habits, their pleasures and aversions, even their pretentions. Rising to their apartments in the service elevators to which I was ordered by doormen, I felt the kind of repose that comes, I imagined, during the recovery from a long illness.

When I had gone to see Uncle Federico to ask him if he knew of any work for me, he had told me the final news of Nana's fate had not been determined, that it was only realistic to assume she was dead.

Although he blustered and boasted about his ability to find a job for me, I guessed nothing would come of it. I asked him if he had ever heard from Maura. She had not told me why she had left the employ of the Salamanca. He shook his head and shrugged. "These people," he said, "they don't fit in. Of the village. Do you understand? They have the habits of village life. Miss Cruz was like a Red Indian in the kitchen."

I observed that she had been born in Havana and had grown up there.

"Compared to the great city we live in," he said, smiling tolerantly, "Havana itself is a mere village."

Before I left, Federico thrust a silver-framed photograph of Atilio toward me. I could see that he was no longer plump but lean and handsome in a brutal way. He was attending classes in a special technical school, Uncle Federico related, the fees all paid for by the government. "Microelectronics," he pronounced voluptuously, gazing up at the ceiling. "A new field, Luisita, the most important of all. Do you know of transistors?"

"Tell her about the marriage," urged Aunt Aurelia.

"Yes, yes. The marriage. To an American girl. Do you recall my speaking of the priest who dines at the Salamanca? The one whose car I bought years ago? It is his niece, a good Catholic girl, of course, and Irish, very beautiful—"

"—pretty," interrupted Aurelia.

I imagined Atilio ascending the long body of an American girl, pressing his stinging, heated flesh against her like a mustard plaster. They invited me to come to the wedding. I said I'd try, knowing I wouldn't. "*Mira!*" Aurelia cried out to me, running heavily up the hall as I was about to leave. She was carrying a lavender silk dress in her arms, cradling it like an infant.

"The Mamá's wedding gown," she murmured raptly. She hardly took notice of my admiring words or the slow closing of the door.

My work, done and every day undone—was the dull, mechanical

movement of a treadle. I dreamed of another life. I wondered if I had become the ghost of the plantation, if the people of the village, walking along the dirt roads at twilight, gazing up at the slowly darkening sky, would, sensing my presence, shiver and retreat indoors. Yet it was the very monotony of my servant's life that freed me to return in my thoughts to Malagita.

"I have allergies. See to the dust on the venetian blind slats," Miss Mathes wrote in one of her curt notes. Another said: "I like things to be streamlined. Make hospital corners on the bed." Streamlined, I muttered, a new intrusive word which evoked moving metal parts, trains or airplanes, but not her dingy little apartment, its floors hidden by a brown carpet the color of dried mud.

Dwight Gelden, the plump, eleven-year-old son of the Geldens, let himself in with his key after school and delivered his mother's messages to me. "Ma says clean the refrigerator today," he told me. Wherever I worked, he found a seat from which to observe me. In one hand he carried a book, his finger serving as a marker. In the other, he carried food. He ate steadily until his mother came home from the adoption agency where she worked. When we heard her key in the door, Dwight stuffed his cheeks and fled to the bathroom.

"Where is he?" she would demand. "Eating? In the bathroom?"

When Dwight emerged, flushed and furtive-looking, she would smile. "Did you perform well in your history test?" she might ask him.

The cold, finicking fashion with which she behaved toward me roused up a desire to go against her. I deliberately misplaced objects or left undone small tasks. On one occasion, the powerful maternal ambition she felt toward Dwight burst forth from her. "He performed beautifully last night at the dinner party," she said as I was putting away the housedress I wore to clean. She seemed to wait for my confirmation as if, while I had been serving the meal, I had observed only her son.

One afternoon, I discovered a comic book hidden beneath Dwight's mattress. As I stood there holding it, I heard a movement at the bedroom door. Dwight was standing at the threshold, staring at me, his round, dimpled fists pressed against his belly, panic on his face. As he watched me silently, I put the comic book back where I'd found it.

In winter I went to work and returned home in darkness. The brief cold days, the cloud-webbed skies through which on rare occasions the pale winter sun slid, helped to enclose me in my labor. I ate my supper standing up at the sink. I washed my clothes and hung them to dry on a cord I'd stretched across the small bathtub, and I washed hurriedly, seldom glancing in the mirror which hung above one narrow shelf. It held a bottle of aspirin, a tube of Tangee lipstick, and a can of Mavis talcum powder. I didn't use the talcum. I sniffed it because it evoked, not Maura, who had covered herself with it from her neck to her feet, but Mamá watching her, absently smiling and clutching her bathrobe around herself as a shower of powder fell through the air.

When the days grew longer, when daylight lingered in the sky as I walked up the slope of 125th Street to the large tenement where I lived, I was afraid of the hours that would have to pass before darkness would descend. Darkness and cold had made me a shelter. It was blowing away.

I went to the movies or took long walks along the Drive and Broadway, often not returning to my room until past midnight. The fixed lines of routine were dissolving in the growing warmth which brought a pale green haze to the park beside the river. I strained to comprehend the commotion of my spirit. I felt against my face the damp, light spring wind. It was like a voice speaking indistinctly in a room to which I couldn't find a door. A dull, intermittent grief for those gone forever was pressed aside by a sharp fresh grief—but for what? Standing on the Drive, I looked across the Hudson at the huge inclines and peaks of an amusement park roller coaster, an illegible scrawl against the sky. I saw the Jack Frost Sugar sign go on like an expelled breath of light. Was my father standing at his window, listening to his music, seeing what I was seeing?

I felt faint and leaned forward to support myself against the stone wall which separated the sidewalk from the narrow park which sloped to the river. Where had Maura gone among the miles of streets? I gasped at the suddenness with which a longing for Mamá's presence took hold of me. For a second, I thought I heard myself call out for her.

I couldn't sleep. As I lay in my bed, my legs twitching with exhaustion, an enormous idea came to me, so thrilling that I rose and fled to the window to press my face against the glass already cool with morning.

I would return to San Pedro. I would save money. From now on, I would live like a nun. I would work on weekends, at night, anytime anyone wanted me. No more wandering through the streets where peddlers parked their barrows of damaged sheets and cheap sweaters. A nun didn't need such things.

Jaded, clammy with fatigue, I washed the slats of Miss Mathes' venetian blinds. The grime I rinsed from them settled beneath my fingernails. It didn't matter. It was a token of my intention.

I always needed money. My clothes were a jumble of barrow bargains and hand-outs from my employers. I would manage. I took a discarded mayonnaise jar home from the Geldens. I washed it and dried it and put it beneath my bed. At the end of two months, I had collected three dollars in it.

My exhilaration passed. It would take years to save enough for my passage to San Pedro. But a possibility had taken root in my mind. My life was touched with a difference.

In May, I found a letter from Ellen Dove in my mailbox. She had tracked me down through her mother to Eloise Grant. It had been months, she wrote, and she wanted so much to see me. I went out at once to a public telephone on Broadway and dialed the number she had written down. "Not here," a voice said crankily. I went back to my room and waited as long as I could bear to. On the fifth try, I reached Ellen. The fourth time I'd called, an angry female voice had shouted, "Get outa my face! You think I got nothing to do but answer this fucking phone?"

"Hello," said Ellen's familiar voice.

"It's me, Luisa," I said so weakly that she cried out my name twice. "It's all right," I croaked. "Just that—I'm so glad."

The next Saturday, I went to an address off Amsterdam on 143d Street, to a brownstone house with a high, weathered stoop. Ellen opened the door to me. We embraced like two people who had thought they'd lost each other forever while the landlady, an enormous Negro woman, stood down the hall and watched us, her expression unreadable.

"I told her you were Spanish but all she sees is white," Ellen whispered as we went up the stairs to her tiny room. Later, she told me the woman had been a famous blues singer in her day but that arthritis had crippled her so she couldn't walk up a flight of stairs. There were other boarders besides Ellen in the house; everyone pitched in to clean the upper floors and shop for the landlady.

She was thinner than I'd ever seen her. Her face had the starved look of someone who never gets enough sleep.

"I hardly see Momma," she told me. "I have so much to do. She was angry with me for a long time. It's better now. Last week, she even talked about Thad. She said despair was the greatest sin and she was committing it every day. She looked at me like I could tell her what to do."

I saw Ellen whenever she had time left over from her classes and studying. One evening, as I started upstairs to her room, I glimpsed the landlady, who had grudgingly let me in, through the open door of her room. There was music coming from a radio standing on a table next to an empty liquor bottle. She swayed and stepped forward, then backward, shifting sideways liquidly, her huge body keeping exact time to the music.

Ellen didn't ask me about my jobs. It was as if I had a sickness about which it would be indelicate to speak. We talked about her work. I watched her face more than I listened to her words as though I might learn from the intensity of feeling that gave her eyes such a light what it was that drove her so.

She urged me to come to a gathering—not exactly a meeting, she said—of some friends and classmates of hers. Most of them were students at City College, and they met every few weeks, when they could, to speak of things important to them.

"Now don't always say no," she begged.

"I don't," I protested.

"Will you come?"

"All right."

She laughed and snapped her fingers. "Good!" she cried. "I'll get you yet!"

I don't recall much of what was talked about in the room of the Negro student, Julian. I sat on the floor among the others; there were eleven of them, men and women, most of them Negroes. I could feel their consciousness of my presence in the determined way they avoided looking at me. But I stared at them, at their hands and clothes, the way they smoked their cigarettes. Julian gestured fiercely. Negro factory workers, welcomed during the war into industry everywhere in the country, were being dropped back into the pits of American life, he said. Ellen watched him as though he were speaking only to her.

I went to other such evenings; it was really Ellen I came to see in the various rooms we met in where people struggled to change their lives with speeches. But perhaps, because the charged atmosphere of those hours—intermittently crackling with talk that went off like a string of firecrackers lit and flung into the quiet of a hot, still summer evening—was so unlike that of my subterranean days, I began to look forward to them. People greeted me, although distantly. I remained anonymous as I did during a dinner party where I served guests and later heard the murmur of their conversation from the dining room while I plunged my hands into soapy water and washed up the dishes. Julian never spoke to me.

"I'm involved with him," Ellen told me in a severe voice. More softly, she added, "Sometimes I forget Thad."

I waited, afraid she would say more, afraid she wouldn't. I made an effort not to stare at her narrow bed with its worn chenille coverlet.

"It's not what I imagined," she said. "It's more terrible. But better, too." She laughed suddenly. "Don't say anything," she said.

She didn't refer to Julian in any special way again. I watched for signs of pregnancy. I asked her, "Aren't you afraid?" when she was speaking about Mrs. Dove's failing health. She frowned. "God, yes. What's going to happen if she gets seriously sick?"

Poor people, she went on, had no reserve of money for sickness. For an instant, I thought I heard a note of gratification in her voice, almost of triumph.

"I meant pregnant," I said. "Don't you worry about that?"

"Haven't you ever heard of contraception?" she asked irritably. Before I could reply, she began telling me about a program she had learned about at New York University for minority students that provided complete tuition. With a busy, fussy insistence, her hands gripped in her lap, she seemed to be burying my question beneath stones. Sometimes Ellen was poisoned with information.

Several weeks later, despite my resolve not to bring up Julian, even indirectly, I found myself asking her if she was going to marry him.

"You're such a little girl!" she said angrily. Then she cried, wiping away her tears with her knuckles. "I didn't mean that," she said, her voice quavering. "It was unfair. But you want me to tell you something I can't tell you. Nobody can tell you."

Maura had said something like that, too.

.   .   .

There were no more gatherings during the summer. Ellen got a job working in the kitchen of a resort hotel in upstate New York, and I didn't see her until the fall. By then Eloise Grant had left New York and I was looking for more work. When I found a day's job with an old couple on Central Park West, I had to change my other days around. Miss Mathes didn't care what day I came, but Mrs. Gelden was affronted.

"We can't reorder our lives at a moment's notice," she said. "Just for your convenience."

Did she really believe it was a matter of convenience? Her dark eyes were narrowed with resentment. Her hair in its tight knot drew her skin up toward her forehead.

"We're due some consideration," she went on. "There's Dwight. He expects you on Fridays. It will disturb him, such a change, even though, of course, he's such a well-adjusted boy. I've never asked you to do woodwork. A child must have consistency. Now I have to ask Professor Stevens to give him his music lesson on a different day. Then the Professor will have to change his entire schedule, I'm sure. I can't have Dwight coming home to an empty apartment. Mr. Gelden can't possibly send his shirts to the laundry. He expects them to be ironed on Fridays. The starch those laundries use gives him a rash. You know how delicate his health is. If there are too many shirts for you to iron—"

I couldn't stand it. "I need the work," I interrupted, raising my voice. "Miss Eloise Grant left the city and I have to fill that day now."

"Eloise Grant, the actress?" she asked in surprise. "I didn't know you worked for her. You didn't tell me that." She looked at me with a certain interest. When she spoke again, her voice had softened somewhat although there was always something metallic, hard, about it. "I can't see why that couple has to have you Fridays. You said they're home all the time."

"Their daughter's job takes her out of town that day," I explained.

"They're both very frail. She doesn't want them to be alone when she's out of reach."

She sniffed and went to her closet to get her coat.

"Well," she said, sighing, shutting her pocketbook with a snap. "I suppose we'll just have to work it out."

After she left, I seized the dustmop and dusting cloths. Like Ellen, I had my lessons to learn. A servant can disrupt the order of her employer's life only in dire emergencies, but it is her own connivance in bringing them about that is the accusation made against her. A servant's face must be blank. I shouldn't have shouted at her and let her hear my private voice.

I didn't eat the soup she had left me but went out to a cafeteria nearby. Sitting there in a booth, at midday, I suddenly imagined myself to be a person who could go into coffee shops when she felt like it, whose afternoons belonged to her, who had money in her pocketbook and could stroll along streets boisterous with autumn wind and bright with sunlight.

     .   .   .

Ellen and her friends were to hold their first fall meeting on the ground floor of an apartment house on Morningside Heights. I stood for a few moments outside the yellow brick building looking out over Harlem. I felt a powerful disinclination to see her and the others, particularly Julian. They came together out of a sense of common experience and purpose; their anger could speak. These embattled few had each other. Because Ellen had asked me to, I had taken home with me, each time I had come, a few mimeographed sheets stapled together, their newspaper, and I had tried to read the accounts of administrative neglect of Negro students, their persecution by teachers, advice on what recourse they had, and sometimes a short poem of lament and angry resolution. My mind had wandered; I had remembered the rough pink sheets of songs Mamá had so prized and Papá had so scorned.

To please Ellen, I had come tonight. I didn't think I would come again. As I stood there watching the dark fill up the eastern sky, I heard laughter and turned to look through the window of the apartment. I saw Ellen in a dimly lit room, Julian standing next to her. A white man was speaking, one hand holding a cigarette and gesturing. He was older than the others. I could just make out his light hair, his high, narrow forehead. Ellen was listening, but Julian's head was bent over his pipe. He was scraping it out with a small knife whose blade shone as he turned it violently to and fro. Sometimes the man looked down. I guessed someone sitting on the floor had spoken to him or asked a question. People often sat on the floor, even when there were plenty of chairs.

He looked through the window and saw me. Ellen, following the direction of his glance, began to wave. Reluctantly, I went in.

In the room, people were moving about and talking. I had missed Mr. Greer's talk, Ellen told me reproachfully, and she knew it would have been especially interesting to me. He had been auditing a class she took on constitutional law, and she and he had become acquainted. She'd asked him to come and speak to the group. I didn't pay attention to what she said. I was looking at Mr. Greer's mouth, his thin blonde hair that curled around his ears, and the tweed suit he was wearing, not unlike the tweed of the suit Mrs. Miller had given me and which I had rehemmed yesterday evening. She took my arm and led me to him. "Tom, this is my friend, Luisa de la Cueva. Tom has been living in Ecuador this past year," she said, turning to me. "He's written a book on American business interests there and what they're up to."

"It isn't finished," Greer said quickly. It isn't finished, I repeated silently, trying to name to myself the quality of his voice.

"Luisa grew up on a sugar plantation," Ellen went on. "She knows all about Yankee exploitation."

"The plantation was owned by a Spanish lady," I said.

"I'd be interested to hear about it," he said, looking at me steadily. There was a kind of roar from Julian in which I could make out Ellen's name. She went to him at once.

"Are you a student?" Mr. Greer asked.

"I'm a maid."

He was silent so long, I wondered if I'd managed to end our conversation and should move on.

"Temporary?" he asked at last.

I laughed without knowing why. "I don't think so," I replied. "But you're not a student," I added boldly.

"I've been one here and there," he said.

What could he mean? Here and there—the wide-ranging world. In one swoop, he had claimed learning and dismissed it. I grew aware that I was leaning toward him; I saw a slight flaring of surprise on his face. I moved a step away. I tried to repress the smile I could feel forming on my lips, tried to look at him sternly like a person with strong, ready convictions.

"The book I'm writing," he began, his unblinking eyes fixed on my face so closely, I felt he could detect the faintest involuntary movements of my flesh, "actually, it's a study of cocoa plantations. But I'd like to hear, very much like to hear about sugar cane. How it was in Cuba. It was Cuba?"

I shook my head. "San Pedro," I said, and at his blank look, added, "It's a little island. But not at all—" I broke off and looked at Julian across the room. "It wasn't the way they talk here—my life."

"That's what I would be interested in," he said. "The human side. I can make up my own rhetoric."

He waited. Speech abandoned me. He touched my hand lightly. I heard only dimly the voices of other people. "Could I telephone you?" he asked.

"I don't have a telephone," I said.

"I have," he said. He took a pencil and a notepad from a jacket pocket and wrote down a number, carefully tore out the page and held it out to me. When I continued to stand there motionless, he reached out and took my hand and closed it around the paper. His skin was dry and warm.

"Were you standing out there on the sidewalk a long time?" he asked gravely.

"I think so."

"Are you going to call me?"

"Yes," I said. His hand dropped away. A man from a group which had been speaking together nearby approached him with a self-important scowl, his mouth opening in anticipation of whatever he was going to say. "Yes," I said again.

"*Hasta luego*," whispered Mr. Greer.

After several weeks had passed, I couldn't recall the words of my brief exchange with Tom Greer, remembering only that he had said something to me in Spanish, a commonplace phrase his whisper had made eloquent. His features grew less distinct although there were moments which took me by surprise when I could see clearly his thin, rather childishly curling light hair and the narrowness of his skull, and the way he had held it, poised and motionless, as an animal does when it raises its head to listen—an antelope or a fox—alerted by some sound.

I had no reason to telephone him. I imagined having to remind him of where we had met, my voice faltering.

Yet the emotion I had felt in his presence would not leave me; it had enveloped me like the garment of a religious order, both a material thing and an emblem of unearthly things—just as, when he had leaned toward me, speaking, he had been so densely there yet intimating, beyond that room, a world not known to me. When his hand had enclosed mine, he had seemed to gather me up entirely.

One morning the urgent desire to see him again died away. I worked that day with a light heart. But at night when I lay down in my bed and turned out the light, I was overcome by such anxious, bitter loneliness that I cried out.

I would have to call him. He had asked me to. It was only a telephone call. It was nothing. I would hear his voice and then I would be all right again. I would do it in the morning. Nothing would come of a phone call. I got up and turned on the light and walked about. The bed was barely disarranged; my room held little. There was no human brightness in the room, only an indifferently wrought order. I have been ill, I thought. This long meditation on Thomas Greer has made me ill.

Just after seven o'clock the next morning, I stopped at a public telephone booth on Broadway, the same one from which I had called Ellen months ago. I knew I had only enough courage for one attempt. If he answered, I would simply remind him he had asked me to call. Or I might inquire after his book.

I didn't know what I would ask him. I entered the booth wondering fleetingly if I would have felt such apprehension if I had ever entered a confessional box. I knew his number by heart and I dialed it. He answered at the third ring.

"Hello," Mr. Greer said.

"This is Luisa de la Cueva."

"I'd nearly given up hope," he said.

I could tell by his voice that I had waked him. He must be lying in bed, the bed linen crumpled around him.

"So had I," I said. I had to lean against the booth, such was the wave of joy, of hope, that washed over me.

.   .   .

Until I saw Thomas Greer through the apartment house window, I had not thought of my life ahead but always of a place and a time lost long ago, when the bounty of life had been charged with unreasoned meaning and where spirit had not been severed from body.

I told Tom the story of my life. I sat at the foot of our bed. He lay against the pillow, one leg extended toward me, the other bent, a sheet draped across his belly and groin. The lamp light shone on his raised thigh and its thin covering of fair hair, on the bones of his kneecap. I held his foot in my hand. Sometimes I leaned forward and rested my head against his leg. His hand caressed my face and hair. "Nana's hair grew like a scallop shell," I said.

Astounded, I traced the passage that had led me to him. All was chance, Papá had said. If Ellen's mother had been able to afford the Catholic school tuition, I would never have met her. If he had not been writing an article on constitutional law, he wouldn't have gone to Ellen's class at the university. Chance! I pressed my face against his pale skin. How could it have been chance?

He told me about himself, suddenly, abruptly, stories that were like secrets rashly offered, as we were coming home from a movie, or drinking coffee in a grill. The names of places and people often changed in his recitals. I might have questioned him, reminded him that the other week he had said he'd lived in Oregon during the first years of his life, not Washington, that he'd described his father as a sheep rancher, not a farmer, that an ulcer, not rheumatic fever, had kept him out of the army, but although I was puzzled, I came to believe that the inconsistencies in his telling were simply a reflection of the hard, bitter life he had led.

A life could not be tried. I gathered up his sorrowful, lonely years and learned them, freeing myself from any belief that depended on mere names and dates.

When I came home before he did, I looked at all the places where we had made love and had talked, and I said his name aloud to myself. Later, it seemed to me, we had held one long uninterrupted conversation the first year we lived together. My desire for his presence often had in it the shock of physical pain. I didn't know how much more severe it was going to get and I held my breath, knowing nothing could stop it.

Sometimes he would ask me—even though I'd told him many times —how long I'd stood out there on the sidewalk before I'd come into the room where Ellen's meeting had been taking place, and I saw that my strangeness, when I'd still been an unknown woman, continued to hold mystery for him.

"But you were thinking of not coming in at all, weren't you?" he asked.

"Yes. I didn't really want to."

He put his arms around me and slid his fingers through my hair and pressed my face against his neck. "And then you did," he said.

.   .   .

In 1949, we drove to a small town in Pennsylvania and were married by a Justice of the Peace. A few weeks later, when I could no longer bear the troubling sense of something left undone, I sent a note to my father telling him of my marriage. As I wrote, my scalp prickled faintly. When I had mailed the letter, when it slid away beyond my reach, I felt I'd given away my location to an enemy. His acknowledgment arrived a month later—an insured, carefully wrapped package containing a thick album of records, his wedding present to us. "Wagner!" exclaimed Tom, laughing. When I looked at him, not comprehending, he said, "A Nazi favorite." I put the album away, holding it gingerly—a joke shared by two men who didn't know each other.

Tom didn't finish his book on the cocoa plantations of Ecuador but we carried the manuscript with us wherever we moved. The pages yellowed, the box they were in filled up with crumbling rubber bands. For a while, I continued to work. Tom wrote articles and sold a few. When he was paid, the money astonished me, the amount seemed so immense. He wanted me to quit domestic work, saying I could get a job as a salesgirl or a receptionist in an office. Although I wanted to give way to him in all things, I refused.

"Why?" he demanded.

"We need the money."

"You're not answering me."

"It's easy work for me. And I don't have the clothes for the kinds of jobs you're talking about."

"We can manage some clothes."

"But it won't be for long, just until you—"

"I don't understand you," he interrupted. "Who wants to be a domestic if they can be something else?"

"Maybe that's why. Because I can't be anything else."

"You won't try," he said. He looked grim. I said no more. I couldn't. My thoughts were turbulent, inchoate. The brief exchange we had had stirred only the surface of my refusal. I sensed, as I imagined he had, a shapeless lump of obduracy in myself. But I could not lift it up into light. He didn't talk about it again. And as it turned out, shortly after that conversation he got a regular job on a company magazine published by a large coffee importing business.

Miss Mathes left me an extra week's pay and a brief note that wished me good luck. But Mrs. Gelden complained bitterly that my two weeks notice barely gave her time to find someone sensitive enough to understand her family's needs. Was that what I had been, I wondered? She was wearing a blouse I had pressed. What an odd, awful creature she was! I felt a flash of sympathy for her, that beleaguered general, guiding her wretched army, a sickly man, a fat, unlovely boy through the dangerous world. The Birnbaums, the elderly couple on Central Park West, seemed genuinely to regret my leaving, although it was only Mrs. Birnbaum who could say so. Mr. Birnbaum was, as his old wife said, ga-ga by then and bedridden. "You've been good to us," she said, clasping my hand in hers. They were soft as cotton and covered with the baby powder I had always bought for her at a neighborhood drugstore. "Age is the biggest surprise," she said.

Tom and I lived for several months in a borrowed apartment that belonged to a wealthy acquaintance of Tom's, Howard Thursby. Then we rented an apartment a block from Riverside Drive on the top floor of a house. It had once been the servant's quarters, the landlord told us. There was a fireplace in the living room; one of the small bedrooms had been converted into a kitchen. I was mad with happiness the first day we moved in. Tom bought a few small logs from a florist's shop, and we made a fire and sat in the living room among our few pieces of furniture. I'd been granted a new life.

One night, Tom brought Howard Thursby home for supper. I'd not met him before, and I was startled by his ragged raincoat, his dirty tennis shoes. I listened silently to them talking during supper, and after I had washed the dishes, I went to the bedroom and began to look through Tom's magazine. Thursby came and stood in the doorway and smiled at me. "What big eyes you have, Grandma," he said.

How agreeable the conversation of men was at a distance! I lay there, dozing, the magazine falling to the floor. Later, I heard the front door close then Tom calling me. I went out to him, smiling.

"Why did you leave?" he asked. "You acted like a maid."

I began to gather up glasses and ashtrays, unable to answer him. Why had I left? Men were supposed to be left alone together.

"Stop cleaning up," he demanded. He took a glass from my hand. "You're not the maid," he said patiently. I began to cry and he began to laugh. He shook me. He removed the pins from the coil of hair at my neck. In haste, we undressed. But there was no freedom, no repose in lovemaking for me that night. I was imprisoned in an inner darkness; I was trying to grasp hold of that elusive presence that ordered me to do this or that. My body grew weary. I was glad when love was done with.

We began to quarrel. Tom told me to stop buying such cheap cuts of meat—most of the time, he complained, he didn't know what the hell he was eating—and I must buy myself some clothes in a good store, not those holes on Broadway. Where had I managed to find that terrible lamp with the silk fringe? It was like the one Ellen's mother, Mrs. Dove had, I told him. It was time we invited people to dinner, he said.

I wondered why the lamp was terrible. I shuddered as I recalled the pink armchair Mamá had bought for Papá. I set myself the task of trying to learn a different way of seeing.

Ellen visited us several times. There was something wrong about our evenings together, a false ease, an intimacy that vanished in a moment of silence. Was there irony in the way she looked at me, at Tom, at the apartment? He behaved toward her with rough camaraderie that seemed immoderate. I was relieved that she was too busy to visit often.

Tom brought home a woman from his office, Gina Cohen. A stale odor of powder, a rich, throat-tightening perfume rose from her clothes. "I knew how you'd look," she told me. "He talks about you all the time." I bent over to open the oven door and look at the chicken I was roasting.

"Tell her about the plantation," Tom said. "About your grandmother."

"My grandmother worked in the sugar cane fields," I said curtly.

"No, no. The other one," Tom said insistently. "De la Cueva."

"I only saw her once."

I set down Gina's plate. She was smiling at Tom. She was always smiling or chuckling. "You ought to wear your hair on the top of your head," she told me. "The shape of your face would show more. It's such a perfect oval."

I served coffee. Tom held my hand. "Stay," he said.

"I'll be right back," I promised. How relieved I was to be away from them, my hands at work in the sink, the dishes draining on the counter.

When I came back to the table, their saucers were filled with cigarette butts. In the smoke, they leaned toward each other speaking excitedly.

"Tommy has a wonderful idea for a magazine," said Gina. "All these marvelous new products made from plastic . . . a hundred things! He said you can get companies interested in a Spanish edition. Think of the markets! All of Latin America!"

"It wouldn't be easy to raise the money. They're shortsighted. Greedy and shortsighted," Tom said.

"You can do anything," avowed Gina. "Can't he?" she asked me.

Before she left, she gave me a recipe for chicken. "It won't keep you away from the table so much," she promised. "That's the important thing."

The summer that I was pregnant, Gina found us rooms on the top floor of an old wooden house near the ocean, an hour by train from the city on Long Island. She often spent weekends with us. One hot morning in August, she appeared at our bedroom door with my breakfast on a tray. She had brought me a brush for my hair. "I love your baby already," she murmured. I heard the radio in the kitchen, and I was suddenly relieved to think that Tom was there—as though there had been some doubt until that moment where he was. Gina laughed. "You did ring for breakfast, Madam?"

I was faintly embarrassed, thinking, I'm an audience for a play I don't understand. Gina said, anxiously, "You remember? The bells in the plantation kitchen?"

Had he told her everything I told him?

We walked on the beach at twilight. I looked out at the sea, aware how they slowed their steps for my labored progress. "Let's sit down, Tommy. Luisa is tired," she said. It was not tiredness. A terrible pain ripped through my belly. "Oh!" I cried. "I think—"

They half carried me back to the wooden house. Gina's short, heavy body seemed about to sink into the sand with my weight. She kept up a running comment of extravagant encouragement that oppressed me as though it had been bullying. Tom said nothing. I saw fear on his face. They lowered me to the still warm steps of the house, and Tom went to find a cab on the main street of the little beach town. Gina's short arm couldn't reach around me but she tried to. I pulled away from her suddenly. "It's my baby," I cried out.

Charlie was born a few minutes after three in the morning. I struggled up out of the anesthesia. "A cab will cost too much," I said loudly. Then I saw them both by my bed. Tom held my wrist; Gina wept. I felt, for an instant, a paroxysm of love for them. Almost at once, I wanted Gina to disappear.

After they had left, I saw the day was coming. I felt a vast, sweet relief in my body. Poor Mamá had only been sixteen. I was twenty-five. A nurse wheeled a crib next to my cot. She picked up a bundle and handed it to me. The faded blue blanket swaddled the baby. His eyes were closed. He opened his mouth and gave out a faint cry that seemed to travel from a great distance. I held him to me. Now there were two of us.

.   .   .

Tom's work went well. He became in time the executive editor of the magazine. Gina was made associate editor. He went to the conventions in Detroit and Chicago, even California. When he was gone, Gina would drop in to visit me.

It was easier to listen to her when I was holding Charlie. Didn't I think I wrapped him too tightly? Was I feeding him too often? The stores would deliver groceries—why did I exhaust myself by going out to shop? I smiled, and rested my cheek against his damp, warm head. Gina's voice was papery as though she lacked enough saliva for the tremendous work of her talking. She talked so much, she imagined she listened.

One evening as she watched me bathe Charlie, she said, "Tom is going up. He's going to be important." She paused and looked at me significantly. "Important," she repeated. She slipped her hand into the water. "Isn't that too cool?" she asked. I lifted Charlie out and wrapped him in a towel. "You'll be the wife of an important man," she said. I sat with my back slightly turned away from her as I nursed him. I didn't want her to see my breasts.

"Do you know what I'm saying?" she asked intently.

She was telling me a way I ought to be. I glanced at her over my shoulder. There was an expression of desperation on her face. Her thick, milky neck throbbed like a frog's. I knew suddenly that Tom had complained about me to her.

"What is it I'm to do?" I asked. Charlie wailed. I was holding him too tightly.

"It isn't the Great Depression, you know, Luisa," she said in a thin, wheedling voice. "You behave as if it is. I mean, you could buy some clothes. You'd look wonderful in good clothes. And you could think about fixing up this darling little place. And you could—there are people in the company Tom needs to cultivate and have to dinner."

Charlie had begun to cry steadily. "I'd better take him to his room," I said coldly.

"Yes, yes . . . I have to meet someone for a drink," she cried. "What a big bore! I'd rather stay here with you and sweet Charlie." Smiling, pulling at her dress, she walked to the front door. Still smiling, she turned and looked at Charlie. "You'd better check for open safety pins," she said. But I looked back at her stonily, and her gaze fell away.

.   .   .

There were times when Charlie cried for so long his face became a candle flame, and I walked through the apartment with him, desperate with his desperation. The discomfort of life begins at once. When I was able to ease his, I felt I had prevailed over it for a little while. I was always tired, yet oddly at rest. I neglected the laundry, the apartment. I ordered groceries on the phone for hastily put together suppers, steeling myself against the wordless criticism on Tom's face, telling myself with a certain aggrieved satisfaction, that I was doing as he and Gina wished me to do, spending twice as much money as I needed to spend. It had been a month since Papá had sent me a fifteen dollar money order after I'd written him of Charlie's birth. I'd not yet cashed it. "For your son," he'd written. Not his grandson. I felt neither grieved by his words nor resentful, only bored and wearied by his old refusal.

Tom came home late one night. I had been missing him all day, full of a melancholy longing for our first days together. I watched him take some papers from his briefcase. I could see beyond him into the bedroom. My thoughts flew ahead to that moment when, his clothes put away neatly as they always were, he would kneel on the bed, his body clenched against the chill, and pull back the blankets to burrow beneath them. When I first put my arm around him, he would seem massive. Then as the warmth of our bodies heated the tunnel we were in, he would become lighter, smaller, and the featureless flesh would turn, under my hand, into a cold earlobe, the silken hair on his chest, a nipple, the rougher skin of his hand, the small sack of his belly, the cluster of his genitals, the heat of his groin and long muscle of thigh, and if I reached down, I could hold in my palm the heel of his foot drawn up against the cold.

I grew aware he was staring at me.

"There's a woman's dress shop on Broadway, up at the corner," he said flatly. "Tomorrow, you can go and buy a bathrobe of your own."

I looked, dazed, at the money he was holding out to me and I plucked nervously at a thread from the old cotton bathrobe of his that I was wearing. His face was expressionless; he looked the way he might have a week, a year before we had met, if someone had said my name to him, before the enormous intimacies that had taken place between us.

I tore off the robe and threw it toward him.

He picked it up from the floor and folded it carefully over his arm. "You'd better put something on," he said. "It's quite cold tonight." He left the room. I was in despair. I reached my hand toward his coat on the chair where he'd dropped it. He returned at that moment in his pajamas. Without glancing at me, he went to the bedroom where he turned on the lamp. I went to the bathroom. He had hung the cotton robe on a hook. I dropped it on the floor and left it there.

He was sitting on the edge of the bed, removing a large paper clip from a sheaf of papers. He placed it with finicking care on the base of the lamp. His white, unblemished feet looked inhuman.

"Please. Don't speak to me that way," I said breathlessly.

"I merely asked you to buy yourself a bathrobe," he replied, not looking up from his papers. "I'm tired of seeing you in mine every day I come home."

"But it's late. I was getting ready for bed."

"You don't go to bed at six," he said. "When I come home at six, there you are, trailing around in it."

"I don't trail around!" I exclaimed. "I didn't know it bothered you." He glanced at me briefly. We were speaking in low voices as though conspiring. "I don't *know* what bothers you!" I suddenly cried out.

"I didn't say it bothered me," he said coolly.

He had disappeared down a twisting path, twisted into himself. Only his posture, a sullen warning like some faint response as he sat there deliberately attentive to his papers, aroused in me a kind of excitement that seemed like hope.

"Please. Tell me—" I couldn't think now of what he could tell me. His unavailing remoteness had made me an intruder. Argument would have been a luxury.

"Is that an article for the magazine?" I asked, pointing to the papers. He didn't reply.

I fell on him, grabbing the papers and scattering them across the bed and the floor. His arm stiffened across my back as he gathered up the folds of my nightgown and moved me off him like a sack. I stamped on the papers.

"Stop it!" he ordered. He began to gather them up. I raised my fist. He caught my arm and held it above my head.

"I don't want this," he whispered. "I won't have this."

I burst into sobs. "Don't cry!" he commanded me. My head fell forward until it rested against his shoulder. His grip on my arm loosened. After a moment, I stood back. He bent to gather up his papers.

"I'm sorry," I said.

"Come to bed," he said. We stayed apart on opposite sides of the bed making our own warmth. He fell asleep only a few minutes after I turned out the light.

The next morning, Saturday, a heavy snow was falling. We took Charlie out to the park below the Drive. Barking, excited dogs coursed along the slopes; people held up their faces to the soft languorously falling snow flakes. On our way home, we passed a small crowd gathered around a sobbing boy who struggled to remove his legs from the rungs of his bicycle wheel around which his pants leg was tightly wrapped. Tom gripped his waist, then with his glove in his mouth, deftly unwound the cloth and freed him. "Not a day for a bike," he said mildly to the boy. People looked at Tom admiringly. They hadn't heard what I had in his voice—contempt.

He took Charlie home, and I went to the store on Broadway and bought a bathrobe for myself.

The snow continued, a slow, white drowning of sound and movement. The street lamps went on. There was no traffic. The city had ceased its life as a city; the shapes of cars and garbage cans became ambiguous. I stared down from the window at a new world of ownerless objects never to be reclaimed.

Tom didn't go to work on Monday. He had bought himself a new typewriter. Most of the day he sat in the living room working at it. We hardly spoke. In the white, withering light, I carried Charlie as I went from one task to another. Tom sat straight in his chair, his fingers tapping on the typewriter keys, a cup of coffee on the floor next to him.

When had he made the coffee? I hadn't noticed him going to the kitchen. How swiftly he took care of himself! I tried to think up topics of conversation. It would have required invention in that blighted silence. I lowered Charlie to Tom's lap. His head bobbed against Tom's shoulder. He looked over Charlie to the sheet of paper in the typewriter. I picked up the baby and took him away.

I put on my new bathrobe in the late evening. Tom studied it and rubbed the sleeve between his fingers. "There's a little gap in the seam," he noted. "It's not very warm, it it?"

"It's nylon."

"I can see that," he said. He smiled and patted my shoulder.

I went to the window. Behind me, I heard a rustle of paper, the creak of a chair, a match struck and blown out. There was an odd numbness in my shoulder as though he had given me a thump instead of a quick, dismissing touch. The people I glimpsed through their windows in the apartment building across the street were bathed in a light made poignant by the black sky above, the hard glitter of frozen drifts on the street. A woman clutched a small child, lifted it up, then embraced it and rained kisses on its tousled hair; a man spoke to someone I could not see, and laughed and brushed back his hair with both his hands.

Now I heard the rush of water into the bathroom sink, the flushing of the toilet, a brief clatter of the wooden hangers Tom had bought on which to hang his business suits, all the nighttime sounds of his implacable orderliness.

Motionless on his side of the bed, he slept without waking until a pencil line of gray light framed the dark shade at the window. When he left for work, he seemed to take with him a noxious air that had made it difficult for me to breathe. I hung up the nylon robe carelessly, not even turning when I heard it slither to the floor.

He came home with a long box under his arm.

"Try this on," he said gaily, smiling down at Charlie, who had crawled to him and was trying to grasp his ankles. In the box lay a white wool bathrobe, thin and fine like silk, embroidered with tiny violet flowers. When I put it on, he said, "Lovely. I wasn't sure it would fit."

After supper, after I had put Charlie to bed, Tom taught me a card game. We were playing it when the telephone rang. He put down his hand carefully, fanning out the cards, and went to answer it. His unemphatic replies gave no hint of what he was hearing. He returned to the table and picked up his cards. We finished the game. He said, "My father is dead."

I cried out. He shook his head in mild rebuke. "It doesn't matter," he said. "It doesn't make any difference."

      •   •   •

Had I been so dazed with love in our early days I'd been unable to take in what he had told me? Who had called him on the telephone with the news? Was it an older sister or an older brother? All I knew for sure was that his father had been living in a place called Biloxi, down south. Sometimes I'd mailed the checks Tom sent him once a month.

"Will you go to the funeral?" I asked him the next morning.

"No."

"Is your brother there?"

He stared at me with the same expression with which he had looked at the foolish boy caught by his bicycle wheel, an expression which seemed to contain an unfaltering judgment on human folly as well as female inattention.

"My sister," he said dryly. "Bernice. She's taken care of everything."

"What did he die of?"

"Heart," he said. "And alcohol."

Charlie wailed from his crib. Tom went to get him and walked around the living room, carrying him, until his sobs subsided. His hair was brown like mine, but his eyes were like his father's. Patiently, Tom held him; it was such a strange patience, answering what had called it out, yet without sympathy. As he lowered the baby to the floor, I glimpsed Tom's slightly swollen mouth, his blistery child's lips.

But he had told me about a brother. Ben, he had called him.

What hadn't he lied about? I thought of little else. On an afternoon a week later, as I was carrying Charlie home from the grocery store, I saw Tom alight from the Riverside Drive bus. I stopped to watch him as he strode toward me, his head down, his walk so quick and contained. He didn't see me, but went up the stairs to our door, paused to look up briefly at our windows, then went in.

"The subways are improving," he said as I walked into the living room. "It took only twenty minutes to get here from the office."

There must have been a look of shock on my face. He began to talk at once, uneasily and disparagingly, about someone on his staff whom he would have to fire. His voice grew louder, his comments on the man's inefficiency wilder, his eyes never leaving my face as though desperately trying to hold my attention so I wouldn't see some awful thing in another part of the room.

He knew he had lied. Like me, I was suddenly convinced, he didn't know why.

.   .   .

I bundled up Charlie and took him to see Papá. I suppose I was play-acting. I hadn't heard from him since he had sent me the fifteen dollars. Perhaps there was mischief in what I did. When I put Charlie down on the scrubbed floor of my father's room, he crawled rapidly to where Papá sat, vigilantly, in his old chair close by his records. Although he had spoken to me without his usual aloofness, and had even scrutinized Charlie's face with some interest, I saw the truth of his feeling when he hastily drew back his feet until they were nearly pointing sideways. His movement made Charlie halt; he leaned on one plump hand, the other suspended above where Papá's feet had been, and stared up at him. As if bewildered by what he saw, he turned around and righted himself until he sat facing me. I ran to him and picked him up, patting his back. He stiffened in my arms and turned to look at Papá again.

"You comfort him too soon," Papá said reprovingly.

We didn't stay long. At the door, Papá suddenly leaned forward and placed his thin mouth against Charlie's forehead. Charlie was still for a moment, seeming to reflect upon the brief touch of his grandfather's lips. Then he thrust his head between my neck and shoulder; I felt the moisture of his breathing on my skin. I said a quick good-bye to Papá, who only looked at me quizzically.

The wind was blowing off the river. I held Charlie close to me as I walked down Broadway through the old neighborhood. The Red Robin movie house had been boarded up. But the variety store was still there, and I peered through its windows. In Mr. Dardarian's place behind the register stood a young man with bristling black hair. I paused at the corner of the street where our last flat had been. The door that led to the hall was open and had pulled away from its hinges.

As I stood there, thinking, I don't know what, a little girl skipped out from the hall and onto the steps. She wore no gloves. On her feet were light patent-leather shoes like those Mamá had once bought me, digging them out from a sagging box in front of a dry goods store. The button was gone from one shoe and the strap hung loose. The uneven hem of a cotton dress hung just below her coat. The coat's hood, fallen between her narrow shoulders, was lined with soiled white fake fur. She lifted a thin hand to her mouth and blew on it. Suddenly she caught sight of me standing there, staring at her. She gazed at me solemnly until, slowly, a smile widened her lips and her eyes crinkled. I wanted to say something to her, to call her *nena* or *querida*, to tell her how sweet she was. She turned her head toward the door and seemed to listen. With a last glance at me, a small wave of her hand, she ran back inside. My eyes stung with tears, and I clutched Charlie so hard that he cried out as I hurried to the nearest subway station.

.   .   .

Another light snow fell, coating the hardened drifts of the last storm. I stood at the window looking down. People coming home from work at that hour were making their way down the sloping street, their hands pressed against their mouths and chins. Among them, I saw Gina trudging through the fallen snow with tremendous determination. As she passed beneath the amber light of a street lamp, her unsmiling face was as grim as that of someone who has been charged with an arduous and bitter duty.

Charlie, clutching at the edges of a low table, his round face taut with excitement and intent, hooted as he wobbled and swayed. I snatched him up despite his protest and was holding him when Tom opened the door to Gina.

"You see how he already knows me?" she gurgled when Charlie stretched out his arms toward her. "Babies always know me."

Tom made her a drink. She couldn't seem to keep her hands from me. I found the feel of them unbearable, as though the damp tips of her fingers communicated to me more directly than speech that she knew of our trouble.

"Tell!" she exclaimed. "Does the robe fit? I told the salesgirl that I had a beautiful, tall, thin friend. Much taller than me. I can't wait to see you in it!"

My God. What had he told me? Hadn't he said he'd been afraid the robe wouldn't fit? Had he actually said he'd bought it himself? I looked at him, and he smiled agreeably. "Luisa's made stew, plenty for three," he said.

"Oh, I was hoping you'd ask me," Gina said archly. She felt in her pocketbook until she had pulled out of its depths a bright yellow mechanical duck. Charlie grabbed for it. "Wait! Wait!" she cried indulgently. She wound it up and set it on the floor. Around and around it waddled as Charlie shouted with delight. Tom and Gina rocked simultaneously back and forth in paroxysms of inexplicable laughter until the duck ran down and was still, a tin webbed foot suspended above the floor.

·   ·   ·

Charlie walked, then ran. He began to talk. When he played with a toy, he was grave and intent. In the late afternoons, he watched at the window for Tom to come home. But when his father entered the apartment, Charlie was shy and clung to my legs.

I learned to give small dinner parties. I had two drinks each night then wine. I welcomed my alcohol-induced detachment toward the transient curiosity of Tom's business acquaintances, toward Gina's sharpening scrutiny of my face, her eternal advice.

Once, when we were alone, she suddenly began to cry. She had no one of her own, she said. There had been a marriage long ago. Disastrous. He had been an emotional invalid, entirely dependent on her. Oh, she was so alone! As I tried to comfort her, I thought—she is asking me to hurry.

When I was hard and sure in the bitter knowledge that the marriage could endure, I pitied her. But when I was weak and hopeless, I knew that all three of us were waiting, Gina and Tom and I.

Howard Thursby telephoned when Tom was at work. "Well, hello," he said. "How is the tolerant Mrs. G.?"

Tom wasn't in, I told him.

"I saw him last month," he said. "In a Chicago rooftop nightclub, dancing away the hours with his buxom lady assistant editor."

I said the baby was crying, I'd have to hang up.

"Guarding the fort, are you," he said huffily.

I hesitated. "No," I said impulsively. "I'm lying so I can get off the phone." I put down the receiver.

On a Sunday, when Tom had gone to get the newspaper, I telephoned Ellen. Charlie was sitting at the table drawing cats on scraps of paper. "I have to get out," I whispered to her. "I'm dying from this."

"It's an awful apartment," she said, "but there's a tiny room you could use. I've stored some old stuff of Momma's in it. I'll find another place for it. Oh, I'm so sorry Luisa!"

I waited another two weeks, like someone, I thought, hanging around a house that's burned down. One day, I packed two suitcases. Tom saw them when he came home. Charlie was turning the pages of a magazine. I saw his lips move as he recognized letters and said them to himself.

"I'm leaving," I said.

Tom looked at Charlie. "I can't stand it," he said tonelessly.

I looked at his heavy shoulders, his chest, remembering their weight upon me. Charlie turned suddenly. "Why are you standing there like that?" he asked Tom with terrible alarm in his voice.

We didn't urge each other to try again. We hardly spoke. It was not a battlefield that lay between us but a desolation. Hope had gone. We were against each other.

"Double-crossed," he muttered once. I averted my eyes from the rancor in his face.

A few weeks after our divorce, when Tom and Gina were married, I recalled something I had read in the Book of Knowledge while the Miller children, restive as always, had urged me to turn the page. The paragraph that had caught my eye described how certain larvae must, in order to develop, attach themselves to the living tissue of another animal. Tom's and Gina's marriage had grown inside of Tom's and mine, fastening itself upon its insufficiency, feeding upon its weakness.

.   .   .

Charlie had been silent when I had told him that we were going to live by ourselves for a while. Daddy would come to see him, I said. But Daddy and I couldn't stay together now.

Silently he ate the supper Ellen had prepared for us. Her apartment down on the lower east side was a smaller version of the ones I had lived in in the barrio. Charlie got up and went to a window that gave onto a narrow shaft.

Ellen told me about her scholarship at New York University. She spoke anxiously about the character committee she would have to go before, along with passing her bar examination. McCarthy had made an inquisition out of the process. She looked searchingly at my face.

"Do you know who Joseph McCarthy is?" she asked. "Do you know about the Korean war? The Brown decision?" Her smile was exasperated.

It was so hot and close in the little room where we were sitting, I began to feel ill. A presentiment of further calamity was given form by the inhumanly sustained baying of a passing ambulance. "Not for us," murmured Ellen, her fingers pressing my arm.

"I know about those things," I said. "Politics."

"Oh, Luisa. Politics aren't separate from life!"

Charlie began to cry. It was an open-mouth wailing I had never heard from him before. I ran to pick him up. He held himself stiffly. I might have been holding his wooden replica in my arms. Ellen caught hold of one of his hands and kissed it again and again. The hot, thick tears which sprung from his eyes dampened my dress and my neck. What is it, we asked. We begged him to tell us. He had seen a bird fall down, he whispered. Its wings had cut his hand, he explained, nodding his head, his eyes wide and unblinking as they were when he invented a story to tell me.

Ellen and I talked until late. I had thought Tom was my fate, I told her. She listened to me speak of him and the effort of tolerance was in her face. The more I told her, the more I sensed how little I could tell, only a catalogue of wounds given and received, of cruel puzzlement, of disappointed expectations that had left us hard and unforgiving—God knows what they had arisen from—ignorance, solitary imaginings, soft lies. How could I speak of different silences, that first, powerful erotic quiet, the final silence of enmity. That kind of love, she said, was an illness. It lacked purpose, and it collapsed without it. She looked once toward the small room behind the painted glass doors where Charlie lay asleep on a couch. Her face softened. "I remember when my father died," she said. "He wasn't much use to anyone by that time, and I was a lot older than Charlie. But I felt a dead chill moving in from the world. You're not the same—ever again."

I was silent, quelled by a prescience of the wordless suffering of small children. Did I have a lawyer, she asked? When I shook my head, she said, "Oh, Luisa, you're making a mistake." I said hastily that I knew Tom would send money, although I couldn't expect him to support us entirely; I'd have to work. She studied me, started to speak, then got up and came to my chair and bent down to rest her cheek on my head. "Well, you're going to need a lawyer before this is over. I'll be ready." She straightened up. "Here we are," she said gently. "I'm still wanting you to better yourself . . . like they say to us colored folk . . . why don't you better yourselves? Do you remember that vile old man who called us 'nigger girls,' that time we went to the museum? Christ," she exclaimed abruptly. "It's awful, being black in this country, like being electrocuted all the days of your life." She sighed. "Listen, I've got to study a while. You think you can sleep now? That's Thad's old cot in there that I made up for you. He was such a hopeful, sunny boy. You remember?"

I lay awake. I tried to think of Thad. It was Tom's lies I enumerated, adding them up as though their sum might contain truth.

A week later, I returned to the apartment, stopping by the grocer to pick up some cartons. Tom had kept the rooms neat like my father kept his room. I packed away some bed linen and cooking things. The apartment was already unfamiliar to me. I felt like an exhausted thief who must rest in rooms he has robbed. I lay down on the bed. On the floor next to it was a book. Love, its title read, was a many-splendored thing. I guessed Gina had given it to him. It wasn't his usual reading.

I wouldn't have to ever see her again, I told myself. There was some comfort in that. I fell asleep in the hot, stuffy stillness. When I awoke, Tom was standing in the doorway looking at me. I sprang up. "What time is it?" I asked dazedly.

"Where's Charlie?" he asked accusingly.

"Ellen's taking care of him."

He moved toward me suddenly and embraced me. We sank back onto the bed. He slipped his hand beneath my blouse; it was cold, I shivered. At once, he removed it and stood up. He looked down to where I had dropped the book. I felt a jolt of fear. I ran out of the bedroom, then I longed to be back. Oh God! It had all been my doing, from the beginning. "I'll be back to get the boxes," I called out, my voice breaking. When there was no answer, I said, hopelessly, "I'll keep the key until then."

Charlie and I stayed with Ellen until the middle of September. At her suggestion, I looked on Long Island for a place to live and found a small, partly furnished apartment near Kew Gardens, not far from where the Miller family had lived. It would be cheaper for me there, Ellen had said, and easier for a woman alone with a child. She gave me Thad's cot and a few other pieces of furniture. They had belonged to Mrs. Dove who, two years earlier, had gone back to Ohio to live out her days. A classmate and friend of Ellen's from the university, a pale, exhausted-looking young man with reddish hair who vaguely resembled Thad, picked up my things in a dilapidated station wagon, and drove them and Charlie and me to the apartment. He was silent throughout the trip as he lit one cigarette after another. When he had carried up the last carton, he said shyly, "I have to study in my head all the time. Just want to say, sorry for your trouble. You don't have to thank me. It's like a holiday, getting away from the books."

In a box, Charlie found an old rag doll of his beneath a frying pan. He climbed onto a small, upholstered chair that had come with the apartment. He curled himself around the doll, holding its head next to his own. I lifted him, still gripping the doll, and sat him on my lap.

"We'll be all right," I said. "Charlie?"

The long twilight gave way to darkness.

One weekend before we were married Tom and I had taken a train up the Hudson to an inn in the hills. In the late afternoon, we had set out on

a walk. We had found a lake and an old rowboat on its pebbled shore.
Tom rowed us out to the middle of the lake and let the oars rest. We
floated on water streaked with the color of violets. I had started at a
sound. A fish jumping, Tom said. I heard a heavy rustling as though a
wind close to the ground had started up. Then I saw four horses walking
down a slope through the trees. Down they came, the twilight golden on
their moving flanks, their bobbing heads. They had been the spirits of
that hour, guardian spirits, I had thought.

I began to tell Charlie about the horses as though it was a tale from long
ago, how the great beasts had raised and lowered their hooves among the
twigs and fallen leaves, how one, whinnying, had slid and nearly fallen,
how the light had glimmered through the tree branches and struck gold
from the horses' bodies, how Tom and I had watched until it had grown
too dark to see.

"I think I'm hungry," Charlie said.

When I put him to bed in Thad's cot, he reached up and gripped my
hand. "Tell me again about the horses," he said.

.   .   .

Tom's monthly checks paid the rent, the utilities, and not quite two weeks
worth of groceries. In those first months of disorder, of pervasive worry,
and a wrenching regret that would catch me up suddenly as fear does, it
was Charlie, leaning against my knees, at four still amused by baths, by
sudden storms, by the stories I told him at night as he lay drowsily on
Thad's cot, who gave me moments of tranquility—even of resolution—
when I recalled to myself that what we had, all anyone had, was simply
life itself. To foster it, I must become quick and cunning and ready.

One thing led to another. A notice left on the scored table in our lobby
gave me the telephone number of a baby-sitter, Maureen Mackey, a high
school sophomore, available for weekday afternoons. I found a part-time
job in a small nursing home near the public school Charlie was to attend
until he began high school. As I scoured dishes and pots and pans in the
sink, and wiped off the metal trays which would hold the meagre por-
tions of food to be carried to those patients who, through incompetence
or illness, could not hobble into the dining room, I suffered convulsions
of panic when I visualized the distracted look on Maureen's face as I

opened the door to her each afternoon at 3:30. At 7:30, I began running toward home as soon as the door of the nursing home swung to behind me.

Nearly always they were sitting on the floor, Maureen, calm, plump, smiling as she played cards with Charlie or watched him draw with a crayon on stationary I'd taken from the nursing home.

"He doesn't know about God," she said to me once, reprovingly. "He knows a lot of big words. But you ought to tell him, you know. About God." I would later, I promised. "I'm Catholic," she said complacently. She held up a small gold medal she wore on a chain around her neck. "See? St. Christopher. I told him about him. He liked it."

When the time of Maureen's graduation drew close, I went to the supervisor of the kitchen staff in the nursing home and asked her if there was a chance I could work in the mornings. When she replied, her voice swelled with the alerted consciousness of her power over other lives. "We got our full staff in the ayem," she said. "I can't go round switching people to suit you—or anyone else for a matter of fact. I understand you got a kid but others got their troubles too."

The next afternoon as I hurried into the staff entrance, I found a middle-aged Negro woman blocking the narrow path that led to it.

"Are you Luisa Greer?" she asked with a tremor in her voice. When I nodded, she said, "Don't take my job away from me. Miss Ludlow told me you was trying to get on the morning shift. That's my job. She'll do what you want before she does what I want. I got three children." Her hands shook as she fumbled in her pocketbook and took out a cigarette and lit it. She stared at me through her exhalation of smoke, her face impassive.

"I won't take your job," I said. "I need more money than they pay here anyhow." I felt ashamed. Did I need more money than she did? "I mean—I have to get a full-time job." She looked at me expressionlessly. Only her voice pressed. "Will you tell her? She's in there now with the dietitian. Will you go there and tell her you don't want the morning shift?"

I nodded, wanting only to get away from her hard, bitter beggary.

As it turned out, Maureen, after her graduation, continued to live at home for nearly a year. Then, two months after Charlie had begun the second grade, I arrived at our apartment on a cold, dark evening to find him asleep on the hall floor in front of our door.

"Where's Maureen?" I cried. He sat up rubbing his eyes. "I don't know," he said. I knelt and held him until he began to wriggle away. On the few occasions Maureen had been unable to come, she had always telephoned me the evening before.

The next morning, after I had left Charlie at school, I stopped by the two-family brick house where Maureen lived. I had not met her mother, but the stolid woman in a housedress who opened the door to me could have been no one else.

"She's run off with some dago kid," she said desolately. "The kind of people that are moving into this neighborhood! Next there'll be niggers."

"My son had to wait four hours in the hall," I shouted at her, tears springing to my eyes. "I depended on her!"

"The poor little kiddie," she said with sudden softness. With her rough red hand, she touched mine. "I'm truly sorry. She's always been a responsible girl till he come along. I know she'll be back. She really liked your little fellow."

Maureen didn't come back, at least not to us. I began to look for work again. Through an advertisement in the newspaper, I got a job with Mrs. Marylou Justen. Later, a friend in our apartment house sent me to Mr. Edwin Clare, an antique dealer, and when Charlie was eleven, Mrs. Justen referred me to Mrs. Phoebe Burgess. Among these three households, I spent most of the rest of my working life as a servant.

.   .   .

In my first interview with Mrs. Justen's mother, Mrs. Doreen Early, I slipped underground as easily as Charlie slid down the heaps of earth above the great trench in front of our apartment house where a new highway was being put through to eastern Long Island, and I assumed once more, as though there had been no interval, the shallow compliance of a menial.

"I do the interviewing for my daughter," said the gray-haired woman who opened the door to me in the foyer of the apartment on the upper east side of New York City. She waved at the large room where seven cats slept or cleaned themselves upon shabby armchairs, their upholstery clawed and ragged. On the floor, lying half underneath a piano which had no lid—and made me think of a person without an upper lip—a bearlike dog snored wetly, its head on its paws.

"She had one of her urges," Mrs. Early said as I looked around, gauging the untidyness of the room. "She took one of what I call her disapproving-looks walks." She appeared to judge my incomprehension to be a matter of impaired hearing. "Marylou has her peculiarities," she shouted. The dog lifted its head and yawned. "She imagines she can actually change people by glaring at them, people who speak too loud, people who drag their animals by their leashes, fat people eating conspicuously, women wearing tall ugly hats, and funny gentlemen, sissies in other words. Do take off your coat. I don't live here. It's just Marylou and her menagerie. I hope you can iron. You won't find it hard working for her. She's fair—" She broke off as the door opened in the foyer. The dog crawled out from under the piano and stood wagging its tail. A tall woman carrying a large bag of groceries came into the living room. "Hi!" she greeted me in a girlish tremolo. She clumped across the room, the dog following her, through a door I supposed led to the kitchen. Mrs. Early was staring at me fixedly with an odd, abashed expression. Mrs. Justen returned with a can opener in one hand, a can of dog food in the other.

"I'm not much good at this," she said. "But I guess I'm supposed to ask for references. You said on the phone you hadn't done domestic work for a while." Her voice trailed off as two of the cats jumped off their perches and came to sit in front of her. "Look at that," she said musingly. "Is there anything tidier than a cat?" I stared at her startling green eyes, her fuzzy fair hair; she seemed weighed down by her own large bones. On the telephone, I had explained what I could of my situation. Now I handed her a copy of the old letter from Mrs. Miller, still in the same envelope in which she had given it to me so long ago.

Mrs. Justen dropped the can and opener on a chair and read the letter intently. "Well," she said, handing it back to me. "What a nice letter! I think it would be really swell if you could work here. Do you think a day and a half? I work at home myself. I'm a reader for publishers." She looked down at the cats who had both begun to purr loudly. "I'm not tidy," she said, "like cats. Do you like animals?"

"I like animals," I said. She sighed with what I took to be relief. "That's great," she said.

After our supper that evening, I told Charlie about the dog and the cats. "It's like a zoo," he said excitedly. "Could I go with you? To see them?" I explained as well as I could that I couldn't take him with me. I said, you have to go alone to your job. "I see," he said bravely. It was something he often said when he didn't see at all.

.   .   .

On Sundays, the huge road-building machines were motionless in their trenches. Charlie liked to go out and examine them closely, his hands in his pockets because I had told him he mustn't touch them. Sometimes we took a picnic to a place where there had been a World's Fair, where long avenues had been laid down on a marsh. They were empty now. Debris blew through dismantled exhibition halls. On spring afternoons, we took walks in an old cemetery a mile or so away from the apartment house. In a green stillness, Charlie leapfrogged over low tombstones, and I pretended we were in the country. Just beyond a slope where the last line of new grave markers stood, I could see the rising walls of a new apartment house. They were being built everywhere, casting their shadows over the old community of small wood and brick houses and slightly stunted trees.

One day, as we passed the nursing home where I had worked, the Negro woman who had been afraid I would take her job emerged onto the sidewalk and paused to light a cigarette. She looked at me without recognition.

On those mornings I went to the city to work, as Charlie sat sleepily over his breakfast, I moved with frightened efficiency, making our beds, checking his school lunch bag, making sure he had Mrs. Justen's phone number in his shirt pocket. We parted on the sidewalk, breathing air made dusty and gritty by the road-building. I bent to kiss him, already feeling a painful fluttering of vague fear that would not abate until we were together again. On weekend mornings, we ate long breakfasts and lingered at the enamel table.

"Will you tell me about the hurricanes in San Pedro?" he asked.

"I've told you a hundred times."

"I know."

"What's the hardest in arithmetic?"

"Subtraction."

"Maybe I can help you."

"You get too nervous, Ma."

"Let's go to a movie tonight."

"Oh, let's!"

At the early show in the local Loews theater, I sat in a state of blessed ease, hardly aware of what the movie was about but mindful of Charlie sitting next to me, his intent face turned up toward the screen, both of us safe for the moment.

We had little money to spare for movies. I knew I would have to get more work. But on those Saturday mornings when we had the whole weekend for ourselves, I felt a kind of triumph. Drinking too much coffee, I'd watch Charlie as he roamed about the room, and catch an expression of gravity on his face that reminded me of Nana's look. He loved to hear stories about her, about things she had said, or the way I'd find her, one day stirring a kettle over an open fire, another, sitting in her doorway, smoking her pipe, waiting for me.

What I dreaded most during those early years was illness, Charlie's or mine. Mrs. Justen wouldn't pay me if I didn't turn up. At a sign of a cold in Charlie, I could hear the panic in my voice as I asked him if he'd been sneezing the day before. Toward the end of the month, before Tom's checks arrived, I couldn't bring myself to open the drawer in the kitchen where the pile of bills seemed to multiply like cockroaches.

On one Saturday a month, sometimes two, Charlie went downstairs to the small lobby of our apartment house to wait for Tom to pick him up. He would return in the late afternoon and tell me in a careful voice where they had eaten lunch. He was often carrying a new toy Tom had brought him. By the time I had filled my weekdays with work, Charlie went into the city on the subway by himself to see his father, and after that, he didn't tell me much about what they had done together, only looked at me with solicitude when he came home as though I had been the child who had gone away, not he.

"Do you think we'll ever go and visit my grandfather?" he asked me one Saturday in May. We were walking to the business section of the village where there was a new shoe store.

"We never got along well," I said.

"Like you did with Nana."

"Yes."

I bought him new sneakers. He wore them home, running far ahead of me and coursing back, his face bright with pleasure. It must puzzle him, I knew, to think he had a relative not so far away whom he had never seen.

A little cat, mewing, its fur dull and patchy, came out from beneath a rhododendron bush and began to follow us. Charlie stooped to pet it. "It's lost, Ma," he said, and looked up at me with anguish.

We took it home. Charlie said he was going to call her Bird, and he glanced at me with a smile that was both shy and sly. I was amused by the perversity of the name. He looked thin and shanky, holding the cat. I was suddenly aware of his singularity, his self that was not my self. I went out and bought food for the cat. After she had eaten, she curled up on Charlie's lap and went to sleep, purring. From time to time, he called out to me—"still sleeping." I hoped the cat would distract him from thoughts of Papá.

.   .   .

For a few months, I worked as a chambermaid in a hotel which claimed to be a luxurious home away from home. An identical design of thick, yellow bamboo stalks with blunt green leaves covered the walls. In each room, along with beds and chests, stood a spindly writing desk, its drawers outlined in gilt. The desks swayed on their thin legs when I touched them with a dusting cloth. Nothing could have dispelled the anxious melancholy of these rooms where only a kind of organic evidence remained of the passage of human bodies, all that I scrubbed and rinsed away from basins peppered with the stubble of shaving, from tubs where wet whorls of hair collected in drains, all the everlasting secret leakings that betrayed the simmering internal marsh hidden in people, their flesh that left damp blotches and stains on bed linen. Once I found a set of false teeth grinning in cloudy water in a hotel glass, and another time, sheets and mattress so soaked with blood, I opened the closet door fearfully, half expecting in that Sunday quiet to discover the victim of a gruesome killing.

As I went about my cursory cleaning, I imagined Charlie lying in bed, planning his breakfast. The wound of separation from him didn't heal.

The pain of it stunned me, took away a careless lightness of heart I vaguely recollected from a time and place I had forgotten.

He grew more competent every year, making his meals when he had to with intent invention, rarely complaining of my absence, offering me, when I got home, a quick smile, a welcome of washed dishes and home-work done. But in the middle of the night, I sometimes heard him walking about restlessly, ending up at the side of my bed in the living room, staring down at me whom he thought asleep. I would get up and sit with him at the table and tell him about the places I worked, the people who hired me, hoping the details of my life away from him would bring it closer. "We need a magic telescope," he said, "that way we'd always know what the other was doing." We were both wounded, I saw; the sharp cut of life had struck him twice, leaving him with an unchildlike pensiveness.

He had found a friend, Jack Gold, and often when I had walked home from the subway, I would find him playing with Jack in the empty lot that separated our building and the one where Jack lived with his mother. He was a sleek boy with deep-set eyes and black hair like an Indian's and thin, grown-up hands. I had gotten to know Amy Gold one bitter winter morning after Jack had tied up Charlie with his belt, set him against the apartment house wall and pelted him with snowballs. Jack had been nine then, a year older than Charlie. When Charlie came crying to our door and told me what had happened, I asked him why he hadn't run away from Jack. "Because then he wouldn't play with me," he said.

Mrs. Gold came over a few minutes later. Jack had confessed. She was apologetic, bending over to embrace Charlie with such easy warmth that I felt hopeful, sensing that the incident might result in a larger life for Charlie and me. She stayed for coffee. She was a widow, she told me. Her husband had been killed in a jeep accident at Stuttgart where he had been on overseas duty. She had been working for an antique dealer at the time. Her husband's pension and a small bequest from an aunt a few months later had made it possible for her to stop working.

"Mr. Clare is not one of your run-of-the-mill queers," she said. "He's an expert on Shaker furniture. American stuff of all kinds. He's always getting called in as a consultant to museums or private collectors. I liked him a lot. He was smart. But when I had the chance to stay home with little Jack, I grabbed at it. I've been working all my life, and I was glad to stop, believe you me!"

When I visited her the first time, she watched me closely as I gazed at the sofa and chairs covered in white linen, straw baskets holding plants, and on the windowsill, a row of blue glass tumblers through which sunlight wavered. I murmured how beautiful it all was. Shyly, she said that Mr. Clare had done it all, getting furniture for her at a discount, and helping her sell off hideous Flatbush furnishings she had inherited from her mother.

"When Hal was killed," she said, "Mr. Clare was so kind to me, kinder than a normal man would have been. We keep in touch on the phone and he always sends Jack a birthday present. But it's hard to know what to do with a man when you don't have a sexual lever on him."

Once away from the distraction of her apartment, her apparent ease in life which I admired and envied, I wondered at the tough echo of "sexual lever." But as I came to know her, I paid less attention to her imperious statements: "Depression is self-indulgence . . . there's no such thing as friendship between men and women . . . boys need an iron hand . . ." These were notions she fooled herself with, for, in fact, she was often sad, she had several male friends she had known for years, and the hand with which she touched Jack was gentle, almost timid.

We all had supper together at least once a week. She had a little car. In the hot weather we went to eastern beaches on Long Island for long afternoons, sun-drugged, ringing with the released, joyful cries of our children.

It was, perhaps, from such an afternoon that Charlie invented a history for himself. I was usually unable to attend the special days for parents at Charlie's school, but I went to see his homeroom teacher.

"Charlie has told me, of course, how your husband drowned at the beach trying to save an old man caught in the undertow—" She stopped abruptly. I had risen straight out of my chair. "Oh, it's not true!" I blurted out. After I had told her what was true, she looked grave. "Well, we mustn't let him go on with this fabrication," she said. I was frightened. I was imagining Charlie alone in the apartment, as I gathered up soiled sheets in hotel bedrooms miles away, thinking up this story of heroism and death to explain an absence he hadn't understood.

"He's a good student," the teacher said. "Don't be too hard on him."

When I entered the apartment, Charlie grabbed up the cat and held her close to him, regarding me uneasily over her head.

"You lied about Daddy," I said.

He dropped the cat and went off to the bedroom. I followed him. He was sitting on his bed, looking haunted. "You told the teacher he'd drowned saving an old man."

"I didn't say he had saved him," he said, his voice quavering.

I sat down beside him. I felt his embarrassment as though it were mine. "Don't lie anymore," I said. "It's no good. Try not to."

He began to cry, holding himself apart from me. The cat came and crouched at his feet, purring loudly.

"Look at Bird," I said softly. "She doesn't know what's the matter."

He wiped away his tears with one thin bony wrist. "It's not so hard for her," he said.

On the rare occasions Tom came to the apartment to see Charlie, he would stand silently next to the front door until I had gathered up my pocketbook and coat and was ready to leave. He would stand aside then, his face blank as I passed him. During that minute, Charlie, too, stood in arrested motion at the window. Only the snap of the clasp of my pocketbook broke the stillness. Although I knew he would be taking Charlie out somewhere, I wouldn't return until late in the day when I was sure he would have gone. I could not bear to enter that polar region twice in one day. I walked for miles, pausing only to drink a cup of coffee. I invented a scene of reconciliation, of some kind of mutual forgiveness. It was no less farfetched than Charlie's tale of Tom drowning. I knew the vacancy of Tom's face when he stood by the door was a way to tell me how he loathed everything about the apartment. "Don't!" I wanted to protest. I was always uneasy about looking at him directly, but I couldn't help seeing his expensive new clothes. He was getting prosperous. Once I thought I caught the flash of polish on his fingernails. He had a car now, big enough for ten people, Charlie said wistfully.

As I walked, I pondered. It was all a sham, his hatred, my bewilderment, our silence. False! Charlie stood there, waiting by the window, the bones and flesh of our connection. All the rest was pose, confusion, dismay at a life that had died by our hands. There were moments when I craved his presence. As they ebbed away, I felt ravaged as though I'd not gone from my apartment on my own volition but had been driven out.

.   .   .

By the time Mamá had been able to buy me shoes, my toes had bent and curled inside the old ones. I was ashamed of my crooked toes. I bought Charlie a new pair of shoes every two months so there would be no blemish on his slender high-arched feet. I couldn't afford them. I couldn't afford anything. Amy said the money Tom sent was a pittance, a sin. I ought to get a lawyer. He was probably making a mint. "You have to force men to support their children," she said sternly.

I would have to find more work. Amy shook her head and sighed. "I hate to see a woman so bullied by a man," she said. But she offered to telephone among her friends to see if she could find me something. I waited, without the energy to pursue jobs in newspaper ads, or present myself to the dead-faced women who so often ran employment agencies, hoping instead that Amy would turn up something. An inexplicable torpor had overcome me; my life seemed senseless. Yet I felt an intensifying dread each time I counted out the crumpled dollars from Mrs. Justen, or when I opened the pay envelope from the hotel. When Tom's checks arrived, I was grateful for the brief days of relative ease which would follow. I had only vague impressions of lawyers and divorce courts, mostly gathered from accounts I'd read in newspapers which told of inconceivable sums of money awarded to the aggrieved, luxurious-looking women in the blurred pictures that accompanied the stories.

In hotel rooms, I watched the dust settle back upon the desks. I tightened my lips against ammonia fumes, against the vomit-tinged odor of wax. One Sunday morning, as I slowly walked to a rumpled bed, an elderly man, naked except for his leather slippers, emerged from behind the bathroom door and minced toward me, softly mouthing obscenities.

"Stop that at once," I shouted.

"All right!" he cried. "Don't get so mad, little honey."

He trotted back meekly to the bathroom and closed the door. When I got home that afternoon, Charlie was out somewhere. I looked at the shabby furniture. The apartment was no more than two flimsy boxes.

When he came in, he seemed to have grown a foot since I had left him sleeping that morning.

"You've got to leave me a note when you go out," I said harshly.

"Take it easy, Ma," he said. "I was just over at Jack's. See? We made this." He held out a balsa-wood model of an airplane. I wanted to crush it in my hands. I went quickly to the kitchen and turned the tap on full, as though the rush of water would wash away my unreasoning anger.

.   .   .

One morning, I arrived half an hour earlier than usual at Mrs. Justen's apartment. I changed into the slippers I wore to clean in. The kitchen sink was filled with dirty dishes. She was sleeping, I guessed, so I couldn't start the vacuum-cleaning yet. I went down the hall toward the bathroom, passing her bedroom. I stepped back. A man was lying next to her, his bare shoulders rising from the blanket, his head nestled between her shoulders. As I stared, I felt a flash of guilt. A servant is often an old child, aged by wearisome labor that is without resolution and issue, but childishly flustered at some unexpected, intimate glimpse into the life of her employers.

I tiptoed back to the kitchen. As quietly as I could, I began to wash dishes. Later, I heard the bathwater running. Mrs. Justen came into the kitchen. We looked at each other silently. She picked up a cat. The dog groaned a greeting from the living room. "I've found a home for him in Westchester," she said brightly. "Isn't that nice? A friend of mine has hired a car and we're taking him up today." I didn't speak. "Leave the bedroom until last," she said curtly as she left the kitchen carrying a tray with two cups and the pot of coffee she had made.

I'm not thinking about you, I wanted to tell her. Only about myself. Blindly, I reached for a dish towel. A cat Mrs. Justen had rescued from the street the week before, was crouched on it, staring at me and hoping for its breakfast.

.   .   .

Mrs. Justen was in her early thirties. Some weeks, she left me piles of dirty dishes and soiled laundry scattered all over the apartment. Other times there was little for me to do. She cleaned up after her strays her-self. She was unpredictable but fair. She gave me two weeks vacation with pay and an extra week's wages at Christmas. In the mornings, she sprayed herself with a heavy floral perfume before she combed her hair or dressed. During the years I worked for her, she went away twice, once to Maine for a week in late summer, and once to Bellevue Hospital for three months.

Her mother, Mrs. Early, often came to spend the day. She had a kind of irritable vigor, an energy that seemed accusatory, that proclaimed no one else did as much as she did. In her presence, Mrs. Justen grew sullen, moving in her heavy way out of the room where her mother was sitting pasting blurred snapshots in an album, or consulting a cookbook for help in planning a dinner party for Mrs. Justen's birthday. "I just want to please you," she said to her daughter's back, her expression half-pleading, half-scornful, full of strange pride.

They bickered continually, ignoring me as I worked around them. I began, in time, to think they were not indifferent to my presence, that it allowed them to declare their powerful, angry attachment, and that if they had been alone, they might have smouldered in silence.

"One of the books Marylou read for her publisher and recommended is being made into a movie," Mrs. Early said to me as I washed the window sills. "She's very literary," she added. She only spoke in order that Mrs. Justen would hear her admiration. Beatriz de la Cueva would have de-stroyed herself before she would have pretended to speak to a servant as an equal, I thought to myself.

Mrs. Early smiled appeasingly at her daughter who bent over to buckle on one of her many pairs of broad-strapped sandals. "Darling! Why on earth do you wear those things? You look like an Indian beggar."

"Because I'm not vain like you, mother," Mrs. Justen said, glaring at Mrs. Early. "Look at those terrible shoes you've got on! What do they have to do with the shape of a human foot?" Even on snowy days, Mrs. Justen's feet were sandalled. When she had to go out on an errand, she would pull on a pair of huge black rubber boots that could accommodate the sandals which reminded me of those on the feet of the plaster saints I'd glimpsed when Mamá had taken me to Mass.

"And I wouldn't make so much out of a book being made into a movie.

It's the modern equivalent of a public hanging. We'll all be made into movies one of these days," she said. Mrs. Early continued to gaze at her with an admiration that, I had learned, was only another form of provocation. Mrs. Justen snorted and left.

After I had worked for her for a year, Mrs. Early whispered to me that her daughter had been nearly unbalanced by her marriage, and divorce a few months later. "She was a mere child," she said. "He was one of those fellows, you know, the kind that like other men. I had to manage everything."

I imagined Mrs. Justen in one of her great peasant skirts, towering over a Mr. Justen who had sheltered briefly in her shadow like someone taking refuge under a tree from a sudden storm, then run away from her. How dismayed she must have been at such an absolute rejection of her large pale body, her fuzzy blondeness, her heavy female self. How had she gotten herself into such a fix? She had kept his name. Had she loved him? I observed her closely that day, but I remained unenlightened.

Mrs. Justen read two newspapers every morning. Her mail, which I usually brought in from the doormat where it was left, consisted largely of appeals for money from various organizations mostly dedicated to protecting animals. When her mother wasn't visiting her, she would read the manuscripts she got from publishers, lying on the couch while I cleaned around her. Sometimes, she would go to stand at a window, her body arrested like a stone on the edge of a cliff.

The animal population dwindled and swelled as she found homes for strays or took in more.

"As long as people are cruel to animals, they'll be cruel to each other," she told me one morning when I found her warming evaporated milk for a battered tom cat she'd found under a bench in Central Park. "This poor creature, Luisa . . . he goes back to the beginning of his tribe. When Dr. Ingle fixes him, that's the end of his line." She spoke in a fluting voice, self-conscious and somewhat affected, the voice which people often used to express their deepest convictions, or perhaps those they wished others to share.

The cat suddenly hissed and ran out of the kitchen. "He felt the strangeness," she said, "just as we do sometimes." She placed the saucer of milk near the refrigerator. "So he'll get the warmth," she explained. She peered into the living room. "Come, kitty," she called. "Poor puss. He has reason to be afraid."

Some years later, she quoted something said by an American Indian: "White man think everything dead." She had repeated the words with weary gravity, but as soon as they were out of her mouth, we had both burst into laughter. The blunt assertion seemed to reveal the madness of the world. "Certain people," she said a few minutes later, "have told me my feeling for animals is just hatred for people turned inside out. It makes me wild. My mother is one of them."

.   .   .

Tom was in Chicago at a conference, Gina told me. I had telephoned Tom infrequently, and then only at his office, but there was an emergency. It was the first time in six years I had heard her voice.

"Charlie has to have his tonsils out," I said. "I'm taking him to the hospital tomorrow."

"Poor child," Gina said. "Isn't he a little old for a tonsillectomy?"

I didn't reply.

"He'll need lots of attention afterwards," she said, her voice swelling as though she'd been reminded of something wonderful about herself. I said good-bye abruptly and hung up.

Ellen came to spend the night with me in the hospital children's ward. We paced the dimly lit corridor. A little boy wailed heartrendingly when a doctor and a nurse approached his bed to change the dressings on his burns. "I won't put up with this every damn day," the doctor cried.

"Hurts," Charlie croaked. Ellen and I held his hands and he fell asleep. A few feet away from him, in another narrow cot, a boy arched his body convulsively to escape the thermometer a nurse was directing toward his small clenched buttocks. His mother was bent awkwardly over him, her head close to his. Later she walked to the plastic couch where Ellen and I were sitting. "It's like a concentration camp here," she whispered.

We talked and dozed through the desolate hours of a hospital night in a silence broken now and then by indistinct mutterings, untranslatable messages from the dreams of sick children. Sometimes there was a wordless cry, awful in the hush. Ellen and I gripped each other's hands. In the morning, we took Charlie home in a taxi, stopping only when Ellen raced into a store to buy ice cream for him. The fare on the meter made me tremble. I didn't know how we'd manage the last week of the month before Tom's check was due. Ellen pushed my hand away from the outstretched hand of the cabdriver. "I'm a lawyer now," she said. "I've had my name in the newspaper, and I can pay for this taxi."

"Oh, boy!" Charlie said hoarsely when I opened the door to our apartment. I held him close for a minute, then led him off to his room. There was a lump under his blanket. Clutching his throat, Charlie started to laugh. The cat crawled out, blinking and mewing. "Poor old Bird," he whispered, "all alone."

I looked at Ellen. "How will I thank you?"

"Don't," she replied. "I've got to go. You're all right? I have a job interview. I won't have time to go home and change."

"You always look fine," I said fervently.

After she'd left, I searched through my pocketbook. If I'd had to pay for the taxi, I would have had three dollars and change left. The hospital bill had wiped out our money. I sat at the table while Charlie slept, pennies and nickels and three quarters heaped up before me. I was in the dead center of the worst money trouble we'd had. In two weeks, I told myself, we'd be all right. Tom's check would come, Mrs. Justen would pay me, the hotel paycheck would be in the staff box. I sank back into the chair. Two weeks without anything. I'd go to Papá. At last, I'd have to go to him. I stretched out my arms on the table and rested my head on them. The cat jumped on the table and lay against my head. The warmth of the small body, the regular rise and fall of her soft flanks against my forehead bore me off into sleep.

I woke in the dark, the telephone ringing. It was Tom. "I hope you checked up on the surgeon," he said. "These so-called simple operations can be dangerous."

"He's all right," I said. "He's asleep."

"If there's any further medical situation, I expect to be notified well in advance. I don't want any more last minute calls."

"Tom, I don't have any money. The hospital bills took it all."

He didn't answer for a time, then, "I'll send you a check as soon as you've sent me an itemized list of your expenses."

His voice reminded me of another voice—Uncle Federico's.

"Fuck you!" I said distinctly.

"I'm familiar with your vulgarity," he said quickly. I heard a note of surprise, the sudden collapse of his deranged condescension. I started to laugh and he hung up on me.

I took Charlie his supper. I felt mysteriously happy, at rest in the moment. The cat lapped up the little pool of ice cream left in Charlie's dish. "This is our island," I said. "We've been washed up on a beach. Now we're safe. I'm going to gather fruit from the trees, mangoes and papayas and chirimoyas, and we'll have a great feast."

He smiled and closed his eyes. I looked at him for a long time. Like a strong net that was drawing me out of the dark sea, I felt the force of his existence.

.   .   .

Amy tried to press a coat on me. I had been wearing a raincoat over two sweaters. "I know it doesn't fit you well," she said, "but you can't go out like that in this weather."

I wanted to refuse it for another reason than its fit. I knew how unjust it was, but I had begun to find Amy hard and blind in her complacency, unaware that she lived in a world of choices beyond my reach. I was ashamed of my feeling, wearied by it, and disgusted with myself. Yet it rose up in me when I noticed Jack's new tweed jacket, when I mentally toted up the amount of money she must spend on keeping her linen upholstery so white. In the end, I accepted the coat, as much to thwart my own envy as to keep warm.

It was Amy who got me a new job. It hadn't occurred to her to call Mr. Clare, she explained to me, until she'd exhausted all her other friends. "Those men are always so fastidious and silly about their things," she said. "I wouldn't have thought he'd allow anyone to lay a hand on his antiques."

When I first saw the old stone pile of an apartment house on Riverside Drive with its great dusty windows, my heart sank. The lobby floor was marble, the mirrored walls reflected in their perpetual dusk the white hair of the doorman and his red face which grew redder as he told me I was to use the service elevator. I caught a glimpse of myself in the mirrors as I walked toward the door that led to the elevator, the collar of

Amy's coat under my cheek, my hair undone by the wind on the Drive. The doorman followed me and jabbed a bell and cursed someone named Henry. When the elevator doors clanged open, the doorman expostulated, "What the hell you doing down there, Henry? Playing with yourself? Take this woman up to Mr. Clare's."

Henry gave me a cold, bored glance. He was an old Negro with long horse teeth which held clenched between them an extinguished cigar. His fingers came through his cotton work gloves. He left me on the eighth floor, slamming the doors behind me. I stood in the service hall delaying the moment when the door must open, when I would have to cross a new threshold. A firehose was coiled upon the wall. A neatly tied sack of garbage stood on the floor. I lifted my hand to knock. Before I had touched the door, it opened. Mr. Clare stood there looking at me. A small, long-haired dog came to sit by his feet.

I wondered if the same look was on my face that I saw on his, a kind of blankness across which, like light stealing across a wall, the first pale impression of another person, a stranger, played. The first moment of meeting seemed very long.

"Mrs. Greer?" he said at last.

I nodded, gesturing slightly with the paper bag in which I carried my working clothes.

"You're not to come up in that filthy old elevator again. I'll speak to the doorman. You're to come up in the elevator we all use. Come in. You must be frozen, the Drive is hellish on cold mornings. I've got some hot coffee ready for you."

At the kitchen table, he pulled out a chair for me and put down a cup of coffee. He sat on the other side of the table and lit a cigarette. "Amy values you so much," he said. "You mustn't be intimidated by all the stuff in the other rooms. I've made my living from it since I sold the store. Together, you and I will keep it up to the mark. You have a little boy, Amy said."

"Charlie, he's ten. Sometimes he gets sick and I won't be able to come."

"Of course not," he agreed briskly. "And you can always bring him here, too. Do you think you can spare me two days?"

I held out Mrs. Justen's scrawled note of reference written on a publisher's stationary. He brushed it away. "Never mind that," he said. "I know it will all work out beautifully." He fiddled for a moment with the scarf he was wearing around his throat, his finely shaped hands rearranging the folds. I caught the aroma of a perfume with which, I learned later, he only doused himself when he planned to spend the day at home. His thin brown hair was carefully brushed. He suddenly smiled at me, the corners of his large blue eyes creasing. "I've made a potato soup for our lunch," he said. "I hope you like potato soup."

"Oh, yes," I said.

"Now," he said, standing up, "come along and we'll see what's in the store." The dog danced around him. "Her name is Greta," he said. "She's my darling."

.   .   .

When I began working for Mr. Clare, it was a prosperous time for him. He was sent for by museums all over the country to advise them on early American furniture. The large rooms of his apartment—he called it his "digs"—were filled with valuable pieces. Occasionally, he'd sell one off. He had money in those days. He spent it quickly, saying it burned a hole in his pocket, and he didn't care to become too attached to it. When he went out to a consultation, he wore a homburg and carried a furled umbrella. Seeing me glance at it one brilliant, sunny morning, he said, "It gives me courage."

He was curious about me. It wasn't until I'd been working for him for several months that I told him much. Before I left one afternoon, he called, "Wait!" He showed me half of a chocolate cake in a box he was about to tie up. "Take it home and you and Charlie have a little treat tonight," he said. He saw me flinch. "For mercy's sake! You don't have to take it, dear," he said, laughing. He tossed his head back. I realized I had made him uneasy.

I began to tell him, at first defensively, about my island in the sea of islands, about Malagita and the servants from Spain, and the servant who had been my mother. When I told him about the great plate she had brought home so apprehensively that night long ago, he asked me to describe it again. He went to his books in the living room and came back with one open which he set down before me. "Like that?" he asked me. I stared down at the picture of a plate. "Very much like that," I said, stirred by the photograph, evidence of a life I had begun to only half believe. "Lowestoft," he murmured. I took the cake home.

Unless he was away, we ate lunch together, and after that first bursting tale of mine, he asked me to tell him more; he seemed to want to know everything, even the songs Mamá had sung along the path to the canal. Always there was the soft urging of his voice, resonating with interest. I began—years away from the helpless yearning time of the barrio, a mile or so from where I sat talking—to recall more the more I told, my hand resting on the table, smelling the French polish I had waxed his furniture with that day, my eyes fixed on his handsome, still young face, through the cloud of his cigarette smoke.

He paid me well above the minimum wage. When he gave me a Christmas present, I knew he had given it thought—a pair of mocha leather gloves, a brown canvas bag in which to carry my work clothes, a leather change purse from Italy.

Charlie and I were better off until the time when Tom's checks began to arrive erratically. I wrote him, saying I counted on the regularity of his checks, that Charlie was growing taller every month and needed new clothes. He didn't reply. After a few months, the checks arrived the first of the month again.

On the day after my thirty-sixth birthday, we were down to fifteen dollars and change. At supper that evening, Charlie broke a chair leg with his drumming feet. I struck him suddenly on his shoulder. He gave me a stunned look and ran to his room. I heard him trying to work the paint-encrusted lock and key. I went swiftly to his door. He peered at me through a crack.

"It was wrong of me," I said, my voice breaking. "I can't explain it. But it was wrong."

He opened the door wider, but he turned his back to me and went slowly to sit on his bed.

"Charlie? I'm sorry."

"You didn't have to hit me."

"I know it. I wasn't even mad at you."

"I don't hit Bird when I'm mad at something else."

"Maybe we can fix the chair."

He stood up and we went back to the kitchen. We examined the broken leg. His gaze was intent. I wanted to clasp him to me. Instead, I held up the chair so he could chip away the dried glue from the hole where the leg had fitted.

"We'll have to find some really strong glue," he said.

"We'll find it," I said.

       ·   ·   ·

"I don't know what I'm getting you into," Mrs. Justen said. "But since you need work, you can give her a try. Phoebe Burgess telephoned me Sunday—for the first time in years. She wanted something, of course—asking me if I knew of anyone. In the days when I saw something of her, I recall she had an old Irish woman working for her. I heard her husband skipped off a few months ago with some young girl. She has a child, a brat. I may not be doing you a favor."

I took down Mrs. Burgess' phone number and address. "It'll be an awfully long trip for you, won't it?" Mrs. Justen asked. "All the way out there?" Her voice held a note of remote, speculative sympathy. She went to the couch and stared down at a new dog she had found. It was curled up in one corner trembling faintly. "Look at him," she said. "He's been burned with matches. What a hopeless species we are! I can't understand it. How can people torture such innocents?"

It would be useless to inquire of her how I could get to Quogue, the village on the south shore of Long Island where Mrs. Burgess lived. She'd shake her head violently and wave her hands in front of her face. She'd probably say, "I'm no good at details," something she frequently avowed to her mother when Mrs. Early persisted in asking her where a certain store was that sold embroidery thread, or where she could buy corn plasters, or how to get to some movie house.

"It's because they're innocent," I said, wondering how much the trip to Quogue would cost me, and whether Mrs. Burgess would give me the fare.

She gave me a gratified look. "That's right, Luisa. That's exactly it. But why it should be so, God knows."

With five full days of work, Charlie and I might be able to manage. I could quit the hotel. Even after I learned it would take me over an hour to reach Mrs. Burgess' house, the trip weighed little against the prospect of easing the fright which gripped me as each month drew to its close, when all my attention narrowed to the metal mailbox in our lobby into which, one of those days, the postman would slip an envelope containing Tom's check. I knew what I knew. Work was a hook I had to swallow to be saved.

.   .   .

I woke at five o'clock. It was not thought that summoned the effort to begin; I rose because I had risen yesterday. Water flushed away the webs of dreams. I dressed in the dark, my eyes still closed. Somewhere nearby, the cat purred. At the door, she rolled on her back offering her belly to be stroked, and I stooped to caress her, murmuring wordlessly, longing to lie down beside her and go to sleep.

I stepped outside into the numbing cold. My nerve nearly failed. I crept along the front of the apartment house on the frozen surface of last week's snowfall until I was out in the open on a barren, treeless stretch of earth where great holes and piles of dirt, rimed as though with age, looked more like an abandoned battlefield than the real estate development it was. I fought to stay upright as the wind sifted through my clothes. I met no one on the way to the Long Island railroad station. Everything living had vanished. On the platform, one elderly man, his neck wrapped in a yellowed piece of flannel like a baby's old blanket, waited motionless beside me, his hands in cotton work gloves gripped against his narrow chest. In the train, only a few passengers stared straight ahead with the lifeless immobility of statues.

Over an hour later, I was walking cautiously down a narrow lane, avoiding patches of ice hidden by sweepings of snow. Snow-covered fields lay on either side of the lane, luminous in the growing light. The sky was vast, still, pale, like a frozen gray sea above. Here and there, a cleared driveway led to a house; some were surrounded by high hedges, others huddled beside evergreen trees. I read the names on mailboxes, several decorated with drawings of seagulls, and finally found Mrs. Burgess' name, underneath it the words *Larch House* like the title of a book or the name of an hotel. I stood for a moment and looked at the house at the end of a winding path. It was large, rambling, an old farm house, I thought. Near the front door stood a tree with a slack red ribbon tied to one of its lower branches. As I walked up the path, the door opened and a thin boy of seven or eight flashed out and past me, into a drift of snow. He wore only underpants and a sweater the sleeves of which didn't reach his thin wrists. A woman's voice called, "Brian! Brian, you get back here!"

The barefooted boy stayed where he was. He was shivering violently. I started toward him, intending to lift him up out of the snow, but he cast such a wild, baleful look at me, I halted. A woman draped in a blanket ran out of the door, grabbed him up, and dragged him back toward the house. They struggled at the door, the child punching the woman's shoulders, snatching at folds of the blanket as she tried to catch his flailing arms. "You damned bastard!" the child yelled. The woman caught sight of me and burst into laughter. She heaved the boy into the house and slammed the door shut, rearranging the blanket around herself.

"Mrs. Burgess?" I asked.

"That's me," she answered. "Come on. We'll freeze to death."

In the hall, the boy was sitting in a huge chair like a throne. He was eating honey, dipping his finger into a jar and licking it.

"I'm Luisa Greer."

"Nobody else would be here at this time of day," she said amiably. "Get dressed, Brian."

The child didn't stir. Mrs. Burgess said there was coffee ready in the kitchen and why didn't I go and have a cup? She smiled. I saw the gleam of her large white teeth. I guessed she was in her early thirties. Her black curling hair was uncombed and damp as though she'd just emerged from a bath, and a pair of gold-rimmed glasses sat precariously on the curls. One plump arm nestled among the blanket folds. In the dark hall, her eyes and skin looked incandescent. She took hold of my arm with a large square hand and led me firmly to an entrance to a dining room. She gestured toward a door at the other end. As I walked toward it, I heard her say, "I don't want any more shit from you. Get dressed. You're going to be ready for that school bus or you're going to be in serious trouble." I felt a touch of nervous hilarity at the casualness with which a word I had only heard in angry exchanges in the barrio had been used by Mrs. Burgess to her son.

"Mammy, I'm sick," came the honey-thickened high voice of the little boy. "You're so mean, Mammy."

In the kitchen, I searched for a cup. One cabinet held jars of marmalade and jams. Several china plates sat on a marble table on one of which a fried egg had congealed. I poured myself coffee. It was extraordinarily bitter. I put it down just as Mrs. Burgess walked into the kitchen. She had dropped the blanket somewhere and was wearing, I saw, a long peach-colored satin slip. Perhaps it was an evening gown.

"That's Italian coffee," she said. "If you aren't used to it, you'll fly up to the ceiling."

She sat down at the table and gazed at me silently a moment, her chin resting on one hand. "Brian hates the cold," she said. "We have this battle every morning in the winter. Poor thing. I don't blame him. They don't heat the bus. I've been thinking of moving to New York."

"Mrs. Justen said you were."

"What did she say?" she asked.

"Just that," I answered, uneasy under her intent gaze.

"Look at that egg," she said. "I fry one every morning and every morning I have to throw it away. Sedley, our little dog, used to eat them. I don't know where my child gets his eating habits. Like a drunk's . . . Do you think honey is enough for him? I wonder if he'd eat a muffin if I toasted it?"

She pointed to a package on the counter. I took a muffin from it and began to break it open with my fingers. She was instantly at my side. "No! No!" she cried in a horrified voice. She took two forks from a drawer and, inserting the tines into the muffin, balancing it on the marble table, gradually worked it open. I stood back, abashed, wondering what I'd done wrong, and watched her bang down the control of the toaster. A minute or so later, she ran out of the kitchen with the toasted muffin and I heard her pleading with Brian to eat it.

I opened drawers and cabinets and found boxes of English tea, silverware and silver teapots, and a variety of earthenware cooking pots the likes of which I'd not seen in any other kitchen, and which surprised me by their resemblance to those, I now recalled, Mamá and Nana had used in Malagita. But these were refined, their glazed surfaces reflecting my hand as I touched them and visualized those other, coarser versions. Many of the dishes I found in Mrs. Burgess' kitchen resembled those Mr. Clare displayed in his china cupboards. I looked for but could not find any kitchen plates, daily ware of the sort Mrs. Justen, and other people I'd worked for, used. A crate of wine stood in a corner, the long wire from a wall telephone curling among the bottles. As I glanced at the phone, I thought at once of Charlie in whose school workbook I'd written down Mrs. Burgess' number, and I felt an habitual worry sharpened because I was further away from him than I'd ever been.

The phone rang, and Mrs. Burgess hurried back into the kitchen and grabbed the receiver, saying hello with a touch of alarm. "I can't talk now," she said. "My new little Spanish maid is here." I had been looking at her. At her words, I dropped my gaze and began to put dishes in the sink. The personal interest that she'd aroused in me, and which I'd not been aware of until that second when I lost it, had made me forget what I was doing in her kitchen. I was not little; I was a maid. I heard her laugh. She said, "I'll call you back after I go to Westhampton to get the dog." I stood with my hands in the sink, hesitant about turning on the water to wash the dishes, hesitant suddenly about everything. I felt her come toward me, and I turned but didn't meet her gaze.

"The thing is, Sedley, our little dog, ran away. Poor Brian is absolutely broken-hearted. Really . . . He's been gone two weeks—one of those goddamned farmers probably shot him. I have to go to a kennel and get a new dog for him. I mean—two weeks is anybody's limit! That's the best thing, wouldn't you say?"

Was she asking me a real question? I remarked that the roads were icy. "I know, I know," she responded impatiently. "I'll get a taxi to take me." She looked down anxiously at the egg. "Let's talk a bit," she said. As I sat down on the chair she had waved me to, she lifted a man's woolen jacket from a hook near the back door, gave it a disgusted look and dropped it around her shoulders. She raised her hand to her mouth and bit at a nail. She appeared so distracted, I wondered if she'd forgotten who I was.

"Luisa," she pronounced slowly. "Well, Luisa, a month ago my husband skipped off for good with a baby girl from one of his shows. It was some concussion. There's been a lot of confusion around this place. The house is a mess. It's much too big for us anyhow. I am going to have to move. Oh, Lord . . . And sell it and pack and—poor Brian, he's never lived anywhere else. I won't always be here the mornings you work. I have to go see the lawyer all the time. Marsh wants the piano, for instance, because he says the baby girl has to practice her scales. Scales! The lawyer says, don't let him take anything. What can I do? He drives four trailers up the driveway and loads up the household goods, for God's sake. Could you come Mondays and Fridays? That would be so nice."

I'd have to rearrange my days with Mr. Clare and Mrs. Justen. I was alarmed and about to say something that wouldn't commit me, but she was talking again. "There's a mountain of ironing," she said. "Brian changes his clothes five times a day like an English gentleman." She frowned and muttered something I didn't catch then looked directly at me, smiling. "That fool, Marylou Justen, wants me to take one of those strays she picks up on the streets. She told me it was immoral to buy a dog when there are so many without homes. That's how she thinks she's going to straighten out the world!"

She rose suddenly and put the coffee pot on the stove and lit the flame. "I'm out of cigarettes," she said dreamily. "Oh, dear me . . ."

Running her hands through her hair, she discovered her glasses and put them on, murmuring inaudibly to herself. A clock ticked somewhere in the house. "Jesus!" she exclaimed softly. She poured her coffee into a small glass and stirred it with a tiny spoon. "Things fall apart," she said. "By evening, I think I've got them in hand. I don't know how to fix anything. I'm scared of the thermostat. Can you imagine? And that shitty car! Buy a new one, he says, holding a box of my books in his arms." She sighed. "Well, Luisa, tell me all about yourself."

She was staring at the spoon. "I have some letters, references. I've been working for—" I began.

"—Look!" she interrupted, holding out the spoon. "You can see my great aunt's name engraved on it. It's nearly worn away. See? *Letitia*. Isn't that a darling name?" She held out the spoon. I had taken two envelopes from my pocketbook. She put one hand over them, gradually she slid them back toward me. "I don't want to read them," she said. I took the spoon from her. "You have to look close," she said. I made a show of examining it. She laughed suddenly. "To hell with it!" she exclaimed.

She was a person without secrets I thought that first morning, and for a long time afterwards. I came to her home to clean and was caught up almost insensibly by her absorption in her own life. So many of the people I had known had been hellbent on getting through their lives, not pondering them but fleeing, as though life itself was outside them, an enemy that would pursue them to the grave.

I might have seen her only as a person giddy with herself, transfixed by self-love. I might have stayed aloof and kept myself from becoming part of the dense network into which she drew—with comical intensity—anything that touched upon her concerns. I didn't, I couldn't. To be employed by her induced in people a kind of shifting uncertainty which I saw reflected in the faces of electricians, plumbers, a tree surgeon who came to cut down a diseased elm, delivery boys, the moving men who, not quite a year later, carted off her household to the city.

Often, it was only when she paid my wages, after searching for the money in one of the cloth bags she used for pocketbooks, that I would recollect I was her servant. In truth, it was the very ambiguity of my relation with her that both kept me off balance and charmed me, and continued to, even after I had begun to like her less.

In time, I grew used to her repeating things a friend or an acquaintance had said to her about herself. She liked to think such things over; even sardonic comments seemed to fill her up with a rush of life. Once someone had called her an empress of egotism, she told me. She reported this in an untroubled voice, another phenomenon about herself to muse upon. In any event, she was impervious to what anyone else thought about her. She had simply forgotten to go to a dinner party she had been invited to one evening, and I heard her, the next morning, explaining to the hostess how she'd become absorbed in a book—and had been too down in the dumps to go out anyhow. She didn't say she was sorry, no more than she had when she dropped a cup on my foot one morning. The mode of apology was not known to her, suggesting that one form of self-awareness had eluded her.

She finished her coffee. She seemed to have forgotten she had asked me to tell her about myself. Brian walked into the kitchen wearing a heavy coat and rubber boots.

"You're evil, Mammy," he said. "I know it," Mrs. Burgess agreed, smiling pensively. She rose and enfolded Brian in a long embrace. After they left, I began to search for what I would need. I knew she didn't want to tell me where the cleaning things were or even what to do.

Every room in the house was in disorder except for the hall with its solitary enormous chair. In Mrs. Burgess' bathroom, jars of cosmetics lined the shelves and overflowed onto the floor. An opalescent bowl was filled with silver combs and hair ornaments, a tiny silver razor reposed on the broad rim of the tub next to a huge sponge. Buried among the folds of the quilt on her bed were three novels and a book on lace-making. In Brian's room, dozens of toy trucks and cars lay scattered about the floor. A teddy bear's button eyes stared blankly out of a hill of discarded dirty clothes. And everywhere there were rugs like fields of faded wild-flowers and mirrors framed in gold-painted wood, mirrors which stood on the floor on elaborately carved feet, or hung on the walls of the halls and rooms.

At noon, Mrs. Burgess called me to the kitchen. Above her thick cowl-necked sweater, her face shone as though she'd just scrubbed it with the rough cloth I'd found in the bathtub wrapped around a cake of soap that smelled of roses. She pointed to a sandwich on a plate, a few slices of tomato arranged in a circle around it. She held out a glass of wine. "Want some?"

I shook my head. "I'll try to arrange my days," I said, surprised at the tentativeness of my voice. I realized then that I didn't want her to think she was making any difficulty for me.

"Don't worry about it," she said. "If you can't, you can't. I'll take what I can get." She laughed. "That's me!"

At four that afternoon, it was already dark. I was standing by the front door putting on my rainboots. Brian was complaining in the kitchen that he couldn't find anything to eat. Mrs. Burgess glided down the hall. She regarded me silently for a moment.

"Here's a key for you," she said, holding it out. "At least, I had the sense to get that done. Are you going to come Friday? If you do, I won't be here till noon. I almost always see Father Owen on Fridays." She darted forward suddenly and stared at the narrow collar of my coat. "Wait!" she said. She went into a closet in the hall. When she returned, she was holding a long scarf, pale green like the first grass that grows in the spring. She threw it around my neck, tucking its edge into my coat. Her face, close to mine, was rapt as her fingers quickly straightened and arranged it. "There," she said, standing back and looking at me. "That's better."

"I'll bring it back Friday."

"It's for you, Luisa. Keep it," she said. Her tone of voice reminded me suddenly of a child in some household I'd worked in when she'd found exactly the right article of clothing for her doll.

"Mammy!" howled Brian.

Mrs. Burgess laughed and shrugged and started back toward the kitchen, not hearing, I thought, my thanks or good-bye.

On the long ride home, I thought about her. I touched the soft wool about my throat from time to time. I wouldn't have traveled twice as far to work for Mrs. Burgess, but I would travel this far.

.   .   .

"And how is the rich little match girl?" Mrs. Justen asked me. She was in a mood of restless hilarity, grabbing up a kitten and pressing her face into its fur then dropping it into a chair as though it had been a book, opening, then forgetting to drink one of the bottles of soda she gulped down all day long. "I used to call her Miss *Mange beaucoup*," she said, laughing.

"She's very nice," I replied, pressing the collar of one of her smocked, girlish blouses.

"Nice!" exclaimed Mrs. Justen. "Not exactly the *mot juste*, I'd say."

I wished she was a person who could speak plainly. I would have liked to ask her about Mrs. Burgess, about the husband who had slipped away, and the girl.

"I want you to sign a petition," she said gravely, her lips trembling slightly as though in memory of her laughter. She placed a piece of paper in front of me on the ironing board. "They're murdering baby seals and they've got to be stopped."

I signed it as I had signed dozens of others. Sometimes I wrote Luisa Sanchez or Luisa de la Cueva. Mrs. Justen never noticed. I wondered where the petitions went. I couldn't believe they would ease the suffering of a single animal.

"Look, Luisa," she called from the kitchen. I sighed. It was to be a day when I wouldn't finish anything. I went to her. She was standing in the door looking at a thin female cat who was eating only from the rim of a dish of food, looking around fearfully after each bite. Mrs. Justen's hand stole towards mine; she gripped it. We stood there, watching; I don't think she knew she was clutching my hand in hers. I felt a surge of sympathy for her. "My daughter is extreme," Mrs. Early had said to me. "It's because of her soul," she had explained. "Not all of us have such a large soul."

I washed up several days' accumulation of dirty dishes. I read the scant remains of food—Mrs. Justen was dieting again. Just before I left for the day, she came to me holding the green wool scarf Mrs. Burgess had given me. "Goodness, Luisa, where did you get this beautiful thing?" she asked.

I hesitated a moment. "Mrs. Burgess gave it to me," I said.

She looked at me quizzically, drawing the scarf over her wrist then clutching it rather greedily. "She must have liked you," she said. The sarcasm in her tone didn't escape me, but I didn't think she knew how wistful her expression was.

.   .   .

Tom Greer sent me a theft insurance policy form to sign. The curt note accompanying it said he had neglected to have my name removed from it years ago. Something had been stolen, and would I sign the form and return it at once, he asked. I had not known, years ago, that we'd had any insurance. And I felt abashed as though confronted with new evidence of my ignorance of the rules of a defended life—a charge made against me so often, in one way or another, by Tom and Gina in those faraway days. But when I showed the form to Amy, she grew indignant as she squinted at it through her new glasses. "Well, for Christ's sake!" she exclaimed indignantly. "Look at that! Somebody stole a briefcase from their car with some jewelry of hers in it. You don't have to sign this. In fact, you shouldn't. He's got a nerve! You're supposed to help get money for his wife?"

"I don't care about that," I said quickly, knowing I did.

"You're afraid of him," she accused me.

A month passed. The form lay in a drawer. I had been stung by Amy's remark, and I didn't sign it. But I could not throw it away. One Saturday morning I received a call from a man who announced he was a Mr. Crum, Mr. Greer's attorney.

"You received a form from my client. Why haven't you signed it?"

"I haven't been married to Mr. Greer for years."

"He supports you. The policy continues to be in effect."

"I support myself."

"He supports your child."

I thought he'd dropped the phone, the pause that followed was so long. Then the impersonal voice came back. "You *can* write your name," it said, "can't you?"

The insult, its implications of how Tom had spoken of me to this dead-voiced man, was like a violent blow. For a moment, I wanted to shout at him that I was descended from Spanish nobility who made their own laws and had no need of dog lawyers to remind them of their privileges, including the privilege of being an illiterate bastard. This thought, which struck me with as much violence as Mr. Crum's words, so astonished me that I didn't answer.

"Well?" he asked impatiently.

"The jewelry belongs to his present wife."

"That's hardly your business, is it? Incidentally, while I have you on the phone, there's something else. Mr. Greer tells me that one day last month, he went to get Charlie at the apartment of a Mr. Clare, an employer of yours."

I recalled that Saturday. Mr. Clare had asked me to work the extra morning to help him prepare for an evening party he was giving for some museum people whom he had recently advised on an exhibition of eighteenth-century American cabinetry. Charlie was to have been picked up by Tom at noon. Often, Tom took him to a movie, then to a restaurant supper with Gina before bringing him home. He had looked downcast that morning. He liked me to be there when Tom arrived. I guessed that when Tom stood in the door, and I was still in the apartment, Charlie had both of us in one place, the plain physical proximity of his mother and father righting, for a brief time, all that had gone awry.

I had suggested to him that he come with me to Mr. Clare's. He had telephoned his father to make this new arrangement.

"Are you there, Mrs. Greer? Or rather, Miss de la Cueva?" asked Mr. Crum. "Mr. Greer feels strongly about the incident."

"I don't understand what you're talking about," I said.

"It is hard for me to give credence to that. My client is quick on the mark about such matters. I, for one, would not want my young son to be in the vicinity of a pervert. We are considering asking for an undertaking that you will keep Mr. Greer's son away from pederasts."

I broke the connection.

I had been cleaning Mr. Clare's bedroom when the bell had rung. Charlie ran from the living room where he had been looking at magazines, to the bedroom door to say good-bye to me. I had heard Tom's voice, then Mr. Clare's, then the closing of the door.

I held out for six months, refusing to sign the insurance form. The support payments stopped. Charlie, at Tom's insistence, went into the city to meet him. He came home from each visit with a new gift, a watch, an elaborate German toy racing model we were unable to assemble, and over the plastic pieces of which he sobbed as though he had failed at life, and a navy blue blazer which his father asked him to wear when they were planning to eat in a restaurant.

To make up for part of the loss of the monthly check, I found work cleaning offices at night through an agency called *Ready Man* that appeared to employ only women. In an office building on lower Broadway, I broke the uncanny, dead silence of the long corridors with the toneless roar of an industrial vacuum cleaner. I emptied out vases of dead flowers and wastebaskets and sometimes stared for long moments at framed photographs I found on people's desks, a child on horseback, two girls in graduation dresses, middle-aged women with sculptured hair. All of these children and women were smiling, always smiling. In the streets of that area of the city, there was a vigorous aroma of coffee, a single-note, powerful smell that made me giddy with memories of hot mornings in Malagita when I had stood watching a servant grind the coffee beans for La Señora's breakfast.

When I got home, I always went at once to Charlie's room and listened to his even breathing before I put down my pocketbook or took off my coat. In the kitchen, I found his supper dishes draining, a jam-covered knife that he must have used later and forgotten to wash, the radio on the floor near a chair beside the window that overlooked the dark lots behind our building, his homework spread out on a table, a pencil stuck upright in a crack in the wood. Unable to sleep, I began to set the table for his breakfast. The cat padded into the kitchen, wrapped her tail around her feet, and watched me. Soon, Charlie appeared at the door in his pajamas. "You okay, Ma?"

"I'm okay."

Mr. Clare let me come to him afternoons on the days after my night work. When Charlie had gone to school, I would lie down and try to sleep a few hours before setting out for the city once again.

In Mrs. Burgess' laundry room, among the heaps of soiled clothes, I grabbed up a shirt of Brian's and pressed it against my eyes to staunch tears that seemed to be made of a thicker substance than salt water. It seemed only a few hours, a few months ago, I had been strong. Now I was weak. I had found a limit to my miserable donkey's strength, and for a long while, couldn't forgive myself.

At last I confided in Amy that Tom had stopped the checks, and would send no more until I had signed the insurance form. I didn't tell her, or anyone else, about Mr. Crum's "undertaking" concerning Mr. Clare. She went to her telephone at once and called Lou Varick, a lawyer friend of hers.

"You should have told me right off!" she exclaimed to me. "Don't you know you have rights?"

I hadn't understood until that moment that you *had* to have rights. As had happened before when I'd been shaken by events, I glimpsed the source of an unthinking—and unchanged—conviction in myself, in this case, the contract Nana had given me to read that bound my grandfather to the de la Cueva family until he had escaped in death. Ellen's struggle in pursuit of rights had illuminated briefly the arbitrary, capricious and brutish nature of those who could grant them. I realized that I hadn't believed in the possibility of justice, only in fits of mercy.

Lou Varick, gripping my arm as though he feared I might slip away from him, took me to a huge chamber in Family Court. As we walked down an aisle, a Negro man cried out, "Where am I going to get the fifteen dollars you tell me I got to send her every week? Every week! Some angel's supposed to drop that money in my pocket?" The judge, a short man in a black robe, swelled like tar on a burning day. "Get that man out of here," he shouted, and a sallow-faced clerk led the Negro, now unprotesting, out of the room. Behind him, a young pregnant Negro girl followed, her soft child's face set grimly as she stared at his back.

My case was postponed eight times over a six-month period. On the ninth day in the courtroom where I met Mr. Varick, I turned around to see Tom sitting in the row behind me, whispering to an elderly man dressed in a suit of a peculiarly lifeless blue. As I turned back, I heard the elderly man whisper loudly, "We'll murder her."

I started to get up. Varick gripped my arm. "Lawyer's talk," he murmured. The case was postponed once again. I felt their movement at my neck as the two men rose behind me and stepped out of the row.

Varick gazed at me sadly on the sidewalk in front of the courthouse. "It's the court calendar, you know. Partly. You can't let these delays discourage you. It's in the nature of the thing."

"I'm going to sign that form," I said.

"If you could hold off for just a little longer . . . I'm going to talk to Crum this afternoon again. We get along, you know, brother lawyers and all—"

"I can't, Mr. Varick. I can't," I declared passionately. "Not another time." I didn't tell him that it wasn't simply exhaustion that had worn me down.

It was Tom's hatred, which I saw reflected in newspaper stories of murder and calamity and which sometimes seemed to me a kind of natural force, one that could cause an earthquake or a tidal wave, human animus and the indifferent world of natural catastrophes all made one. I had once loved him and still bore the weight of it like a dead infant that must be carried to an indefinite term.

I signed the paper. The support checks began at once. I quit *Ready Man*. For a long time, I felt like a dog I had heard yelping one night when its drunken owner beat it on the sidewalk below our apartment.

I heard directly from Tom only once in the next year. He wrote a note: "I don't want Charlie vaccinated with the new anti-polio vaccine, in the event you've heard about it and intend to have a doctor give it to him. It has not been tested sufficiently to assure me it's safe."

I heard no more from him or his lawyer about pederasts.

"Tom and Gina may move to California," Charlie told me one afternoon in September as we walked toward the shoe store. I said nothing. I no longer wanted to speak of Tom.

"He says I can go out there to visit him in the summer."

We walked into the store.

"Ma?"

The salesman came to us. I glanced at Charlie's face, contorted with some emotion. We sat down on the hard seats.

"Aren't you surprised?" Charlie asked.

"That's a good, big foot you got there, son," said the salesman with a stale grin.

"I'm not surprised," I said.

The salesman looked up at me reproachfully as though I'd spoiled his professional joke.

.   .   .

"Hard times?" Mr. Clare asked me diffidently.

When I nodded wordlessly, he said, "Me, too."

He was standing in the sunlight which poured through a living room window. He put up his hand suddenly as though just aware of the bounty of the light, shuddered, and moved out of it. I caught the intermingled smells of his perfume and the whiskey on his breath. Greta sat on the sofa, her tail wagging slowly, eyes fixed upon him ardently.

"I was able to sell the highboy, thank heavens!" he said. I noticed that the tall Queen Anne chest was gone. Where it had stood, the wall was ridged with dark streaks, successive tides of dust.

I had not explained to him why I had had to take up night work. Often, I felt shamed and disgraced as though I alone had brought about the hours I had spent in that courtroom with its close smell of fear, of unwashed bodies, its mutilated chairs, its hateful clerks who had not seemed able to imagine that anyone in that chamber had ever been alive. When I looked at Mr. Clare, I thought of Tom's "undertaking," another outraged shriek from the happy many. I didn't think I would have signed such a thing, although the thought of spending an eternity as an employee of *Ready Man*, knowing I'd sacrificed the small ease Tom's checks provided us with, might have made it hard not to.

Mr. Clare tucked the ends of his scarf inside his shirt. His face was blotched; his fingers moved nervously. I'd not seen him so undone.

"I'm in a dying profession," he said pensively. "Houses are being torn down, not restored . . . they're tearing down the past . . ."

In the months that followed, he gave no dinner parties. In a week he sold a valuable wall clock and a sofa in the Sheraton style. He told me he was holding on, no matter what, to his Hudson River paintings. Art has its seasons, he said, like everything else, like people. Someday the paintings would be worth a good deal.

I told him I wouldn't be able to come to him the following week. I was to help Mrs. Burgess prepare for the movers. She had finally put her house up for sale, sold it within three weeks, and was moving to the city. I think he was relieved because he wouldn't be obliged to pay me. I recalled that day often. It was when I first realized Mr. Clare was beginning to go broke. Except to take Greta for her walks, he rarely went out. I would discover him sitting in his Duncan Phyfe chair, smoking his cigarettes, a little drunk. When I was dusting around him, he said, "I must get rid of all these trade magazines I've been piling up for a thousand years, all this clutter. It's a good thing, actually, that I've had to sell off a few things. I must cultivate a less material view of life. What happened to your hand?"

I told him that one of Mrs. Justen's strays had scratched me when I'd been making her bed and dislodged the cat from its hiding place beneath the blankets. "She must be a saint," he said. "Although one does wonder about these animal lovers. Well—one mustn't judge. The facts are never entirely in. I spent a few weeks in Morocco years ago. Oh—the patient animals there! Beaten, crippled . . . they expect nothing else. The Arabs are very attractive, but they're horrible to animals. A dog is supposed to have betrayed Mohammed. Religion unleashes the most terrible brutality." His voice trailed off; he gave me a bright empty smile and got up and disappeared into the kitchen. I heard him struggling with the ice-tray, then the clink of ice cubes. I went to finish up his bathroom. When I was ready to leave, he was sitting in a lyre-backed chair. He had drawn it from its customary place near a window into a dark corner of the room.

"Are you all right, Mr. Clare," I asked softly.

"I'm fine, dear," he replied. "Thank you for asking. One must bear up." His voice was utterly dispirited.

.   .   .

Charlie had gathered the mail and left it for me on the kitchen table. There was a telephone bill, a circular from a magazine, and a letter from Papá. In it, folded into a tiny square, was a five-dollar bill. The note read:

"Here is something for your son's birthday which must be some time around now. I have a telephone. Here is the number." He had underlined it with red ink.

"I'll call him up," Charlie said, giving me a questioning look.

"All right."

"Should I?"

"If you want to. Well, maybe not."

"Yes, I'd better not," he agreed.

It had been easy enough to tell Charlie Papá had been unhappy all his life; it meant little to him, and for me it was a lifeless conventional phrase which spared me the trouble of explanation. It was more difficult to say that I was still afraid of my father.

I had related so much about Malagita to Charlie that he often spoke of the plantation as though he had lived there. And when I first showed him the two massive silver forks, his hand had stolen slowly toward them as though they were magic relics. Once, when we had been walking along a city street, we had passed a hunchbacked man. "*Enano,*" Charlie had whispered, smiling up at me.

How determinedly I had sought out Nana! I wondered if that same desire—to find his grandfather—stirred Charlie, frustrated by more formidable obstacles than a herd of small pigs.

After he had gone to bed, I telephoned Papá to thank him for his gift.

"You might bring the boy to see me sometime," he said.

"If you tell me when . . ."

He said he had news—he was getting married. "I'm tired of being alone. You know, I've retired. I'm getting old." He paused. "She's a nice woman, competent. When is your son's birthday, by the way?"

"He'll be eleven next Saturday," I said. "How old are you, Papá?"

"Sixty-seven," he said in a bored voice.

"I asked—when should we come?"

"This Sunday if you want. I'll have Rose here to meet you. We're getting married next month."

"Congratulations."

"Thank you," he said stiffly.

I sat down heavily in a chair. My first thought upon hearing his news had been—but he *is* married. Now, once again, I buried my mother.

Those deaths that touch one's own flesh and spirit must be repeated everlastingly.

.   .   .

Mrs. Burgess had agreed at once with my suggestion that Charlie come with me the day before her move to help pack those books and objects that were too valuable to be left to the movers.

When I told Charlie, he looked woebegone. He had planned a day with Jack Gold. "What about Bird?" he asked. "She'll be alone all day."

"She's alone every day."

"Not weekends. She's going to go crazy."

He kept away from me on the train, finding a seat at the other end of the car from where I was, and when I touched his shoulder and told him our station was coming up, he didn't raise his head. But by the time we were walking along the lane leading to Mrs. Burgess' house, he had regained his good spirits. A fresh breeze was blowing from the sea, half a mile away. Two dogs raced past us. A man with a handkerchief tied around his head, his expression drugged, was cutting grass in front of his house. In his driveway, a child on a tricycle waved to us.

"It's so different," Charlie said. He gazed across a farmer's field planted with wheat, one of the few fields still in cultivation in that area. He was happy, pausing there, his dark hair ruffled by the breeze, his fists clenched in the tension of expectation and happiness. He looked so merry, I hoped some northern gaiety in his makeup would spare him Latin dejection and its whittling-down irony. I would have liked to have given him that field, that lane along which a few last wild roses bloomed. As I looked at him, the knowledge that Mrs. Burgess would see him in a few minutes filled me with pride.

In the back of my mind, I was thinking—Tom will take care of him in the future, help him, when he's older, out from under my shadow.

Mrs. Burgess' door was open and we walked into the hall. Brian, his hair sticking out in all directions, wearing only his blue blazer with the gold buttons, was squatting among the crates holding Sleepy, the cocker spaniel. He was trying with one hand to grip one of the animal's long silky ears while keeping his thumb in his mouth. He didn't glance at us.

"Jesus!" cried Mrs. Burgess from somewhere upstairs. "Damn it,

Brian, you haven't packed a damned thing!" She appeared at the head of the stairs and looked down at us. Her red Chinese robe hung like a tent around her. In one hand she carried a goblet of red wine. The dog yelped suddenly and ran outside. Mrs. Burgess let out a ripple of low laughter. "What a tableau," she said as she walked barefoot down the steps to us.

"This is Mrs. Burgess, Charlie," I said. "And that is Brian."

"Charlie," repeated Mrs. Burgess with the fond emphasis she gave to people's names when she first spoke them. He looked at her and grinned. "Do I need help! Charlie. Wonderful! I've made us a lovely lunch. Brian, go get that damn dog before it gets run down by a tricycle. And for God's sake, put on some underpants!"

"Your shirt buttons are missing," Brian said, glaring at Charlie.

Charlie looked down at himself. "There's two still on," he said mildly.

Embarrassed, I started to explain he was wearing old clothes, but Mrs. Burgess reached out and tugged gently at his hair. "Never mind," she said, "I'll sew some on later," and sent him to the living room to pack books into boxes. I went upstairs with her to help wrap the dozens of little ivory jars and other cherished objects she kept in her bedroom. As we walked in, she looked around the room with an odd, characteristic haughtiness that, often as not, could give way to a screech of laughter as though she'd caught herself out—a child behaving pompously in imitation of a grown-up. She disappeared into her large closet and at once burst into loud sobs. I went quickly to the closet door. She was standing beneath the light bulb, her hand holding the cord, her face flooded with tears.

"It's horrible—the way I've spent money on these rags. What am I going to do with all this shit?" She gestured at the clothes, the tumbled piles of shoes. "What's the damn use? Who'll take this crap? I don't want it anymore. Should I cart it to some church around here and dump it on the steps? I can't take it to Father Owen's church. He'd be scandalized if he knew what I—don't step back! The top of that Roman box is just behind your foot. It's ages old. Careful! Marsh came yesterday and took, among other things, my medical books." She sniffed and wiped her face with the stiff cloth of her sleeve. "That son of a bitch is as much interested in medical books as I am in those disgusting musicals he produces. What's a poor body to do? Where did I leave my bottle?" She disappeared behind a wardrobe box for moment and emerged waving a bottle of wine. "If I live through this, I can live through anything."

In the kitchen now cluttered with packing cases, Mrs. Burgess set out our lunch at noon. There was cold chicken, string beans, and slices of tomato, over which she began to sprinkle bits of scallion. I was struck, as always, by the intensity of her concentration when she prepared food.

Charlie was hungry. When he'd finished what she'd put on his plate, he looked at me uncertainly. "Could I have another piece of chicken?" he whispered to me. She glanced at him as she poured herself a full glass of wine, put down the bottle and lifted the glass high. "Sure!" she cried.

It was such a gay, boisterous *sure*! We all laughed, even Brian, who had inserted his index finger through three slices of tomato and was trying to see through them. "Everything's red, crazy Mammy," he said with a sly smile.

By early afternoon, Mrs. Burgess was slurring her words and bumping into the packing cases and crates Charlie had lined up in each room where he worked. She staggered as she led me to the cellar, crowded with dusty, broken furniture and boxes of books.

"Things!" she groaned despairingly. "Oh, my God! Maybe they aren't even mine! Maybe they were here when we bought the house." She tripped and wailed and squatted down on the cement floor. The hem of her robe fell away revealing her smooth-skinned calves. "My little foot," she mumbled. "I've hurt it, poor thing," and she leaned against a stack of empty wooden liquor crates, her eyes closed. "Are you all right?" I asked her. "No," she said dully. "I'll never be all right."

She opened her eyes and gazed at me without apparent recognition, then reached into a nearby box and gradually brought what her hand had found in front of her eyes. Her mood shifted. She laughed contentedly. "Christmas! Wait till you see my tree decorations! Look at this . . . isn't it heartbreaking?"

She held out to me a large brilliantly colored ball concave on one side, and in the concavity a tiny infant in a large bonnet all of it made of glass. I took it to return it to the box.

"No! I want it in my hand," she said. "I don't care what's in the other boxes. I'm not leaving anything for the rich fart who bought the house. I don't care how long I have to store it all. Everything's mine!"

Later on, there were phone calls. I had come to recognize the voices of a couple of the callers, Mary Fender, who was married to an accountant who had worked for Marsh Burgess, and with whom, Mrs. Burgess told me, she spoke nearly every day of her life, and Georgia Casten about whose fourth marriage to a Negro delivery boy, fourteen years younger than herself, Mrs. Burgess had remarked, "She only did it to get attention. He's pretty dumb but awfully good looking . . . they really are rather fabulous . . ."

The conversations she held with the two women were nearly the same. I was wrapping plates in newspaper at the marble table, and it seemed to me that she even laughed at the same places in the accounts she gave them of our day of packing. But it was her way to tell everybody everything, just as it was her way to make comedy out of an incident someone else would have passed over without comment.

The long afternoon drew toward twilight. Golden streaks of light lay upon the rolled, rope-tied rugs and filled boxes. Mrs. Burgess, holding a small straw basket in her hand, said, "All right. Let's take five. You thought I forgot. I never forget. I found three beautiful pearly buttons and I'm going to sew them on Charlie's shirt."

"It's just an old shirt," I muttered. She laughed and shook her head. "That's not what matters," she said grandly.

Brian was somewhere upstairs chasing the dog whose claws clicked upon the bare floors. We were in the hall. Charlie drew back toward the front door. "It won't hurt, Charlie," she said. "I'm a wonderful sewer-on-of-buttons. I've done it for Marsh a thousand times, and for Howard and Leon and hundreds of others."

Charlie looked bewildered. I was accustomed to the way she spoke of events and people as though I must know about them. Or as though anything which concerned her life must be known to everyone.

"Come in here," she called from the living room entrance. "I'm going to sit in that beautiful chair and Charlie, you're going to stand right in front of me. You don't even have to take that shirt off. Let me get my glass. Now, Charlie . . ."

She sat down in the chair which she'd backed up to the french doors and began to arrange the folds of her robe with great fastidiousness. She felt for her glasses, on her head as usual, held them out, seemed to admire them for a moment, then hooked them around her ears. She placed her hands on either side of the basket in her lap as though it was a small living animal. Charlie moved toward her hesitantly. Looking up at him, she picked up her glass of wine from the floor and drank deeply. She beckoned. He took another step, another, until he was directly in front of her. He turned to glance at me questioningly.

I smiled but not only at Charlie. Mrs. Burgess bent over the needle she was threading. The sunlight fell on her dark head, on the skirt of her robe that was as red as a berry on a branch, on her hand reaching up to take hold of Charlie's shirt, the flash of the needle going in and out of the luminous little pearl buttons as she sewed them on. The silence, the light now fading, shadows softening the outlines of the two figures, induced in me a kind of drowsiness, and when Brian burst into the room wearing an enormous straw hat that fell over his ears, I had an impulse to push him out so nothing would break the spell of that scene which had the dreamlike quality of something glimpsed through a window at dusk.

"Oh, Mammy, you're going to sew his front to his back!"

Mrs. Burgess leaned forward and bit the thread with her teeth. "Shut up, Brian! There, Charlie. You're an elegant new boy."

We were ready to leave. In my bag was a set of keys to her new apartment on West Sixty-eighth Street where I was to meet her the next day. She would drive Brian and the dog to the city as soon as the movers had left. She lingered at the door. "Luisa, you'll be there, won't you?" she asked wistfully. "I don't know what I'd do without you." She appeared sober but tired, and vaguely chastened as Brian was after he'd ravaged a whole day with his caprices.

"I'll be there, Mrs. Burgess."

She was looking at Charlie. "Wait!" she commanded. She ran back into the house, grabbing up the skirt of her robe as she did so and giving me a humorous glance over her shoulder. When she returned, she was holding something hidden by her curled fingers. "Hold out your hand," she said, smiling, to Charlie. When he did, she placed a small object in it. We all leaned forward to see it, an ivory carving of two dancing monkeys. Although it was no larger than Charlie's thumb, it was so intricately carved I could see the sharp teeth in the monkeys' mouths.

"There," she said. "For good luck. It's very, very old."

Charlie said nothing about our day until we had got home.

"She's rich, isn't she?" he asked.

"She must be," I said. "There's money she inherited when her parents were killed in a plane crash. She was only three years old. Now she's sold that house, for a lot, I guess. And Mr. Burgess gives her money, too."

"She's nice," he said, "even if she is rich."

.   .   .

When the telephone rang later, I was sure it was Mrs. Burgess. I had been thinking about her, her last night in that house where she had lived with her husband, alone now with her child as I had been with mine. She would want to make sure I was coming to her in the morning. I was alarmed at the thought of speaking to her after she had been drinking steadily, but I went quickly to the telephone, determined to try and reassure her. It was Tom.

I assumed he had called to make arrangements for taking Charlie out somewhere on his birthday the following day. "I'll get him," I said.

"Just a minute. We're moving to California next month. I'll be writing to you about suitable arrangements for Charlie's visits out there. I want the whole thing to be without trauma. I hope you will try to reassure him. Hello?"

"I'm here," I said. "Charlie told me you were going away."

"I'm not going away. I'm going to California," he said. He spoke without emphasis, colorlessly. I held the phone away from my ear as though he was shouting. I had heard his implacable antagonism conveyed in the only word he had raised his voice to utter, a word made familiar to me by the conversations of various of my employers who appeared to find comfort in speaking of suffering as trauma.

He cleared his throat. I didn't want him to go to California. As debased as our involuntary tie was, I depended with unreasoning hope on his goodwill toward Charlie. But toward whom did he have goodwill? I recalled suddenly how frigidly he had spoken more than once about Gina, her unction, her sentimentality—he could see right through her, he had told me, right to her ambitious, hungry heart.

Charlie came to the door carrying the cat. I pointed mutely to the phone. When he took it, I went off to the closet to get a package of tissue paper to wrap his presents, a new stamp album and an envelope of stamps, a winter sheepskin coat I had bought in May from a local store, paying for it over three months.

After Charlie was asleep, I obeyed an impulse to telephone Ellen in Atlanta where she had moved to work for a black legal firm after passing the state bar examination there. I had seen her twice in the last two years, once when she came to New York for some professional meeting, and then when she stopped to see me for a day after she had gone to her mother's funeral in Dayton.

Time and distance divided us, but we were bound by our first powerful affection for each other. It had, perhaps, become something of a monument to which we returned now and again to lay a wreath in memory. We occasionally exchanged letters. She had written to me that she was seeing a man considerably older than herself, Jim Creedmoor, a history teacher in a black college near Atlanta. She didn't write of love but of commitment and struggle. When I had seen her, she looked more beautiful than ever. She was thin and elegantly and expensively dressed. When I commented on her clothes, she had said, "I'm like everybody else, honey. I put a lot of what I earn on my back."

She was home. We talked as long as I dared. She told me to reverse the charges. It was my call, I said. She laughed and said I was getting uppity. I described Mrs. Burgess, how working for her was hardly like being a servant. I heard a certain breathlessness in my voice. I was trying to persuade her of something, that my life had changed.

"She won't forget who you are," Ellen said sharply. "Don't you forget."

"You can't always classify people."

"You have to," she said with conviction.

She was still carrying Julian's laws of life in her head, I guessed. I tried to speak of the complicated feelings I had about Tom going to California. He talked to me, I told her, as if I was a drunken maid he'd discovered lying on his kitchen floor, groceries tumbled about her.

"You scorned him," she said.

"I didn't," I said defensively. "I couldn't live with him."

She laughed, saying I couldn't expect a man to make such a distinction. She pleaded with me to come and visit her. "Don't those Madams of yours ever give you a vacation? I'll help with the fare for you and Charlie."

"It's nice to have a rich friend," I observed.

"I'll never be that," she said. I inquired after Mr. Creedmoor. They might marry soon, she said. "That's wonderful," I said but I heard the flatness of my voice and knew I was envious.

After I'd hung up, I was nettled, restless. We had been at odds. I thought of my halting effort to describe Mrs. Burgess. I had a sense of having had one last, decisive comment to make about her. I stared at the phone, tempted to call Ellen back. But I couldn't afford to. In any case, I didn't know what the decisive comment could be.

In the morning, I tiptoed into Charlie's room and left his presents beside his bed. The August heat was like a soft metal poured into the mold of the little room. An hour or so later I picked my way across a street blistered with patches of melting tar and escaped from the burning sun into the foyer of the cream-colored building into which Mrs. Burgess was moving.

Her apartment faced Central Park. As I walked through empty rooms smelling of fresh paint, I was aware of a tinge of green in the light, an imminent green flood arrested at the windows which were level with the tops of trees across the broad avenue.

I didn't have anything with which to scour away the hardened grease from the stove. Mrs. Burgess wouldn't like that. Untroubled as she was by disorder, she was panicked by squalor, by the slightest suspicion of decay in leftover food—she always averted her face when I scraped the remains of food from plates into the garbage can—and drains clogged by her own hair combings drove her cursing and holding her face from the bathroom until I'd cleaned them out.

I had been sitting on a window sill looking down at the street for only a few minutes when the door was flung open and Mrs. Burgess staggered into the large foyer dragging two laundry bags.

"You're here!" she shouted with such manifest relief, I wished Ellen had been there to hear her. Who, among my employers, had ever valued my presence so much?

"Brian had a shit fit—absolutely impossible—so I left him and that damned dog with Mary. She hates animals and children. Wonderful! The dog was singing Madame Butterfly and pissing all over the car upholstery. Oh! Look, I've brought sandwiches for us." She felt around in one of the bags and produced two bottles of scotch. "For the movers," she said, adding, "Some of it."

The phone wasn't working, I told her, and I'd like to go out and call Charlie in an hour or two from a public phone to wish him happy birthday. She looked frightened. "Can't you do that later? He's such a smart, adorable boy. He'll know you're thinking about him. Oh dear—the phone company was supposed to—maybe they'll send a man later. You won't have to go out at all. I think I might have just a little shot. I'm so stupid. I should have made sure of the phone. We're positively cut off. You won't go out, will you, Luisa? I think I'll feel better when I see my things."

I took the sandwiches she was holding out to me, and as I went to put them in the kitchen, she lifted a bottle to her lips, the cap of which she had been removing while she talked to me. When I returned, she was standing at one of the large living room windows. There were streaks of sweat on the back of her long-sleeved blouse. She turned to face me slowly, her expression vacant.

"My life," she murmured.

"The view is beautiful," I said.

"Views!" she exclaimed. She bent down, seized her pocketbook, and opened it. "Look, Luisa," she said softly, holding out a small faded photograph. "I found it in the cellar. A picture of my great-uncle Wilfred at eighty-eight. You must know who that baby is he's holding. He was my guardian. I lived with him six years. Then I went to someone else. He's dead . . . everybody's dead."

In the picture, nearly invisible among yellowed patches like sickly sunlight, I could barely make out a short bearded old man, a bundle in his arms, an indistinct infant face. When I looked up, Mrs. Burgess pointed to a tear as it fell down her cheek.

"Poor old me," she said.

"I know how you feel," I began. "My grandmother—"

But she was hastening away to the kitchen. "Look at this vile stove!" she shouted. "Those bastards, with the rent I'm paying—what pigs!"

I joined her in the kitchen. "I would have gone out to get cleaning things," I explained. "But I was afraid you'd get here while I was out."

"Yes, yes . . . but I suppose we can't just sit here waiting. Maybe you *had* better run out and buy stove cleaner. I can't stand this! Did you ever see anything so disgusting?"

I telephoned Charlie from a pay phone. He was already pasting stamps in his new album, he said, and Bird and he were eating the bacon I'd left for him in the frying pan. I found a market on Columbus Avenue and bought what I needed. When I returned, a huge moving van was drawn up in front of the apartment house. On the fourth floor, Mrs. Burgess' front door was open. She was standing in the middle of the living room, a cotton scarf tied around her head, directing the young movers who were carrying Brian's wooden bed frame to his bedroom. She was flushed and smiling. When I passed her on my way to the kitchen, I could smell the whiskey on her breath. "I'm feeling a *lot* better," she said.

By late afternoon, she was too drunk to stand upright. The movers stood in the living room. One slowly removed a broad leather belt from his waist and wound it around one wrist. The other two were watching her closely as she peered at a small key in her hand. She was swaying in front of a standing clock made of fruitwood, a moon and a sun painted on its face. She tried and failed to fit the key into its narrow door.

"This marvelous object belonged to old Wilfred," she said thickly. "I must hear it ticking. He found it in Provence. It came all the way from some little whitewashed room in France. Can't you understand how I feel about this thing?" She swung around and glared ferociously at us. The movers glanced at each other. "Mrs. Burgess," said one of them, holding out a bill. "If you could just—"

"Wait!" she cried. She put her fingers to her lips, gave them a canny look, and staggered to the kitchen. "We *must* have a drink together," she called back. She returned carrying her checkbook and a bottle of whiskey. Smiling all the while, she felt around in a crate of china until she'd found a small object wrapped in newspaper. "Anyone care to bet this isn't a glass? Luisa, give it a rinse."

"That's all right, Missus," said one of the men. "We'll share the glass. Newsprint won't hurt. But if you'd sign this and pay, see? Right here, it says . . ."

Mrs. Burgess had bought the clock a few months earlier in an antique shop in East Hampton. The strain of moving, the amount of liquor she'd poured into herself—I'd noticed that one of the bottles of scotch on the kitchen counter was nearly empty—had driven her temporarily out of her head.

When I came back with the rinsed glass, she was leaning against a tall crate, her glasses on askew, writing a check. She tore it free with a dramatic gesture and waved it in the air until one of the movers managed to grab it from her hand. "You've been princes," she said. "Kings . . ."

When the door closed behind them, she sat down on a pile of bed linen. "Done . . . it's done . . ." she muttered.

I made up her bed and hung up some of her clothes. I unpacked all the boxes in the kitchen and put things away, knowing she would change everything around.

She slept curled up in a corner of a couch. It grew dark. There was a faint touch of coolness in the air. She had drunk so much, she might sleep through until morning. But she might wake. Queasy with fatigue, I went back to the market on Columbus and returned to the apartment with bread and eggs and coffee. She wouldn't care for what I'd bought, the white loaf, the American coffee, but it was all they had. At least, she'd have something to eat when she awoke.

I stood for a moment looking down at her. She was breathing heavily through her open mouth. She seemed so stranded. What would she do now? The divorce agreement had been signed months ago, the house sold. She hadn't cared for anyone in Quogue; she wouldn't be going back there. Brian would be sent off to boarding school in a few years, she'd told me. Mrs. Burgess was all set. Set for what? Perhaps she would marry again. Perhaps she'd meet someone she could love and pity. Love, the pity in love, I thought, feeling wretched as I stood there, aware of the monotonous noise of traffic coming through the open windows. Should I close them? But it was too hot. If only she didn't drink so much! I had to leave. Tomorrow, Mary Fender would come to the apartment and help her. Gradually, she would rediscover her possessions, find places for them, and so reassemble her world. I would miss the farmhouse out on Long Island. It had been full of surprises. There had been a wire-covered light above the front door, a quiet-looking light she turned on at twilight and which, as I walked away down the lane toward the station, I had always turned back to see.

Charlie arrived home a few minutes after I had. He was carrying a record player his father had given him and a record from Gina—*Great Classical Hits*.

"Did you have a good time?"

"Pretty good."

"Did you like your presents?"

"Especially the stamps."

"Shall we have some iced tea?"

He nodded and gave me a measuring look. "Gina said I was the only person in New York she was sorry to leave." He picked up the cat and held her above his head. I fixed our tea.

"She made a cake," he said after a while. "The icing slid off it."

He was watching me across the table. I knew he wished he hadn't told me what Gina had said to him. It was so like her, that complacent claim on Charlie's affection with its intimation that nobody else was worthy of hers. He was looking worried. "She always liked you a lot," I said with effort.

I couldn't speak of her with ease, although she had been only the occasion of the finishing off of my marriage, just as the theft of her jewelry had led me to Family Court.

"We'll murder her!" Tom's lawyer had pronounced. Under that sentence, I had been cast loose from my link with Tom with a finality more absolute than divorce papers had been able to bring about. I had been made to understand that even the most elementary equality was not my right. And no pity. Ravaged and abject after my days in court, I had realized at last that Tom was my foe.

Gina had nourished an idea in him. But it had already been his. I had grasped it finally as I signed the insurance form. It was an idea which had taken root in Tom's and my first conversation: through an error in judgment, Tom had married the servant when all along he had been meant for the lady of the house.

I laughed suddenly. "Madam Gina," I said.

Charlie laughed, too. "That's a good name," he said. After a moment, he asked, "Did Mrs. Burgess get moved and all?"

"She got moved. I won't have that long trip anymore."

"That kid of hers didn't help much, I bet."

"He wasn't there."

"You know, when I helped pack the books? The kid suddenly jumped up at me and said I couldn't eat anything or even have a drink of water unless I got his permission first because everything in that house was his."

"Brian's not housebroken," I said.

"Like the dog," he remarked pensively. I held the glass of cold tea against my cheek. "Maybe they switched babies on Mrs. Burgess in the hospital," he said.

.   .   .

"I brought you to visit Papá long ago," I told Charlie the next morning as we stood in front of my father's apartment house, looking down at the Hudson. "But you were very little then."

"What did I do?"

"You tried to untie his shoelaces."

The door to Papá's room was ajar. I pushed it open and we went in. Papá was standing with his back to the window. A few feet away from him, erect on a straight-backed chair, sat a middle-aged woman. Her hair was white at the temples, her face, large and plain. Her feet were placed together side by side, her hands clasped in her lap. She gazed at me wordlessly. When Papá greeted me by uttering my name, she smiled very faintly as though at first she had been unsure but now knew who I was.

"Mrs. Rose Lafferty," said Papá. She got up and came toward me, holding out her hand. She shook mine, nodded to Charlie, and returned to her chair where she removed a handkerchief from the sleeve of her blouse and wiped her mouth thoughtfully.

"Charles," my father said loudly. Charlie started toward him. At once, Papá pressed his back against the window and Charlie halted, casting a quick glance at me. I went to stand beside him. "I hope you're working hard in school," said Papá.

"He's a good student," I said.

"Can't he speak for himself?"

"I'm not so good at math," Charlie said apologetically.

"As long as you can add and subtract," Mrs. Lafferty spoke up with abrupt, nasal brightness. "And," her voice trailed off, "multiply and divide."

"Mrs. Lafferty is an accountant," Papá said with the barest softening of his expression as he glanced in her direction. "Well, would you like some coffee?"

"We've had breakfast."

"That isn't what I asked." He walked stiffly to the stove where I saw he had already made coffee and was keeping it hot on a low flame. His hair was white. His nose was sharper than ever. I stared at him fixedly. He had become an old man.

"After we're married," he said as he poured coffee into cups he had already lined up on the counter, "Mrs. Lafferty and I are going away for two weeks. I've not been out of this country since we first came here."

"Are you going to San Pedro? To Malagita?" I asked with sudden suspicion, my heart beating in my throat.

He turned to face me, holding two cups of coffee. "San Pedro? Malagita? Why would I go there? We're going to Puerto Rico. There is no Malagita. Some American businessmen bought it several years ago. What I believe is called a consortium." He looked at Mrs. Lafferty as though for confirmation. She smiled placidly.

The extreme relief that went through me with the involuntary force of a shudder when Papá had said he wasn't going to San Pedro, emerged into the open as a short loud laugh, a kind of unmelodious *ha-ha-ha* that took me as much by surprise as it did everyone else. The cups rattled in their saucers. My father held out one toward me, frowning. "Here," he said brusquely, "take it."

"The *vivienda* will still be there," I said resentfully. How could he claim there was no Malagita as though place was merely an idea that could be dismissed at will?

"The house," he said in English, and with emphasis, as if he was speaking about some four-sided affair with a pointed roof like a child's drawing, "was built to endure everything but neglect. I suppose it is still there. For the Americans, it will seem only an inefficient structure full of wasted space. Although Americans like to waste space—to show they can throw away what other people need."

He held out the other cup to Mrs. Lafferty upon whose face, as she looked down at it, there stole an expression of alarm as if she was about to do violence to the potato impassivity of her large body by introducing into it the bitter Caribbean coffee Papá had made, and which Mamá had always diluted with boiled milk for me. I tried not to stare at her. She was so square, so massive, I thought, Mamá's ghost would not get past her easily. She suddenly smiled at me. "How do you like it out there?" she asked. "Queens, is it?"

"It's near Forest Hills," I said. "It's quiet."

"Are there shops near you?"

"Oh, yes, a street of shops."

"I like to have my shops handy," she said snugly. "My, your son is tall! Of course, it's better to be tall."

I had forgotten for a moment that Charlie was there. When I glanced at him, I saw how uncomfortable he looked. "You can sit down," I said. He sat tentatively on the edge of a chair.

"Do you have something in mind to be, as they say here," Papá said to Charlie. "One of those Yankee occupations, piloting an airplane?"

"I don't know yet," Charlie replied.

"You don't know yet," Papá repeated as though in disbelief.

"Where will you go in Puerto Rico?" I asked quickly.

"Federico advised me to stay in San Juan," he answered. Did Papá still see him? Did he take advice from a man he thought such a fool?

"How is he?"

"He's not changed, I imagine, since he was Charlie's age."

"I'm very excited," Mrs. Lafferty chimed in. "A foreign country and all."

"It's Federico who goes to San Pedro," Papá said, looking at me keenly. "Yes. That's where he goes. Estremadura. They've built several of those resort hotels there, and a gambling casino and a golf course."

"But it's a swamp!" I exclaimed.

"The swamp was drained years ago. Federico says there's no trace of it—except sometimes at night when there's a faint marsh odor, especially during the rainy season." Papá smiled sardonically. "The tourists wouldn't notice that as long as it didn't affect the plumbing."

"My grandfather died there," I muttered.

"People die everywhere," said Papá. "Charles, do you like classical music?"

"Your grandfather loves classical music," announced Mrs. Lafferty forcefully.

"We have a music period in school," Charlie said.

"What do they play for you?" asked Papá intently. Charlie gave me an uneasy look. "*Marche Slav*," he offered. At Papá's bleak expression, he threw in, "Dvorak's *Unfinished Symphony*."

"Papá, you're asking questions like a policeman," I protested. Mrs. Lafferty scowled and carefully crossed her feet. I noticed that her shoes had been recently resoled. I got up and took my cup to the sink and reached for the tap. "Leave that!" Papá's voice ordered.

Mrs. Lafferty, at that moment, burst into speech like an actor who has arrived late on the scene and intends to make up for lost time. She had been born and raised in Rhode Island, she said, and the grand beaches had been her own playground. An odd girlishness lightened her voice. She must have spent better years there, I thought, than she had since seen. After her husband, Mr. Lafferty, had passed on, she had come to New York to make her way. Her older sister in Providence had tried to discourage her, but they had never gotten along, although as far as she was concerned, getting along with your family was the most important thing—blood was thicker than water—and where else could you turn in times of trouble? So when her niece got married, to try and make up with her sister, she had sent a present, and that was how everything began, because the niece and her husband were going to Nova Scotia for their honeymoon, on the boat from Boston, and after all, what was more appropriate for a sailing than a basket of fruit? And so she had met my father in his lovely shop, luckily just a week or so before his retirement. And now, after years of friendship, they had decided to make an honest woman out of her. Very romantic, she thought, the whole thing.

She smiled at me broadly, cheerfully. I smiled back, somewhat dazed by the facility and speed with which she had related her life story. Mamá, I thought, could never have told such a coherent, unadorned tale, but then, I supposed, it was easy if you left out so much. On an impulse I hardly understood, I went quickly to her and pressed my cheek against hers, aware at once of the damp cellar smell of pancake makeup. Charlie and Papá regarded me with surprise. For a second, I saw a resemblance between them, and it struck me as comical.

At the door, Papá said, "Well, come again. I will put some records aside for Charlie, real music, that is." He reached into his jacket pocket, took out a bill and examined it, then held it out to Charlie. It was ten dollars. Before Charlie or I could thank him, he closed the door.

"Was he always like that?" Charlie asked me as we went down the subway stairs.

"He's better than he used to be," I replied grimly.

"We won't have to go again for a while?"

"Not unless you want to," I said, grinning at him.

He took and held my arm, a thing he had not done for some time.

.   .   .

Mrs. Justen and her mother were sprawled on opposite sides of the sofa. On the floor, within reach, stood a bottle of dark rum. "Mother and I are taking a day off," Mrs. Justen trilled at me. Mrs. Early emitted a coy giggle.

The sink overflowed with dishes. The litter boxes were foul and had not been attended to, I guessed, for several days. As I went about my work, I could not help but hear the rumble, low and monotonous, of a quarrel between them, interrupted now and then by a flow of irritable weak laughter from one or the other. I blotted them out with the vacuum cleaner. At some point, Mrs. Justen staggered into her bedroom and fell on her bed. In the living room, Mrs. Early remained rigidly upright on a chair, her feet at an odd, clumsy angle on the floor. Although her eyes were wide open, I didn't think she saw me.

I found stale cheese in the kitchen and ate it for my lunch. One of the women was now snoring loudly. I had little hope of getting my day's pay. I had never thought of my labor as an indignity; the work had its satisfaction. But my dependence on my employer's knowing that I continued to live when I was out of their sight, that the money they searched for in the clutter of their pocketbooks was vital to my existence—it was that that filled me with choked-down rancor. There was something about a woman working in the house, I had long ago concluded, that blotted out an essential distinction between hirer and hired, almost as though the need my work filled should be wages enough.

I was relieved to see, as I started toward the door in my street clothes, that Mrs. Justen was not going to forget, that she was hurrying toward me, pocketbook in hand. She veered suddenly toward her mother, still in the straight-backed chair, but slumped over, her skin ashen.

I waited uncertainly at the door. "I've got it straight," Mrs. Justen said triumphantly. "It wasn't you who phoned me Saturday. It was I who phoned you!"

"Oh, Marylou," her mother said faintly, lifting her hands then letting them fall back on her lap.

"Yes! Yes! Yes!"

Mrs. Early smiled insipidly. "What does it matter, sweetheart?" she asked.

"But that's what made you so angry! You say I never call—it's always you who calls . . ."

"What do such things matter?" Mrs. Early asked again in the hushing voice of a mother with an unreasonable child. "All right. You did phone me. Does that make you feel better?"

"That's not the point!" cried Mrs. Justen.

"The maid is waiting," Mrs. Early said patiently. "I think you've forgotten her."

"Don't you give me lessons in memory and forgetting," Mrs. Justen said in a strangled voice.

"That is unforgivable," Mrs. Early retorted with more spirit.

"I'm going now," I said loudly.

"For heaven's sake! Pay the poor woman," Mrs. Early shouted.

"You'll drive me mad!" Mrs. Justen muttered. She took some bills from her pocketbook and came toward me with them in her hand.

"I'm sorry," she whispered to me. "But you see how it is."

"Are you discussing me with the servant?" Mrs. Early called out throatily.

I hurried away from the apartment house. I guessed that soon Mrs. Early would grow tearful and begin to utter extravagant and imprecise accusations against herself. Mrs. Justen would grow bored and run out of the apartment. There could be no resolution between them. Mrs. Early was either lofty or self-abased. In any case, they were mired in their attachment to each other.

Something did drive Mrs. Justen mad that year. She fell into a black depression. She would not get out of bed except to use the toilet. One day, she didn't do that. Mrs. Early took her to Bellevue Hospital.

Although I disliked Mrs. Early, I continued to clean the apartment as she asked me to when she moved into it, partly out of necessity, but partly out of pity I felt for her daughter. Week by week, Mrs. Early got rid of the animals until there was only one female cat left. "At night, it paces back and forth outside the bedroom door," she told me. "Do you know my daughter often slept with all those animals piled up on her like a blanket? My Lord! She used to kiss them!"

One afternoon Mrs. Early drew me to a bureau where she had placed her husband's photograph in its silver frame. He was wearing a soldier's uniform, and it was hard to tell much about him from the blank military posture and stare with which he had faced the camera. "He was a hero," she murmured. "A patriot. He died for his country."

I left her there brooding over the picture. Mrs. Justen had told me her father had been killed in a car smash-up on a New Jersey highway. Mrs. Early would find a way, I was sure, to join that fact with her story of her husband's patriotism. When you were like Mrs. Early, you could say anything.

Mrs. Justen came home after two months. She was pale, very thin, and she had a new air of resolution, even in the way she picked up a pen or opened a window. It was as though she felt she had missed the concrete feel of things all her life and was now determined that nothing should pass her by. She continued to rescue animals, but she didn't keep them long. She discovered places out of the city which sheltered them while trying to place them. "I love this little creature," she would tell me in a firm voice. "But enough is enough. I can only do what I can."

Mrs. Early moved back to her own apartment but visited her daughter nearly every day and fussed over her as she always had. When her mother sat gazing at her as she read a manuscript, Mrs. Justen would say, "Mother, go away. Go to another room. I can't concentrate." Dutifully, Mrs. Early would go to the kitchen where, when I went to fetch a can of wax or a rag, I would find her sitting tensely at the table, still watching.

One day Mrs. Justen asked me, "Is Phoebe Burgess terrified of multiple sclerosis and other exotic diseases the way she used to be?" I was startled but tried not to show it. Only last week, Mrs. Burgess had been telling me how she'd have moments of agonizing panic because she thought she'd detected the first symptoms of some disease. I had seen her reading through medical books but quickly passing over the luridly colored photographs of diseased flesh that accompanied the text.

Mrs. Justen looked down at the magazine she was holding. "When my—" she hesitated, began again, "when my husband and I gave up," she said, "I thought I was dying." She paused. "And I went to Phoebe. All the time I was crying, she was telling me about multiple sclerosis, how horrible it was. Finally, I just grabbed her arm and shook it so she'd listen to me. She looked at my hand and tapped it twice and said, 'You need a psychiatrist.'" Mrs. Justen laughed harshly and shook the magazine.

"Look at this," she said. I bent over her to look at the full-page ad she wanted me to see. It was of an elaborate wheelchair with some sort of motor attached to one arm. "Just the thing for her as the disease advances, wouldn't you say?" Mrs. Justen asked.

If I'd not been a servant, I might have defended Mrs. Burgess, although I wasn't sure what Mrs. Justen's charge against her was, only the ordinary one that could be made against most people—against Mrs. Justen herself—that they lacked genuine sympathy for anyone else's troubles.

But Mrs. Burgess never pretended she felt it. She made her own offering—her exhilaration, her life, at its best, like a parade full of spirit and gaiety. Perhaps it was envy that accounted for Mrs. Justen's resentment.

.   .   .

Some people, I had learned over the years, didn't think about taste, good or bad. But for others, it had the consolation and arbitrariness of religion, and like religion, excluded from grace those who deviated from its pronouncements.

Mrs. Burgess laughed when I asked her for a tablecloth one afternoon. I was about to set the table for a dinner party she was giving that evening. "Nobody uses them anymore," she said. The round table Mr. Burgess had bought in England years before, and had had shipped all the way home, was scarred and stained. When I began to work for her, I had asked her if I should use steel wool on its surface. She'd shrieked and thrown up her hands in mock horror. When she had found me brooding over it, she'd said, "Now, Luisa, stop worrying about that table. It looks just the way it ought to."

She went to special stores to buy things, figs packed in wooden boxes, dark, malt-smelling loaves of bread, French preserves in jars I would have kept but which she threw away once they were emptied, and imported bottles of olive oil, their labels adorned with drawings of olive groves or elaborate scrolls in vivid colors. Each of the many demitasse cups on a pantry shelf was different. I asked her why she didn't have a matching set—had Mr. Marsh taken some away? "They're not supposed to match," she said reprovingly, then giggled. "Well, maybe you're better off, Luisa, not knowing these things."

For her dinner parties, she prepared one or two dishes. "Will there be enough?" I once asked her anxiously. "Not for the swine who are coming tonight," she replied. "They won't know what they're getting. But the hell with them . . ."

I learned to cook a few dishes from watching Mrs. Burgess, although I had trouble finding the ingredients in the stores in my neighborhood. But the clothes she gave me never looked right. I couldn't carry them off the way she did. Amy looked at them longingly but they didn't fit her. I ended up taking them to a church a few blocks from home and stuffing them into a large wooden box that had Vincent de Paul written on the side of it in black paint.

.   .   .

Several years ago, I had given up Greer and reclaimed Sanchez as my name. But the wedding ring Tom had bought for me in a Broadway store when we began to live together, remained in the bottom of a small felt bag where I kept a few pieces of jewelry he had given me, an opal necklace, two silver bracelets, several pairs of earring studs. Searching in the bag, my fingers would come upon the ring. Sometimes I took it out and slipped it on and looked at it, the narrow gold circle which had once contained me, and that I had imagined I would wear all my life until it would sink into my flesh as Nana's wedding ring had sunk into hers. I couldn't give it away or throw it away. I would stare at it lying on my palm; where it touched my skin, it provoked a faint sensation, a tingling. It was a mystery, a fish swallowing its own tail, a thing in pursuit of itself.

.   .   .

Ellen wrote that she was working with back country folk outside of Atlanta. For the first time, because of the Voting Registration Act, she felt her legal services were of real use.

"A lot of black people are scared to death by what we're trying to do," she wrote. "In this place where I'm staying, they have to register at the sheriff's office, the last place they want to be. I've been boarding with a minister and his family. His children go to a swimming hole in the afternoons to cool off. The other day I was about to jump in when I saw a snake swimming right at me. I can hardly stand it, I'm so scared one of the little kids will get bitten. Or I will. The first night I slept in this house, a snorting old car drove by jammed with men. Shotguns were poking out the windows. Despite all this, I love the south. It's not safe for my skin, but it's a lot safer for my mind. I loved getting your letter and hearing about Charlie. He sounds like such a nice serious boy, like Thaddeus was. I think of all our days together. They made me happy and they still do. Don't worry about me when you read some of the horror stories in the papers. (Luisa, you *are* reading the newspaper, aren't you?) In the thick of things, it's different from the way it sounds. I've never felt such an informed joy."

I didn't worry much about Ellen. I couldn't believe anything would happen to her. I pondered over "informed joy." Perhaps it was what I'd felt when Charlie was born.

.   .   .

"He deserves it," Mrs. Burgess said, her eyes bright with tears as she told me she was taking Brian to Quebec and Montreal in July. She hugged Brian who stared at me over his mother's shoulder with owlish eyes. At ten, he'd shot up like a weed after a rainfall, his dandelion hair falling over his eyes, his usual expression mocking or else disappointed. The telephone rang. "Fuck it!" exclaimed Mrs. Burgess. Brian flung himself down in a chair. "That'll be the day," the boy said, "when you don't answer a phone." Mrs. Burgess gave him a look full of gratification. "Look how he understands me," she said. "But just watch me not answer it this time. I know it's Mary Fender and she'll have to wait. Come on, Luisa. We have to do the marketing."

Every Friday, I went with her to the big market three long blocks away. They didn't deliver, and she always had a long shopping list for weekends. I didn't like going. In the hardware store where she might want to stop for some small item, her loud disparaging remarks about the cheap, decorated cooking utensils earned us hard looks from other customers. In the market, she would call out comments about the meat she was examining as though I was standing across the street. "Why does she start yelling the minute she gets into a store?" Charlie asked me after he'd gone with us one Friday. I didn't think she knew she was making such a racket, I told him.

I hadn't been candid. I suspected she did know. I wondered if she thought she was a famous person. Everything about her interested me then. She was, I thought, beyond the reach of judgment just as Beatriz de la Cueva had been, issuing pronouncements from her great bed. Mr. Clare had remarked that some people were marvels because they were so absolutely what they were, their styles so true to their natures, "like crocodiles," he had said.

As I ironed, I heard her on the phone telling one friend or another her opinions on politicians, movies, each other, and especially on what Father Owen had said to her, and how wonderful he was. I guessed when a friend was trying to report on her own life when Mrs. Burgess began to worry a cuticle with her teeth. And I sensed she was waiting eagerly for a chance to bring the conversation around to herself. When she hung up, still smiling at a joke she'd been told, her face flushed with pleasure, she would clap her hands together and describe to me the delicious supper she was going to make for her friend George, and George's fool of a girlfriend, or for some other couple, one of whom she usually disparaged, although she might take the sting out of her remarks by saying that she had once been just as besotted with Marsh as dumb Lila was with George, or just as ignorant as Georgia Casten was about love before she learned so much about herself and life, from Father Owen. She had told me several things about the Episcopal priest whom she saw more often than anyone in Malagita had ever seen the village priest. He had been a close friend of her mother's, and after the death of her parents had become, she said, her unofficial guardian. "Great-uncle Wilfred was so old and he didn't know beans about babies," she observed. I had no way of knowing if she went to Father Owen's church on Sundays—she never mentioned that. I guessed she didn't. I couldn't imagine her sitting in a pew surrounded by other people hearing God's unexclusive word.

She was so open, so lacking in caution; I had come to realize how wary and secretive I was, and I admired those opposite qualities in her, trusting what I saw to be the whole truth about her.

And there was her luxurious playfulness. It was that, I knew, that so entranced Charlie. During vacation days, when he might have chosen something else to do, he would often come with me to Mrs. Burgess'. I could hear them laughing in the kitchen where she was preparing lunch. Coming upon them suddenly, she, leaning against the sink, her hands held to her flushed cheeks, Charlie grinning, looking at her with delight while Brian leaned his long length against him and tweaked his hair, it was as if I'd awakened from a sleep troubled by forlorn dreams to find myself in an atmosphere of light, of pleasure, of children playing in the sunshine, children like the two cousins I'd never met but had glimpsed years before in the beautiful gardens of the *vivienda*.

.   .   .

Tom wrote that he'd changed his mind about Charlie visiting him for six weeks. Three weeks would be less traumatic for him. I realized that with Mrs. Burgess in Canada, one day each working for Mrs. Justen and Mr. Clare—he'd given up my second day, he couldn't afford it now—I would have more time for myself than I had had in some years.

Mr. Clare had pulled himself together, and once more went out with his umbrella in hand, his homburg hat placed rakishly on his head, wearing his best blue suit. "There's nothing better looking than a chap in a navy blue suit," he had said to me somewhat ruefully. He got small jobs decorating or advising people on their collections of antiques. I was glad at the thought of free days, but when Mrs. Burgess asked me if I would do two days a week cleaning for an old school friend of hers, Gerda Mortimer, during July and part of August, I agreed at once. We always needed money, although with less desperation than we once had. Mr.

Mortimer, Mrs. Burgess told me, was a professor of French. He was going to teach a course at one of the city colleges during summer semester. Mrs. Mortimer took the children to their country house in Connecticut for the summer. "Wait'll you see them!" Mrs. Burgess said. "She can't clean, she can't cook, and her idea of style is to dress up in a dirndl and three heart lockets. He's Mr. Bandbox, a great beauty with the brain of a lobster. And no heart. Another impossible little couple like Marsh and me."

The Mortimer apartment was directly across from Mrs. Burgess', on the east side of the city. I went for my interview on a Saturday. A plump girl of about fourteen opened the door and peered at me shortsightedly. She was wearing a black brassiere beneath a transparent blouse. Her eyes were sooty with makeup, and the toenails of her bare dirty feet were painted green. She gave me an icy stare, turned her back, and slouched off down a long hall. A boy, a year or so younger, workman's boots on his feet, hanging from his bony shoulders a thin Indian shirt of the sort that had begun appearing in store windows recently, leaned against the wall and stared at me insolently.

"Is Mrs. Mortimer—" I began. He held up his hand. A thick red cross was painted on his palm.

"I'm the maid," I said.

"Okay, sister," he squeaked, then called out over his shoulder, "Hey, Gerda!"

A woman appeared at the end of the hall wearing tennis shoes and a cotton bathrobe printed with red hearts. "Hi!" she said. "You Luisa? Come along, dear, to the living room."

I followed her into a room in which I was at first aware only of piles of clothing on every chair. Then I saw the handsomest man I'd ever seen lounging in front of a bookcase. He smiled at me gently, almost, it seemed, commiseratingly. Mrs. Mortimer pushed some clothes off a chair onto the floor. "Summer stuff," she said. The girl padded into the room, a huge canvas bag hanging from her shoulder. "You're not going out without shoes!" exclaimed Mrs. Mortimer. "It's a free country," the girl said sullenly. "Free for what?" murmured Mr. Mortimer.

"You think there are worse microbes on the street than there are in this apartment?" demanded the girl.

"Sit there," Mrs. Mortimer said to me, ignoring her daughter who stood behind the sofa glaring at her menacingly. "Here's the setup. I'm leaving Tuesday with the children for the country. Gerry can't manage things alone. He comes to us weekends. He'll need shirts picked up, a few errands . . . you can see the place is a mess. Housekeeping isn't my bag."

The girl emitted a jarring shriek of laughter. Her mother made an odd gesture with her hand as though brushing away a cobweb.

"Our regular is in Mobile," she continued, "with a sick mother, or so she told me. Phoebe raves about you. She must be crazy about you to recommend you to anyone. She's not great for doing favors. Gerry, do you have any questions to ask Mrs. Sanchez?"

"Miss," I said, thinking about Mrs. Burgess raving about me.

"Not a one," Mr. Mortimer said, the musing smile still playing about his lips.

"So long, Gerda," the girl said in a hard voice.

"Tell her not to call me that," Mrs. Mortimer said to her husband in a tight voice.

"She'll outgrow it," he said.

She turned to me. "Can you start the first week of July? Any two days that suit you." I nodded. She held out a key.

.   .   .

"I haven't been apart from him since he was born," I said to Amy. She was poking sections of orange into a tall drink. "Now I've hurled him into the sky."

"Try this." She held out the drink to me.

"Do you miss Jack?" She had sent him off for six weeks to a camp in New Jersey.

"I do," she replied. "But I love the time to myself. I've got a lot to do in the next few weeks."

Amy was moving away to Michigan. She was getting married in September to an engineer, a Mr. Cost, a widower with one grown-up daughter. I had met him briefly and been struck by his large, innocent eyes, his quality of almost supernatural calm.

"Drink that down," she ordered me, "and then I'll make you another. Then we're going to eat dinner, a lot of nasty, creamy things your Mrs. Burgess wouldn't approve of from what you've told me."

"She's not like that," I said. I felt a wave of exuberance. I had time. Only Bird awaited me at home. "She doesn't pay attention to what other people do. She's not ready to be angry the way most people are—at least, the ones I've worked for."

"Why on earth should she be angry," Amy asked. "She gets what she wants, doesn't she?"

She took my glass and began to make another drink. "That was strong, Amy," I said.

"Wait till you drink this one!" she said. "I want you to break out for a while."

"Of what?"

She looked at me with mysterious wisdom. I felt that alarm that can arise from the friendliest exchange when you sense, backed up behind a casual remark, a long-held judgment about yourself.

"I do what I have to," I said.

"That's what I mean."

"So do you."

She ignored that. "I've had a feeling about you," she said. "You remind me of a nun I used to hear about from her niece who was a pal of mine—how the nun gave up a wicked life full of husbands and love affairs to devote herself to the poor."

"Perhaps you don't know what a servant is," I said uncomfortably, nettled now, yet struck by an echo in what Amy had said of Thad's joke about our disguises. "I can't finish this," I said, putting the drink down on one of her glass tables. "Loosen you up," she said.

"Liquor makes me silent. I got into the habit of it for a while when I was married. I don't know if Tom ever noticed how much I drank."

"Another religious order," Amy said. "Marriage. It's not everyone who can stand it. When Jack's father was sent overseas I was close to being glad. Well, relieved."

"But you're getting married again!"

"That's different. I don't love him so it won't be so hard."

I laughed at that, and she did, too, protesting, "It's not a bit funny!"

I watched her fussing over dinner. I would miss her, I knew. I would miss her simple ideas about everything in the world, the banners she hoisted up emblazoned with slogans about men and children. She knew about lawyers and makeup, about furniture and clinics and school scholarships. You had to be comfortable, she often said, it was the only way to bear up, and you had to find out how everything worked, or else you'd go under.

"Charlie must be flying over Arizona now," I said.

"He'll be fine."

"You never told me how you met Mr. Cost."

We were lingering at the table over coffee. She was silent a moment. "In a bar," she said at last. "He was looking for someone, just like I was."

"He didn't seem like the kind of man who hangs around bars," I said.

"He isn't," she said. "He was miserable there. That's why I noticed him."

.   .   .

I let myself into the Mortimer apartment the following week. It took me two hours just to clean the kitchen. I started to explore and discovered Mr. Mortimer in a small, very neat room off the living room. He was bent over a pile of papers on his desk. He lifted his head to gaze at me, then put down a pen slowly. "Do you need anything?" he asked. "Have you found what you need?" I nodded and started to withdraw.

"I leave for my class after midday. So if you do need anything—"

"No, I'm fine. I've found everything."

"Sorry it's so awful."

"I've seen worse." I started to leave again.

"Where?" he asked curiously. "Not at Phoebe's," he added reflectively.

"I've worked for a lot of people."

"Are you Spanish? Well, of course you are. With that name."

"I am and I'm not," I answered, wanting urgently to go. It was difficult not to stare at him.

"The Antilles? Ecuador?" he questioned lightly.

"I'll start on the living room now—if the vacuum cleaner won't disturb you."

"Did you find the bags? Gerda drove Lizzie crazy. She never got enough bags. I ordered ten boxes for the vacuum cleaner, enough, I estimated, for ten years."

"I found them."

"I hope there's something for your lunch in the fridge."

"I can go out and get something."

"So it was empty. I'll go out and get some bread and cheese. Do you like bread and cheese? Is that—"

"—Really, Mr. Mortimer. I'd better get back to work. There's a lot to do."

"I'm sorry," he said. "I'm keeping you. The absentminded professor . . ."

He wasn't a bit absentminded, I thought, as I began to work on the living room. He'd kept me in his study with an iron grip.

The next day I came to work, he said, "I admire your efficiency." He was wearing a light cotton bathrobe and leather slippers that morning. His skin shone from his bath.

"You've had maids before," I said stiffly.

"They don't stay long, or else they fall under my wife's spell and start rioting in the kitchen, drinking the white wine, and dropping coffee grounds on the floor. Gerda is possessed by a demon of disorder. If I replace a book on the shelf, Gerda thinks it's the day after the funeral."

I was alarmed and embarrassed by the way he was speaking to me, the confiding note, the social tone, as though I was someone else. I stared down at my old black shoes. They were so ugly, they reminded me forcibly of what I was doing there. I caught sight of his foot; he had slid it out of his slipper. It was a narrow, high-arched foot, the skin golden.

"You have an alert expression," he said. "As though you were listening."

I picked up the brown paper bag which held the rags and polish I would be using and went out of the kitchen. Later, while I was ironing a dress I had washed when I found it balled up and dirty in Mrs. Mortimer's closet, I heard the front door close. If he spoke to me in such a way again, I'd have to leave, I resolved.

I had less to do the following Monday, and I intended to go right after Mr. Mortimer left. The apartment was clean though disorder threatened. Mrs. Mortimer, like Mrs. Burgess, was a collector. She didn't have Mrs. Burgess' selectivity. Dozens of antique bottles stood on shelves gathering dust along with empty jam jars, some of which still bore their labels. The kitchen was bare, a few blackened pots in one cabinet, a set of plastic dishes in another. Dinner dishes and glasses were in a glass-fronted cabinet in the dining room. Among them were spools of thread, scissors, writing implements, and scraps of paper on one of which was written a long list beginning with: *get moth balls*, and ending with a sentence: *I must do everything I have ordered myself to do.* It was dated a year earlier and signed, Gerda Lyle Mortimer.

Behind the Mortimer bed, an enormous object that extended across half of the room, hung a great whorl of dusty beige satin. In her closet, half of her clothes lay on the floor among the worn shoes. Mr. Mortimer's shirts and sweaters were on flat shelves in another closet; his beautiful suits hung from padded hangers. Marriage between two such closets seemed improbable.

I was eating a sandwich I had brought from home when Mr. Mortimer walked into the kitchen. The folds of his soft white shirt rose against his strong neck.

"Oh, you've found something to eat. Good." It was noon. A sallow, almost tropical light from the inner court of the apartment filled the kitchen. We stared at each other. I felt overcome by an immense fatigue as though I'd not slept from the first moment I'd seen him, through all the looks and glances that had passed between us, the averting of eyes, the brief instants when our eyes had met, to this silent staring which made me want to cry out in protest. I put down my sandwich and went to the sink and turned on the faucet. I held out my hand and water flowed through my fingers. He was coming nearer. I won't, I told myself. I won't.

"Are you lonely?" he asked. "I'm lonely."

I shut off the water and circled away from him. In the girl's bedroom, I changed into my street clothes. When I emerged, the apartment was silent. He must have gone. I sat down in the living room and put my cold hand against my cheek. I must leave and not return.

The front door opened. A moment later, Mr. Mortimer came into the living room, halting at once when he saw me sitting there. I leaned my head against the back of the chair. He stood still, his hands hanging inertly at his sides, his head slightly bowed.

"I don't actually have classes today," he said.

The curious humility of his stance sent a shock through me as though I'd been wounded but didn't yet know where the blow had fallen. He began to walk slowly toward me. The waiting was almost unbearable. I didn't move. He reached out and took a pin from my hair. I held out my hand for it, not knowing I'd done so until I heard his faint laugh, his words, "You are fastidious."

For a few weeks that summer, I believe I was in a state of happiness. It was not a simple thing. Unlike misery, I could find no reason for it. Or perhaps it did bear some similarity to a certain kind of misery—that which Mrs. Justen had suffered, a darkness rising up that swallowed the past, the imagined future. We had few conversations. He was far less interested in my past than Tom had been, than Mr. Clare was. I don't think I ever asked him a question about himself, even so ordinary a one as where he had been born. It was the immediacy, the being out of time, that made me understand how worlds were lost to sustain it. In an instant, I'd abandoned the calm I had taken so long to find.

The ending of it came in a brief conversation between us. He had taken me to lunch in a French restaurant in the neighborhood. I was uncomfortable because of the way I was dressed. The other customers there looked rich and careless and at ease. Some of the women were middle-aged, silken layers of creamy fat girdled their wrists and hands and seemed part of the food they were consuming. I looked timidly at the menu, "What's the matter?" he asked. "You shouldn't have brought me here," I said. "I don't have the clothes . . ."

"Why are you afraid of these people?" he asked. "They do what shopkeepers tell them to do." A waiter came and stood leaning over us. Mr. Mortimer ordered for both of us. When the waiter left, he said, "Will you stay on with us—after Gerda comes back?"

"No," I said at once.

"We haven't had a word from Lizzie," he went on.

"No," I whispered passionately.

"It won't make any difference."

"It won't make any difference," I repeated in disbelief.

"Gerda probably knows," he said conversationally. "She knows most things about me."

"My God! Why do you stay married to her?"

"Do you think that's a poor reason to stay married? I know of worse ones."

I saw the waiter coming in our direction. I got up and moved quickly to the door and out to the sidewalk. A man knocked into me and gave me an indignant look. I didn't know which way to go, what to do. Mr.

Mortimer was suddenly at my side. "What are you doing," he said in a low voice, gripping my arm, and leading me uptown, toward his block. "I said something stupid," he said. "I wasn't thinking. I wanted to hold on."

"Please let go of me," I said fiercely. I saw him glance uneasily at a couple staring at us. He released my arm. I said, "I'm going now." For a second, he closed his eyes. I turned away and ran down the street, threading my way through people until I came to the subway. I caught hold of the railing and tried to breathe normally. An elderly man asked me if I was all right. I could only nod.

The subway was uncrowded. I sat across from a family, a brown-skinned old woman, her three daughters, and asleep on the lap of one of them, a child. They were Latin, and from their Spanish which I could hear clearly at each station stop, they were from the Caribbean. The three young women spoke with animation and confiding, impatient gestures but the old woman was still, her face calm, dreaming as she gazed from time to time at the sleeping child. Her blouse was embroidered with bamboo shoots and large red flowers. She might have picked it out and bought it only fleetingly aware that it reminded her of another country. On the wedding finger of her wrinkled brown hand, a wedding band glowed. Her broad feet were shod in Chinese slippers, red and embroidered with gold thread. One of the women reached out and stroked the old woman's crinkled silver hair. She grew aware of my stare; she leaned toward me slightly, her gaze sharpening into a faint challenge. I turned my head away. When they left the train at the last stop before it went under the river to Queens, I leaned forward to catch a glimpse of her as two of the women gripped her arms and hurried her down the platform. I thought of Nana for whom everything made a difference.

On the way home, I passed a squat, new brick church, except for its short spire and small cross as ambiguous as any other suburban place of commerce. I would have confessed to a priest that I had fallen into the master's arms with lewd haste, discarding my clothes as eagerly as he had. I would claim I had known it would end as abruptly as it had begun. If he had asked me what I had expected, I would have told him, severely, that that was not a proper question for a priest to ask. Like Amy, I had been looking for someone, but not in a bar, in an apartment I was obliged to clean. I would not have told a priest that. Would I have cared at all if Mr. Mortimer had not said his wife probably knew, and that I had instantly imagined her looking at us all the way from that country house to where we lay entangled and sweating against the back of her living room couch on a workday summer morning?

What penance would a priest give me as cruel as the embarrassment I felt which loosened my bowels and made me want to grip the arms of the people I was passing and beg them to distract me from the unbearable shame I felt over a thing that had made no difference, not—as had been my first outraged thought—only for him, but for me.

Against the contemplation of that cold love, I tried to evoke the old intoxication of images of Malagita. Nothing rose up in my mind except Mr. Mortimer's beautiful face that had so transfixed me.

.   .   .

Charlie came home two days later. I saw him at once among the other debarking passengers. He was tanned, and he looked much taller than when I had left him at the airport.

I hugged him. He felt muscular, strong.

"How was it?"

"Pretty good. The beaches are great."

"Your father?"

"I'll tell you later. I want to get home and see Bird."

He never told me much. After he had unpacked his suitcase, he said, "He's got a big real estate agency out there. He makes a lot of money. I went out with Gina once to a drugstore to pick up some medicine for him. The prescription wasn't ready, and she started shouting that she was Mrs. Greer, didn't they know? And what was the meaning of the medicine not being ready? She goes on like that all the time."

That evening he was quiet and preoccupied. In slow motion, he looked through his books and old school papers and stamps. Just before he went to bed, he came to stand beside the chair I was sitting in, sewing a tear in a pair of his trousers.

"Most of the time, he didn't even notice I was there," he said. "I wish he wasn't that way."

I put my arm around his waist but he pulled away from me. In the middle of the night, I awoke. Charlie was in the kitchen. He had made himself a pot of coffee and a pile of toast. He had never cared for coffee before.

"I like it now," he said, smiling at me. "I liked getting up and making it. I'm really glad to be home."

       •   •   •

Mrs. Burgess came home that week, too. They'd had quite a time, she said, rolling her eyes. Brian had driven hotel staffs crazy all over Canada. "That boy!" she exclaimed proudly. Right after they'd gotten off the plane, Brian had developed a high fever and still had it, but he desperately wanted to visit a school friend that afternoon. Mrs. Burgess hadn't called the doctor yet. Did I think she should let him go? "Not with a fever," I said.

"But he'll be so disappointed. He hasn't seen anybody for a whole month. I don't think it's anything really serious. Don't you think he could go for a couple of hours?"

"No," I said with more irritation than I had meant to show. I was dusting bookshelves and had not been looking at her as she spoke. At her silence, I turned. She was standing a few feet away from me. In one hand, in the middle of her palm, lay a gold maple leaf pin. As I looked, her fingers slowly closed over it, and she slipped it into the pocket of her skirt. I had the impression she had meant to give it to me.

"I'm going to let him go," she said, with not a trace of the uncertainty that had been in her voice only a moment earlier.

I moved uneasily under her glance. It was such a strange, fixed expression; it immobilized her features; it made her eyes go dead.

Years later, Mr. Clare showed me a Mexican stone carving of a mythical animal a young friend had brought back from a trip to Yucatan. Its lidless eyes started out of its head and were as round as marbles, unseeing, neither animal nor human. It was Mrs. Burgess' look when she was crossed.

       •   •   •

For a long time, I brooded about Mr. Mortimer. Fleeting recollections left me breathless, drained of the strength I needed for the tedium and labor of cleaning. My mortification had slowly drained away, leaving a pale emptiness in which images of the prodigality of carnal life played out their scenes without color or sound.

Mrs. Burgess asked me how it had been to work for the Mortimers, trying to elicit from me with her own ironic comment details of their household which she could laugh over. I told her little, agreeing simply that Mrs. Mortimer was certainly something. The chilling fear I had had, that Mrs. Mortimer would tell Mrs. Burgess that her husband had been making love to the maid she'd sent her, had evaporated. In the event, I had determined to claim those hours, to say, "Yes, that is what happened."

"Were you alone with him ever?" she asked.

"Some mornings," I said, turning to the sink to wash away the silver-cleaning paste from my hands. I could sense her waiting.

"He made a pass at me," she said.

The range of what she would consider a pass was great, I thought. He might have complimented her on a dress she was wearing.

She left the kitchen after a moment. In the living room, I discovered her standing at the window.

"Come here a moment," she said pensively.

I went to her. "All the leaves are gone," she said, gesturing at the park below. "How sad it looks. The tree branches fork like legs. Doesn't it look like a field of women with their heads buried in the ground?"

I saw what she meant, how the thicker branches swelled like thighs. Later, I watched her prepare her lunch. She was cutting radishes over a mound of cottage cheese. Absorbed, unaware of my scrutiny, she sprinkled parsley over the radishes and held up the dish and murmured, "Pretty . . ." She gave me a quick glance then. "I'm on a new diet," she said, and laughed. I listened intently as one listens to a whisper. I thought I heard her forgive herself in her laughter for what was only a child's innocent greed.

.   .   .

For the first time since I'd begun to work for Mrs. Burgess, she began to question me about San Pedro. Was the food like Mexican food? Had I heard of any bad incidents involving American tourists?

I described the countryside around Malagita. She fidgeted.

"What I want to know is if the beaches are safe. In Cuba, they have those shark nets, or used to."

"I don't know about beaches," I said. "But the food isn't Mexican."

She waved her hands impatiently. "Oh, never mind that," she said. "We'll eat in the hotel restaurant. Stupid imitation French crap. They're all the same, those islands. I just don't want Brian and me to get murdered by crazy people."

I stared at her mutely.

"A lot of trashy types spend holidays in those places," she said regretfully. "But Brian has to have some sun during the Christmas break. So why not?"

"You're going to San Pedro?"

"Well, it's not the moon, Luisa. It's only a five-hour flight."

That she should go there in the passing of an afternoon was as incomprehensible to me as the idea of men in weighted suits being shot out into space to circle the earth. When I had heard from Papá about Federico's trips to Estremadura, I had imagined it had taken him weeks, yet I knew as well as anyone else that people flew to the Caribbean night and day.

I ironed their clothes, saw them packed in suitcases, listened to the ruckus of their voices lifted in anticipation and excitement and argument. Mrs. Burgess asked me no further questions about San Pedro.

She was perched on the arm of a chair as I pressed a linen blouse. She was leafing quickly, impatiently, through a woman's fashion magazine. I started to put the blouse on a hanger, but she reached for it and took it from my hand without looking up.

Part Four

On an impulse, I walked to Broadway, thinking I might find a gift for Brian's seventeenth birthday in one of the new shops that had settled into narrow spaces once occupied by small markets or cheap shoe and hosiery outlets, and which now displayed seaweed and rosehip concoctions, heelless footwear with toes that swelled like derby hats, paraphernalia for drug use, surplus military uniforms from wars unremembered, or unknown, to those who bought them, and craft stores which exhibited in their windows pottery and jewelry and leather articles. In one of these last, I pushed open the door, a bell rang, and the young woman lounging behind a counter, apparently sunk in thought, turned her head ever so slowly to give me the benefit of a lofty gaze. At the back of the room, a bearded, long-haired young man worked at a rough table on a leather bag. An enormous black cat suddenly leaped to the counter. The girl's face softened. "Lumumba, man, that's no place for you to take a walk," she said, lifting him and lowering him to the floor.

"I'd like something for a young boy," I said. She yawned.

"A belt," I said, "or a wallet."

"Which?"

"A wallet."

I picked out the plainest one she showed me—the others were covered with designs of snakes or steer horns—but it cost more than I could really afford. Still, I bought it. It would be the first gift I'd made to anyone in a household where I'd been employed as a servant.

It wouldn't be noticeable in Brian's pirate's hoard of gifts. But as I walked toward Central Park, the box in my hand, I was pleased by the thought he might use it. It was August, and the sidewalks were filled with strolling people. The trees were motionless in the park, their leaves glittering where light from street lamps touched them.

In the elevator, I heard the bone-rattling racket of amplified music. The living room was empty, every light turned on. From the speakers of the record player, a male voice moaned. The music thumped with the irregular pounding of an ailing heart. On a table set aside for the purpose reposed Brian's presents. In the morning, Mrs. Burgess had stood over them, brooding, picking them up, rearranging them. I started toward Brian's bedroom, wanting to put my gift in his hand. Mrs. Burgess rushed in, her eyes wide with excitement, her long jet earrings quivering among the ringlets she had let escape the mass of hair piled on top of her head, held there by a long silver pin.

I held up the box. "Is Brian dressing? I brought him—"

"—No, no!" she interrupted urgently. "Put it on the table." She snatched the box from my hand and placed it among the other things.

"Will you listen to that shit! I told Brian to turn the sound down. We'll have the cops!"

I lowered the volume on the record player and went off to the kitchen. Mrs. Burgess followed. On a counter stood a nearly empty teacup. I started to wash it, but she grabbed it from my hand, muttering, "Bourbon, leave it . . ." She filled the cup with more liquor and drank, then rolled her eyes toward the ceiling. "I'll be glad when this day is over," she declared. "But they are sweet, aren't they, Luisa?" The doorbell rang and she ran out of the kitchen.

I picked up one of her cookbooks and idly turned the pages. I thought suddenly of Mr. Mortimer. In the morning, after she'd gotten a phone call, Mrs. Burgess had come to where I was vacuuming and stooped to turn off the machine. "You remember the Mortimers? Those people you worked for, years ago, when I took Brian to Canada?"

I nodded. Her eyes had glittered with amusement. "Well—they've broken up!" She looked at me expectantly. "He ran off with a girl?" I asked neutrally. "No!" she cried triumphantly, "that's the joke! *She* did!"

"Perhaps they can all live together," I said, turning the machine back on. I glanced at her. She was staring at me with a touch of surprise.

From the living room I heard the shouts of Brian's guests as they arrived and Mrs. Burgess' welcoming explosions of laughter. The system of Mr. Mortimer's life, as I had reflected upon it over the years, had grown to seem like a fortress, less susceptible of change than marriages made rigid by unspoken laws like those of the Millers and the Geldens. Now there would be more packed suitcases—more lawyers' work, I thought. But Gerald Mortimer would find another slatternly woman, and in other chaotic rooms show off his precise, uncluttered beauty and devise for himself a monk's bare cell. Those children of his—but they weren't children anymore! He might not recognize me if we passed on a street.

Mrs. Burgess came into the kitchen accompanied by two huge pink boys in linen suits, their glossy black curls tumbling down to their shoulders. "Look at these adorable brothers," she ordered me. "They're *hungry*! Give them some of that salmon, Luisa." The boys looked down at her dumbstruck, their mouths open, their bloodred lips working slightly as though they nursed on some substance in the air. After they had fed on salmon and toast, observed dotingly by Mrs. Burgess, and left, I forced my thoughts away from Mr. Mortimer to Charlie.

He was coming to pick me up and walk home with me at midnight when the party was to end. It was dangerous to be out on the street so late alone. He had been home a week from Florida where he had been spending most of his time these last few years. It was easier to get work there, easier to live, he had told me. Only two of his high school classmates had gone on to college. "Everybody's a carpenter now," he'd said with a smile, "with some exceptions." One boy he'd known had become a millionaire and gone into real estate. He'd made a fortune growing marijuana on a neglected piece of land in Delaware that belonged to an uncle, planting a border of corn around the weed to hide it from the police. "Maybe I'll end up in business, too," Charlie had said. "Everybody in this country seems to in the long run."

He had started working after school hours when he'd turned fifteen. He didn't ask me for money although I gave him what I could spare. The child support, my last material connection with Tom, had stopped after Charlie's eighteenth birthday. He'd gone to California to visit his father last year, and Tom had said he would pay the tuition if Charlie would go to college.

"I don't know whether I'll go or not. I'm thinking about it," he had said. He had been feeling tired this last year, he told me; he thought it was because he didn't know anything, his ignorance depressing him more than lousy jobs, running a tractor in a prison farm camp, or putting a new roof on somebody's jerry-built house. There was worry in his face. He guessed the carpenter days were coming to an end, he said. It was strange to me, the idea of Charlie in college and I felt a kind of vague hilarity at the unexpectedness of it. I began to arrange the food Mrs. Burgess had prepared on the platters she had put out earlier in the day. Charlie suddenly walked into the kitchen.

"The front door was open," he said. "It smells like a dope den in there. Is Brian pushing these days?"

"He's too lazy," I said, "even for that."

"Are you going to be ready to go soon?"

"After they're fed," I answered. We smiled at the same moment.

A dreadful shriek cut through the rock music like a line of fire. Charlie and I ran into the living room where Mrs. Burgess stood alone, one hand covering the lower part of her face, the other pointing toward her bedroom.

Brian's guests were crowded around Mrs. Burgess' bathroom door. I followed Charlie as he pushed them aside. Someone flushed the toilet and a girl giggled shrilly.

Lying in the bathtub was a boy around Brian's age. He was gasping, his hands waving feebly as though seeking a purchase. Charlie knelt and gripped his arm.

"What'd you take?"

The boy groaned. Charlie shook him. A line of bubbles was forming in the corners of his mouth.

"Does anyone know what he took?" Charlie demanded, looking up at the faces of three girls whose manes of hair fell forward like curtains as they leaned over him. One mumbled, "He must have brought it with him. George swallows anything."

Mrs. Burgess, in the living room, was calling upon God and Father Owen. "He's got to go to the hospital," Charlie said. He lifted the boy out of the tub then half-carried him into the living room where the boy crumpled against him. A girl cried out. Mrs. Burgess was backed up against a window. "I'm going with you, Charlie," Brian said.

"No!" groaned Mrs. Burgess. Brian didn't look at her. He and Charlie together dragged the boy through the front door and out into the hall.

In a few minutes, the guests all trailed away. Only the pink boys in their linen suits grinned amiably and bid Mrs. Burgess good night as though this had been an ordinary evening for them and the boy's collapse into the bathtub merely a sign that it was time to depart.

I picked up an ashtray filled with small brown butt ends like animal droppings and went to the kitchen. Mrs. Burgess followed me, saying, "Couldn't it just be pot? Some people can't take pot. But how can you stop them from using it?"

I started to take the vacuum cleaner from the closet. "Don't," she said in a low voice. "I want some tea." She was standing in the middle of the kitchen, her hands clasped against her stomach, her shoulders bent, giving her the bundled-up look she had when she was troubled.

"I know Brian uses it—a little," she said. "But he's not crazy," she added aggressively. "He knows when to stop." She put out two cups on the kitchen table and after she had poured out the tea, I sat down across from her. She took a sip. "Oh, I feel better," she said with a fluttering sigh. "Charlie's so grown-up. You remember when I sewed those buttons on his shirt? He didn't quite trust me." She giggled at the thought but at once looked solemn. "Oh, I hope everything will be all right."

I looked away from her, overcome with aversion toward rich children, their drugs, their limp passage through youth, acquisitiveness and discontent settling and hardening about the unformed softness of childhood.

"It's awful, isn't it," she said simply, and with such feeling I thought she'd read my mind.

"I wonder if other people know what to do when the really bad thing happens," she mused. "Does anyone ever know what to do?"

"Some of the time, I guess."

"I never know what to do."

We talked in a desultory way about the peril in the streets and how the city had changed in the eight years she'd been living in her apartment until Brian burst into the kitchen, Charlie, a step behind him.

"They think he took acid," Charlie told us. "It can be serious."

"What do you mean? Serious!" exclaimed Mrs. Burgess. Brian gazed at her bleakly.

"Don't you know what serious is, Mammy?"

"I told the doctor we'd found him sitting on the curb on our way home from the movies, that Brian knows him from school but hadn't seen him since June." He was staring at Mrs. Burgess, waiting, I guessed, for an acknowledgment from her that he'd protected her household. She gave no sign she was aware of what he'd done. Brian said he'd telephoned George's mother. His father had died of cancer last winter. "I'm going to bed," Brian said. "Some goddamned birthday party."

"But your father will give you another one," Mrs. Burgess said to him supplicatingly. "Wait! There must be something on the tube. We'll hunt up a movie, darling."

As Charlie and I passed through the living room, I saw that Brian had not gotten around to opening his presents. I looked briefly through Mrs. Burgess' bedroom door. She was huddled against a pillow, Brian, holding another pillow against his chest, leaned against the bed. Already the light from the television set was flickering on their utterly still faces.

"Let's not wait for a bus," I said to Charlie.

"Okay."

I often walked to work to Mr. Clare's or Mrs. Burgess'. I only took the bus to Mrs. Justen on the east side when I was late getting up in the morning; in the last few years I had sometimes overslept. When I'd moved from Long Island, after Charlie had left home, walking was a celebration of my emancipation from subways and buses. I had rented a small apartment on Ninety-fourth Street. Broadway was a few steps away. It was not the Broadway I had known. The neighborhood had filled up with whimsical shops and foreign restaurants and their customers, people who looked as if they could slouch through the world without being surprised at anything they saw—or anyhow, as if it was their intention to appear so.

Two men slammed out of a bar as we passed it. I was glad Charlie was with me, not only because of the late hour and drunks but because the boy in the bathtub had frightened me, the foam on his lips, his helpless, grasping hands, his rolling eyes, an intimation of chaos, of an unravelling of all that had become ordered and comfortable for me. Mr. Clare's heart attack last year had not alarmed me half as much.

"That boy thinks he can have everything," Charlie said.

"I expect he can."

We walked up the two flights of stairs to my apartment. "I still miss Bird," Charlie said as I unlocked the door's three locks. "You remember how she was always waiting for us when we came home?"

"I remember."

The older I grew, the more I missed everyone. I had thought emotion would diminish, cool as the separate years fused, the lines once dividing them all swallowed up by time. But the past had become a dense cloud bank out of which peered the faces of those lost or gone, growing more distinct, more plaintive, with each passing month of my life. If I lived long enough to become old, I thought, I would not be able to bear any loss at all. When Brian's miserable, nervous dog died, I'd been surprised by my own tears. Brian had suddenly leaned against me the day Mrs. Burgess came home from the animal hospital with the news of Sleepy's demise. "We'll get another dog tomorrow," Mrs. Burgess had promised. "Oh, Mammy, I don't want another dog," Brian had protested, his tears wetting the collar of my blouse.

But one loss had taken time to make itself felt—the astonishment at Mrs. Burgess that had broken over me like a great wave of light the first day I had begun to work for her. I was no longer beguiled. I was still yoked to her household, but by a bond that was largely practical. She was, after all, the Madam, as Mrs. Dove had called the woman she had worked for.

.   .   .

In some ways, Mrs. Burgess looked younger than when I'd first seen her on a winter morning wrapped up in a blanket in the doorway of the farmhouse on Long Island.

Laughing, at times piercingly girlish, she attended to the school friends Brian brought home with him, feeding them, listening to their music, sitting among them, undismayed when they abruptly departed like a flock of alarmed birds, quoting them to me, as if everything they said was amusing and enlightening.

When she had moved into her apartment, she had made resolutions to stop drinking—next week, after Labor Day, after Christmas, when Brian went off to boarding school. In the afternoons, she would stop by the kitchen, announce that she hadn't had a drink for a week and was going to the movies to celebrate. When she returned, her face was often radiant, and she would relay to me the message she had found in the movie in a hushed voice, her tone as solemn as it was when she reported something Father Owen had said to her. After all these years she still saw him occasionally. He must have been, I imagined, one hundred years old by then, and I pictured him as looking something like Saint Joseph, leaning on a staff, his beard nearly to his ankles.

When Brian went away to a boarding school in Virginia, Mrs. Burgess' life seemed to run down and become motionless like the hands of the clock in the living room which, of late, she rarely remembered to wind. Now and then she went to dinner at Mary Fender's, a mile or so north on the same avenue, or she would have lunch with an old friend at an east side restaurant, then shop. One afternoon when she was sitting on the sofa, a novel she had just bought on her lap, a glass of wine on a nearby table, she suddenly shouted, "I'm not going to do any asshole vocational testing like Mary Fender says I ought to." The book fell to the floor and she kicked it with her foot. "It's typical of her suggestions," she said resentfully.

"The dishwasher is broken," I reported.

She looked blank. "The dishwasher," she repeated dully and sighed. "I'll call somebody." I started out of the room. "I'm just living my little life," she said.

It was when Brian began to bring friends home from school that Mrs. Burgess took a new lease on life, and made a new friend or two of her own. One morning I walked into the kitchen after passing through the silent apartment and found a naked man sitting at the kitchen table looking through one of her medical books. I went to sit in the living room, determined to stay there until he had left. A few minutes later, she appeared in her dressing gown. She looked at me questioningly. I said nothing. She went to the kitchen door and pushed it open.

"Larry!" I heard her exclaim, her voice breaking into a whinny of laughter. The door shut behind her. I heard the rumble of his voice, then hers, high and bantering. The door opened. She stared at me for a moment. "The refrigerator needs cleaning," she said coldly. I went off to Brian's room and looked through the pages of a science textbook I found on the windowsill until I heard Mrs. Burgess bid good-bye to her friend at the front door. I assumed he'd put his clothes on, by then. I felt braced, relieved, as though her coldness to me had cleansed the air of fakery, and released me from a personal concern for her which I had no right to and which, in any case, she would not return.

I didn't see the man again. Two years later, she began an affair with Mary Fender's husband, the accountant.

She had to tell me about it because I was bound to run into him, she explained. She couldn't seem to control the smile that came and went about her lips. He was unpredictable, she said. He dropped in when it suited him. Her conversations with Mrs. Fender continued with one difference; it was she who listened eagerly, pressing the receiver almost violently against her ear.

Mr. Fender did appear one day while I was there. He sat in a chair in the living room, wrapped in a thick coat, morose and silent, throwing down the wine she gave him. I left as early as I could. When I glanced back into the living room, they were both watching me. I wondered if all lovers looked so wolflike, so crazily vigilant, yet so dazed. I wondered if I had looked like that when I had fallen in love with Tom Greer.

When I opened the door to my apartment, always in dusk except for a brief moment in the early mornings when north light touched the floor beneath the living room window, the impassivity with which I imagined I had observed Mrs. Burgess and Mr. Fender gave way to a raging distress that drove me to pace the small rooms gripping a sack of groceries, unable to pause long enough to put it down on the kitchen counter.

Then I did; I put away the food I'd bought to make my solitary meals and as I set each thing in its accustomed place, I said its name aloud—salt, coffee, macaroni, canned peas, bread—and I recalled my mother's voice as she said her prayers to God whom she wished to love despite his mysterious abuse of her. And I heard in my own voice as it recited the very note of entreaty I had once derided in hers.

I shut my mouth as though someone had told me to shut it. I was not praying; I was drowning out Tom Greer's name and the words that would tell my yearning to feel toward someone as I had toward him.

Since Mr. Mortimer, I had known one man. He had sublet an apartment on the first floor of my building for a few months. We had made love in my darkened bedroom like fugitives on the run. What had passed between me and him was a thing like broken speech, a kind of bodily stammering, clumsy and reluctant, without fluency, or even kindness— no secret voice broke through our wary daylit voices.

I envied Mrs. Burgess, for all the disdain I felt toward her fleeting romances that took place in those rooms where various beautiful and expensive clocks ticked away the seconds of her life. They ticked away my life as well.

Nettled and worn out by self-dislike, and disgust for her, I went wearily to work. If she noticed a change in me, she showed no sign of it.

Georgia Casten came back into her telephone life. She and the delivery boy had been divorced, and for a long time she had been too depressed to take or make phone calls. The depression passed, Mrs. Burgess told Mary Fender, and Mrs. Casten got a job in some ex-prisoners' organization. "Work doesn't let you down," she had said, a remark Mrs. Burgess had reported to Mrs. Fender with the comment that Georgia Casten didn't understand herself any more than a chair understood itself.

One afternoon, she made three calls to Mrs. Casten. During the third which she made on the kitchen extension, I was scraping carrots for a stew she intended to make. She told Mrs. Casten that Mary Fender had invited her to a party and she didn't see how she could refuse to go. "What a disgusting idea!" Mrs. Casten had shouted so loudly into the phone, I could hear her words from the sink where I was standing. "But I've got to find out if I *can*!" Mrs. Burgess had cried. "I can't just stop seeing her."

When she'd hung up, she turned to me. "I'm going," she said calmly.

She didn't know what was the matter with Mary, she said a few days after the party, unless she was plain dumb. You'd think she would have guessed *something* by now.

I wondered if she might become a woman like Mrs. Early, a person who could say anything, a person intoxicated with the pure power of lying.

The affair with Mr. Fender ended a few months after it had begun. She was listless for weeks. She cried while she cooked. "It's not the damned onions," she said. I knew she was unhappy, that it was a large unhappiness she couldn't shake off. I felt sorry for her, and some of my old affection returned, but it was not the same as it had been.

One morning she telephoned Mary Fender. She told her how miserable she had been because she didn't know where her life was drifting. She couldn't bear anything! Maybe she should go back to school and become a librarian. Did Mary know if that took a long time? Could she find out? She spoke in a sad, submissive voice. Mrs. Fender, I guessed, asked her a question about Georgia Casten. Mrs. Burgess began to giggle. Georgia had found herself a tall Korean she was having an affair with, or else she'd found a short Korean and had him stretched. She shrieked with laughter. When she hung up the phone, she caught my glance. I had been thinking that not only Nana but her vision of life had been blown away by the hurricane. Nothing seemed to matter. There were only small comedies of behavior. I winced at the memory of Mr. Mortimer and myself gripping each other, rolling against the back of the sofa in the Mortimer living room.

She was still looking at me. "I can't help it," she said as though I'd suggested she could.

.   .   .

During the Labor Day weekend, Mrs. Burgess was going to visit old friends in Newport, Rhode Island. When she returned, she would have to get Brian ready to return for his senior year at boarding school. Brian was spending the three days with his father at their summer place on Cape May. Charlie said a friend of his from Texas was going to be visiting her family in Philadelphia so he'd take the bus down there on Friday evening. He had found a job in a camp equipment store on Second Avenue, and he hoped to find a room for himself in a couple of weeks when he had a few dollars for a rent deposit.

"Did they give you Saturday off?" I asked.

He was twiddling with the dial on the television set. There was a jumpy readiness in the way he stood, like a runner waiting for a signal to start the race.

"I wouldn't take it off if they hadn't," he said irritably.

I wanted to ask him about his friend from Texas. Usually he told me about the girls he knew. I wondered if this one was more important than the others. I put my hand on his shoulder intending to wish him a good trip, a good time. But he moved away hastily, beyond my reach.

I was glad to have the apartment to myself. It was crowded with both of us. I missed my solitude. He had not yet unpacked the duffle bag he had brought back from Florida. I suspected it held dirty clothes, and

I began to pull things out, towels, socks, a few cotton shirts. Far down in the bag, wedged against the canvas, were the carved monkeys Mrs. Burgess had given him years ago. I sat down, holding them in my hand, remembering how it had been, Charlie and I walking down the road, and then that day, like a birthday party we hadn't known we were going to.

I walked a good deal on the weekend, one day to the zoo in Central Park, the next, along Fifth Avenue to Gramercy Park where Mrs. Burgess had first looked for an apartment.

"I love the city when it's empty," Mrs. Justen had said, "when everyone has gone away." It must be full of servants, I thought, as I stood among a crowd watching a melancholy ape watch all of us, a crushed orange in one of its knotted black hands. I went to a movie, then watched another movie on television. My eyes ached, yet I craved still more flat images and preposterous talk.

When I lay down on my bed in the dark, feeling the damp elusive coolness that sometimes follows a day of city heat, I realized I was obscurely frightened.

It was the way I had felt the morning of the day Charlie was born, and years further back in Malagita, when the trees were motionless beneath a sallow sky, and everything living waited breathlessly for the dangerous winds blowing from the south. It must have been Mr. Clare I was worried about, I thought. He had been in the hospital a week for tests. I would see him Tuesday, my regular day.

Charlie came home early Monday. I threw my arms around him as though I hadn't seen him for months. His body was rigid. My arms fell away. I realized that such an unexpected embrace can be intrusive. I nearly said I was sorry and was at once puzzled by the thought of saying such a thing to Charlie. He laughed uneasily, "Come on, I'll treat you to a Chinese supper."

"It's pretty early for that," I said.

He looked momentarily confused, then he threw out his arms. "Okay, we'll be different," he said.

We sat beneath the orange-shaded lamps of the Chinese restaurant on Broadway, late afternoon sunlight streaming through the thin nylon curtains on the windows. We picked at the bowls of food Charlie had ordered with such prodigality, the smell of rice heavy and unmoving in the air like the smell of ironed sheets.

"How was Philadelphia?" I ventured.

"Fine," he said quickly.

I was glad when the meal was over. Charlie said he was going to a movie, and I had the apartment to myself that evening. By Tuesday morning, my apprehension had disappeared. I had missed Charlie so far away in Florida. Now that he had a job in the city, he might stay for a while.

I opened the door to Mr. Clare's apartment. His old friend, Mr. Darby, was in the kitchen putting a cup on a tray.

"Hello, Luisa," he said as I walked in. "The old boy is feeling a bit peaked. He'll be glad to see you. I shall never go to a hospital. At the first symptom of illness, I'll throw myself over a cliff. In Scotland, I think. They have nice cliffs there." He poured boiling water into the cup. "It's herbal tea," he said. "It will be good for him. Don't look so worried. He's cheerful. You know how he is."

I followed him into the bedroom where Mr. Clare, a week's thin growth of beard on his cheeks and chin, lay propped up on cushions from all over the apartment. At the foot of the bed, her muzzle as white as Mr. Clare's whiskers, lay Greta.

"So glad to be home," Mr. Clare murmured. "Poor Greta. Dan says she wouldn't eat while I was gone." At her name, the old dog wagged her ratty tail. "Phew . . . that hospital, Luisa dear. The way people talk to you!"

"That crushing cheerfulness," interjected Mr. Darby.

"It's like the conversations of those astronauts when they rattle around the earth . . ."

"Don't be un-American, old boy," Mr. Darby said.

Mr. Clare smiled at him, glanced at the tea he had set down on the bedside table and reached out slowly to touch his hand. "Bless you, Dan," he said.

After Mr. Darby had gone, I made lunch for Mr. Clare, a bowl of tomato soup and some stale crackers I found in a nearly empty box.

"How will you manage?" I asked him. "There's hardly anything in the kitchen."

"Is there dog food?"

"Plenty of that."

"It's all right then. Dan will look in on me every morning," he said.

"And there's a young couple down the hall who've been lovely to me. They'll do errands."

"Can't your sister come?"

He shook his head. "That wouldn't do," he said. "You know, I'm going to get better." He laughed. "I prayed for friends. I forgot to pray for a sound heart."

I did some errands for him, bringing him newspapers and magazines and the cigarettes he said, with uncharacteristic insistence, he had to have. I bought him a bouquet of yellow asters with my own money. As I arranged them in a vase on a table, he suddenly held up both his hands.

"I'm so cold," he said wonderingly. "And in this weather! Isn't it odd?"

His fingers had a bluish cast. "I'll get you some woolen gloves," I promised. "I saw some yesterday in a shop near here."

I found a cotton undershirt in a drawer. He held up his arms like a meek child. I unbuttoned his pajama top, pulled the undershirt over his head and chest and buttoned the pajama over it. "Much better!" he said, his voice high like a tenor bursting into song, a sound I had missed.

"How long have we been together, Luisa?"

"Nearly ten years."

"I hate to have you clean up after Greta. But she can't help it. You know that." The dog bellied up to him across the coverlet to place her muzzle in his hand.

"I don't mind," I said. "Can I get you anything before I go?"

"Dan's stopping in this evening. There's money for you over there on the bureau."

I put my pay in my bag and stood for a moment at the foot of the bed.

"Luisa, darling. I do love you," he said lightly. "You're a brave girl." His eyes glistened.

"Oh, Mr. Clare . . ."

"I know how you feel about me," he said. "Now, will you get me a little drink. Dan fusses so. But it does me good. Even if it didn't, I should want it and have it."

I went to the kitchen and made him a drink with what was left in the bottle. "You're out of whiskey," I told him.

"I'll be up on my feet in a day or two. Then I'll see to things."

I leaned over him to plump up the cushions. He drew his hand along my cheek, the touch of it very faint. I bent and kissed his forehead. And my heart gripped at the feel of his flesh; it was as though life's warmth had been nearly extinguished.

.   .   .

My father answered the telephone at once as though he'd been sitting beside it waiting for it to ring.

"How are you, Papá?"

"How would you expect?"

"I thought it was around your birthday . . . I wanted to—"

"Last month," he said dryly.

"I'm sorry."

"I hardly expected you to call. Let me estimate—it's been a year and a half since we've spoken, hasn't it?"

"I've had a birthday, too."

"I'm aware of that."

"How is Rose?" I asked quickly.

"Rose is always well," he replied.

Our exchange seemed exhausted. "Charlie," he uttered loudly as though pressing his lips against the phone.

"He's back here from Florida. He may stay."

"You might tell him—I'm putting records aside for him."

"I have told him."

"He might want to look at them sometime."

"I'll tell him you'd like to see him," I said, and at once wished I hadn't.

He muttered something. I said I had to go to work, and hung up Mrs. Burgess' kitchen extension phone. I was ashamed. I had been the tyrant, forcing a wish into the open that he could only bear to express indirectly. I would be obliged now to press Charlie to visit him. The old rancor I felt toward him, roused by his wariness, was with me still; its stale bitterness soured the morning, and I wished the day was over.

I took a bottle of glass polish into Mrs. Burgess' bedroom. She was sitting on the edge of her bed, staring at the floor, an opened jar of face cream in one hand. She looked up at me dazedly as though I'd waked her from an intricate dream. I sprayed the mirror that hung over her bureau, and as I looked into it, I noticed that the mahogany desk she had bought for herself recently had been moved from the living room to the front of her bedroom windows.

"How did you manage to move the desk?" I asked her, not really interested but wanting to distract myself from thoughts of Papá.

"Charlie helped me," she said brightly. "That night of the party . . . that awful party . . . I asked Charlie then. He came by one evening last week—we all moved the desk, he and Brian and I." She got up, stumbled over a slipper and laughed. "Clumsy . . ." she murmured. She started toward the bathroom, paused. I felt my eyelids flicker. The spray had dried on the mirror. The cloth had fallen from my hand, and I leaned over to pick it up. Why hadn't he told me? What night had he come here?

"It looks better over there, doesn't it?" she asked. "What do you think, Luisa?"

I nodded.

"Brian's leaving in a week, thank God! I've been feeding armies!"

Why didn't she go on into the bathroom? I began to wipe the glass, and as I cleared away the white fog of polish, I saw that she was watching me closely.

"I really like to be alone," she said, a tremor in her voice. "I've just discovered that about myself. I like—" Suddenly she went into the bathroom and closed the door. I heard the lock click into place. For all I knew, she was still there when I left.

There was a chill in the air. Summer was gone, the city was brilliant in the golden light of the year's decay. I stopped by a delicatessen and bought ham for my supper. Charlie didn't come home until late. I was awake in my bed. He turned on the television set, and I heard the mumble of voices rising and falling with eruptions of hectic laughter, all of it as incoherent as my thoughts.

　　　　　·　　　　　　　　　·　　　　　　　　　·

On Tuesday I went to Mr. Clare's. A slow autumnal rain drifted against the windows. I hung up my plastic raincoat and went to his room, calling out his name.

He was kneeling on the floor, slumped against the side of his bed. Greta lay beside him, her muzzle against his thigh. She turned her head toward me with effort. Mr. Clare's skin was blue. His cheek rested on one hand that clutched the bedcover.

I don't know how long I stood there in the unearthly silence, looking down on a body turned to stone, remotely aware of a smell, acrid yet weakly sweet, that had nearly overpowered the perfumed air. At some moment, when I could look no longer, I went to the kitchen and found Mr. Darby's office number on a list of numbers tacked to the wall beside the telephone.

We sat together in the kitchen after the ambulance had taken away Mr. Clare's body. Greta was still in the bedroom; when the ambulance men had marched in with their stretcher and lifted Mr. Clare onto it, she had feebly shifted herself under the bed. A policeman had dumped a can of coffee into a frying pan. "For the smell," he'd said, turning on the gas flame. The pungency of the burnt coffee was vile, overwhelming, and I got up and opened the window. The rain, stronger now, spattered on the floor.

Mr. Darby was crying. "He was all right last night. So frail . . . but I thought—" he covered his face with his hands.

"Did you call his sister?" My eyes burned painfully.

"I called her last week," he said as he took a fine lawn handkerchief from an inner pocket. He blew his nose, choked, sobbed, blew his nose again. "She said his life was his affair. She wasn't surprised to hear he'd had a heart attack with the life he led. She hated him, you know, alive or dead."

We sat silently. I looked around the kitchen, at the antique cookie molds hanging on one wall, an aluminum-foil-covered dish, Greta's water bowl near her old wicker basket which, Mr. Clare had told me ruefully, she would use in the daytime but not at night when she claimed his bed. The gloves I had brought for him were in a paper bag on my lap. I put the bag on the table.

"When is the funeral?"

"There'll be none," Mr. Darby said. "He arranged things months ago. He signed some horrible form so that his body would be used for research. He showed me his will right after he got out of the hospital last week. It was *stupid* of me to try to stop him smoking and drinking. He knew he was dying, Luisa. He knew."

"He was alone."

"It must have been right after I'd left him."

"He was trying to get into his bed."

"Yes."

"No funeral, not anything?"

"That's how he wished it. He was a useful person. Not at all sentimental. I even begged him, Luisa—just a little memorial service, anything." Mr. Darby suddenly smiled. "He said—what a bourgeois idea."

My raincoat was hanging from the peg where I always hung it. Soon, I'd put it on and go and never come back.

"He left you something, Luisa, that Chippendale desk in his bedroom. I promised I'd sell it for you—unless you want to keep it. He thought the money would come in handier. I think it's worth quite a lot."

Greta suddenly appeared at the kitchen door, looked at us briefly and sank down on her short legs, resting her muzzle on her paws.

"I'll have to put the doggy down," Mr. Darby said. He began to cry again. "She can't live without him. Anyhow, she must be a hundred years old. Lord! What agony it all is!"

I walked home. The rain was heavy. Through restaurant windows, I glimpsed the slow fluttering arms of waiters as they prepared tables for midday customers. A few storekeepers stood in their doorways, looking out morosely at the street. At the newsstand where I had bought newspapers for Mr. Clare, the old news dealer, a woman in a knitted black cap, sat motionless and staring at the damp edges of the papers which protruded just beyond the peaked roof of her shelter. I thought she sighed just as I passed, but it was the exhalation of my own breath. I tasted the rain, the pavement, the newsprint, and the faintly sickening odor of frying meat from the ventilator of a restaurant kitchen, and for an instant, I registered a headline with the word *Vietnam*. Though the war had been over for nearly nine months, it had continued to evoke in Mr. Clare an indignation and gloom that was uncharacteristic of him. "The waste!" he had exclaimed once. When Charlie had drawn the number 364 in the draft lottery, Mr. Clare had bought a bottle of champagne. "They'll never call him now," he had said. "We're going to drink up this bottle in celebration of one piece of good fortune. I'll tell you now, Luisa, I had already spoken to a doctor friend of mine who's gotten several young men out of the draft. We couldn't let Charlie go to that criminal war!"

He would have spoken to Greta, told her he was going to bed now, that he was feeling a bit under the weather. I had often heard him speaking to her in an amused, confiding voice, laughing out loud when I suddenly appeared, saying, "Well—at least I'm talking to *somebody*—not myself!"

He must have known at the first coarse blow of pain, the heart clutching at itself, that he was near death—and had tried to reach his bed, and fallen beside it a second, two seconds, short of life for the final effort to pull himself up on it.

I wept as I walked, rain and tears mixing on my cheeks. I went around the corner of Ninety-fourth Street. The wind shifted and blew the rain directly at me, blinding me for a moment. I wiped my eyes. From the entrance of my building, Charlie stepped out opening an umbrella, holding it out, turning briefly to look at someone behind him. Mrs. Burgess emerged. For a moment, his arm went around her shoulders. It fell away. They walked slowly up the street toward Central Park West.

Like a devil, a stinging, strangling thing took hold of my throat. I couldn't move. Run! Run! Kick them into the street, I ordered myself. Far away now, the black umbrella rode steadily in midair until it was obscured by rain. I felt a slow, sick collapse of my body, my hands' power to grip flowing so softly away.

A hard object, a running boy in a yellow slicker, slammed into me. "You fuck," he said through perfect, rosy lips. "Get outa my way!" I moved then, and gained the steps and walked into the hallway of my building.

.   .   .

I heard Charlie come home. I was sitting in my bedroom in a chair from which I'd not risen in hours. The refrigerator door opened, closed.

Had he been at her apartment, helping Brian carry his suitcases to a taxi? They would have had the place to themselves once he was gone.

Had she asked me about Charlie's girls? He must have girls, she'd said, he was so nice. Had I told her about the girl in Philadelphia? I must have. Why else would she have said on Friday that Charlie would soon be on his train to Philadelphia? How benevolently she had spoken of him! Young men and their girls, she had seemed to suggest, were the dearest creatures in the world! What *was* I recalling?

I fell asleep and waked ten minutes later. The apartment was silent.

Had they used my bed? I tiptoed into the bathroom. I looked at the washbasin, my towel folded on the rack.

But she wouldn't have cared if Brian was at home. Hadn't she told me that it was wonderful the way children knew everything these days? Not like when she had been a girl, all that shame and guilt. How had Charlie looked when he told me he was going to see the girl in Philadelphia? He'd said she was visiting her family. We had all gone away that weekend. I had walked to the zoo, and he, to her apartment, the son of her little Spanish servant. Hers. When had it begun? I went back to my room. I was afraid to turn on the light.

I strained to remember something. Why had she come to my apartment? Because it belonged to her. Everything did.

I remembered. What I remembered were the faces of Señora de la Cueva's servants. They had belonged to her, too, and to her son. They flocked to my mind, my mother's face among them, and they seemed to look at me with contempt, and the cook pulled down his lower lid in the sign of disbelief, and shook his head. They had known better than to trust La Señora, to imagine the bond between them was more than that of mistress and servant. And Papá had not lied to my mother.

But it was not my servitude that Mrs. Burgess had violated—it was my trust in her, and it was that that was the very stuff of my own fatuity. And Charlie. But I could not yet think about Charlie.

Early in the morning, I heard Charlie fold up the cot and push it into the corner of the room. Had he invented his job in the camp equipment store? Did she give him money? The door closed. I ran into the living room and listened at the door. I heard his steps going down the stairs. I drank some water and lay down on the floor in the living room.

She phoned at noon. "Luisa? Are you sick? I've been so worried . . . it's not like you, not to phone. Are you—"

"What are you doing with my son," I said, my voice seeming to come from a long distance away, reaching my own ear at last as though it had traveled through a hollow tube.

After a moment, she said coolly, flatly, "I don't know."

"You've made a liar out of him," I gasped. "I won't let you do that. Don't you have enough?"

"I don't know," she repeated.

I held the phone down hard for several minutes.

Charlie came home before dark. I was looking down at the street, at the parade of people, at their clothes and the packages they carried. I did not much want to be disturbed from this intent watch.

"Mom?" he said uncertainly.

I understood at once. He had called her or seen her during the day. She had told him that I knew.

I continued to look down at the street.

"I'm twenty-three, Mom," he said.

I turned from the window then. We looked at each other. He knew nothing! But how well I knew him, the faint smile that touched his lips that I'd seen a thousand times. He looked down at the floor. Why was he stooping so? His face looked pasty, swollen.

"It has nothing to do with your age," I said.

I felt such a boiling of my mind, I couldn't say anything more. Awkwardly, he opened the door with his hand behind his back. "I'll be back. Later. I've found a room down on the east side. I'll be back, Mom." He gave a last sad, stubborn glance in my direction and went out the door.

.   .   .

"Come down here right away," Ellen said. "Jim and I can get you work. There are some Cuban refugees. They need every kind of help. We've got committees—"

"Ellen. I can't do anything. I haven't gone out for a week. I once told her he was my luck."

"Luisa!"

"Do you see what I did? I took him there. I brought him to her."

"She was too lazy to get out of bed," Ellen said.

"I'm ashamed."

"Come for a week, then. Visit us. Get out of the place where it happened."

"Is happening."

"It won't last."

"How do you know?"

"I know. Let it go. Let it go, Luisa. Don't talk about it anymore."

"How do you explain there are people who must have everything?"

"You don't have to explain . . . You won't believe me, but in a month, two months, you aren't going to feel this way."

I didn't believe her. I didn't press her further with my misery. There was a point where the knowledge of my own folly overshadowed my pain, where pain itself wore a comic mask. "I've got to get back to work. I've got to earn my living."

"Yes. You must do that," she said gently. "I'm not going to tell you now about other people—how many times this has happened before. The servant's child . . . Oh, Luisa, I could tell you tales! What I'm thinking about is how it will be when you come down here to us. How glad I'll be."

The echoes of her voice warmed me though I'd left the windows open and the apartment was cold. But I wanted to hear noise in the streets, even the wail of police cars and ambulances.

                   .   .   .

I walked the streets, rode subways and buses, waiting for an ordinary disaster, one I could put a name to. On streets I crossed where cars had been halted by a red light, I waited for the one that would break away to run me down. People picked up packages I dropped; an old woman offered me her seat on the subway. I found myself on a nearly deserted train going to Pelham. An elderly black man gave me directions, following me down the platform, repeating them firmly several times, until I got on another train that returned me to the station where I had made the mistake.

Benumbed, my bed unmade, I thought of Mr. Clare. Mourning him, I had moments of quietness, a grief that eased me.

I kept the television on until I fell asleep, waking from time to time to watch gray images sliding across the screen. One night, while the news was droning on, I heard the words: San Pedro. An army-supported coup, led by a former veterinarian, a Dr. Avila, had overthrown the government of José Gonzalez who had fled to Mexico, taking with him most of the country's treasury. There were reports of some casualties in a remote mountain district. One source attributed these to a fight over the outcome of a soccer game between two village teams. It was the third coup in eight years. Dr. Avila had vowed there would be no more foreign exploitation of San Pedro, and had ordered out of the country a team of American mining engineers who had been exploring the possibility of redeveloping the island's neglected nickel ore deposits. The sugar cane industry had fallen off drastically in recent years. Because of San Pedro's political instability, American investors had gone elsewhere. Dr. Avila, a shapeless man in a planter's shirt, glared briefly and fiercely from the television screen and held up two thick fingers in a victory sign.

In the morning, I telephoned Mrs. Justen and said I'd come in today, that I was feeling better than I had last week. There was a pile of laundry, she told me. She'd been a bit down herself and hadn't gotten around to much cleaning.

When I arrived, I started for the kitchen, determined to start cleaning at once.

"Luisa?" I had not seen her standing at the window in her pink woolly bathrobe. "Gosh! Are you okay? You look like someone's after you."

I sat down abruptly in a chair. After a moment, after I swore to myself—this is the last time I will speak of this thing, I told her about Charlie and Mrs. Burgess.

"Just a minute," she said when I had finished, as though I might run off. "I'm going to bring you a cup of tea."

I sat there listlessly. A black tabby jumped onto my lap and reclined across my knees, purring. I rested my hand on his warm flank.

"Jumper knows you're upset," Mrs. Justen said. She placed the tea on a table. "When mother died, I thought I'd never get over it. The relief, I mean. I felt as if my life had caught the wind like a sail. No more watching. I began to miss that too. And it passed. It all passes."

"Until it does—" I began, then let the thought go. "I'd best get at the washing."

"Never mind that. People lie about sex as much as they do about money. As for fucking—everybody fucks everybody. It's not even the point most of the time."

I bent over the cat, afraid I might laugh. *That* in Mrs. Justen's girlish treble voice.

"It's simple, really," she said. "She took advantage of the situation.

She was always excited by intrigue. She'd get a blind, exalted look on her face, and I'd know she was up to something. It made me laugh— what Marsh did to her. She flirted with Luke Justen. Even if he wasn't a homosexual, he wouldn't have looked at her twice. He has too much sense." A tender, musing look had come over her face when she spoke her former husband's name. She shook her head. "She can't help herself," she said.

I sat up straight. "Please don't say that. It's what she always says."

"There are just so many words a person can use, Luisa," she said sharply, "and it's not a compliment to say she's given up the exercise of her will to be merely willful." She stared at me thoughtfully a moment. "Let's go to the movies. Let's leave the laundry and dishes. There's one down the block, some science fiction thing. It's bound to be distracting."

So we went and sat in the theater, sharing a chocolate bar she had selected, watching a space ship full of corpses sail through galactic emptiness while a waltz thundered in the dark. Afterwards, she took me to a bar on Lexington Avenue. "We'll have martinis," she said. "I meet Luke here every week."

"You still see him?"

"Oh, yes! For years. When I was in the crazy ward, he visited me, every day nearly. He'd hide and wait till mother had gone. She pretended to hate him—to show she was on my side. She didn't understand. Luke and I have been friends since we were children. He never lied to me. We thought we'd try it—marriage. He couldn't. He's my dearest friend. We never got divorced—and never will."

She wanted to give me a day's pay. I refused. "We had a day off together," she said, and awkwardly placed her long arm around my shoulders.

The next morning I went to an employment agency and the following week I began to work for Mr. and Mrs. Carter, who had one child, a gentle girl of ten named Jenny, who liked to help me clean, and who made cups of instant coffee while we waited for her parents, both of whom worked, to come home. She told me stories about Paris where she had spent the first six years of her life. "You must speak French," I had said. "I'll probably forget it pretty soon," she said. "That's what Mama says."

"Someone once told me a person wasn't truly cultivated unless they could speak French."

She laughed at that. "Cultivated? I thought that's what farmers did, you know, with the wheat."

"That must be it."

"Is the coffee good? Do I make it the right way?"

"It's perfect," I said.

In the basement of the Carter apartment house where I took their dirty linen to wash in the laundry room, I met a young black woman who worked for another family in the building. Her savage comments on the characters and habits of her employers made me laugh with bitterness and relief. "Do you like them?" I asked.

"Like!" she shouted, giving me a look of disbelief. Her laughter resounded through the basement corridors, striking echoes from the pipes.

.   .   .

I ceased to be a reader of signs. I washed dishes without noting what had been eaten. I no longer read the titles of books on the bedside tables of my employers. I did my work. Powerful memories of earlier days returned to me like springs starting suddenly out of earth where there had been none. Once again, in thought, I wandered the paths of Malagita.

I missed Mr. Clare. But more than Mr. Clare, I missed the old unthinking ease with Charlie. I knew that he, no more than I, knew what to do with the weight of our unspoken thoughts. Were they thoughts? So inchoate and fleeting. In silence, as though it had been determined at our first wordless encounter twenty-three years ago at his birth, we were reconciled. Sometimes when he phoned me and once when he stopped to pick up a box of books, I felt again the seizure of horror, of bewilderment, at the sight of them walking together up the street in the rain beneath Mrs. Burgess' umbrella, and I felt hatred toward him as deep as my attachment to him.

"My place is next to a Ukrainian church," he told me. "It's a funny neighborhood, people selling drugs on the street and this bunch of old Ukrainians walking around staring at the hippies like they flew in from hell."

"Do you want supper?"

"No. I ate right after work. I just stopped by." He picked up a detective story I was reading and turned it back and forth in his hands as though he didn't know what it was.

"Why have you gotten so thin!" he burst out. "You look terrible!" His face worked the way I'd seen the faces of mutes work as they spoke with their hands to each other on some street corner.

"It hasn't got to do with you."

"It does! It was serious for me. It wasn't nothing."

Yes, it would have to be that, I thought grimly. He had said—was.

"If I could say something—I can't," I said. He knelt and put some books in a box. I felt afraid; words themselves could form a new false event. I looked down at him kneeling, reading the titles of the books. I was weary with him, with myself.

Mrs. Burgess made senseless profit, brief distractions for herself, out of the trust of people whose lives touched upon hers. In her gluttonous violence of soul, how would she have been able to distinguish the trust I had given her from the opportunity it provided?

Charlie stood up. "I'm starting night courses in the spring," he said.

"What are you going to study?"

"Everything."

After he had gone away with his books, I ate my supper standing up at the counter. The ticking of the alarm clock in the bedroom was very loud. I had set it for the wrong time last night, and it had wakened me an hour early in the morning in the middle of a dream.

I recalled it now all at once. I had been standing in a forest half-hidden by a tree. I was dressed in rags like a beggar. I had known, as one knows in dreams, that I appeared menacing. Charlie came walking down a path. He saw me and drew back in fear. I stepped out on the path. I said, "Don't be afraid. I'll lead you by."

.   .   .

I received a note and a check from Mr. Darby. He had sold the Chippendale desk Mr. Clare had left me for thirty-six hundred dollars. "Of course, I haven't taken a commission," he wrote, "because you know that Edwin would come to haunt me if I had."

It arrived a week after my forty-ninth birthday. Feeling historical, I had stayed up to watch the New Year celebrations on television. Charlie stopped by the next evening with a present from his camp supply store, a thick sweater whose label bore a drawing of a black sheep. "It's beautiful," I said. "Well, it'll keep you warm," he remarked.

It was a very American article of clothing. It looked large on me although it was the right size. My skin had darkened as I had grown older, and a few coarse, strong white hairs were springing up all over my head. I looked in the mirror at myself, encased in wool. A Spaniard in sheep's clothing.

On my way to Mrs. Justen's, I deposited the check in my savings account at a bank on Broadway. I had over five thousand dollars, what was called a nest egg. I thought of my nest as I walked cautiously across the frozen slush to the bus stop. I visualized the apartment, its neat emptiness, its two-cup coffeepot. I didn't care if I never saw it again.

As soon as I opened the door, Mrs. Justen sprang toward me.

"This country is going Fascist," she cried. "Listen to this—a neighbor told me there was a sick dog on the street, just down where that row of houses begins, toward Lex. He was a big old dog. I thought he was dead until he lifted his head. I took him water and food and a piece of old rug to cover him. He wouldn't move from the steps of the house but he did drink a little water. He must have been on the street for months, his nails were so worn down. I went out a dozen times yesterday afternoon. Once he wagged his tail a little when he saw me. Then, just when it got dark, and I went back with his supper, he was gone! A woman was watching me from the window of the house. She opened it and told me three youths had seen the dog and come over and pissed on him! Pissed on the dog!" Her voice had risen to a shout. She sank into a chair. "It's degeneracy," she said hopelessly. "People who'll do that will burn up babies in ovens."

I looked at her clenched fists. Her long bare feet were dirty and her hair was lank, unwashed. I was alarmed. She might be going mad again. She glanced up at me. "Don't worry," she said sardonically. "I'm not losing my mind."

"Let me make you some breakfast, some coffee."

"Do you think it's only crazy people who feel horror?" she demanded.

"No. It's an awful story."

"It's not a story. It's what happens. I'm sorry I shouted," she said. "These things tear me up. I don't know what to do about creation." She stood up, sighing and clutching her old robe around herself.

"I'll wash and pull myself together," she said brusquely. "Fall apart—pull it together. On and on."

By the time I was ready to leave, she was dressed, calm, smoking a cigarette, a manuscript on her lap.

"Mrs. Justen," I began, then fell silent. She began to look worried. I repeated her name. Her face cleared. "Oh, the money," she said. She opened her pocketbook.

"I'm going away," I said. "I'm going back to San Pedro." Now that I had said it, the idea seemed even more immense than it had when it came to me that morning when I was mopping the bathroom.

"Where I was born," I said at her look of incomprehension.

She held out my pay. "Right away?"

"In a week or so. I have to find out about getting there."

"It seems a nice thing to do, although I wouldn't want to go back to Buffalo where I was born."

I took the money. She stood up and held out her hand. I shook it carefully. She towered over me, but she looked frail, dusty and pale like a huge moth.

"I'll miss you," she said. "I'm sorry I sent you to that woman. It's all because of that."

"No, it isn't," I said firmly.

"But you'll telephone when you get back? Will it be just a few weeks?"

"I don't know," I said. "I'm very tired."

"I understand that," she said.

.   .   .

I gave the Carters notice. I told Jenny I was going back to a place I loved, where I had been born. How lucky I was, she said wistfully.

"*Au revoir,*" she called to me as I went down the hall to the elevator. "*Adios,*" I called back.

I went to a small Puerto Rican tourist agency on the west side. There were four desks in the room, and on one of them a large card read *San Pedro*. An elderly man sat behind the desk. He told me to be careful when

I reached Tres Hermanos. "Things have settled down," he said. "But when you get those rural boys in uniforms . . . I was born in San Isidro myself."

"Why did you leave?" I asked curiously.

"No job," he said. "No food."

I asked him if I needed a passport, and he grinned and said, "No, no. You only need passports for real countries."

I gave Charlie the address of the hotel where I would be spending the night in Tres Hermanos. After that, I told him, I would go to San Isidro and catch a morning bus for Malagita. There was a guest house there where I could sleep and take my meals.

"I'd like you to take these forks," I said. "They're the only thing of value I have."

He took them and rubbed at the tarnish with a finger. "You can polish them," I said. "They ought to be used."

"You're coming back, aren't you, Ma?"

"I used to think it was as far as the moon. The moon isn't far anymore. San Pedro is just a few hours flight."

"You're not saying . . ."

"Will you go and see Papá? I've been bad about that. Now I want you to do it. He'll be dead one of these days. He's saving records for you. He'll be better to you than he was to me."

"I don't like this. How long are you going to stay there?"

"I tell you—I don't know. When I do, I'll let you know."

"I'll pick up the mail," he said, "and look in on things."

I'd forgotten he had a key to the apartment.

"I've met a girl," he said.

I was silent a moment. "That's—" but I couldn't think of a word, and he rushed in, saying, "She's a musician, working in the store now to put herself through music school."

I didn't ask him anything. In Mrs. Justen's bathroom, I'd begun to leave the city, even Charlie.

He was looking at me with such a stillness on his face, I knew he was willing it. I might have asked him questions about the girl musician, but I was afraid of evoking in him an equally willed animation. It was this premeditation in the most ordinary exchanges between us that was the spoiling, the lingering sign of injury. I spoke what truth I could, that I was glad I was going to see Ellen who was flying from the South to some legal conference in New York, and who would meet me at the airport and spend as much time as she could with me.

"She bought me the biggest box of ice cream I ever saw," he said, relief edging his voice.

"When you had your tonsils out."

He nodded and seemed about to say something, but I spoke quickly, "I think I'll do some packing." He picked up his coat and slipped the two forks into his pocket. "We'll be eating in style," he said. We kissed each other with a certain haste. "How's school?" I asked, suddenly remembering. "Good," he said. "Half good, anyhow."

After he had gone, I went to the bedroom. I stared at my new suitcase, packed two days earlier.

I couldn't have broken with Charlie as Nana had done with Mamá. It was unthinkable. And between Beatriz de la Cueva and Nana, there had been no faith to breach.

.   .   .

Ellen and I wandered through the corridors of the airport, now and then sitting for a while in waiting rooms where exhausted children ran in circles around piles of luggage and their blank-faced parents. In a cafeteria, Ellen went to stand in line and get us rolls and coffee.

She carried her cigarettes in a silver case. A garnet necklace hung round her throat, disappearing into the silk folds of her blouse. She tossed a raincoat over the back of her orange plastic chair. We had talked about her work and her marriage. She was staring into her cup. I looked at her hair, close-cropped and curly, without a gray hair. When she smiled, she seemed hardly to have aged.

"Do you remember Julian?" she asked suddenly. I nodded. "I suppose it made his life easier—to hate everything. In the end, he hated me, too. I can't forget him. He was the first. A man. I thought I knew everything then."

"When I told my father I was going to San Pedro, he said he had never understood anything I did. I agreed with him, for once. But I didn't say so."

"What are you thinking about doing when you come back?"

I didn't answer. "Luisa! You're not thinking of staying there!"

"I'm not going to be a servant anymore."

She looked so distressed, I began to laugh. "Now—after all these years—I've given it up . . . what you always wanted me to do!"

"Because of that woman and Charlie?"

"I don't know. I know it's finished for me."

"San Pedro won't be what you remember. You know that?"

"Yes. I know that."

"I suspect you," she said softly.

"When I was little, I sometimes thought my father was a king, riding a borrowed mare, angry because someone had stolen his kingdom. He's shrunken now and walks with a cane and has a fat old wife who crochets orlon bed-jackets. How could I think everything will be the same in Malagita?"

But she was right to be suspicious. Beneath common sense, images gleamed and stirred, out of time, beyond the reach of sense.

My hands began to tremble and I put down my cup. Ellen brushed her cheek. "What is it?" I asked.

She covered my hand with hers. "I was thinking . . . Do you remember that poem we had to learn? 'They flash upon that inward eye which is the bliss of solitude.' *Daffodils* . . . I have trouble recalling where I was last week at this time, but that line never fades away."

"Oh—I remember."

"I have to go."

I walked with her outdoors to the taxi rank.

"Please think about coming south," she said. "We'll find you work, something you'd like. You'll have a different life. Will you call me right away when you get back?"

"I'll call you."

We embraced. Through her heavy coat, I felt the tension of her body, braced as always for battle.

    .   .   .

"*Anda! Anda!*" muttered a woman behind me as I paused on the platform above the flight of stairs leading to the ground. "The air is like silk," I

said in Spanish. She pushed past me, laden with string bags and packages. "Silk!" she exclaimed resentfully.

In the airport terminal, no more than a rough shed, I was questioned
by an official who appeared alternately bewildered and indignant when I
explained to him in Spanish that I was an American citizen who had been
born in San Pedro. I showed him my Social Security card in its plastic
case and, reluctantly, he let me go. Beyond the bus waiting for the passengers to the capital stood a royal palm. It rose from amid building debris, cement blocks, and lengths of rusted steel.

"Someday soon, a new airport," said the bus driver, following the
direction of my gaze. A starved mongrel, all ribs and blood-red gums,
scrabbled across the blocks. Other passengers settled into the bus, and
with a metallic grinding of gears it rumbled off down the narrow road,
the driver wrenching the wheel violently to avoid huge potholes.

Despite the promise of the travel agent in New York, the small hotel,
with its six rooms, had no record of a reservation for me. It didn't matter.
There were only two other guests.

In the dining room with its four round tables, a waiter in a wrinkled
suit jacket and dirty apron brought me a bowl of coffee and milk and two
hard crackers on a plastic plate. For his trouble, he expected me to tell
him why I was there. I had been trying to get back to San Pedro for forty
years, I said.

"There are great changes," he said. "Did you notice the foundations
of the new airport for the tourists? Dr. Avila is a realist, a man of the
people. From the tourist trade, we will have the money for new schools,
nurseries for the working mothers, free medicine for all." He glanced
quickly around the tiny empty room, stooped toward me to move the
plastic plate an inch or two out of its place, and made the sign of disbelief, his index finger pulling down the lower lid of one eye. I burst into
laughter. He looked alarmed at once and shook his head rapidly. "The
coffee," I said in a loud voice. "It's like wine!"

In my room that night I pushed open the great wooden shutters of the
window and leaned out. What noise there was was more like that of
evening in a village rather than a city. Far away, two car horns sounded
exactly two notes, question and answer. Nearer, I was sure I heard a
rooster crow. Across from me, I saw a house larger than the hotel. A pale

glimmer of light shone in a room. It was from the flame of a candle, and near it, a young woman in a thin white gown slowly bent from the edge of her bed to wash her feet in a basin of water, then rose and with both of her hands lifted a mane of dark hair away from her face.

In the morning, I walked down a broad avenue. The balconied houses, the few cars that drove along the street, were bathed in a pale blue light that came from the sea as though the day began there in the harbor, and the edge of the light was white so that each thing, a car, a house, a man walking rapidly across the street, the overarching branches of the trees above the central *rambla*, were luminously outlined, and this ever-widening whiteness of light drowned the years between this moment and the one when my father and my mother and I, gripping our suitcases, had walked down this same avenue on an early morning to the wharf, to the ship that would take us to the United States.

I turned down a narrow street where a woman washed cobblestones in front of a small house painted the dusky mottled color of a peach. Across from it was the tourist office to which I'd been given directions by the hotel clerk. A soldier stood in front of it, watching the woman who ignored his presence there. His face was sweating, he held a machine gun in one hand as loosely as a string bag, his buttocks were pressed against a glass window where a solitary poster advertised a weekend in Cuba, meals, room, tours included in the price of the flight.

With a brisk hand slipping from a frayed sleeve, the woman at the desk wrote out the name of the family who ran the guest house in Malagita. She would telephone Mrs. Diaz to prepare my room. "I come from near there myself," she said. "You won't find things the way they used to be. There's decent housing for people now." She spoke with severity as though I'd made a mistake in having seen Malagita before the great new changes.

I took the afternoon train to San Isidro. The streets there were filled with people, the atmosphere was excited, busy, a provincial town free of any obligation to look like a city. Barrows of fruit, vegetables, shoes were pushed along the gutters. I passed underneath a line of wash hung between two narrow houses and a woman leaned out singing as she tested a man's trousers for dryness. The cafés overflowed with men so that some stood in front of the doors shouting to their friends inside.

The light here was rose, like the colors of the houses, and the sky was tinged with green. My bus for Malagita left from in front of a garage where a dozen or more battered cars appeared to have collapsed all at once in front of a shed that was like a dark cave.

The bus driver had surrounded himself with emblems; a bouquet of wax flowers hung from a string above his head, a small crude painting of the crucifixion was tacked on the wooden crossboard of the window to his left, and a transistor radio leaned against the windshield near the steering wheel.

A few miles from San Isidro, the paved road ended. The driver didn't moderate his speed, and the passengers swayed and clutched their bundles, staring at me fixedly, vacantly. The little bus shuddered and shook through the dusk, the light that had gradually turned yellow, halting now and then in places no different from other places where passengers got off to walk away, as though there were markings, invisible to me, that would lead them to their destinations in a landscape that appeared to have no human habitation. The red dust kicked up briefly shrouded them. When I looked back, pressing my face against the window, they seemed to have traveled great distances from the road. Far away, groves of trees rose like feather dusters. From the east, a vast slow wave of darkness moved across the sky. I was the last passenger.

The driver continued to sing along with the rattling, drum-clotted music from his radio, barely audible above the banging, grinding noise of the bus. The slopes of a mountain rose; on its peak a beacon of light shone. Straight ahead, I saw the stacks of the mill.

"Last stop," the driver called. But I was unable to stand. He turned to stare at me, the smoke of the cigarette he was lighting swirling about his face. I gripped the back of the seat in front of me and pulled myself up. It was nearly dark. I was in Malagita; it lay outside the dimly lit bus. The momentousness of it thinned out my senses as a faint does. "Thank you," I said in a high, shallow voice that hardly seemed my own. "Okay," he said, blowing out smoke.

I stepped down on the ground. The driver threw himself across the wheel like a crab and turned it. The bus drove off.

I was standing in a square given its form by rows of small identical cinder-block houses. As I stooped to lift my suitcase, the square was suddenly washed with light from street lamps. A woman standing in a doorway slowly lifted her hand to her brow, and keeping it there, walked down two narrow steps which hung from the threshold and came toward me.

"You are the guest," she said.

My heart gave a great thump.

"My sister, Adela Diaz, is in charge of the guest house." She came to stand very close to me. She smelled like my mother when she had come from the cooking shed carrying a platter of yellow rice and beans. "Listen to me," she said. "You walk down there, then a little more, past the soccer field—"

"—I don't know the soccer field."

"You speak Spanish very well. Never mind. I'll take you."

She gripped my arm and we began to walk. "I was born here," I said.

She peered at my face. "I heard," she said. "Well, I'm sure it will look very different to you."

"The mills aren't running."

"Why should they be?"

"It's the time now for grinding the cane."

"Sugar! It ruined the country. No more sugar. We have a factory, plastics—cups, pails, spoons, everything."

I halted suddenly as I glimpsed a section of rusted rail that ended a few yards away. I rested my hand on it.

"The *plazuela*."

"The soccer field," she corrected me. "The last trees are to be cut down next week."

"I don't remember there being a light on the mountain."

"For the planes," she said. "From the prison. Where we put Gonzalez' gangsters. Locked up where they can't harm us."

She stopped. "Adela!" she called.

A woman ran from a house toward us. "Ah!" she exclaimed. "The guest. Welcome. You must be tired. The bus ride is so long and bumpy. I have your supper waiting, but no meat tonight. Next week the meat truck comes." Without a word, her sister turned and walked back toward the square.

Adela said, "Over there." She led me to a building more substantial looking than the cinder-block houses, older.

"You'll be comfortable," she promised. "I'll bring your supper right away and in the morning, I'll bring you breakfast. Don't be startled if the lights fail. The generator is not entirely trustworthy. Gonzalez' criminals ate well from the public services. It will be fixed soon."

She swung open the wide wooden door and reached inside to press a switch. The light showed a large square room. Adela crossed it to a narrow door. "A bathroom," she said proudly. "I will bring the hot water for bathing. The toilet flushes except sometimes."

There was a bed, a table, an overhead light, a naked bulb like those I had glimpsed in the cinder-block houses, and three shelves on the wall. On the top shelf, an unframed mirror leaned against the wall reflecting the bars at the window. "For your belongings," Adela said, pointing at the shelves.

I suddenly knew where I was. The guesthouse had been Dr. Baca's surgery.

.   .   .

As it had been when the cane was harvested, the village lay somnolent, nearly empty. In the early mornings, I saw men and women trudging off to the plastic factory, the dead white glare of its flat roof visible from the new road that led toward the mountain and the prison fortress. For three days, I had wandered about Malagita. A few old people stared at me with curiosity, but the younger people gave me no more than a glance. I visited the graveyard. The angel that had stood on Antonio de la Cueva's tomb had fallen and lay in pieces on the ground, one wing like a shark fin riding above the thick weeds. In the neglected field of bones lay those of Sebastiano, my brother. There was nothing to mark his grave.

Elsewhere the land had been cleared of trees; weeds flourished in empty stretches which, unshielded from the sun, burned like pavement. In the afternoons, a breeze sprang up. Cement dust blew through the village; the air carried an acrid taste, chemical and lifeless. The plastic factory had its own shrill whistle.

The hands on the face of the clock tower had stopped at a few minutes after noon, and the arrow on one of the hands had broken off. The grilled fence which had once surrounded it was gone, its door stood ajar, and I walked into the darkness. I ran my hand along some rough planks piled up against the stone steps that rose to the top, far above, where a corkscrew of light fell on brick.

In the church, a brown, torn bit of lace cloth hung from the altar. The door behind it was open. I stepped through it and onto the ground. The schoolroom was no longer there. In the distance, I glimpsed the only *bohío* I had come across. Its roof had fallen in, and it leaned sideways on three stilts. I went back inside and sat for a while. Even there, there was a chemical smell. Though it had the dead feeling of a deserted place, Adela had told me a priest came now and then—to officiate at funerals, marriages, or baptisms. I went up to the altar and touched the lace. It came apart in my fingers and I rolled it into dust.

That morning, I had followed the living green fence, now grown thick, tall, and impenetrable, that had once surrounded the gardens of the *vivienda*. I had crossed the canal by a new metal walkway—the wooden bridge had collapsed at some time; I saw a piece of it resting against the bank of the canal, one end crumbling in the sun, the other in the water—and had found myself in another vacant expanse through which ran a new road that stopped abruptly a few hundreds yards away. I couldn't see the *vivienda*. Each end of the walkway was buried in thick undergrowth. The new road shimmered with heat.

No stick or stone remained of the house of the Chinese. The ground was as blank of clues as the sky. But I thought I recognized the ceiba tree at whose base I had once buried the skull of some small animal, and I went to stand beneath it for a while. I had walked back to the surgery in ten minutes. There had been nothing to impede my way.

.   .   .

"Have you visited the day nursery and the clinic in the office of the people?" Adela asked me as she set my tray on the table. "Also the village council is there, and the office of the director of our factory."

"Where?" I asked. I was lying on the bed. She folded her arms and looked at me worriedly.

"You've been out in the sun too much," she said. "My father said you were tottering when you returned to the guest house this afternoon."

There were still watchers in the village. That hadn't changed.

"I think it was the sun," I said. "Where is the office of the people?" She pointed out the door in the direction of the *vivienda*. Each morning, after the road to the factory was empty, I had gone out and looked at the tiled roof beyond the mill stacks.

"The great house," I said.

"We don't call it that," she said.

"There were other things I wanted to see first."

She looked at me hesitantly, then leaned forward to ask in a low voice. "Were you ever inside it, when you were a child?"

"My mother was a kitchen maid. I was inside it, in the servants' quarters, and once in the bedroom of Señora Beatriz de la Cueva," I answered.

"In the old times," she said politely, straightening up.

"Yes, then."

"My father worked in the mill until he injured his hand. Then it was very bad for us."

I raised up. "You come from here? I thought—" But what had I thought? That these people I had seen on their way to work, eating their suppers beneath the dim light bulbs in the evening, were all from some other place?

She gazed at me with a certain shyness. "My father knew of you," she said.

I had not known of him. I had known only of La Señora, of Nana, a few others. She seemed to sense what I was thinking, for she said as though to console me for that earlier ignorance, "Well, you were only a child. A child is like a little bug, an ant, seeing only what is in front of her." She sighed. "Then you find out—about the others."

"You were here during the hurricane."

"I wasn't born yet. But my mother told me about it. She and my father were in the capital for medical treatment for his hand. When they came back, my mother said it was as if a family of giants had fallen on the village all at once, then gone away. Everything had to be built again— except the main house, of course. And there was a lake in the center of the village. Little by little it disappeared."

"My Nana disappeared, too."

"My father said your Nana knew every child who was born in Malagita, that after she was gone, it was as if no one knew who we were. He said —if Señora de la Cueva had known about us, she would have thought less of herself. Of course she was dead before I was born and the Americans came for a while. They made lists, and things were a little better— better than after the hurricane; there was a medical officer and electricity and two stores so that people didn't have to go to San Isidro for necessities."

"What lists?"

"Of names, families."

"And the Frenchwoman and her children?"

"I don't know about them."

"And now? How is it now?"

"Now it is much better, naturally." She looked at me with a melancholy intensity and seemed about to say more. She glanced at the tray of food. "Oh—everything will be cold! Eat your supper now. I must go home to my family. I'll try to remember to bring you a straw hat tomorrow. They say the blood thins when you live in the north, and the sun can make you ill."

.   .   .

I was still in bed when she brought my coffee and bread in the morning before she went off to the plastic factory. At her expression of concern, I told her I was going to rest in bed for a while. In the afternoon, I would visit the office of the people.

"You will see my child in the nursery," she said. She laughed. "He is the only one with red hair. He looks like the sunset."

Later, after I had dressed, I went to the window. It was so silent; there were no animal sounds. I wondered what had happened to them all, the pigs and donkeys and roosters. The children, Adela had told me, were taken by bus to a new school in a neighboring village, perhaps the very one, I had thought, where Nana had gone to Mass in order to avoid my mother on Sundays.

I had said I was going to the *vivienda* but I had no desire to see it. I had no desire for anything. In the lassitude that gripped me, I was even unable to wish it would end.

I heard sounds, two weighted syllables, a horse's hooves striking the ground. I gripped the bars and pressed my face against them. Shortly, the bobbing head of a horse appeared, then its harnessed body, then the driver on a wagon seat wearing a cap of the sort which baseball players wear. In the wagon there were stacks of worn and dusty automobile tires.

I went back to my bed and picked up a mystery story I had bought at the airport in New York and read a few pages without knowing what I was reading.

"*Hola!*" croaked an ancient female voice. I looked up. A crone was staring at me through the bars where women had once gathered to comfort a woman in difficult labor. She grinned at me. "I heard there was a guest!" she said, nodding her head rapidly.

I went outside and stood beneath the shade cast by the roof of the house. She looked me up and down carefully, leaning on her stick and swaying slightly.

"You haven't heard everything," I said feeling a sudden resentment at the nakedness of her scrutiny. "I was born here."

"Everyone is born somewhere," she said dismissingly. She coughed and spat. "What is your name?"

"Luisa Sanchez."

She looked thunderstruck and let go of her stick. I bent to pick it up. Her little feet in their black shoes were moving agitatedly in the dust. I pressed the stick into her hand. "Ah . . ." she groaned as her hand closed over it. She looked confused, troubled for an instant. Then her face cleared. "Well, of course, I knew that. But memory goes. You'll find that out. I knew it was you. I knew you were coming. Don't you remember me? I forgot for a moment. My son told me, of course. I am Isabel Galdos, your Nana's dearest friend, your mother's, too. How often I took care of you when you were sick!" She lifted one arm and held it out dramatically, a finger pointing upwards. "The toys I made for you! And you went away and we never heard from you. How many years you've been gone! Your poor Nana's bones have turned to dust. What a storm that was . . ." She moved closer, sliding her feet forward as though feeling the ground.

I took a step back away from her. "Nearly everyone is dead," she said. "Only a while after you left, Dr. Baca was carried off by a fit. But I have been here all the time. I have six grandchildren. What of your sweet Mamá?"

"She died many years ago."

She shook her head but was unable to express the smallest suggestion of sorrow although her features were clearly attempting to convey it, the colorless, wrinkled lips turning down, eyes squinting as though to press out tears. She gave up the attempt and asked, "And your Papi?"

"He's alive," I said, and added emphatically, "and in good health."

"How many children do you have?"

"A son."

She was advancing toward me slowly; already I felt her breath on my face and heard the rustle of the black cloth of her dress, and I smelled its mustiness as though it was on my own body.

"Do you know what happened to my Nana?"

"How would I know that? I took my baby into the clock tower and it filled up with water all the way to here," and she struck herself on her bottom. "When we came out, there was a lake."

"Doesn't anyone know?" I cried out with a desperation which had increased every day, deepening with each discovery I made that every landmark was lost, cabins, trees and paths, fragrances and stench, the voices of animals and human voices, all vanished.

She was watching me very carefully now, with an almost medical intentness. "Well," she said in a lighthearted voice, "all our houses were crushed like eggs. What would you imagine with such winds?" She coughed again, her mouth wide open so I could see the convulsive working of her chalky tongue. "Did you marry a rich American, Luisita? You must have so much money, after all, to come and visit us here in the country."

"I was married, but I'm not anymore," I answered dully. "I've worked as a maid to support myself."

She smiled with such perfect malice, it nearly made me laugh, she was so indifferent to hiding it. "A maid!" she exclaimed, chuckling. "Just like your Mamasita."

I couldn't bear her presence another minute, and I glanced toward the *vivienda*, trying to think of a lie that would make it possible for me to leave her. She caught the direction of my glance.

"Do you recall my little Pedro?" she asked. "That brute, Baca, swore I was too old to bear a child. Now Pedro is the head of the village council."

Her hand shot out and gripped my wrist and I grabbed it and tried to push it away. I was flooded with an old revulsion toward her, a contempt

I had felt for her as a child; those elaborate sighs, I remembered now, that had been meant to show her capacity for sympathy, her false caresses in which I had sensed the deadness of her flesh—the gestures of a person senselessly, greedily, after information. Her fingers tangled with mine like a gripping plant. I shook my hand but still she clung.

"Let me go," I protested. "I'm going to visit the *vivienda*."

"My son has been to the *palacio* in the capital," she said, a momentary youthful strength in her voice. "Dr. Avila himself embraced my son."

"A horse-doctor," I muttered.

She pinched my thumb hard as she finally released my hand. "Arrogant," she said angrily. "Always arrogant." She struck her foot on the ground. I caught sight of an elderly couple in the doorway of a house across the way, their faces working with worry.

I started to go into the guest house, but she was not through with me. She stamped her foot again. "Malagita isn't yours!" she howled at my back. "And now it's all ours!"

"I never thought it was mine," I cried, turning briefly to face her, upon which she lifted her stick high in the air as though she intended to bring it down upon my head. I felt faint and leaned against the wall. Suddenly her face, so violently twisting, so hideous in its rage, smoothed out and grew calm. She nodded formally toward me as if ending an ordinary conversation, and turned to hobble away down the road. The old couple were still standing in their doorway, transfixed, staring at me.

I went inside and lay down on the bed. "I never thought that," I whispered, even as I knew I had thought only that all through the years of my servitude. I had been waiting.

The realization of it shut me away from conscious thought, broke its willed links. I seemed to be staring at some object I'd never seen before yet was obliged to name. Or was it a face, not quite human, yet like any human face in which there is reflected one powerful consuming notion? Disembodied, but as distinctly seen as the fingers of my hand against which I now rested my cheek, rose the ancient, ashen features of La Señora, her eyes shadowed by thick black brows. I heard a voice as it dredged up a briefly recollected social asset from a dead world and told me to learn to speak French, then demanded pettishly a little cup of coffee, looking at me, oblivious of me. I had been awaiting an inheritance promised me only in dreams.

Although I lay there apathetically while the barred sunlight, growing ever more intense, fell in lashes of heat across my legs, I was as out of breath as though I'd been running.

After a while, I fell heavily into sleep. A voice woke me, calling softly, "Señora Sanchez?" I sat up. Adela was at the door, carrying my midday meal.

She set the tray down on the table, her face intent. "I'm going away tomorrow," I said, "back to the capital, then home."

"Oh—but I arranged for you to visit our factory," she said. "I thought you would come tomorrow to see it. Didn't you go to the nursery this morning?"

"I wasn't able to go. I'll be sorry not to see the place where you work."

"There's only one bus for San Isidro. It leaves so early, even before I go to work."

"I'll take it," I said. She looked at me curiously. "You've been disappointed?" she asked.

Any answer would have been untrue. I told her no, to spare her pride. Already the curiosity was fading from her face. I had seen how proud she was of the way she managed her work, her family, her responsibilities toward the guest. I knew she would be relieved, too, when the guest had departed.

I ate as much as I could, but I no longer had the stomach for such a dinner in the middle of the day, in such heat. In the afternoon, I went back to the square where I had been dropped by the bus, then went on beyond the village, along the road the bus had followed for several miles, until I was weary. When I came back in the late afternoon, a few old people nodded at me from their doorways. If I met Señora Galdos, I would run away from her as I had once run from the witch whom I had glimpsed at a distance beyond the herd of pigs as she lifted her stick in the air, bawling mindlessly.

I didn't go near the *vivienda*. I didn't look toward it.

The night was calm and clear. The old surgery glowed in the moonlight. The moon was full. One morning, Mrs. Justen had flung down her newspaper and said to me, "Even the ocean has become a fake just like the moon where all those men tramped around and dropped their beer cans." The moon traveled in a great ellipse, moving ever deeper into the sky; its movement seemed noble to me, with a grandeur that was not earthly.

Even without its light, the old fortress prison would have been visible because of the enormous beacon on its tower. I looked through the bars at the house across the way. Had that anarchic scene in the morning frightened the old couple because anything uncommon—even if they only had witnessed it—led them to thoughts of the prison in the fortress? The fear they might be imprisoned themselves?

For such a reason, hadn't Adela lowered her voice to ask me if I had ever been inside the great house? Was it better now in this village or worse? They were going to change its name, Adela had told me. Malagita was from plantation days when a single person could own a village and its people. She didn't know what the new name would be. She had heard it rumored that it might be called Pueblo Avila, after the president.

As I stared at the little square house, the door suddenly opened and the old man looked out. He was staring at the guest house window, and he started violently. He must have seen my face, as white as his in the moonlight. He put a finger to his lips as though he feared I would call out to him, then he withdrew slowly and shut the door. I heard it click.

We had had no door in the house of the Chinese. People were shut away now, or shut themselves away, and that was no less singular a difference than the cinder-block houses, the *vivienda* that was now the office of the people, and the plastic factory that had been built on what had once been land where cane had grown.

In the morning, I put all the pesos I had left under the pillow for Adela, keeping only what I would need to reach the airport. I had paid the tourist office for a week's visit, not thinking a minute ahead when I handed over the money, possessed by more than hope; an intention that everything in my life would become clear when I set foot in Malagita.

      .   .   .

The official at the airport who had so closely studied my Social Security card a few days earlier was cordial. "When you return," he promised gaily, "we shall have a new airport. You'll be able to fly here directly from New York. Great changes," he said, gesturing toward the low dirty ceiling to which were roughly affixed large uneven squares of sound-proofing material.

The small plane that would take me to San Juan lifted. I saw Tres Hermanos, the governor's palace, gleaming and white, the central avenue where trees arched over the *rambla*, the narrow side streets lined with houses the colors of flowers or fruit, the harbor where fishing boats clustered like nurslings around a small warship, thickets of guns upon its decks, then the shore road curving out of the city, the very one, I imagined, upon which Señora de la Cueva had been driven for her afternoon outings when she visited the capital, and where her car had once been stoned. I pressed my forehead against the window as the plane leveled to fly westward. Just below me, the light blue sea touched a ribbon of pale sand, perhaps the beach where four hundred and fifty years ago three Spaniards had landed to claim the island for Spain. One had been called Pedro. I could not, at the moment, recall the names of the two others although I remembered that one had been murdered. I didn't care what their names had been.

I had begun to think about something quite different, a woman who had been our boarder for many years when we lived in the barrio near Broadway. From flat to flat, she had followed us, carrying her suitcase and her bundles. I was wondering what had happened to her. If she was alive, she would be in her late sixties. I was thinking of Maura Cruz.